"LET'S PAY A VISIT TO YOUR WIFE."

A pang of fear stabbed Ulman's heart. He felt the gun barrel jab against the base of his skull—metal to bone—as he sat there gripping the wheel with both hands, trying to think of something to do. Anything. Liz would be sleeping. She was five years younger then he and more beautiful than he deserved.

"Nice place," LePonty said. "All the time you were screwing with my head, I was thinking wouldn't it be great to visit your house."

"Please, Frank." He closed his eyes and held back the scream.

"I almost forgot. I got something to show you."

LePonty's voice was friendly, almost intimate. He fumbled in his pocket, then dropped something in Ulman's lap.

It was soft and felt like a piece of wet cloth with threads attached. Then Ulman realized what he was holding: part of a human scalp.

"I cut that off the guard after I blew his brains out," LePonty said. He put his mouth close to Ulman's right ear. His breath was warm. "Maybe you can explain why I did that, Doc."

The
KINDLING EFFECT

PETER HERNON

AVON BOOKS  NEW YORK

This is a work of fiction. The events and characters portrayed are imaginary. Their resemblance to real-life counterparts, if any, is entirely coincidental.

AVON BOOKS
A division of
The Hearst Corporation
1350 Avenue of the Americas
New York, New York 10019

Copyright © 1996 by Peter Hernon
Published by arrangement with the author
Visit our website at **http://AvonBooks.com**
Library of Congress Catalog Card Number: 96-736
ISBN: 0-380-72634-3

Published in hardcover by William Morrow and Company, Inc.; for information address Permissions Department, William Morrow and Company, Inc., 1350 Avenue of the Americas, New York, New York 10019.

First Avon Books Printing: September 1997

AVON TRADEMARK REG. U.S. PAT. OFF. AND IN OTHER COUNTRIES, MARCA REGISTRADA, HECHO EN U.S.A.

Printed in the U.S.A.

WCD 10 9 8 7 6 5 4 3 2 1

To the men and women who are exploring—
often at professional risk—the secrets of the
brain to control violence and crime.
The next century belongs to you.

We know less about the perpetrators of violent crimes than about their victims.

—*Understanding and Preventing Violence*
National Research Council, 1993

The
KINDLING EFFECT

ONE

Dr. Mark Ulman climbed out of bed, making sure he didn't wake his young wife, who lay curled next to him. It was just after two in the morning, but he'd given up on going back to sleep. Ulman dressed quietly in the kitchen and noticed how his hands shook as he fumbled with his shirt buttons. That had never happened before. He figured it was fear.

As he jogged to his car parked just outside the front door, Ulman ran through a hard, cold rain that soaked him to the skin.

He slipped his aging hatchback into first gear and headed for the clinic. Ulman knew he should have done more to halt LePonty's treatments. It had taken him far too long to figure out what was going on. He'd finally put it all together only yesterday. He regretted that bitterly. It was probably too late to stop it. Ulman doubted he'd be able to stabilize LePonty's radically altered behavior, even with lithium or one of the experimental drugs.

Ulman glanced at the speedometer, which glowed a luminescent green. He was normally a cautious driver, but he was doing nearly seventy as he came up Kingshighway, the blowing rain blasting against the windshield. It was like driving through a car wash.

He wasn't sure what he was going to do, but he'd made up his mind that one way or another he was going to halt the treatments. The session yesterday still haunted him.

He'd watched through a two-way mirror as LePonty came out from under the anesthetic. Moments after he woke up, he'd lunged hard against the straps holding him to the gurney. The response was so explosive it had startled Ulman. He vividly remembered the expression on LePonty's face. It was like some of Goya's drawings he'd seen in the Prado during his honeymoon in Spain. Faces drawn in pencil in a lunatic asylum. Twisted, tormented faces from hell.

Ulman and his wife, Liz, lived in one of the once-elegant but run-down homes that lined Tower Grove Park in south St. Louis. Their three-story Federal townhouse needed a new roof, new plumbing and a fortune's worth of other repairs, but at least it was close to the clinic. Within seven minutes Ulman passed the Lafayette Hospital-Pike University medical complex, turned right onto Forest Park Boulevard and drove the five blocks to the Hartigan Clinic, where he'd worked for nearly two years.

He pulled into the fenced, brightly lit parking lot and slammed to a stop by the building's side entrance. The rain beat down on his head and shoulders as he pushed his security card into the door lock and waited for it to buzz open.

As he hurried to his second-floor office, Ulman was surprised that he didn't see a security guard on duty. He figured someone was probably watching him on one of the closed-circuit television monitors that scanned every floor in the building. Then he forgot about it; he had other matters on his mind. The first thing he wanted to do was look in on LePonty.

Ulman slipped on his white lab coat—at least *it* was dry—and walked into the hallway to take the elevator to the clinic's subbasement. A buzzer was sounding on one of the lower floors. The elevator was apparently stuck there. Ulman tried the button twice, then gave up and hurried down the steps to the first floor. He stopped when he reached the lobby. He thought he'd heard footsteps. The recessed lights were dimmed and shadows played out in dark patches on the floor.

"Doctor, wait." The voice, soft, almost whispered, was right behind him.

Ulman turned and froze. Just two feet away, LePonty was smiling at him, his hard, suspicious face obscured in the shadows but his teeth flashing with the whiteness of bone.

"Glad you stopped by."

The words and tone were chilling.

"You should be in your room, Frank," the doctor said, forcing himself to speak with clear precision.

"Let's take a ride."

"I don't think that's a good idea, Frank. We can go back . . ."

A burst of pain suddenly exploded in his head as LePonty hit him across the face with something hard. He tasted the blood pouring from his lip.

"I don't want to repeat myself," LePonty said, pressing a pistol barrel against the doctor's temple. "Let's go to the back door off the parking lot." He smiled when Ulman glanced at him. "Yeah, I know about that door," he said, grinning.

Ulman heard a sound.

Someone else was there, watching from the doorway of the receptionist's office. In the dim shadows, Ulman couldn't make out the face; he barely glimpsed the dark silhouette before the figure withdrew into the office and closed the door.

Ulman shouted for help.

LePonty laughed and said, "Scream your lungs out."

He nudged Ulman in the small of the back to get him moving. The door that opened onto the parking lot had a push-button combination lock. LePonty punched in the four digits without hesitating. The door clicked open.

"I'll kill you if you try anything. I'd just as soon waste you after all the fucking shit you bastards have done to me. Let's go."

They walked to Ulman's car. In the bright light, Ulman noticed LePonty's blood-encrusted hands. It looked like he was wearing crimson gloves. LePonty made the doctor get in first, then slipped into the back seat.

"Take the car, Frank. You can have my wallet and money," Ulman said, struggling with his panic. "Please don't take me with you."

"No can do." LePonty's voice had fluctuated crazily from almost serene calmness to a madman's shrill cry. "Let's pay a visit to your wife."

The doctor opened his mouth but couldn't push out the words. He looked wildly over his shoulder at LePonty. He remembered telling him during one of their interviews that he was married. It was an inexcusable mistake. You were never supposed to give a patient even the slightest glimpse of your family or private life.

They turned onto Magnolia Avenue and drove along the northern edge of Tower Grove Park. Through the cracked window, Ulman smelled the wet leaves that carpeted the ground. His mind was racing. They were approaching his block.

Ulman looked desperately for a cop. There'd been a lot of patrol cars in the neighborhood in recent days, following a rash of house break-ins. But the wide street that paralleled the park was deserted.

When they started to drive by his house, Ulman couldn't bring himself to stop. Instantly he felt the gun barrel jab against the base of his skull—metal to bone.

"Hold it right here, you fuck."

Another pang of fear stabbed Ulman's heart. LePonty must have looked up his address—or someone had given it to him. The same person who'd given him a gun and helped him escape. Even in Ulman's state of almost total mental paralysis, that thought bored deeply into his consciousness.

He parked a half-block up the street from his house, in the first available space. The homes along the block, all big places with spacious yards and mature trees, were dark. Ulman sat there, gripping the wheel with both hands, trying to think of something to do. Anything. Liz would be sleeping.

She was five years younger than he and more beautiful than he deserved.

"Nice place. All that time you were screwing with my head, I was thinking wouldn't it be great to visit your house."

"Please, Frank." He closed his eyes and held back the scream.

"I almost forgot. I got something to show you."

LePonty's voice was friendly, almost intimate. He fumbled in his pocket, then dropped something in Ulman's lap.

It was soft and felt like a piece of wet cloth with threads attached. Then Ulman realized what he was holding: part of a human scalp.

"I cut that off the guard after I blew his brains out," LePonty said. He put his mouth close to Ulman's right ear. His breath was warm. "Maybe you can explain why I did that, Doc."

A thought came to Ulman: Honk the horn. Maybe someone would look outside and call the police.

LePonty wrapped an arm around the doctor's neck and pulled his head back. Ulman felt a knife blade against his throat.

"Give me your house key."

Ulman realized that LePonty was going to kill him in the car. He couldn't let him in the house. He was suddenly thinking with vivid clarity.

"The key."

The blade nicked his chin.

Ulman started praying. He hadn't done that in years. *Hail Mary, full of grace. The Lord is with Thee.*

He was fumbling in his pocket for his key.

Blessed art Thou among women . . .

He raised the key, then threw it onto the floorboard of the car and pressed both hands against the horn.

And blessed is the fruit of Thy womb.

He pressed down on the blasting horn even as LePonty cut his throat open, even as he saw his dark, arterial blood spray out against the windshield. The knife slashed at him again and again, but he had the steering wheel and horn mechanism clamped down.

Ulman forced himself to hold on, even as he began to lose consciousness.

A light blinked on in the house next to his. The front door opened. The last thing Dr. Mark Ulman saw in this world was his neighbor looking out his door and LePonty sprinting up the street away from his house.

TWO

DR. ROBERT HARTIGAN EASED into a parking space at the state mental hospital on Arsenal Street, turned off the engine and opened his briefcase. He wanted to glance at John Brook's impressive résumé one more time.

Brook and the five other finalists who had applied to join his staff as research associates were equally impressive on paper. They'd all gone to fine medical schools; three had already published in top journals. Each was keen to do breakthrough research in the treatment and cure of criminal behavior.

For months Hartigan had meant to hire another associate. He'd even authorized key staff members to interview a handful of the most promising candidates. But now a new urgency drove the talent hunt. Ulman's death three weeks earlier had been a devastating blow. He needed to replace him—and as soon as possible.

The choice wasn't easy, but Hartigan had finally settled on Brook because of the personal recommendation of Phil Mila, professor emeritus of neurology at the Pike University medical school and an old friend whose opinion he valued over all others. Brook had done exceptionally well at the University of Chicago medical school and was finishing up a fellowship in forensic psychiatry at Pike, where Hartigan had once taught.

His résumé indicated that he had strong research talents. Mila had sung his praises, saying he excelled in neuropathology and liked to get into the brain. He was a team player. All critical attributes. Hartigan also knew that Brook was six three and weighed 195 pounds, that he jogged and worked out.

In a showdown with a violent patient, physical strength counted for something. Brook's rugged good looks didn't hurt, either. Hartigan had done enough fund raising for his clinic to appreciate the importance of making the right impression.

Hartigan had driven to the state hospital to offer the job personally. He wanted Brook on board no later than the following week.

It was a sunny afternoon in early fall—a day of rare good weather in St. Louis. A few psychiatry residents and patients sat outside the hospital—the residents in white jackets, the patients in their blue robes and slippers. Hartigan, who was fifty-seven years old, got out of his car and walked toward the entrance. A fifteen-hundred-dollar cashmere sports jacket hung perfectly on his tall, slender frame. His thinning white hair was combed straight back, and his trademark bow tie was a ribbon of gold-and-red silk beneath his prominent Adam's apple. His nose, cheekbones and chin were sharply defined, his stride brisk and purposeful.

He entered the forensic unit, smiling politely as the medical staff warmly greeted him. As a world authority in the treatment of psychopathic behavior, he'd grown used to such recognition. The clinic he'd founded eight years earlier rivaled the Menninger Clinic in Topeka as the leader in treating violent, criminal behavior and the most severe forms of mental illness. Hartigan was a member of every national and international medical board that mattered, and in some circles he was considered a dark-horse candidate for a Nobel Prize. But he knew better. His work was much too controversial.

Hartigan rarely visited the state mental hospital. It was too depressing. The complex was badly run down. Even the graceful copper rotunda of the main building, a landmark, was encased in scaffolding. The whole place looked poor and underfunded, the paint peeling and faded, the grass uncut. Its drab, heavy masonry made it look exactly like what it was—a warehouse for the mentally ill, a dozen or so of whom happened to be violent killers.

The director of the forensic unit, a small Pakistani with an unpronounceable name, stepped forward with his hand extended, smiling brightly. He'd been expecting him. Hartigan knew this man was just barely competent and that his idea of treating the criminally insane never went beyond administering neuroleptics or lithium.

"Doctor Brook will be down shortly," the director said. "He's been detained. There is a slight problem on C-four."

C-4 was the ward that housed the NGRIs—the not-guilty-by-reason-of-insanity cases. There were about thirty men locked up there on the fourth floor.

"What kind of problem?" Hartigan asked.

A scream rang out somewhere upstairs.

"That would be Doctor Brook's patient," the director volunteered.

"May I observe what's happening?" Hartigan asked.

"It would be an honor," the director said, showing Hartigan to the elevator.

As they waited, another scream, feral and loud, shattered the building's oppressive silence.

"What did he do?" Hartigan asked.

"Shot his wife, I think."

"What else?" There was always something else.

"I believe he beat her somewhat with a hammer."

Brook had been examining charts in the small office off the front desk when the commotion broke out in the hallway. Running to investigate, he found one of his patients lying unconscious on the floor. The duty nurse, Betty Rawling, was bent over him, trying to stop the flow of blood with a towel. His nose looked broken.

"Randall," Betty said, not looking up from the patient as she went about her work with cool professionalism.

Brook caught the edge in her voice and immediately knew why. Two days earlier, Randall Mitchell, a bipolar patient, had been diagnosed as HIV-positive. He was carrying the virus that caused AIDS, which, for someone as dangerously unstable as Randall, was like walking around with a loaded shotgun.

Someone screamed in the dayroom at the other end of the ward.

Betty tersely explained that Randall had struck the patient with a telephone receiver he had ripped off the wall. Then he'd run for the dayroom. Two orderlies, Smith and Williams, had gone after him. She'd also sounded the "all available help" alarm. Orderlies and a few doctors had hurried to C-4 from other parts of the hospital. They were already locking the other patients in their rooms. Upset by the excitement, a few were howling and clapping.

Brook swore to himself. He'd noticed this morning that Randall looked mildly agitated. He hadn't eaten breakfast and had started pacing the hallway, trying to borrow cigarettes from patients, which was against the rules. Smoking, strictly regulated on C-4, was permitted in the dayroom only at certain hours.

Brook had spoken briefly to Randall, but now he regretted that he hadn't examined him more carefully. He was still trying to establish the proper haloperidol dosage to control Randall's rapidly cycling mood swings.

Randall was about five nine, heavyset and slow moving. But he had an explosive temper. He'd pounded his wife to a pulp with a hammer, then set fire to their home. He almost didn't make it out, suffering third-degree burns on his arms before he jumped out a window. He liked to show the scars off to other C-4 patients by wearing short-sleeved shirts. It wasn't pretty. Both arms looked as if they'd been melted.

Brook ran for the dayroom, slipping on a pair of plastic gloves he'd snatched from the red box mounted on the wall for quick access in emergencies. Brook knew this wasn't going to be easy. His hope was he could calm Randall down long enough to get a syringe of lorazepam into him. Used to reduce agitation, the drug was especially effective with violent patients.

"You get these fuckers out of here!" Randall shouted as soon as Brook arrived at the dayroom, a large sunny space with floor-to-ceiling windows. "I'll give 'em AIDS! I got it. You know I got it!"

He waved the telephone receiver over his head like a war club. He was breathing heavily through clenched teeth.

Patients had attacked Brook twice during his psychiatric career. One had broken a rib, swinging on him with a lampstand when his back was turned. But he'd never had to handle anything like this, a violently unstable patient who was HIV-positive.

Brook's strategy was simple: Talk to him, rush him, get him sedated. Nothing fancy. He felt something cold on his face and realized he'd broken out in a sweat.

"I got to call my lawyer," Randall shouted.

"We can discuss that."

Brook wanted to keep him talking. That was critical. He stopped next to Williams. He liked the soft-spoken orderly who'd worked on C-4 for five years, far longer than most. Williams was well over six four, heavy and thick-shouldered, and he knew how to intimidate. Like Smith, he was wearing gloves.

"Why don't you put the telephone down, Randall," Brook said. "We can talk that way."

He moved a few feet closer. So did Williams.

"You keep that big nigger away from me, man!"

Randall dropped the telephone receiver and pulled a jagged piece of brown glass from his pocket. About six inches long, it was shaped like an ice pick. He slashed it across the palm of his hand, opening up a thick red line.

"I swear I'll give you AIDS. I'll splash you with my blood."

Brook and Williams stopped in their tracks. Blood was pouring from Randall's wound. He gripped the glass shard like a dagger.

"We can talk," Brook said softly, taking another step. He

carefully watched the patient's darting, fevered eyes. He knew he had to do something and do it now.

"Randall, just give . . ."

The patient slashed at his head. Brook ducked out of the way, then went in fast, pinning Randall around the arms and driving him hard to the floor. Williams and Smith moved in quickly, grabbing the patient by the shoulders as he thrashed wildly. Dropping the piece of glass, he bit into Williams's right forearm.

The orderly pulled his arm away without making a sound or releasing his grip.

Betty Rawling hurried up with a hypodermic; she was a stocky woman with thick strong arms who knew what she was doing. She gave Randall an injection through his clothing, straight into his upper chest.

The patient's head snapped back; he stared up at the ceiling. Williams and Smith held him firmly. Within thirty seconds they had him in a padded seclusion room, where he lay on a mattress on the floor, his eyes closed as if he were asleep.

"You get any blood on you?" Brook asked Williams.

"Naw," the big orderly said. "I'll get a bandage on this bite, and I'll be fine." Saliva from a bite didn't matter with AIDS transmission; blood was the key.

Brook hadn't been splattered, either.

That was a close one. Randall was a lethal weapon, and Brook knew there wasn't a doctor working in any big-city emergency room in the country who would have disputed that. Treating a shooting or stabbing victim was like playing Russian roulette. An ER doctor had to assume that every patient was HIV-positive—even the babies. It was the same with the mental cases like Randall.

"Let's get him back to his room," Brook said. "Make sure he doesn't swallow his tongue."

They'd been damn lucky. If they couldn't get Randall stabilized, Brook was going to recommend sending him to the state forensic hospital at Fulton. He was too violent—even for C-4.

He was pulling off his gloves when he turned and saw Hartigan watching him.

"You handled that well," Hartigan said.

"I had great help," Brook said, clearing his throat. He wondered how long Hartigan had been watching. He'd found out less than an hour ago that Hartigan wanted to see him, and figured that it was a follow-up to the interview he'd had six weeks earlier with one of the doctor's associates.

Brook normally didn't get uptight, but this was different. He wanted badly to work with Hartigan and, almost unexpectedly, here he was, one of the most eminent doctors in the world, standing a few feet from him. Brook tried to look relaxed, but doubted he was fooling anyone.

"Let's go to your office and talk," Hartigan said, ignoring the medical director, who lamely tried to say something flattering about Brook's performance.

Hartigan suggested they take the stairwell instead of the elevator, and described how he'd once seen a psychotic patient sever a man's windpipe. It had happened when he'd been a second-year psychiatric resident.

"In this very building," he said, with another hundred-watt smile. "My god, that must have been back in 1966."

He explained that he'd just finished his daily rounds when the man ran into the hallway with a butcher knife, and opened up a patient's arm to the bone and slashed his throat before three security guards clubbed him unconscious.

"The lesson I learned from that," Hartigan said, "was that it took extraordinary skill and courage to face down a dangerously agitated patient. You did very well back there, Doctor."

Brook wore typical resident clothes—khaki chinos, a blue button-down shirt and knit tie. As he took in the elegantly dressed Hartigan, he wished he'd worn his sports coat and his one good pair of slacks. They entered his office, and Hartigan motioned for him to sit down. The room was sparely furnished—two chairs, a gray metal table and two gray metal bookcases filled with back issues of *Psychopathic*

Behavior and other journals. A well-worn copy of the *Diagnostic and Statistical Manual of Mental Disorders* lay open on the desk.

Although he'd never met Robert Hartigan, Brook had read everything the older doctor had written. He especially admired his work on brain dysfunction, a theory that explained the most violent antisocial behavior. Hartigan had targeted the hypothalamus, the thermostat that regulates the most primitive part of the brain, the seat of emotion and awareness, as the source of hormonal imbalances that precipitate savage outbursts. His work was controversial.

"I guess you're wondering why I'm here," Hartigan said, his voice a rich baritone.

Brook was waiting for the questions about why he wanted to join Hartigan's staff. An oral test of some sort. Why the hell else would he come all the way out here? Brook tried to pay close attention to Hartigan's every word.

"I'd like you to join my staff," the doctor said matter-of-factly. "Are you agreeable?"

"Damn yes, I'm agreeable," he said, as a smile spread across his face.

Brook couldn't believe it. No more interviews; he'd been offered the one job he wanted, a chance to work with Robert Hartigan, one of the recognized leaders in developing new treatments for the most severe forms of mental illness— schizophrenia, bipolar affective disorders and major depression. His clinic had also broken new ground in treating criminal pathologies, Brook's goal ever since he'd finished med school. His good luck floored him.

"I had a long talk with Phil Mila the other day," the doctor said. "He told me you're one of the best students he's ever had."

Brook knew this was high praise. Phil Mila was a legend at the Pike University med school. Nearly eighty years old, still razor sharp, and still doing research. Whatever Brook knew about the role of dopamine and the other neurotransmitters he'd learned from Phil Mila.

"What kind of research will I be doing?" Brook was

having trouble believing this was really happening, that he was actually going to join Hartigan's staff. Even with Hartigan himself sitting there, smiling and passing along compliments, it didn't seem possible.

"For the moment, let's just say that you'll be doing some interesting things with the brain," Hartigan said. "That's why I wanted someone with a good neurological background." For the first time, he hesitated, choosing his words carefully. "We'll talk about it in more detail after you start."

He suggested they discuss compensation. "Could you give me a ballpark idea about your salary requirements?"

Brook was thrown by his bluntness. "I was hoping it would be in the seventy or eighty range. I've got some student loans to pay back and some other . . ."

Hartigan waved a hand. "I should think we'd pay about a hundred to start with, and a ten-thousand-dollar raise after six months."

Hartigan watched for the inevitable smile, which slowly spread out from the corners of Brook's lips across his entire face. He didn't try to conceal it.

"That's a very generous offer, Doctor," Brook stammered. It was an incredible offer; he knew that he couldn't have made nearly that much at Case Western, which also wanted to hire him.

"Don't feel too pleased with yourself. You'll make it up to me in overtime within the first year," Hartigan said. "Tell me something about your background."

Sooner or later the question always came up, Brook thought with irritation. He should have expected it, but the job offer and the salary had put him off balance.

"My mother's a high-school teacher. I don't have any siblings. My father died when I was an undergraduate."

Brook explained that his father had been a high-school English teacher and varsity baseball coach in a small town in northeastern Tennessee. One night at a shopping mall in Knoxville, he had run to help a woman fight off two purse snatchers, a pair of husky teenagers. Brook's father had laid one out with a blow to the head; the other shot him in the chest.

"Not to dwell," said Hartigan, "on what must have been a long, troubling episode, but I assume you became a psychiatrist partly because you wanted to find out why so many people kill and do other horrible things. Is that more or less accurate, doctor?"

"Close enough," Brook said. He was upset with himself for letting his anger slip out.

"I appreciate your honesty," Hartigan said.

He went on to explain that, while much of the clinic's routine work involved treating the usual array of psychiatric patients, most of whom were handled as outpatients, their most exciting research focused on ASPs, the antisocial personalities. Brook was well aware that this group, the sociopaths, constituted the overwhelming bulk of the nation's nearly one million prison inmates—the most widespread criminal condition of all. The behavior pattern began in childhood. Lying, stealing, truancy, vandalism, fighting and physical cruelty were common traits. ASPs tended to be recklessly aggressive. They usually lacked a sense of remorse and invariably felt justified in hurting others.

"That's the group we need to address, the one that's destroying the country," Hartigan said. "The one I intend to do something about."

He glanced at his Rolex and stood up. "When can you start?"

Brook hesitated. He would have loved to start tomorrow, but didn't want to leave the hospital without giving adequate notice.

"Would two weeks be all right?"

"I'll expect you in a week," Hartigan said. "I'm sure the director here will understand."

THREE
⊢◆⊣

TOM BRODY SAT IN the front seat of his Jeep and glanced impatiently at the digital clock on the dashboard. It was nearly midnight. They had made good time since leaving St. Louis a little over an hour earlier. They were almost to Effingham, a small community that sat on the desolate Illinois prairie about a hundred miles east of St. Louis, on Interstate 70.

The call he'd been waiting for had arrived two hours earlier. They'd finally gotten a hit on LePonty at a truck stop just outside Effingham. The three-man team he'd sent there had been spreading fifty-dollar bills around like confetti, as they showed LePonty's photo to prostitutes who worked the fringes of the sprawling complex.

They had found a girl who thought she'd seen their boy the night before.

It wasn't a complete shot in the dark. LePonty was from Effingham. His sister and brother still lived there. He'd stayed close to them while he was in prison, and Brody figured he might try to go back home. LePonty's police record showed that he'd been a regular at the Red Bull truck stop, where he'd been arrested for soliciting when he was seventeen. Brody thought there was a chance he'd pay a return visit. He figured LePonty probably needed to get laid.

Until this lapse, LePonty had played it smart ever since

his escape. He'd probably hidden out somewhere in the St. Louis area, pulled a few holdups for money and got a gun. If they were lucky, they'd find out the make and caliber before they had to move on him.

Right now Brody didn't want to think about that. A few miles back, they'd crossed the Kaskaskia River. He figured it had to be some sort of Indian name.

"You know what Indians lived around here?" he asked. He took another sip of hot coffee, then set the thermos back on the Jeep's floorboard.

"Beats me," said the driver. "Maybe they were the Fuck-heads."

"You're the fuckhead, Eliot," Brody said, staring at him. "Too fucking stupid to know this whole area was the center of one of the biggest Indian civilizations in North America. Sacs, Osage, Osceola, Cherokees. They all lived here about a thousand years ago. You ever hear of the 'mound build-ers'?"

"You mean the candy-bar Indians?"

Eliot laughed. He gripped the wheel tightly with both hands. He wore driving gloves. He'd been pushing it well over eighty since they'd left St. Louis.

Brody shook his head and stifled a yawn. This late work was a bitch. Hell, everything was getting more difficult. Pushing forty, he had to work harder than ever just to stay fit—two hours a day, every day. An inch over six feet tall, he filled out his gray turtleneck and brown-suede jacket with muscle. His legs were hardened by a lifetime of mountain roadwork, cycling and martial-arts training.

It had been easier to stay in shape back when he was a U.S. marshal. He'd been with the service nearly ten years, spending most of his time tracking down federal fugitives who skipped abroad just before indictment. Most were drug dealers. Brody's assignment was to find them, then notify the local police, so they could make the arrest and handle the extradition. But if you snatched one of the bastards and got him onto a private plane bound for Miami, none of the bosses back in Washington complained, not even if you had to break a few bones. A little money to help the local *policía* look the other way and the job was done—neatly, quickly, with minimal risk and expense.

He'd quit five years earlier to go into private security work. Except for times like this, the hours were better. So were the money and fringes.

Brody hoped he wouldn't have to kill LePonty. The biggest worry was that he'd do something stupid and get into a jam with the local cops. If that happened, all bets were off. They'd have to take him out quickly, which meant they might also have to take out a couple members of Effingham's police force. It could be a mess.

Eliot turned off the interstate at the Effingham exit and quickly found the Red Bull. Hard to miss, it was one of the largest truck stops between Chicago and Los Angeles—a thousand pungent acres of oil-streaked asphalt, restaurants, two well-equipped garages and a cluster of seedy motels. It was also one of the largest brothels east of Nevada. The girls came from the Windy City, St. Louis, Cincinnati and points in between to hustle the four to five hundred drivers who parked their big eighteen-wheelers on the lot every day to eat, shower, catch a few winks and maybe buy an hour of a woman's time.

Most were freelancers, who stayed in nearby cheap motels or rented trailers. The truckers knew where to go and whom to ask for; dates were usually arranged over the CB. The cops for the most part looked the other way. Vice raids were rare.

Eliot pulled onto the lot. The damp night air reeked of diesel fuel. The trucks, many with their engines rumbling in idle, were lined in long, ragged rows that fanned out around the main terminal like the spokes of a wheel.

Eliot parked next to a trash Dumpster behind the restaurant. A woman quickly walked out of the shadows and slid into the backseat.

She was still young and good-looking but going hard in the face from years working in smoky bars and truck stops. Her shoulder-length hair was streaked blond. She wore black boots, a red mini and a sheer silk blouse. Making herself comfortable, she unbuttoned her fur-lined jacket and crossed her long legs. The musky scent of strong perfume filled the Jeep. She said her name was Joy, and she'd been waiting for them.

Brody handed Joy a 10-by-11-inch black-and-white glossy of LePonty. Two one-hundred-dollar bills were clipped to the picture.

"Tell me what you know," he said.

"You sure you aren't cops?" Joy said.

"If we are, we just bribed you."

"He was here yesterday and I think the day before," Joy said, staring at the photo. She folded the bills and tucked them into the top of her right boot. She took a cigarette and a cheap lighter from her silver handbag.

"Don't smoke," Brody said.

"You could say please," Joy said with a pout. Then she directed a fresh smile at Eliot, who grinned in response.

"Let's keep this focused on the guy in the picture," Brody said. "Where and when did you see him? Be precise."

"Yesterday, about seven. He stopped by my place."

She explained that she rented a one-bedroom trailer just across the interstate from the truck stop. A lot of the girls did the same thing, paying by the month so they could work out of their living quarters.

"How'd he get your name?" Eliot asked.

Joy gave him another hundred-watt smile.

"You do a good job, your name gets around."

"Tell us what happened," Brody said.

"I sent him on his way. He was into the kinky stuff, the handcuffs and ropes and all. He wanted to tie me up and give me a golden shower. Then I was supposed to go down on him. He offered two hundred and I told him, no way. I'm not letting any John piss on me. Especially when he gives me the creeps."

"Why did he give you the creeps, Joy?"

"You sure I can't smoke?"

Brody shook his head.

"You spend ten years getting laid, you get a sixth sense about creeps. That boy's a sicko. I told him to look up Gloria. She'll do anything."

"Where do we find Gloria?" Brody asked.

Joy offered the details. Gloria rented a cabin in an old motel court just outside town. She was a striking black girl from Chicago. Unusually tall, with world-class tits. She cruised the truck stop wearing a tight red raincoat with only a G-string on underneath. Gloria had plenty of regulars.

"Good-bye, Joy," Brody said. He handed her another hundred-dollar bill. He liked the way she took the money and didn't ask questions.

"You've never seen us."

She said she understood as if she meant it. She paused to look at Eliot after wiggling out of the backseat.

"Anytime you want a freebie, give me a call."

FOUR
⊳◆⊲

BROOK SPOKE HIS NAME into the small intercom and waited
for the clinic's front door to click open automatically. He'd
parked his car on the street—a battered Audi with over a
hundred thousand miles on the odometer. He liked the look
of the place. The sandblasted facade was painted a light blue;
with its black-marble, art-deco entrance, the renovated, four-
story building had a decidedly modernist look. It was also
strategically located. The Pike University medical school, the
Missouri School of Pharmacology and three affiliated hospitals were all within a few miles of each other.

Brook was more nervous than he thought he would be
about seeing Jenny Malone again. He'd called her the night
before, and she'd suggested this meeting.

He'd known Jenny back in Chicago when she was a grad-
uate student in neuropsychology. They'd gone out for maybe
three months. Jenny was lovely and bright and he'd started
to fall pretty hard, but then all of a sudden she'd dropped
him.

There was no other way to explain it. One day they were
seeing each other, the next he was history. He remembered
how he'd stopped by her apartment on a blistering summer
afternoon in Hyde Park and caught her on her way out with
an armload of books. She was pleasant but firm about it, and
it seemed to him later that she was repeating from memory

when she told him that she'd decided their relationship didn't have any future and that it was better to end it cleanly so they could get on with their lives.

He could still remember standing on that stairwell landing, feeling like he'd just been clubbed on the head. It had taken awhile to get over her. He'd called her two or three times and left messages with her roommate, but she didn't return them, and he finally gave up trying. Perhaps by mutual design, their paths rarely crossed after that.

Brook had pretty much forgotten about Jenny Malone until four or five weeks ago when he was focusing on trying to get hired at the clinic. He'd made some inquiries about the staff and found out that she worked there as a research psychologist. It had surprised the hell out of him. He had long since gotten over his anger about their breakup, and wondered what she'd think when she found out that he was joining the staff. He hoped she wouldn't be upset. It was crucial that they work together and get along. He wanted to make sure they did.

He also wanted to pump her for information about his new colleagues, especially Hartigan. Any details she could offer would be gold.

As Brook waited for her in the building's small lobby, he glanced with irritation at his scuffed pair of Timberland brogues and reminded himself he needed to buy some clothes. He was pretty sure that Hartigan expected his staff to dress well, and he was tired of looking like a med-school retread.

Brook was tense, edgy, but recognized that they had to put this encounter behind them—and the sooner the better. They would have to work together. And, besides, he wanted to know what she had to say about Hartigan, the clinic and their research.

He saw Jenny Malone come out of an elevator. If she was nervous herself about this encounter, she didn't show it as she enthusiastically offered her hand to Brook.

"It's been a while," he said, smiling, but feeling the corners of his mouth tighten. He knew exactly how long it had been—six years.

"You're sure you really want to work here?" Jenny said, greeting him as if he were an old friend. Her voice, pleasantly natural and warm, seemed a little forced.

"I'd better. I just gave notice at the hospital this morning."

Brook tried not to stare. He'd remembered her as being attractive, but still he was struck by how good-looking she was. Her short black hair and green eyes were a riveting contrast. Back in school, she'd worn jeans and loose-fitting sweaters, and now she was dressed in a tailored blue blazer, a long gathered skirt and smart black pumps.

"We can get coffee upstairs," Jenny said. "Maybe there's still time for me to talk you out of this crazy decision of yours."

Following her, Brook saw that it was a deceptive building, larger than it appeared from the street and tastefully, almost elegantly, furnished. A pair of chrome-and-leather Eames chairs graced the lobby's parquet floor. An audacious red-and-yellow print of Donald Duck dressed in a doctor's white jacket hung on one of the pale-gray walls.

"An original Lichtenstein," Jenny said. "We don't have much artwork here, but it's all first rate. Doctor Hartigan is quite a collector."

They went to a room on the third floor, walking up an ornate, wrought-iron staircase that the building's renovators had wisely left open and exposed. The paneled conference room was softly lit; a table and buffet offered a selection of sweet-rolls, bagels, fresh fruit and coffee.

They got coffee and sat in a corner at one of the room's café-sized tables. Jenny was close enough for Brook to smell her perfume. That was something new; she hadn't worn perfume when he'd known her in school. Brook hadn't planned to mention those days at all. In fact, he'd decided in advance to avoid the past. But to his surprise, she brought it up herself, matter-of-factly suggesting they fill each other in on what they'd been doing since they left the University of Chicago.

"I'll go first, but you're next," she said leveling her gaze at him.

This time Brook thought her smile seemed artificial.

Two months after their last "meeting," a word she chose with deliberation, she'd left the university for good. Brook had known that, but hadn't known where she'd gone. By then he hadn't bothered to find out; he hadn't wanted to know.

"The short version is that I transferred to Yale, managed to talk them into accepting most of my credits and got a Ph.D. in neuropsychology in two years. Dr. Hartigan hired me while I was writing my dis. I've been here nearly two years, which still doesn't seem possible."

By unspoken mutual agreement, it was clear they weren't going to mention that they'd once shared drinks in the smoky Hyde Park student bars, or prepared for lab tests together or even known one another.

Brook was more than willing to go along with that strategy, but couldn't deny to himself that something had turned deep within him when he first laid eyes on her a few minutes earlier down in the lobby.

Jenny's speciality was the development of new testing procedures for antisocial personalities—the ASPs who were rapidly filling the nation's prisons to bursting. The standard battery of tests—everything from the Minnesota Multiphasic Personality Inventory, the famous MMPI-2, to projective techniques like the Rorschach and the Thematic Apperception Test, or TAT—had long been the main tools in diagnosing potential offenders, especially at an early age.

Brook had always found the area of psychological testing dry as toast. T-scores, norming, subscales. Too much statistics for his taste. And yet it was crucial. He could tell from the way Jenny's eyes brightened that she was full of the subject, but you'd never know that from her carefully chosen words. Her answers were reserved, almost clinically spare.

Jenny quietly explained that she was also working on new cognitive-behavior-altering treatments for violent sex offenders. She didn't mention that this was an area in which she was rapidly gaining a national reputation.

"That's enough on me," she said. "What about you?"

Brook described what he'd been doing for the last five years—med school, a long psychiatry residency at Pike University and the state mental hospital, where he'd worked almost exclusively with NGRI psychopaths, and now at the Hartigan Clinic. He kept it brief.

"He's tickled that you've decided to join us," Jenny volunteered. "I've never seen him so excited about one of his recruits."

She seemed more relaxed once they'd moved beyond the awkward discussion of their past. She crossed her legs, leaned forward and took a sip of coffee, which until then she hadn't touched.

"Did he pay you to say that?"

"Absolutely."

Brook asked her about her work with sex offenders. "That's a hot area. How did you get interested?" Brook wasn't just trying to make conversation; he really wanted to know, and was struck by the incongruity of this lovely woman doing research in that field.

"I had a class with Margaret Dwight Listing. She taught a fall seminar at Yale."

Listing was considered the leading authority on serial sexual killers. She was on the medical faculty at Cornell and had gained celebrity status through her interviews with killers like John Wayne Gacy and Ted Bundy. She'd also written extensively on the neurological and organic basis for their deadly rampages.

"She played a video of her interview with Bundy," Jenny said, smoothing her napkin on her lap. "He could name every one of his victims, the way they looked, the kind of clothing they wore. The most chilling part of it was when he said he'd moved from Seattle to Florida because it had the death penalty. Knowing that he could get the electric chair if he got caught added to his high."

Jenny explained that she was interested in the theory that

serial killers "troll," or hunt, for their victims in cycles much like a woman's menstrual period. She thought the episodic attacks resulted from irregular hormonal rhythms that also produced fear, anxiety and sexual arousal.

"Have you ever met a serial?" Brook asked.

"Two of them. I interviewed Bobby Lee Davis four times."

"The man they just executed."

Davis had recently been given a lethal injection at the state prison in Potosi. He'd murdered seven women in five states during a week-long rampage through the Midwest. Each was raped, bound with elaborate knots and stabbed to death.

"I was there," Jenny said. "He wanted me as one of the witnesses. He was heavily sedated, but he recognized me as he lay on a gurney. They'd already put the Pentothal IV in his left arm." She glanced at Brook over her raised coffee cup. "He was the most frightening man I ever met. He once told me he'd love to cut off one of my breasts. It was high praise. He said he only took the breasts from the pretty ones." Jenny paused. "Whenever I think I've hit a dead end, all I have to do to keep working is remember that another hundred or so just like him are walking the streets."

"The problem's always been that we can't really do any more than interview these people," Brook said. "We can't do any systematic testing when we catch a serial. Hell, we can't even run routine lab work on them."

Jenny looked at him and, for the briefest moment, thought about discussing that point. No, this wasn't the right place, or time.

Brook asked about Dr. Hartigan.

"Obsessive, brilliant, a world-class workaholic. He'll push you like you've never been pushed before and make you do the best work you're capable of. Should I go on?"

"Please."

"He'll give you anything you need, no matter what the cost. He's impatient and has a temper that has to be seen to be believed. Feel free to disagree with him; he encourages that. But don't make the mistake of saying something stupid.''

Brook had already heard all that about Hartigan; his explosive temper—part of his persona as the hard-driving, break-through scientist—was carefully cultivated for effect. He wanted to know about the work the doctor had under way at the clinic.

"So, how many research associates work here?'' Brook asked.

"Six,'' Jenny said. "We all have our own labs and assistants. I think you'll be impressed when you see the place. I've been to all the major research centers—Hershey, Yale, Stanford. Nothing compares.''

"Am I filling a new position?''

For the first time, Brook detected an awkward hesitation on Jenny's part.

"We've needed to hire another researcher for months, but Doctor Hartigan could never make up his mind. Then something happened a few weeks ago. . . . One of our doctors died.''

"God, I had no idea. How did it . . .''

Brook saw how uncomfortable Jenny had become.

"I probably shouldn't tell you this, but you've got the right to know that the man you're replacing was killed in an accident with one of the patients.'' Jenny looked unsure of herself, suddenly.

"Accident?'' Brook was surprised. "What kind of accident? Some kind of car wreck? What happened to him?''

Jenny hesitated as if she wanted to say more. "Maybe it would be better if you discussed this with Doctor Hartigan,'' she said.

Realizing how curtly she'd spoken, she immediately apologized.

"Most of us haven't gotten over it. We just don't know very much about what happened. Hartigan isn't talking about it, and we're not supposed to ask.''

"What was his name, if you don't mind my asking?'' Brook wondered whether he knew him.

"Mark Ulman," Jenny said softly. "He'll be missed."

He didn't recognize the name. Jenny took another sip of coffee, and he noticed that her hands trembled. She clearly wanted to change the subject.

Jenny glanced at her watch. "I'd better be getting back," she said. "I've got a meeting in five minutes." Another smile. "You'll find out about all the meetings in this place soon enough."

She led him back downstairs, and at the front door once again offered her hand. Her eyes—clear, deep, penetrating— briefly held his.

There was so much more Brook wanted to talk about, so much the two of them had left unsaid. He was still puzzled by her cryptic comment about Ulman's death. As he walked to his car in the glittering, mica-hard sunshine of a late fall afternoon, Brook had to admit that he'd found Jenny intriguing and appealing. Just as he had once before.

FIVE

GLORIA SYLVESTER RENTED BY the month at Coral Estates, a cluster of fifteen decrepit one-bedroom bungalows with attached garages, about a mile outside Effingham. In the late thirties they had been the ultimate in roadside chic, with pulsing facades of coral-red tile, but the place had aged badly and only three of the units were occupied. Overnight guests were rare. The elderly couple who managed the property seldom left their two-story cabin at the main entrance.

Brody figured Gloria probably liked the isolation. From what Joy had told them, she had a regular clientele who enjoyed rough sex.

They'd been watching her for nearly a week. She'd turned a couple tricks at her place, and spent most of her time there—sleeping, eating in, watching movies on the VCR. She didn't have a telephone and relied exclusively on her beeper, driving to a pay phone to return calls and arrange appointments.

So far, no LePonty.

But on the seventh day, at four P.M., she climbed into a late-model Chevy Caprice, wearing her business suit, the distinctive red raincoat. Cut off just below her thighs, it showed an expanse of incredibly long legs. Gloria was at least six one.

Brody decided to take a chance. While two men followed

her, another used a screwdriver to pry open the rusting metal frame of her bathroom window. Slipping inside, he planted two bugs—in the kitchen and bedroom. The work was done crudely but efficiently. He placed the dime-sized cylindrical microphones in small holes chiseled out of the window caulking in the two rooms. A dab of gray caulk sealed them in place. A strand of wire thinner than a human hair ran down the outside wall to a cigarette-sized transmitter. The man finished the job in five minutes. He also shot Instamatic photographs of the small apartment's interior.

Brody and Eliot waited in the Jeep. They'd parked behind some shrubs that bordered a road in back of the motel court. Two others sat in a van, which was also hidden in shadows. Both vehicles were equipped with radio receivers that would pick up every sound inside the apartment.

The bed was outfitted with ropes at the head- and footboards, so that Gloria could indulge her clients' unique tastes; two wrist chains hung from a wall bracket, and she had a collection of leather halters, whips, straitjackets and other S&M paraphernalia neatly arrayed on a table.

Her cabin was at the back of the motel court. The units were ranged along an S-shaped blacktop lined with oak trees.

The two other occupied units were near the entrance.

Brody thought the setup was as good as they were likely to get. With luck, they could do what had to be done without being seen or heard. He realized that he was trying to reassure himself; something usually went wrong on jobs like this.

He'd already explained the plan twice to his men. Plain vanilla, nothing fancy. If LePonty showed up, he and Eliot would go in after him. They'd already jimmied the garage door so it couldn't be locked. They would roll in under it and enter through a side door that opened onto the kitchen.

Brody studied the interior photographs and made a pencil sketch of the floor plan; the bedroom was entered through a short hallway. He handed the drawing to Eliot.

"Memorize this," he said. "We'll move in as soon as they get comfortable."

Eliot's job was to go as far as the kitchen and keep Brody covered.

"It's going to be damn tight," he said, scanning the drawing. "That kitchen's like a closet."

It was getting late in the day. The shadows of trees slanted across the road when the team tracking Gloria reported by radio that she'd just made a telephone call from a drive-up pay phone and was heading back to the motel.

Minutes later her car pulled up in front of her cabin; she was alone. She got out, opened the garage door and drove inside.

Another ten minutes passed. A red, mud-splattered pickup swung into the driveway. From his vantage point across the road, Brody focused his binoculars on the driver, who wore a navy windbreaker. He was starting to grow a beard. After turning off the engine, the man removed his sun glasses and sat behind the wheel a moment, staring up at the cabin.

"It's him," Brody said softly. Their patience had paid off. He radioed word of LePonty's arrival to the team waiting in the van.

"Get your vest on," he told Eliot.

They slipped on their black, bulletproof Kevlar vests.

The two bugs picked up the dialogue inside the cabin. Brody and Eliot heard LePonty tell Gloria to take off her raincoat. He whistled.

"You're one tall cunt," LePonty said. "Those legs could wrap around me twice."

Gloria laughed. But she was all business.

"You said you wanted it rough. How rough?"

"Tie you down. Maybe some oral sex."

"That kind of fun's gonna cost you two bills," Gloria said. "In advance."

When they spoke again they'd moved to the bedroom.

"Put on the neck collar."

It was LePonty's voice. He was polite, almost pleasant. Brody thought he might as well have been telling her what to order for dinner.

"You do got a nice pair of tits, baby. Why don't you slip on that leather halter."

"That'll cost you another fifty," Gloria said.

"No problem, baby. That's very nice. Lie down and let me tie you up."

Brody and Eliot heard the bedsprings creak.

"Not too tight, big boy," Gloria said as LePonty fastened her wrists and ankles to the bed.

Brody glanced at Eliot. Sweat had beaded on his forehead; he was breathing heavily.

Gloria told LePonty to wrap her with a blanket if he used a whip.

"I'm not fucking joking about that," she said.

There was more movement on the bed.

"You look like a *Playboy* foldout instead of a nigger cunt."

LePonty's voice had turned hard.

"That's not a nice way to talk," Gloria said. For the first time, she sounded frightened.

"Look what I brought along to play with, baby."

"Jesus, no!" Gloria wailed in panic. "Don't you fucking do that to me."

A scream—sharp, loud, piercing.

"Did that hurt, cunt? That was a short one. This one's a couple inches longer. You like the way your tits look now?"

"What the hell's he doing to her?" Eliot said, looking at Brody.

"I don't know."

Gloria screamed again.

"Let's move on this guy," Eliot said, slamming his fist against the dash.

More screams followed, then curses and the sound of the chains rattling as Gloria writhed on the bed.

"Stop," she begged. "Please stop this!"

"Not while I've got so many nice things to decorate you with," LePonty said.

"Let's pull the plug on this bastard," Eliot growled, reaching for the door-handle.

"Stay where you are!" Brody snapped. He wanted to hear more; he was also worried about making his move too soon. He wanted to be sure LePonty was totally distracted.

The screaming continued intermittently for another ten minutes. Then they heard LePonty climb onto the bed.

"Now I'm going to fuck you, cunt, but first let me help you get in the mood."

Gloria's scream escaped from deep within her as if torn from her soul.

"He's screwing her," Brody said. It was time. "Put your hood on." Then over the radio: "We're going in."

They jogged across the road to the garage, lifted the door a few feet and rolled under. They wore black facemasks, hoods and black trousers. Each carried a 9 mm Glock equipped with a silencer and laser sight.

The door to the kitchen wasn't locked. Brody slipped inside and looked up the hallway to the bedroom. He could hear Gloria moaning.

Motioning with his left hand for Eliot to stay behind, Brody inched his way to the bedroom door, keeping his back flat against the wall. He held his pistol at eye level, took a breath and stepped into the bedroom.

"It's over!" he shouted.

Chained to the bed, Gloria raised her head and let it fall back.

LePonty, who lay next to her, reacted with surprising speed. He grabbed a gun from under the pillow, rolled over on his side and might have gotten off a round at Brody if he hadn't wasted the first bullet on Gloria. He shot her in the head.

Brody fired twice as LePonty swung the pistol in his direction. Both rounds hit him in the upper chest, knocking him onto the floor. He was a spindly man with a Nazi cross tattooed in blue ink on his sunken chest. He'd peeled off his shirt, but still wore his jeans.

Eliot was in the room.

"Damn, look at her," he said.

The bullet had blown away the back of Gloria's head.

Brody had seen wounds like that before. But what LePonty had done to her breasts was as original as it was sick. He'd stuck thirty or forty hatpins into them, along with several pieces of cheap rhinestone jewelry that glittered in the dim light.

"Why did he shoot her?" Eliot asked. His face was pale. Brody worried that he was going to throw up.

"Maybe he figured it was a double-cross," Brody said.

A troubling thought entered his mind. Nothing in LePonty's prison profile or background had remotely suggested that he was capable of carving up a doctor, or a prostitute—or of taking on a man in a bulletproof vest in a no-win gunfight.

He knelt next to LePonty and picked up his pistol, a heavy Browning. LePonty's eyes fixed on his face. The right pupil had already dilated and turned white. The two small, dime-sized wounds in his chest made a sucking sound. He was dying.

He tried to say something. Flecks of blood bubbled from his mouth.

"Say it again," Brody said, slipping his arm under Le-Ponty's head. "I don't understand you."

LePonty's teeth were clenched. He mumbled something again, spitting blood.

"I'm listening," Brody said, putting his ear near Le-Ponty's lips. "Come on, speak to me."

This time he understood every word.

LePonty thanked him.

SIX

AT EXACTLY NINE A.M. ON a cool autumn Monday, Brook was buzzed into the clinic's lobby. His first day on the job. He'd been up since five that morning and was eager to get started. He wore a new tweed jacket and dress slacks. Anticipating a hefty salary increase, he'd bought a couple outfits off the rack at Brooks Brothers—a little too conservative for his tastes but a nice fit. He carried a well-traveled, blue-canvas briefcase. The strap was looped over his shoulder. He was more nervous than he'd expected to be.

Dr. Hartigan was waiting for him.

"Glad to see you, John," he said, striding across the lobby and vigorously shaking Brook's hand. "I want to show you around a bit. Then we can talk."

Hartigan wore an immaculate white shirt and a small bow tie that added to his professorial image. They took the elevator to the second floor.

The tour began at the library, the clinic's bustling heart. Two librarians were on duty from eight A.M. until eight P.M., six days a week. "We have a computer link with the libraries at the state hospital and at Pike University," Hartigan said. "We also subscribe to over ten thousand journals. If you need something and can't find it, just let our librarians, Martha or Debra, know."

"We'll also get you any lab assistance you'll need," Hartigan said. "We can talk about that a little later."

They had a lot to discuss. But his questions could wait. Hartigan seemed so intent on showing him around that he didn't want to interrupt.

They climbed the stairway to the fourth floor. Brook admired the hardwood floors that were polished to a sheen.

"We'll start with Marty Conner's PET scanner," Hartigan said. "I know that must impress you."

"You've got a PET scanner?" Brook asked, trying not to sound like a boy asking about a new toy. He was flabbergasted. Most hospitals couldn't afford a positron emission tomography machine—much less a psychiatric clinic, even one as prestigious as Hartigan's. The starting price was around a million dollars.

"I would have fired you if you hadn't been impressed," Hartigan said lightly. "You'll be seeing a lot of Marty."

Brook was familiar in a general way with PET scans, which offered a noninvasive window into how the brain worked. PET imaging was based on the fact that mental functions, even vision and emotion, are accompanied by increases in blood flow, oxygen and glucose metabolism. The PET scan measured these metabolic changes by injecting radioactive tracer molecules into the bloodstream, then photographing the gamma rays that flashed like lightning in the affected parts of the brain.

Few fields in psychiatry offered more promise than PET neuroimaging, and Brook was well aware of its exciting potential. By injecting subjects with small amounts of a radioactive material, it was possible to take computer-generated pictures of how the brain "lit up" when it performed certain tasks. Its applications to psychiatry were only just being realized. The technology offered a way of studying how neuroreceptors work in living subjects and—more important for psychiatrists—how psychoactive drugs affect these neuroreceptors.

For the first time, brain function could be tracked.

If Hartigan wanted him to do PET research, Brook was

more than willing; he couldn't have asked for anything better.

Hartigan opened a door to Marty Conner's office. Conner was expecting them. He got up from his desk to shake Brook's hand. Conner was a big round-shouldered man, well over six feet tall, a neurologist who loved to paddle Missouri's Ozark streams on long getaway weekends. His four-wheel-drive Chevy Bronco had a canoe rack on the roof. But he didn't have much time to get out on the water these days; he put in ninety-hour weeks working with the PET scanner.

"I think Doctor Hartigan may have plans for us, so what do you say we take a look at the machine," Conner said.

He led Brook and Hartigan into a large adjoining room. The PET scanner, with its unmistakable "donut hole" insertion chamber, filled most of the floorspace. Brook stood in awe in front of the gray machine, which was a good seven feet tall. But the apparatus itself didn't astound him as much as the technology that accompanied it. To do PET scans, most clinics used an on-site cyclotron to produce the positron-emitting isotopes that were used as radioactive tracers. But Hartigan's lab used a linear accelerator to produce the "hot" isotopes.

"It's much smaller than a cyclotron and requires far less lead shielding," Conner explained. "We've got it down in the basement."

Linear accelerators were just coming online. The technology was brand-new. Even the Pike University medical school, a pioneer in PET technology, still used a cyclotron to produce most of the isotopes needed for PET scanning.

"What kind of radioactive element do you use?" Brook asked.

"Oxygen-15," Conner said. "We've found it works better than Fluorine-18. It has a half-life of only two minutes, which means it's extremely safe. That's the good news. The bad news is that it doesn't give you much time to take your pictures. You've got to move damn fast around here."

"I still can't believe this," Brook mumbled in astonishment.

"You'll find that we do a lot of brain work," Hartigan said. "We need the PET-imaging capability. Marty and several of the other doctors on staff practically have a monopoly here. So a word of warning: If you need the scanner, be sure to sign up early."

Brook noticed a strange-looking apparatus suspended from the ceiling by a movable steel arm and draped with a black hood. The device was positioned directly above the patient gurney, which was backed up against the scanner's donut hole. Brook asked what it was for.

"That's a closed-circuit television screen," Conner said. "We put the subject's head into the scanner and cover him to the waist with the hood so that he can see only what's projected on the TV screen. Then we show him certain images and see what part of his brain lights up."

"We're running some interesting experiments on brain function, but more on that later," Hartigan said.

The clinic director was being deliberately vague. Brook knew that Pike and a few other large medical schools were doing similar work on how the brain processes language. He still had difficulty believing that a private clinic could engage in such costly research.

"A one-million-dollar scanner and a two-million-dollar accelerator to study an organ that weighs three pounds," Hartigan said.

"How the hell can you afford this?" Brook asked.

Hartigan chuckled.

"We're a small clinic, but we're extremely well funded. We receive sizable Ford and Rockefeller grants. Only a small portion of our yearly budget comes from the NIH and other federal sources. We've also been endowed by several private benefactors who are very interested in our work. Unfortunately, I can't tell you their names; they insist on anonymity. Suffice it to say that we've got some big money behind us. Enough to get anything we need."

Brook wondered about these benefactors. But Hartigan didn't volunteer any more information, so he didn't press it.

The clinic, Hartigan went on, also had a close working

relationship with a private laboratory in St. Louis that was developing some experimental, made-to-order drugs for them.

"PCZ Pharmaceuticals," he said. "They're doing some incredibly advanced work. They've got computers that can create three-dimensional color images of molecules. You put on a pair of three-D eyeglasses, and it looks like you can reach in and touch them. They're working with Al Silver to come up with some interesting new psychotropics. He's just getting ready to run the drug trials."

Brook already knew about Silver, who published regularly in the leading neuropsychiatry journals. His main work had focused on the neurotransmitters that seemed to be involved in predatory aggression, especially the serotonergic system. Neurotransmitters like dopamine seemed to enhance aggression, while norepinephrine and serotonin appeared to inhibit it. Silver was also looking at testosterone, prolactin and other hormones thought to play a role in aggressive behavior.

Brook had never heard of PCZ Pharmaceuticals, but knew that psychiatrists were often involved in FDA-sanctioned drug tests. He'd worked on several himself. There was nothing all that unusual about it, which was why he found it strange that Hartigan cut him off when he asked a fairly innocuous question about Silver's work. Brook was puzzled by Hartigan's evasiveness. He definitely didn't want to reveal much about the clinic's more interesting projects.

"Trust me, Doctor. All will be explained in good time," Hartigan said, reading Brook's concern. "Let's go next door. There's something else I want you to see."

They left the PET scanner and entered a small, state-of-the-art pathology lab. The room was equipped with a stainless-steel autopsy table. Gleaming dissection instruments were neatly arrayed on an adjoining counter. Stryker saws, used for opening the cranium, hung from a wall.

Brook gave Hartigan another surprised look. First the PET scanner and now this. The clinic was far better equipped than he'd imagined. This was turning into quite a tour.

"You do autopsies here?" he asked.

"Sometimes, but not often," Hartigan said. "Although we do section and stain a lot of brains. Here's what I want to show you."

They entered an adjoining room. Hartigan switched on the light. Two five-gallon plastic buckets were on a table. Brook smelled the strong odor of formaldehyde.

"We just got these," Hartigan said. "We'll be getting several more in the next few months."

Brook looked inside the buckets. Already sectioned, the brains were submerged in formaldehyde.

Hartigan pulled on a pair of rubber gloves and motioned for Brook to do the same.

He reached into the first bucket and gently lifted out a brain hemisphere that had been cross-sectioned to lay open the limbic system—the fibers and nuclei that ringed the brainstem.

Hartigan traced the major parts with a gloved finger—the hypothalamus, the sea-horse-shaped hippocampus, the amygdala.

"The oldest, most primitive part of the brain, and probably the most important," he said. "Fear, the sex drive, anger, our basic emotions. They all originate right here in the limbic region."

"Professor Mila liked to say that we were beasts long before we were angels," Brook said. His favorite professor. White-haired, irascible, pungent in his viewpoints and criticisms. Brilliant even in his old age, Phil Mila had fired him with his enthusiasm for the brain.

Mila's point was that the limbic system had evolved long before the cerebral cortex, the part of the brain that made love, trust, altruism and the other human virtues possible. Beasts before angels.

"I know I've touched on some things that you're dying to question me about," Hartigan said. "I apologize for being so vague. You'll understand why later. For the time being, just be a little patient. We'll talk very soon about the kind of research I want you to get involved in. But for the next few weeks, I'd like you to concentrate on our bread and butter—treating patients. We all love research, but these folks pay our bills.''

Private patients were treated for a variety of psychiatric complaints—everything from severe depression and schizophrenia to sexual dysfunction. As Brook was already well aware, the clinic also handled forensic referrals from the state-hospital system for a wide range of psychiatric evaluations and treatment.

''We also have a very lucrative business doing NGRI evaluations for some of the local prosecutors,'' Hartigan said. ''All of us spend some time testifying in court. We try to rotate these chores. As the new man on the block, you'll get a heavy dose, I'm afraid.''

Brook didn't mind at all. The not-guilty-by-reason-of-insanity criminal cases intrigued him. He was fascinated by evaluating men accused of murder or other violent crimes who claimed they didn't know what they were doing because of mental illness or brain injury. Most were trying to fake it.

Hartigan looked at his watch. ''I think it's time to get you settled in your new office.''

As they descended the steps, Brook casually mentioned what Jenny had told him during their meeting several days earlier—that one of the clinic's doctors had recently died in an accident. He was surprised when Hartigan stopped on the stairway.

''Who told you that?'' he asked curtly. He looked upset.

Startled by the reaction, Brook hesitated. He didn't want to mention Jenny's name, so he said, ''I may have heard someone talking about it at the state hospital.'' Hartigan looked him fully in the face. ''I don't really remember who it was. I hope it's not true.''

Hartigan seemed to realize that he was overreacting. His features softened. ''We did lose a doctor not long ago under tragic circumstances. We still don't know all the details. As soon as we do, I'll feel better about discussing it. I'm sure you can appreciate the need for circumspection.''

Brook nodded that he understood, but he didn't at all. Hartigan's reticence struck him as odd.

They continued down to the second floor, where Hartigan opened a door and smiled. The office was spacious, a far cry from the basement cubicle Brook had slaved in at the state hospital's forensic unit. An expensive oriental carpet covered the floor. He slowly took in the track lighting, the richly upholstered leather chairs and teak furniture. The floor-to-ceiling bookshelves were filled with an up-to-date psychiatric reference library.

A computer terminal already glowed a pale green on the desk.

"We even turned it on for you, John," Hartigan said. "You're online with an e-mail address. Welcome aboard."

Brook tried to smile, but felt an uneasy tightness in his stomach. He knew that this office had belonged to Mark Ulman.

SEVEN

BROOK'S PATIENT WAS A mid-twenties CPA who worked for a large St. Louis accounting firm. He had an ingratiating smile and a problem that had compelled him to seek medical treatment. He was a paraphiliac, a sexual deviant—specifically, a chronic *frotteur*—someone who liked to rub up against women in crowded places like elevators or subways.

He was the most interesting patient Brook had handled during his first two weeks at the Hartigan Clinic, where he'd seen the normal run of psychiatric cases—bipolar depressives, manics, a few schizophrenics. After ordering blood work-ups on each, he prescribed lithium carbonate and tricyclic antidepressants for all but one, a middle-aged woman he put on a low dose of monoamine oxidase inhibitors, MAOIs.

The *frotteur* was agreeable to Brook's suggestion that they try satiation therapy. Brook made an appointment to see him in one week. In the meantime he put him on an SSRI, a selective serotonin-reuptake inhibitor that reduced the compulsive nature of his sexual drive while he was under treatment.

Brook was still writing up his evaluation when the telephone rang. Hartigan wanted him to come to Jim Serra's lab right away.

Brook hurried up the steps, taking them two at a time.

He'd seen Serra several times in the building, but this was their first meeting. The intense, forty-two-year-old bioengineer was from Stanford. He was a handsome man, almost pretty at certain angles that emphasized his sharp profile. He was about five ten, with a delicate face and pale skin set off by dark-brown hair.

Hartigan met Brook outside Serra's third-floor lab. He explained that Serra was doing research in electromagnetic stimulation.

"We call it neuro-stim around here," Hartigan said. "It's one of our hottest areas of research. But more about that later."

"Wait a minute, that's not fair," Brook said, smiling. "You've got to tell me more."

"Jim's working with magnetic fields, especially magnetic nerve stimulation," Hartigan said. "We're only beginning to understand how magnetic pulses can induce electrical currents in the body. Jim's out in front of everyone in the country in this area."

"The real pros are in Western Europe," Serra said, opening the door to his office and joining them in the hallway. "They don't have the same hang-ups we do about new medical technology. They're not afraid to try new things."

Serra introduced himself to Brook and shook his hand. He'd been expecting them.

"Is the patient here?" Hartigan asked.

Serra nodded and led them back into his office.

"I'd like you to watch this," Hartigan said, holding the door for Brook. "I think you'll find it interesting. Jim's going to use magnetic stimulation to induce an electroconvulsive shock in one of our ECT patients, a severe depression case." He ushered Brook into a large, well-lighted room. "This will help you understand some of the work we're doing here."

Brook didn't doubt that magnetic pulses could be a powerful research tool, but he wondered about using neuro-stim to induce an electric shock. He was well acquainted with ECT, or electroconvulsive therapy. Electroshock, as it was popularly called, was an excellent therapy for many severely depressed patients who didn't respond to medication. Brook had given the procedure dozens of times himself, but this would be different.

The patient—an elderly woman with strawlike white hair, a hawk nose and withered face—lay unconscious on a gurney.

Serra fiddled with the controls of a machine Brook had never seen before. Brook had been told about this bioengineer's ability to describe technical matters in clear, precise language, breaking complex concepts down into digestible pieces. He hoped Serra would live up to his reputation.

"We're about ready to start," Serra said. The woman had already been given a 20-ml injection of methohexital, an anesthetic. She was covered with a white sheet, which rose and fell rhythmically as she breathed.

The lab was crammed with equipment that included an electroconvulsive machine. The room also had an anesthesia device, an EEG and oxygen tanks, plus an intubation set (in case the patient started choking), an electrocardiograph and defibrillator (in case her heart stopped) and stacks of trays arranged with assorted syringes, needles and glucose-infusion sets.

Serra motioned for Brook to step forward so he could examine the neuro-stim device, which in many ways resembled an ECT machine. About the size of a large stereo receiver, the console was outfitted with a dial and a row of switches. A lay person might have mistaken it for a shortwave radio.

"This is a Swedish-made machine, a BAT-12," Serra said. "It's widely used in Europe to check neural connections." He pointed to a four-foot-high stack of what looked like automobile batteries. "That's the energy-storage capacitor," he said. "This machine generates a tremendous amount of high-pulse energy, up to five thousand amps or more. It's designed to dump the charge back into the capacitor so it isn't dissipated."

Serra raised a paddle-shaped device attached by a long cord to the neuro-stim console. "This is the stimulating coil,'' he said. ''I designed this model myself. The trick is in knowing how to bend the coils, so you can concentrate and focus the energy fields.''

''The idea is to use brief magnetic pulses to trigger a neurological response,'' Hartigan said. ''You set off the magnetic stimulus by passing a strong electrical current through the coil.''

''Michael Faraday first described the principles of magnetic fields in a famous experiment in 1831,'' Serra said. ''The discharge current passing through the coils generates the magnetic pulse. Faraday used iron rings; I use copper coils wound like the mainspring of a clock.''

Hartigan said, ''A magnetic charge passes right through bone and tissue. It's painless. You don't have to worry about electrode burns, as you do with conventional ECT. The device doesn't even touch the patient. And thanks to Jim's work, we can trigger seizures in the deepest parts of the brain without having to insert subdural electrodes into the skull.''

Brook was impressed but a little perplexed. The scant reading he'd done on the subject indicated that while magnetic stimulation was widely practiced in Western Europe, it remained an experimental procedure in the United States.

''Did you get special permission to do this?'' he asked.

Serra looked at Hartigan.

''You might say that,'' Hartigan said, smiling. ''We have an IDE from the Food and Drug Administration. It wasn't easy, but I made it happen.''

The granting of an IDE, or ''investigational device exemption,'' was tightly regulated. It was definitely impressive that the clinic had gotten one to run neuro-stim experiments.

''We're ready to go,'' Serra said, attaching eight red EEG wires to the woman's scalp to monitor her brain waves. He placed an ambu-bag over the patient's face, and gave her five minutes of oxygen to increase the seizure's duration and reduce confusion and amnesia afterward. Then he inserted a plastic bite-guard in the woman's mouth and attached an inflatable ankle-cuff to her right leg.

The cuff method was the easiest way to monitor a seizure.

Just before he injected the woman with 10 cc of succiny-choline, a powerful muscle relaxant, he would inflate the cuff tight enough to compress the main artery in the leg. That way the drug wouldn't flow into the right foot, leaving it free to show the effects of the current; in a good seizure, the foot jerked in spasm for at least twenty-five seconds.

"We'll give ten to twelve pulses per second," Serra said. "Everybody ready?"

Hartigan nodded.

Serra inflated the ankle cuff and injected the muscle relaxant into the woman's shoulder. He held the neuro-stim wand a few inches from her right temporal lobe and switched on the machine.

There was a rapid series of loud, jarring clicks.

Brook instinctively flinched. He wasn't prepared for the noise. The only sound you got with ECT was a soft hum. His eyes were glued to the woman's right foot, which quickly started to twitch, and continued to spasm for thirty seconds, an acceptable length for a seizure.

"That was a good one," Serra said, checking the EEG's printout. A series of jagged spikes showed clearly on the brain's alpha-wave band.

Brook had never seen a convulsion induced so easily. What he'd just witnessed amazed him. The advantages of neuro-stim over traditional electroconvulsive therapy were striking. No electrodes; no scalp preparation to assure a good electrical contact; no danger of burns. The patient didn't even have to change clothes: This woman wore a dress instead of the usual hospital gown.

"So what do you think?" Hartigan asked.

"I'm still picking myself off the floor," Brook said. "How often does a depressed patient get neuro-stim?"

"It depends on the individual, of course, but about the same as with conventional ECT," Serra said. "Say, three sessions a week for a month or so."

Hartigan's beeper went off. He glanced at the digital number, frowned and said he had to call someone. He looked distracted when he left.

EIGHT
⊳◆⊲

BRODY HAD STATIONED HIMSELF in an office in the clinic's subbasement. A closed-circuit television panel, segmented into three rows of five, small, black-and-white screens, stood before him. There was another, more elaborate bank of television monitors at the control center just down the hallway. The cameras continuously focused on the doors, corridors and, especially, the recently renovated prisoners' wing—a four-room suite separated from the rest of the floor by a wall of clear, four-inch-thick, bulletproof Plexiglas.

At Brody's insistence, the rooms were equipped with hidden cameras and audio hookups. It had been a crash program, but money was no object. The work had been done in a matter of weeks. Brody still couldn't believe he'd had to fight Hartigan about it. The doctor had argued that the cameras would be too intrusive.

Brody had also hired a Dallas company, one of the best security firms in the country, to install an elaborate electronic-surveillance system in the basement. It included new infrared, trip-alarm heat sensors that could detect even the slightest movement. Again, the work had been completed on a fast track at great cost.

Brody knew Hartigan disliked him. They rarely spoke to or saw one another. But that was before LePonty's escape. Since then, Brody had insisted on more access, and if the doctor didn't like it, that was too goddamn bad. With more inmates on the way, security would have to be tightened up.

A red light blinked on the console panel in front of him. Brody glanced at one of the television monitors and saw Hartigan standing outside the office. He looked impatient—as usual. When Brody pressed a button, a steel door opened. Hartigan nodded to Brody and sat down on a small sofa.

"You sent for me," he said without any pretense of politeness.

"We found LePonty."

Brody handed Hartigan a manila folder and watched as he examined the photographs in silence. They showed LePonty lying dead on a shag carpet, with two bullet holes in his chest.

"We put the body in one of the coolers in the path lab," Brody said. "Moved it in early this morning."

Hartigan shook his head as he stared at the blowups. "Everything was going so well."

LePonty had received six treatments before his escape a few weeks earlier. Hartigan explained how he'd administered all of them. LePonty had shown better-than-expected results, tolerating the neuro-stim without any measurable side effects. He'd been the first to get a reduced, brief pulse-stimulus in the 270-mC range. He'd done very well at that level. The PET images and other tests were all promising.

Brody angrily cut him off. "I don't know what you did to the guy's head, and I don't care," he said. "I just know you really fucked him up."

The comment so infuriated Hartigan that he slapped his hands together and stood up. "This discussion is over," he said angrily.

"No, we're going to talk," Brody said. "This thing's been on my mind ever since I had to kill that punk. He was a con with a robbery record. He wasn't a tough guy. Shit, he never even strong-armed anyone. Whatever you did made him one of the worst killers I've ever seen."

It was the same thought he'd had as he'd listened to LePonty's dying words. Something had happened that had drastically changed the guy's personality in a way he'd never thought possible.

"I've got to tell Beckworth about this."

"I'm sure he'll appreciate hearing that you killed one of our best subjects," Hartigan said.

He didn't like the results any more than Brody, but for different reasons. For the doctor, it was the loss of a good guinea pig; for Brody, it was the balls-up aspect of the escape that most distressed him. That, and LePonty having turned explosively dangerous.

What angered him most was that things had been allowed to get so far out of hand in the first place—and that Hartigan, in his arrogance, didn't understand that elementary fact. Or pretended not to understand.

"It was badly done," Hartigan said.

"It was badly done because you didn't have enough security, not enough cameras and not enough firepower," Brody said in a flat, even voice.

The security staff had bungled it. At the very least, Le-Ponty should have been shot dead before he stepped foot outside the building. He never should have gotten that far. That was why Beckworth had insisted they hire Brody to begin with. Len Beckworth had known him for years, ever since their days together at the federal prison at Marion, Illinois. They'd stayed in touch after Beckworth became a state prison warden and Brody had quit the feds and gone into business for himself.

The final approval for hiring Brody had come from the Paulus Foundation. Named for a seventy-year-old multimillionaire from Taos, New Mexico, the foundation had long been one of the clinic's principal financial backers. James D. Paulus was a little-known ultraconservative who had amassed one of the nation's largest fortunes by way of shrewd real-estate investments and a killer instinct for leveraged buyouts of blue-chip manufacturing companies. He had a Western conservative's strong views about penal reform and, after hearing Hartigan lecture once at the University of New Mexico about ways to change criminal behavior, he had become an ardent supporter.

Paulus liked to stay in the background and rarely interfered in the clinic's operation, but he was vitally interested in Hartigan's latest project as well as in Beckworth's role in it. During one of their rare meetings, he'd intimated to Hartigan that he wanted to start a national party based on a strong law-and-order platform; he was convinced Hartigan's research could be politically exploited.

He had provided Hartigan with what amounted to a blank checkbook. But, in security matters, he'd ordered him to defer to the warden.

Once Paulus and several of his foundation members had approved the arrangement, Beckworth had sent Brody to the clinic. They were paying him a great deal—ten thousand dollars a week, plus expenses. He wouldn't have touched this crazy job for anything less than that.

The last test of the new security system had been completed only a few days before. Its installation had been under way even before his arrival from L.A. The entire upgrade had cost over a million dollars; it included infrared cameras at key locations both inside and outside the building, the specially designed living quarters, and extra manpower. Hiring the personnel had been Brody's primary responsibility. He'd brought five handpicked men with him and was getting others.

He told Hartigan how they'd tracked and captured Le-Ponty. Then he handed him a photograph of the dead prostitute, a black-and-white close-up that showed what the bullet had done to her head.

"We've got to get better here, doctor. We can't have this happen again. If someone else gets out, we'll have hell to pay. Both of us."

"Did Beckworth tell you to say that?" Hartigan massaged his temples with the fingertips of both hands.

"He thought we should get things settled before we bring in the next batch," Brody said. "He doesn't want any more problems. What happened with LePonty didn't make him happy.''

''Security is your worry.''

''Security is everybody's worry!'' Brody shot back. ''Get that straight. And I want your hotshot scientists to get it straight, too.''

Brody had not yet met the staff, and doing so was long overdue. He'd already studied their personnel files and knew they were all temperamental, with IQs in the top five percent. A few were certifiable bastards. And it was his job to keep them in line—before another one of them got killed.

Brody was still investigating what had happened to Mark Ulman, but there was no longer any doubt in his mind that someone on staff had helped LePonty escape. It was the only way he could have gotten a gun.

A St. Louis homicide detective he knew had shown him the crime-scene photos. Fortunately, Beckworth and some of his people had managed to keep a lid on what had happened. Ulman had been stabbed savagely in his car. From the way the hands had been slashed to the bone, he must have put up a damn good fight. Brody had figured that Ulman was trying to save his wife when he'd made that disturbance outside his home. It had taken real guts to lean on the horn like he did when someone was cutting his throat.

Brody told Hartigan to arrange the staff meeting as soon as possible.

''I kinda think your docs will pay attention to what I want to tell them.''

NINE

THE ELEVATOR STOPPED ON the second floor just as Brook was preparing to leave the clinic for the evening. It was after midnight. A woman wearing a white lab coat greeted him with a polite nod and moved her large cart to the side so he had room to squeeze in. The cart was covered with a green sheet.

The elevator was going up instead of down, but Brook decided to ride along. He didn't recognize the woman, who had light-blond hair and a splash of freckles across her nose. She wore steel-rimmed glasses and her spiky hair was cropped in a short, boyish cut. He figured she was one of the clinic's lab technicians, most of whom he hadn't met yet.

He heard a noise, a faint squeak, followed by several louder ones.

"Is Mickey Mouse hiding in here somewhere?" he asked, grinning at the woman. She was in her mid- to late twenties, with a nice face and soft, friendly eyes.

"No, just us rats," she said, smiling. She lifted the sheet.

The cart was loaded with at least a dozen wire-mesh cages, each containing a large black-and-white rat. A few of the rodents were nervously circling or pacing back and forth in the cages, which were just wide enough to let them turn around. Most lay still with their pointed snouts pressed against the wiring, eyes open, whiskers twitching.

"Those . . . are . . . big . . . rats," Brook said.

"And not just your run-of-the-mill big rat," she said. "These babies are from the Charles River strain."

Brook recognized the species. The best laboratory test animals available, specially bred to weed out any hereditary abnormalities or pathogens that could alter a test. In the lab business, they were considered Grade-A pure.

Brook was surprised. He hadn't realized the clinic was running animal tests.

The elevator stopped on the fourth floor.

"Mind if I tag along?" he asked.

The woman hesitated, working something over in her mind. Then she said, "You are on staff here, aren't you?"

Brook introduced himself. Her name was Agnes. She said that she'd worked for the clinic for three years. One of her jobs was to take care of the laboratory animals. Every few days she picked up a fresh shipment of Charles River rats from a medical-supply house that provided lab animals to research centers and hospitals in the St. Louis area.

"I make most of my pickups late at night," she said. "You have less chance that way of running into some animal-rights protester."

Brook nodded. He understood exactly what she was talking about, and considered saying something suitably sarcastic.

The fanatics who wanted to ban animal experiments were nuts. He'd run into a few of them in med school. They really believed that it was better to put up with Lou Gehrig's disease or AIDS than run animal experiments that could point the way to a cure.

Agnes pushed her cart past the autopsy room to a door at the end of the hall. She took out a set of keys. "Get ready. We have to go in fast."

Brook started to ask a question, but Agnes had already opened the door and turned on the overhead lights.

The explosion of sound was instantaneous: A feral, high-pitched wail.

Brook hesitated in the doorway, but Agnes grabbed his

sleeve and pulled him into the room along with the cart, slamming the door shut to keep the noise from pouring into the hallway.

The shrill, flesh-tingling howls continued. Brook had never heard anything like it. He was jittery and angry with himself for feeling that way.

But, boy, what kind of cat *was* this?

Agnes said, "That's Tommy. He knows I've got something for him."

Steel cages lined the floor. Brook counted at least ten, each with a cat inside.

Tommy's cage was set on a low table, a place of honor.

When Agnes pointed him out, Brook was startled by the animal's size. He expected a hefty macho-type feline. Instead, he confronted a small, gray tabby with exposed ribs and a wispy tail that would have looked fine on one of the rats. It looked undernourished.

The moment Brook bent over for a closer look, the cat threw itself against the cage's meshed grill, springing as if shot from a cannon, mouth opened wide, fangs bared like some crazed jungle animal. The impact made the cage wobble on its stand.

Agnes grinned skittishly when Brook jumped back. She said, "He'd kill a hundred rats a day if we'd let him. He's an incredible predator."

An exposed bipolar electrode protruded from a spot of white bone in the cat's skull, where the fur had been shaved off. Brook recognized the recording electrode buried in the left hemisphere of the brain; the tip of another electrode rose from the frontal cortex. The third exposed wire was a ground. A triad of small, silver-alloy skull screws fixed the leads in place.

Brook glanced in some of the other cages. The cats were all outfitted with similar electrodes. Most looked asleep or drugged. What kind of experiments was Hartigan running? It was clear they were subjecting the animals' brains to repeated, deep electrical impulses.

Tommy continued lunging at the front of the cage, hissing

in rage, slamming against it. White foam flecked the corners of the animal's mouth.

"How long will he do that?" Brook asked.

Agnes shrugged. "Until I give him a rat." She took a long, sad look at the cat. "I think he knows."

"Knows what?"

"That one of these days he's going to be sacrificed."

Brook took in some of the lab's impressive equipment, starting with the steel operating table in the center of the room. A Leitz microscope with a color tube stood on a counter, along with an electron microscope outfitted with a 35-mm camera. The shelves contained rows of chemical solutions used for staining brain samples—methelene blue, osmium tetroxide and eosin. There was also an assortment of cutting and sectioning boards. Brook took note of the portable EEG. Whatever they were doing also involved monitoring the brain waves of these animals.

"Who works here?" he asked, wondering again just what kind of research they were doing.

"Mainly Doctor Krill and Doctor Hartigan," Agnes said. "I'm surprised one of them isn't here right now. They do most of their work late at night."

She slipped on a thick pair of quilted, padded gloves. "Would you like to see Tommy in action? It's time for his first rat of the morning."

"Sure," Brook said, fighting off another touch of squeamishness.

Agnes opened one of the cages on her cart and took out a huge rat. Sleek and docile, the black-faced rodent was well over a foot long. She held it up by its midsection. The rat was nearly twice the cat's size.

Tommy was on all fours, back arched, hairs bristling. He kept striking his forepaws against the cage, biting at the wires.

"Better stand back," Agnes said. She opened a hatch and lowered the rat into the partitioned cage. Then she pulled a lever that raised the screen divider.

In a blurred move almost too fast to see, Tommy sprang

on the rat's back. He bit into its neck, twisting and ripping with his fangs. The rat, crazed with fright, rolled over with the cat still hanging on. Another darting bite in the neck, then another, and the rat was dead.

Instantly, Tommy whirled around in the tight space and threw himself at Agnes and Brook, slamming into the bars of the cage. His muzzle fur was moist and dark with blood. The cat howled, the sound wild, dark, unnerving.

Brook swallowed and realized his throat was dry as sand. From the way the electrodes were positioned, he thought the experiment might involve the amygdala. His guess was they were triggering seizures with these animals and then monitoring the effects on the brain.

Trying to think through the various possibilities, he didn't hear the door open. Agnes did, managing a smile and a quick, "Good evening, Doctor Hartigan."

Brook turned. Hartigan stood there in his white lab coat, eyes glaring.

"Miss Lightfield, you were told to allow no one into this lab. Please finish your assigned duties, then consider your employment terminated. Your severance pay will be mailed to you. Six months should suffice."

Agnes stood by her cart, frozen. Her fingers came to her mouth.

Brook stammered, "Doctor. I asked her to let me come here. It was my idea. I can't believe you're serious about . . ."

"That's enough," Hartigan said angrily. "I'll see you in my office in ten minutes."

Brook hesitated.

"Ten minutes!"

Tommy stood up, paws on the grill, and howled at them. He pounced back on the dead rat and ripped at its throat.

Brook arrived promptly for his meeting with Hartigan, who motioned him to a chair. Original artwork covered the walls of his office, including a striking desert landscape in vibrant pastels by Georgia O'Keeffe. The soft overhead light gave the O'Keeffe a translucent glow.

Brook had admired the painting during earlier visits, but this time he didn't even notice it. He began by objecting again to Agnes's dismissal.

Hartigan raised his hand, stopping him. "I'll hear no more about that. Miss Lightfield was under orders not to allow anyone into that lab. She violated those orders."

The tautness in Hartigan's voice told Brook not to push this. He sucked in his anger, realizing that his job might be on the line.

Hartigan said, "I hadn't intended to have this conversation so soon. I would have preferred to bring you along more gradually. But after what just happened . . . after what you've seen . . . I don't have any choice."

He took a sheet of paper from a desk drawer and handed it to Brook.

"It's fairly standard," Hartigan said. "Other research labs have them. Our government intelligence agencies use essentially the same form."

The language was legalese, but Brook quickly realized that he was being asked to sign an agreement that would bind him not to discuss his work with anyone outside the clinic. He would also be prohibited from publishing anything about his research without Hartigan's written approval. The prohibition was absolute, remaining in effect for three years if he left the clinic.

"I've got to insist on total confidentiality," Hartigan said.

Brook carefully examined the documents, and leaned back in his chair as he considered it. He had a million questions, doubts—and an intense desire to slow this all down.

After reading the paper through another time, he took out a pen and signed the agreement.

Hartigan smiled.

"Excellent, John." He countersigned the papers and filed them away in the drawer, which he locked. "So how did you like Jim Serra's work?"

"I had no idea anyone was doing anything like that in this

country." Brook wanted to discuss what he'd just seen on the fourth floor, but it was apparent that Hartigan was following his own plan.

"It's insane to allow neuro-stim research to go full-speed ahead in places like England, Sweden and Germany, and do virtually nothing about it here." Anger laced Hartigan's words. "They're years ahead of us in so many technical areas—suturing, cauterization. If you need a serious operation, you're better off flying to Europe. That's the simple truth, and it would shock the hell out of people if they really understood what's going on. We're constantly limited by restrictions on research."

"What does all this have to do with those cats?"

The words came out more curtly than Brook had intended.

"Fair enough," Hartigan said, "but I want to tell you up front that I won't answer all your questions today. There are some things I can't discuss at this point."

The clinic director sat back in his chair and folded his hands. He looked like a benevolent professor about to impart all of his distilled wisdom to a favorite student.

"We're looking at how seizures alter the brain's limbic structure and how those physical changes affect behavior. I'm especially interested in the hypothalamus and amygdala."

"And you're studying all this by using electromagnetic stimulation to trigger seizures in animals?"

"Exactly."

ECT altered the brain's neurocircuitry and produced all manner of chemical changes—everything from the production of dopamine and other neurotransmitters to reduced serotonin levels. The reasons were still largely unknown. Convulsive therapy released prolactin, endorphins and cortisol—probably by stimulating the hypothalamus.

"Some recent work—none of it published yet—suggests that ECT might even alter genetic structure," Hartigan said. "I'm convinced neuro-stim can have the same results. It's radical stuff, John."

"It sounds to me like you're kindling those cats," Brook said.

Hartigan leaned forward in his chair and placed both hands on his desk.

"What do you know about kindling?" he asked. His eyes had locked on Brook, who suddenly felt like he was taking his medical boards and had just been asked a trick question about some obscure detail of neurochemistry.

Brook explained that the idea was to get the brain so sensitized to the current that it eventually "kindled," or went into seizure spontaneously—with little or no electrical stimulation. Researchers trying to develop a biological model for epilepsy and its treatment had pioneered the controversial procedure. Kindling had occurred in reptiles, amphibians, felines, even monkeys, but never in man. The procedure was intensely experimental.

Hartigan's head went up and down approvingly as Brook described the concept.

"Haven't some of the animal experiments shown dramatic effects on nerve pathways?" Brook asked.

"Yes, cells downstream from the region where current was applied change anatomically," Hartigan said. "Once a certain threshold is reached, complex hormonal changes begin. Cells change shape, new ones form, different neural connections are established. The brain completely reshapes itself, becomes neurologically reprogrammed. Behavior changes. And these changes are permanent. They can even occur before kindling is achieved."

Brook began to understand what Hartigan and Krill were up to on the fourth floor. They were studying the neurological underpinnings of animal behavior and how that behavior could be altered through repeated seizures.

Similar experiments had had breathtaking results. Previously aggressive, predatory animals became gentle in experiments that had been repeatedly duplicated. But Brook was also aware that the opposite was sometimes true. If the scientific evidence showed that animals became less aggressive, it also demonstrated that kindling could cause wild, often frightening behavioral changes if allowed to run out of control.

After what he'd just seen on the fourth floor, Brook didn't doubt that for a minute.

The neurological reasons for these striking changes were unclear; one theory attributed it to decreased levels of crucial neurotransmitters like dopamine, chemicals that interacted with specific receptors in the brain.

The hope, of course, was that all this would offer a model for understanding human behavior; kindling was considered the best bet for studying the complex neural mechanisms that triggered epileptic seizures.

"What I've always wondered about kindling is how do you control the seizures once they start?" Brook asked. It seemed to him that the whole thing was like a runaway nuclear chain reaction, one cell firing after another until the entire brain was convulsed.

"We're confident we can limit the neural activity to the limbic region," Hartigan said. He sounded as sure of himself as if he were discussing a routine surgical procedure. "Al Silver's also working on some experimental drugs designed to control the hormonal changes."

Fascinated, Brook started to ask another question, but Hartigan raised a hand, interrupting him.

"I know all this sounds interesting, but it's really something of a diversion for us," he said, signaling he wanted to change the subject. "I expect you to keep what we've just discussed to yourself. The fact is I've got other research plans for you, Doctor. What do you know about the NIH brain study?"

Next to the Human Genome project, it was the largest effort of its kind—a massive attempt to study the brain, its chemistry and thought processes.

"They're funding a full court press on mapping the brain. It's a four-year project," Brook said. "At least seventy labs and over two hundred scientists are involved."

Hartigan smiled. "We're one of those labs. We're using PET scans and other imaging techniques to try to see how the brain processes violent thoughts. The bottom line is, we're trying to isolate the neural structures that play the biggest roles in aggression. I think it can be done. It's what I want you to get involved in.''

''I'd be working with Marty Conner?''

Brook heard himself ask the question without realizing he'd spoken. This was one of the hottest areas in forensic psychiatry. He couldn't have asked for anything better.

''Under my supervision,'' Hartigan said, smiling as he read Brook's excitement.

''What about the subjects?'' Brook asked. ''Are you using med students?'' Medical students and residents frequently participated in research projects like these; it was usually a fast, easy way to make good money.

Again, Brook felt Hartigan's gaze bore into him, the eyes glittering.

''We're using prisoners from the state penal system,'' Hartigan said.

He reminded Brook about the confidentiality agreement he'd just signed. ''I know this is a lot to absorb in one sitting.''

Brook slowly took in what that meant.

''How do you get them?''

''They come mainly from Jefferson City and Potosi. Both are close and convenient. So far, we've seen six men.''

Jefferson City and Potosi were the sites of the state's two largest prisons. Brook had given NGRI evaluations to dozens of men who wound up there; two or three of them were on death row. He wondered how anything like this could be authorized.

''Who approved this in the Department of Corrections?'' He sounded in control, focused, even slightly bemused; and yet Brook was blown away. First kindling and now this. He kept staring at Hartigan's face, trying to see if he was serious.

''Warden Beckworth.''

Len Beckworth was in charge of the maximum security prison at Potosi, the state's largest. Brook recognized the name but had never met him. He knew that the warden was fairly young, early forties—and a Christian fundamentalist raised in the Missouri Ozarks, with a reputation as a tough, no-nonsense administrator.

"He was happy, even eager to help us," Hartigan went on. "At the present rate of incarceration, he figures he'll need ten more prisons within five years. He also knows that Missouri's taxpayers will never go along with that, so the parole board will have to keep releasing prisoners to make room for new ones. Convicted murderers and rapists will be freed to kill and rape again. That's how the system works. So you can understand why the warden wanted to cooperate—even at considerable professional risk."

"And you've already seen six men?"

"Only briefly, for evaluations." Hartigan hesitated. "We had some, ah, security problems we needed to fix before we could handle longer stays. But those have been resolved and we're ready to move ahead."

Brook was excited and disturbed. The thought of working with the very population most in need of careful study and research was almost electric. Prisoners were rarely subjected, even voluntarily, to modern neurophysiological research. The limited amount of work that had been done couldn't compare with what was possible at Hartigan's clinic.

"What kind of prisoners are you focusing on?"

"The kind that meet the criteria for antisocial personality disorder—ASPD—the kind that account for seventy percent of the prison population. Your typical con and a few not so typical. The multiple killers and serial sex offenders."

"Do the men volunteer?"

"Without exception."

Brook felt himself swept along by Hartigan's breathtaking plans. He began to wonder what he'd gotten himself into.

"Does this trouble you?" Hartigan asked, carefully studying Brook's sobered expression.

"I want to know more."

But he didn't have much time: Before he concluded their meeting, Hartigan told him they would receive three more prisoners from Potosi within a week.

TEN

THE SMALL LECTURE HALL at the Lafayette Hospital psychi-atric unit was already crowded when Brook arrived. Many of the doctors had brought their lunches—brown bags and trays of salad and sandwiches from the hospital cafeteria. Jenny had called Brook the night before and invited him to a talk she was going to give to a group of psychiatrists about her specialty: serial sexual killers.

Jenny was the featured speaker for Grand Rounds, a weekly lecture series for staff doctors at the hospital, which was affiliated with the Pike University medical school. She stood next to the lectern in front of a movie screen, talking to three young doctors in white lab coats.

Brook could tell the docs were interested in her and couldn't blame them. Jenny looked wonderful; she wore a hunter-green coatdress, double-breasted with gold buttons, that hugged her figure.

When she saw him, she nodded and mouthed the words, "Thanks for coming." She'd suggested they have lunch af-terward.

Brook glanced around the room. About forty people sat at the staggered lecture tables separated by a narrow aisle. Most were psychiatrists, several of whom he recognized.

Introduced as a rising young star in the study of serial sexual offenders, Jenny told her audience that she often gave this same lecture to prosecuting attorneys. The idea was to help them understand the type of deviant personality they were dealing with, so that they could convince a jury that these people weren't innocent of their horrible crimes by reason of insanity.

For the next two hours she discussed the behavior of Jeffrey Dahmer, Ted Bundy—and also Robert Berdella, who had tortured and killed five male prostitutes close to home in Kansas City.

Serial killers, she said, were among the most intelligent of criminals. They certainly weren't psychotic. A psychotic killer was quickly caught; he made stupid mistakes. A man like Bundy rarely made a mistake.

Jenny defined a serial killer as anyone who killed three or more victims in different locations. A cooling-off, or "dormant," period followed each crime.

Jenny quoted from Richard von Krafft-Ebing, a forensic psychiatrist from turn-of-the-century Vienna and one of the first to study the sadist killer. He described what he called "the lust murderer" as representing the most extreme form of sadism. He did breakthrough work, but then his research was nearly forgotten until the FBI rediscovered it in the 1980s. His theories were now the basis for profiling techniques used to identify serial killers.

For many in the audience, lunch stopped the moment Jenny started her slide show, a series of black-and-white photographs of the killers and their victims. One slide showed a young woman whose left leg had been cut off and neatly positioned next to her upper torso at a right angle.

Several doctors got up and quietly made their way to the door in back. A few more followed.

Brook admired how Jenny was in total command of her audience. Yet he was also struck by the incongruity of a young, attractive woman lecturing a group of doctors about the absolute depths of human depravity. He couldn't help but find the contrast jarring.

Watching her turn off the projector, Brook could almost

feel the tension drain out of the room. He smiled when he noticed all the uneaten lunches.

"Nice job," he said. She'd been impressive.

Jenny gathered up her papers and notes, and put them into her briefcase.

"Where should we go?" she asked. "I don't have much time. I've got to be back at the clinic in an hour."

Brook was irritated by her unexpected abruptness, remembering that this meeting had been her idea. The intensity and warmth she'd communicated during her lecture had vanished. She looked distracted.

Brook suggested they grab a bite at the hospital cafeteria. They took a crosswalk to the main complex. They each got a sandwich, salad and iced tea. Brook found a table in a corner away from the others.

Alone with her, he couldn't help but think of the months they had spent together back in Chicago. He could still remember how much he'd enjoyed being with her.

Jenny looked unsure of how to start. "I owe you an apology," she said finally. "I haven't been honest with you. There's so much going on at the clinic, so much you need to know about."

When she hesitated, Brook said, "Tell me about it. The other night I stumbled onto some experiments Krill and Hartigan are performing on cats up on the fourth floor. A young tech named Agnes showed me the lab. When Hartigan found out, he fired her."

"Agnes Lightfield?" Jenny straightened in her chair and let out a breath. Her eyes wandered out to the cafeteria and back to Brook.

"Agnes is wonderful with animals," she said at last. "I'll make sure she gets another job. I know two labs that would love to hire her."

She looked at Brook and held his gaze before asking if he'd talked to Hartigan about the animal experiment.

"It's something, all right," Brook said. "He said they were running some kind of kindling experiment on cats."

Even against the noisy background, they'd both lowered

their voices to make sure they weren't overheard.

Jenny sat there a moment in silence. The news seemed to have surprised her.

"I wondered what was going on up there," she said, finally. "Hartigan's been very tight-lipped about the work on four. I knew Krill was working with animals. We all did. But I had no idea they were kindling. . . ."

She glanced at Brook. She looked tense, upset.

"What's wrong?" he asked.

"Sometimes I worry about all the secrecy in this place." She hesitated and seemed to regret what she'd just said. But she had something else on her mind. "Did he tell you about the prisoners?"

Brook nodded. "That was some news, too. That was quite a talk we had. He wants me to work with Marty Conner on giving them PET scans."

It bothered him that she hadn't leveled with him earlier about the prisoners. Even taking into account the confidentiality agreement they had signed, there were things she could have told him about the clinic and its research. She'd been far from forthcoming.

Jenny was still having a hard time with this and looked agitated.

"Has he discussed Mark Ulman?" That much she had already told Brook about.

"He mentioned him," Brook said. He still recalled how upset Hartigan had become when he told him he'd heard the doctor had died in an accident. Hartigan's response had struck him as odd.

Jenny frowned, then tried to compose herself. "Mark was murdered."

It was Brook's turn not to touch his food. He put down his sandwich.

"One of the prisoners got out," Jenny continued. "We're still not sure how it happened. He made Mark drive him to his home. He stabbed him to death in his car right in front of his house." Her eyes had turned moist. She looked at her hands for a few moments before saying, "Mark was a fine man, a caring doctor. He had a wife. I liked him a great deal.''

Brook felt his lower jaw drop. Jenny's story had taken him completely by surprise. ''Do they know how the guy escaped?''

''If they do, no one's telling us. We're not supposed to discuss any of this, just go on with our jobs as if nothing ever happened. I'm worried about it. I don't know what kind of work Mark was doing with his patient. It was all kept very hush-hush. We just don't know what was going on.''

From the way her voice wavered, Brook thought she was going to break out in sobs. She made an effort to continue. ''John, I can't forget him. We had lunch together the day before he . . .''

Jenny suddenly brought a fist crashing down on the table. The iced tea glasses wobbled and almost tipped over. A few heads turned.

''I'm sorry,'' she said, twisting in her chair. Her face looked pale.

''Has the prisoner been caught?''

Jenny looked up slowly, focused, gripped her glass. ''He was captured in Effingham, Illinois. He resisted. Our new head of security had to shoot him.''

''Who's that?'' Brook knew next to nothing about the clinic's security staff.

''His name's Brody.''

She explained that all this had happened nearly two weeks earlier but that Hartigan had told her only a few days ago.

''We shouldn't talk about that here,'' she said. Brook wondered whether this was more evasiveness on her part.

Jenny glanced at her watch and said she had to get back to the clinic. Brook wanted to keep talking, but she was clearly too upset to continue. He walked her to her car, which was a few blocks away on the top level of the hospital parking lot. It was a raw, cold day in late October, and they spoke only a few words as they hurried along with their heads down in the sharp wind. Jenny thanked him and managed a mechanical smile as she slid behind the wheel of her car.

As he drove back to the clinic, Brook was aware that two conflicting thoughts had taken hold of him—the desire to help Jenny cope with the tragedy of her loss, and the equally compelling urge to learn whatever he could about how and why Mark Ulman had been killed.

ELEVEN

Brook got out of town that Friday. He was way overdue for a break and spent the weekend hiking in the Mark Twain National Forest deep in the Ozark foothills, a four-hour drive from St. Louis. He went down late in the day straight from the clinic and camped out, pitching his one-man tent in the dark and crawling into his down sleeping bag with a flask of Jack Daniels, a pocket lantern and a detective novel. He hiked the trails Saturday and found a campsite with a hazy view of the rugged hills that swept south to the Arkansas border.

By midafternoon Sunday he was back in the city, refreshed, ready for work and still troubled about his last conversation with Jenny. He'd tried to put it out of mind during his brief camping trip—without success. He was looking forward to talking to her some more.

After showering and shaving at his apartment, Brook drove to the clinic, hoping to catch up on his journal reading and prepare for his weekly round of patients. Hartigan had continued to send him interesting cases, among them a twenty-nine-year-old man from a prominent St. Louis family who had twice hurt his wife during bondage. His sadomasochist tendencies were worsening, but at least he'd taken the first step of admitting he needed help. Brook also had an appointment with the accountant-*frotteur*, who was making steady progress.

He'd just entered the building, when Jim Serra called out from the stairway. Like Brook, he wore weekend clothes—jeans, a black-and-red-plaid shirt, loafers.

"They're here," Serra said, smiling. "They came in last night."

They'd been expecting three prisoners from the state penitentiary in Potosi any day. The men had arrived under heavy guard at four in the morning in a convoy of unmarked prison vans.

"They were pretty drugged up for the drive to St. Louis, but they're starting to come out of it. Want to take a look?"

Brook took the elevator to the subbasement with Serra.

"Anybody else here?" he asked as the doors opened.

"Doctor Hartigan . . . Brody."

Brook had met the new security director for the first time the previous Friday when Hartigan introduced him to the staff. He'd made an impression: a tough-looking man with dark eyes and a frosty attitude. Brody had announced some new security procedures. Among other things, at least two guards would accompany each prisoner at all times.

Brook and Serra hadn't taken five steps before two men in blue jackets stopped them. The guards, built like pro-football linebackers, didn't say more than four or five words as they stiffly examined Serra's and Brook's identification badges and escorted them to the security office.

The prisoners' rooms were on the other side of a bullet-proof plexiglass partition. The hallway reminded Brook of an expensive hotel, with watercolors hanging on the gray walls and oriental carpets on the hardwood floors.

One of the guards pressed a buzzer and a metal door opened automatically. Brook and Serra entered a room, where two other men in blue jackets sat at a bank of black-and-white television screens that showed different views of the clinic's hallways, stairwells and exterior doors. The security cameras also focused on the parking lot and the street and sidewalk in front of the building. Intent on their job, the two men didn't look up from the monitors.

Hartigan was in an adjoining room, which was crammed with television screens, computer terminals and other electronic equipment. He smiled at Brook as if he'd been expecting him.

"Take a look," he said, motioning to one of the monitors.

The screen showed a man slouched in a wing chair with his arms folded. He kept staring at the room's walls and ceiling, trying to spot the hidden camera. He had dark-brown hair, a full face, thick neck and brown, hooded eyes. A putty-colored dent scarred the bridge of his nose, which looked as if it had once been broken. The room was furnished with comfortable-looking chairs, a table, bed, television, video cassette player and a well-stocked bookcase and magazine rack. There was also a private bathroom.

"That's Edward Lind," Hartigan told Brook. "You'll be seeing a lot of him these next few weeks. I want you to have a major role in his treatment."

It was the first time Hartigan had mentioned that to him, and Brook wasn't sure whether to be irritated or elated. Hartigan, to his annoyance, had continued to keep him in the dark even after promising to be more forthcoming about his plans for the prisoners. He hadn't even told him in advance about the men's arrival. Brook hoped he wouldn't have to make an issue out of it.

From a previous discussion with Hartigan, he knew only that Lind was thirty-six, a two-time loser in for bank robbery. His prison record revealed that he was hardboiled, took grim pride in serving his time without complaint and was rarely in trouble. A con from the old school.

"That guy's one of the toughest people in Potosi. Don't forget that and don't make any mistakes with him."

Brody had walked up behind Brook and was looking over his shoulder at the monitor.

Brook nodded as he took in Lind's robust physique. The inmate was heavily muscled from pumping iron in the prison weight room. Even wearing the lemon-yellow polo sweater

he'd been given that morning—all the prisoners received a
new wardrobe—his body-builder's arms and shoulders stood
out in sharp relief. Lind looked quite capable of taking care
of himself.

Hartigan flipped a switch on the control panel. One of the
screens showed a lanky black man nervously pacing in his
room. James Billings, Prisoner Number 056822, was thirty-
three years old and doing seven-and-seven for robbery. He
had big hands and feet and the wolfish, restless look of men
who fill homeless shelters on winter nights. Brook had
treated plenty of them, many with serious mental problems.
One look at Billings was enough to tell him that he'd probably had a crack-cocaine addiction. The darting eyes were a
dead giveaway.

"I'll work with Billings myself," Hartigan said. "We'll
get started tomorrow. I want to do a full battery of intelligence and sociopathy tests. We'll also want to run some
blood work and get a detailed EEG and cranial X ray."

The X rays were needed to get precise skull measurements
before they started the PET scans.

Hartigan switched to another camera. The face on the
screen instantly seized Brook's attention. He'd seen patients
with bizarre physical features before, but never anything like
this. It was Gary Waters, an inmate doing twelve years for
rape.

Still groggy from the sedative, Waters lay on his bed.
About five feet nine, he had thin arms and legs and a sunken
chest. When Hartigan adjusted the camera for a close-up,
Brook noticed that the man's forearms were black and blue
with tattoos, one of them a penis that bore the words, "Born
to Fuck." Another depicted a woman in high heels with her
legs spread.

Waters's sandy hair was clipped short, prison style, and
he had thick, blond eyebrows. His raw, bony cheeks looked
like creased leather, the nose straight and delicate. The eye
sockets were deep, dark-rimmed and set wide apart. The lips,
incongruously, were full and red. The contrast with Waters's

narrow face and pale skin was jarring, but not as much as his other features.

The prisoner's long, clawlike fingers were curved like the talons of a bird. And his ears—slightly off center—looked as if they'd sprouted from the sides of his head.

Brook readjusted the camera to make sure. No, he wasn't mistaken. That had to be a birth defect.

It was a wounded body, and Brook knew enough about criminal physiology to realize that glaring physical abnormalities like these were often associated with violent offenders.

"Pal, you're one fucked-up-lookin' puppy," Brody muttered, taking a long look at Waters, who was thirty-one years old.

Hartigan's summary of the man's prison record indicated that they'd have to play close attention to him. Without a doubt, Waters was the most volatile and dangerous of the three prisoners. Despite his wiry, almost emaciated build and flyweight size, he'd been in repeated fights in the pen, most recently with a black who belonged to the Black Muslims. Waters had broken the man's left arm at the elbow with a metal water pitcher, and spent a month in solitary confinement. The records also showed that he enjoyed hurting people and wasn't afraid of getting hurt himself.

"Who's going to work with Waters?"

"Doctor Malone," Hartigan said.

"The lady doc?" Brody shook his head in disbelief. "You sure that's a good idea? This guy's seriously bad news."

"Doctor Malone's more than capable," Hartigan said, looking irritated that Brody had dared question his judgment.

"I don't understand it," Brody said, shrugging. Brook didn't miss the sarcastic edge to his voice. "How does a good-looking, smart woman like that get into a line of work like this? I've been thinking about that ever since I saw her. Do creeps turn her on?"

Brook stood up. Brody's surly arrogance had already rubbed him the wrong way, but that last crack was way out of line.

"That calls for an apology," Hartigan said. "Doctor Malone is one of the country's best forensic experts on serial sexual killers."

Brody smiled.

"Right now, I mean it!"

"You're right, Doctor. I'm sorry," Brody said. He was still smiling, but his eyes were locked on Brook's. "I had no business saying that. I don't know what got into me."

"I should see to it that Beckworth fires you," Hartigan said.

"I don't think that's a good idea," Brody said, taking another glance at the row of television monitors. "From the looks of those boys, you're definitely going to need me."

TWELVE

JENNY MALONE STOOD AND smiled when Gary Waters shuffled into the room, shackled at the ankles with a three-foot length of plastic cord. He had a guard at each arm and one behind him.

This was Jenny's first session with Waters, and she'd prepared for it until one that morning. A great deal had to be accomplished in the next few days. One of her jobs was to run a series of routine but crucial tests on each of the prisoners before they got started with the PET scans. Hartigan had drilled the staff on the importance of sticking as closely as possible to his tight schedule.

The interview room, one of two in the clinic's subbasement, might have been a comfortable study. A bookcase lined one wall. A pair of plush leather chairs faced each other across a coffee table. The room was also fitted with hidden cameras and wired for sound.

Jenny motioned to one of the chairs. Waters sat down, the guards still flanking him. They were Nordic versions of Brody—blond, fit and young. Both kept their eyes focused on Waters.

The prisoner wore a blue cardigan, twill slacks, brown socks and a pair of cordovan shoes. The clothing was jarringly preppie. But his pale skin and gaunt features made him look anything but collegiate. Jenny was well aware that a monster was hidden within that pinched face and stick-figure body.

Grinning sheepishly, Waters glanced around the room, craning his neck from side to side. He looked like a hillbilly suddenly set down in a Fifth Avenue hotel, but his cold, blue eyes took in everything.

A guard fastened a seatbelt across Waters's waist, locking him securely in place so that he couldn't get up or lunge forward.

Jenny introduced herself.

"I'd like to ask you some questions, Gary, and maybe answer some of yours." Waters's sizable file lay open on the coffee table in front of her. Her tone was informal, yet firmly conveyed who was in charge.

"Whatever you say, ma'am," Waters said. "I know the drill pretty well."

He reminded her of an eager student trying to ingratiate himself with a favorite teacher. He leaned forward in his chair as if straining to hear better. His full, deep voice—and this surprised Jenny—had nothing of a rural twang. As Waters smiled boyishly at her preliminary questions, she found herself focusing on his eyes. Combined with his fine voice, they had an almost hypnotic effect.

"You mind telling me what you've got planned for us here?" Waters asked. "They didn't say all that much back in Potosi when we signed up for this."

"Today we'll be giving you some tests. We'll also draw blood and do a few other minor procedures. I'll explain more a little later what we're all about here. But first I'd like to go over your record for a few minutes."

"Sure, Doc. I'm not too proud of what I did."

Jenny was well aware that Waters was saying exactly what he thought she wanted to hear. The hollow line about remorse was a con job typical of antisocials. She understood the game: He was already trying to manipulate the conversation to his advantage.

Glancing at the papers spread out on the table, she took a quiet breath and tried to clear her head. This was the point where it could get difficult, when the memory of what had happened to her that night in Chicago could unexpectedly force its way back into her mind. For years that hadn't been a problem, even during difficult interviews with sex offenders, and she could usually shake off the feeling by concentrating on the job at hand. But lately she'd had trouble doing this. It took more effort to hold old memories at bay. She still wasn't sure why.

"You were convicted two years ago of raping a woman in Topeka, Kansas."

"Yes, ma'am."

Eyes down, Jenny said, "You beat her up pretty badly."

"It just got out of hand. We'd both been drinking." Waters's voice was sincere, apologetic.

The police record said he'd picked up the woman in a bar, raped her in his car and hit her in the head with a brick. After stripping her naked, he tied her hands and feet with duct tape and stuffed her in the trunk. A short time later, a cop who'd stopped him for driving with a broken taillight got suspicious and searched the car. He was looking for drugs, not a battered, unconscious woman who'd been so badly assaulted that her vagina was torn open.

The victim had been incredibly lucky. Jenny was certain that Waters had planned to torture and murder her.

"You've never killed anyone?"

He smiled and said, "Ma'am, you gotta know from looking over my prison file that I never killed nobody."

His record was one of the most disturbing Jenny had ever seen. Waters had been arrested three times previously for rape, but never charged because the victims had refused to testify. They were too scared. Waters was a leading suspect in the unsolved cases of two Kansas City women who had disappeared without a trace and were believed to have been murdered. Both were prostitutes. Jenny planned to press him on those cases, but not right now.

"And you raped only that one woman in Topeka?"

"Yes, ma'am. I was good and drunk. So was she."

Jenny decided it was time to clue Waters in on a few

things and let him know this might be harder than he'd anticipated. Her strategy with a serial offender was to let him understand from the outset that she read him perfectly and could get inside his head whenever she needed to. The controversial approach was designed to force the patient to admit the brutal truth about himself and forget manipulation and lying, which only wasted time and hindered therapy.

"Gary, let me tell you a little about yourself," Jenny said, folding her hands. "You've raped dozens of women, not just one. You've been doing it since you were in your late teens, and you enjoy it. There are times when the desire to rape and torture a woman, to have a sex slave, becomes so strong you can't stand it. It builds inside you for days, weeks and, when you can't fight it anymore, you hunt down your next victim. You're a serial sex offender, Gary. We'll talk later about whether you're also a serial killer."

Waters's eyes narrowed and his face tightened in a moment of jarring compression that, shadowlike, passed as quickly as it had come. But Jenny had seen enough—the face of a killer who could charm a woman into his car, then do unspeakable things to her. His mask of sanity had momentarily slipped.

"Let's get one thing straight, lady. You've got no proof I killed anybody," Waters said slowly. "The only thing I'm good for is one rape."

Jenny nodded. She'd achieved her purpose. There was no sense pushing it.

As promised, and with some major omissions, she laid out the program for the next few days. They would draw samples of his blood and cerebrospinal fluid for routine analysis, do an EEG to measure his brain-wave patterns and administer a battery of psychological exams, including the Rorschach, WAIS-R and Thematic Apperception tests. There was another test, which she didn't mention—one she'd helped develop herself. In the next day or two, they would use a special instrument to measure Waters's sexual preferences.

The following week they'd start the PET scans.

Before she drew his blood for analysis, Jenny decided to push one more button with him.

"Gary, I see that you've been in a lot of automobile accidents." She took his police rap sheet from one of the folders and started ticking them off. "If I'm counting right, there are over a dozen of them."

Each accident involved a woman driver, each was a rear-end collision in which no one had been injured, and in each case Waters hadn't even tried to get away. He'd sat in his car, waiting for a squad car to arrive. Then he collected his ticket and drove off after giving the woman phony insurance information.

"I guess I'm just a bad driver," Waters said.

"I don't think so, Gary. Here's what you were really up to. You'd pick out a good-looking woman, one that met all your standards. Maybe she had long hair or great legs or breasts, or some other feature that turned you on. You'd already spotted her at a convenience store or gas station. It doesn't matter where. Then you'd follow her car and bump into the back of it at a stop sign or red light. You'd sit there watching her face in her rearview mirror. You were in control, Gary. You were enjoying yourself. You'd entered her life and ruined her day, and you were getting excited just watching her get mad. She'd get out of the car and you'd see how angry she was, and you'd start to feel sexually turned on. You probably sat there and masturbated. Does any of that sound familiar, Gary?"

Waters stared at her. He didn't know what to say. Jenny felt the weight of his gaze and knew she'd reached the first threshold with him.

Two security guards stood behind Ed Lind as he sat on the edge of the examination table with his feet shackled. Lind wore shorts and a green T-shirt. His features reminded Brook of a billboard cowboy's—the chin, jaw and nose were sharply chiseled, and the deep creases at the corners of his mouth looked like knife scars.

Brook shone the pinpoint light of an ophthalmoscope into

Lind's right and left eyes. The exam was a crucial preliminary check for brain injury or any other neurological problem
that could cause violent behavior. The inner structures all
looked normal—the vitreous chamber, ora serrata and cho-
roid (the dark-brownish layer that kept light waves from being reflected out of the eye). So did the orange-tinted retina,
with its spider's web of blood vessels that entered the eyeball
at the optic disc.

Brook wore a new lab coat with his name stitched in blue
script over the right pocket. He was a little nervous but eager
to get started. Earlier that morning he had introduced himself
to the prisoner for the first time, during a brief visit to his
room. After finishing a big breakfast—a double order of pan-
cakes and sausage—Lind had been brought to one of the
clinic's examining rooms.

He watched Brook and frowned.

"I don't like getting stuck."

"You won't even feel it," Brook said, working quickly
under a bank of fluorescent lights. It wasn't unusual for criminals to have an exaggerated fear of needles—or of any surgical procedure, no matter how minor. They almost regarded
it as physical maiming, and, for many ASPs, being maimed
was more terrifying than dying.

Finishing the eye exam and reflex check—both were well
within normal ranges—Brook wanted to draw a blood sample, and was searching through the drawers of a cabinet for
a tourniquet. When he couldn't find one, he resorted to an
old med-school trick. Expertly tying a rubber glove around
Lind's right biceps, he swabbed the forearm with alcohol.
Then, telling Lind to bend his arm, he inserted a butterfly-
infusion valve into the large anacubital vein in the crook of
the elbow.

"That better be a clean needle," Lind said. "I don't want
to wind up with AIDS like half the other shits in prison."

"Not gonna happen, Ed," Brook said, doing a lousy im-
itation of Dana Carvey doing George Bush.

He quickly drew off 12 cc of blood with a syringe, removed the infusion needle and put a bandage over the punc-

ture. Then he transferred the blood into two 5-cc vials, which he capped, marked and placed in a lab pickup tray. He dropped the needle and plastic tubing into a red biocontaminate container. The procedure had taken less than two minutes.

"What's going to happen to it?" Lind asked, nodding toward the filled vials.

"A routine work-up," Brook said, explaining that the blood would be checked for glucose, lactic acid, hemoglobin, protein and the white and red blood-cell counts. Brook didn't mention that he was particularly interested in checking Lind's testosterone levels. Clinical studies had associated higher counts with sociopathic behavior.

"Maybe it'll tell you why I rob banks," Lind said. Once the needle had been removed and discarded, he looked and sounded more relaxed.

"You rob banks because you enjoy it, Ed."

Lind smiled. "Bull's-eye," he said.

So far, Brook hadn't detected that Lind was trying to con him. He didn't have the plastered smirk and wise-guy attitude usually associated with an ASP. On the contrary, the prisoner had answered most of Brook's questions truthfully and with some deliberation.

Still, Brook didn't forget for a minute that he was dealing with a hardcore bank robber. In the cell-block pecking order, bank robbers had the highest standing. Prison royalty, they were invariably bright, tough and usually older than other inmates. They were also incorrigible. Paroled, they would likely go right out and rob another bank. It was nearly impossible to change their behavior. They weren't homicidal sociopaths, but they wouldn't hesitate to kill anyone who got in their way. They were ruthless, intelligent and willing to take huge risks. The prison record told Brook that Lind was a textbook example.

Brook told Lind to lie on his right side. It was time to do the lumbar puncture for the cerebrospinal test.

"Tell me again this isn't going to hurt," Lind said.

"You won't even know what hit you, Ed."

Brook already had removed the plastic syringe from the test kit. He attached a three-inch, large-gauge needle to the syringe and had Lind slide his shorts below his waist. Using an alcohol swab, he rubbed the base of the lumbar spine, an area called the *cauda equina*, or horse's tail, where the spinal cord fanned out in a complex bundle of nerve endings. It was the best place to draw off cerebrospinal fluid, which pooled there in a reservoir.

"What did you say that fluid's for?" Lind asked. He almost sounded apologetic. "I can't remember half the shit you told me."

"Your brain floats in it," Brook said. "It keeps it in equilibrium and helps drain off impurities. It also absorbs shocks to the head."

"I've had a few of those," Lind said. He was trying to stay calm, but the strain was showing. "I guess this is kinda late, but what can go wrong?"

"Not a thing." Brook didn't tell him that the most serious complications included fatal strokes from sudden brainstem compressions.

He had the syringe ready to go.

"This might be a little uncomfortable."

Lind glanced over his right shoulder and saw the needle.

"Fuck, no!"

He started to get up. The guards quickly grabbed his shoulders and pinned him flat on the gurney. He looked up at Brook, teeth clenched, his eyes flashing anger.

"Don't mess with me," he said, the words coldly malevolent. "I didn't agree to come here just to get stuck full of goddamn needles."

"This is a piece of cake, Ed. You've got to trust me."

Brook nodded to the guards, who loosened their grip and let Lind lie on his side.

"Don't move!" Brook snapped. "Or you *will* feel it."

Within seconds he'd plunged the needle deep into the spinal reservoir and drawn off 20 cc of the clear, waterlike fluid, which he injected into a test tube for analysis. Brook wanted to check the fluid's 5-hydroxyindoleacetic acid levels—one

of the chemical components of the neurotransmitter serotonin. Low readings were associated with an increased propensity for violence. Like high testosterone levels, low serotonin
levels had gained widespread attention as a possible indicator
for aggressive behavior and had become one of the most
exciting research areas in forensic psychiatry.

"That's it, Ed. We're done," Brook said.

Lind turned over on his back and took a slow, deep breath,
filling his lungs before exhaling. The doctor had been right;
the procedure hadn't been so bad.

"I'll be fifty-five years old before I can even go to the
parole board," he said slowly. "You can screw around with
my head as much as you want. Just don't make a mistake."

Jenny took out the set of cards for the perception evaluation
test. It included twenty-five black-and-white cards that
showed people in various scenes, many of them ambivalent
or bizarre.

"I want you to make up a story about each picture," Jenny
told Waters. "Tell me what's happening, what the characters
you see are feeling and thinking."

"I know you've already explained it once, but why are
we doing this?" Waters asked, his voice polite, deferential.
After a long morning spent undergoing various personality
tests, he showed no signs of getting tired.

"It lets us get an idea of how you think, Gary."

She watched him settle back in his chair. He'd stopped
grinning. Waters had been lying when it suited him, lying
skillfully as he gave her the answers he thought she expected.
He would probably do it now.

Jenny put the first card on the table, a pen-and-ink sketch
of two people—one, an attractive young woman with short
dark hair; the other, an old man who was pensively touching
his lips with bony fingers. It was a haunting scene.

"What's happening there, Gary? Make up a story." Jenny
was trained to keep her voice and expression neutral as she
asked questions and listened to the responses.

"That's a father and daughter. The man's been giving her

hell all her life. He's a real bastard and maybe he's dying of cancer, and the girl's happy about it. She looks like she's smiling. She's feeling great that daddy's gonna die.''

The next card showed a woman lying naked in bed. A man was standing at the side of the bed, his right arm covering his eyes, which were averted. Maybe he was crying.

''They just had sex.'' Waters frowned. He took a sip of coffee, trying to conceal what he was feeling, but Jenny had noticed that his face had hardened.

''The guy just screwed her, and he doesn't like it,'' Waters said, staring at the card. ''She made him do it, and he wants to get away.'' He took another long, unblinking look at the card. ''Or maybe he wants to kill her.''

''What can you tell me about the woman?''

Waters shrugged and shook his head.

''Is it his mother?''

Jenny was taking a risk. She wasn't supposed to suggest a response or lead the answers, but there was a certain brittleness to Waters's voice that made her zero in on incest. It wasn't as much of a shot in the dark as it seemed. Often, serial sexual offenders have been raped by a parent.

Waters's expression darkened. ''He's been sleeping with her since he was twelve. He wants to kill her, but one of the shitbums she's been living with does it for him. Beats the crap out of her one night, and she doesn't wake up.'' He gave Jenny a wicked look. ''Is that the kind of story you had in mind?''

THIRTEEN
⊷⊶

IT HAD BEEN A rough two days, and Lind was showing
frayed edges. Earlier that morning they'd finished the last of
the intelligence and personality tests. Lind now lay on a gurney in an examination room. Twenty-three red and blue
wires hooked to the "head box" were attached to his scalp
and connected to the electroencephalograph. Two other leads
that monitored his heart rate were affixed to his breastbone.
A wire clipped to the little finger on his right hand measured
oxygen levels.

"That stings!"

"I'm sorry, but it can't be helped," Ted Krill said. He
was rubbing Lind's scalp with a metal stylus, to lower the
skin resistance for better electrical conduction. A trial run
had shown that three of the electrodes were loose and needed
readjustment.

The clinic used a new, state-of-the-art digital EEG. A computer screen and laser printer had replaced the bulky analogue machine, which required pens, graph paper and a
complicated array of switches to set the proper sensitivity
readings. During seizure activity, the clacking pens often
jammed or splattered ink on the walls. The digital models
were a huge improvement.

Lind wore a pair of loose-fitting jeans and a Western shirt.

His eyes were closed, and he looked like he was nodding off. Krill shook the prisoner's right leg.

"No sleeping."

Drowsiness or sleep could disguise the brain rhythms with "junk" artifacts that Krill likened to background noise. They didn't want that to happen.

A Chopin piano concerto played softly in the background. Krill always worked with a CD player switched to classical music. A big, slow-moving man, Krill had prematurely gray hair that made him look older than he was. Brook appreciated his brilliance with the EEG, a procedure that measured the brain's rippling electrical impulses. Both his M.D. and Ph.D. in neuroscience were from Harvard. But he was a pain in the ass to work with—arrogant, irritable, quick to criticize.

Brook was familiar with the basic principles of the electroencephalograph—or at least thought so until he began working closely with Krill, who quickly showed him how little he really understood about it. Krill was a virtuoso with the machine, both in technique—determining the proper montage or electrode placement, controlling the current, calibrating the frequencies—and in analyzing the results.

Using a tape measure, Krill had made a series of twenty-three red crosses on Lind's head and scalp, one to mark the precise location of each electrode. He positioned them according to the international "ten-twenty" grid system. He'd already prepped the scalp with an electrode jelly that looked like white toothpaste and felt like wet sand, swabbing some on each red mark.

Brook had helped by filling the hollow, button-sized gold electrodes with a squirt of electrolyte glue, which made the room smell of ether. He'd attached each electrode with a shot of compressed air; this served to dry the glue. As a final touch, Krill had fitted Lind with a cloth head-covering that resembled a green swimmer's cap; it would keep the electrodes from slipping. All the prep work had taken half an hour.

"We're going to do a photic-stimulation test, Mr. Lind," Krill said. "That means we're going to flash a strobe light in your eyes. We'll slowly increase the speed of the flashes. I want you to lie there and try to keep your eyes open.''

In someone with epilepsy, the strobe could trigger a temporal-lobe seizure. So could three or four minutes of deep breathing. Lind didn't have a history of seizures, but they wanted to make sure.

Hartigan quietly entered the examination room, carrying a clipboard. He nodded as if to say, carry on. Brook noticed Krill's faint frown.

On Krill's orders, Brook turned down the overhead lights, positioned the strobe a few inches from Lind's face, then switched it on. The cycle was ten seconds on and five off, with the pulsing blue-white flashes gradually increasing in speed.

''Look at all these wonderful alphas,'' Krill said.

Brook glanced at the computer monitor, which showed the brain-wave readings scrolling across the bottom of the screen at one-second intervals. With a normal person, alpha waves were in the 8- to 13-Hz range. Lind's were considerably lower.

''He's showing slow activity over both hemispheres,'' Brook said. He was impressed. That's just what Krill had predicted. ASPs had distinctly slower alpha waves, a pattern especially true with the more aggressive offenders. No one knew why, although it was documented that patients in the early stage of such dementia-inducing diseases as Alzheimer's and Huntington's chorea also exhibited slow alphas.

''How we doing?'' Lind said, raising his head from the pillow after the strobe was turned off. ''Have you read my mind yet?''

''Let's give him some caffeine,'' Hartigan said, the first time he'd spoken. The stimulant was used to trigger epileptic attacks in cases where it was necessary to confirm a diagnosis in patients with equivocal EEG readings. If Lind was prone to an attack, he might have a grand mal or less severe fit, complete with unconsciousness, spasms and mouth-foaming.

Krill glanced at Brook. They hadn't planned on doing that.

"I realize it's a change in procedure, but I want to make sure that Mr. Lind isn't subject to seizures."

"Couldn't we wait a day?" Brook asked. He would have preferred delaying that test, knowing how strung out Lind was and how strongly he reacted to needles. He started to explain this, but Hartigan cut him off.

"Doctor, in case you haven't noticed, the EEG is still running."

Brook swallowed the reprimand and prepared a hypodermic with 2 cc of caffeine.

"Jesus, are you bastards going to stick me again?" Lind said. He tried to get up, but stopped when two guards approached the examination table. They'd been in the room the entire time.

Brook had never seen anyone so terrified of needles. He prepped Lind's right forearm with alcohol and injected the drug just below the elbow.

"Try to breathe easily," he said. "This will only take a minute." Provided you don't have a convulsion or an anxiety attack, he said to himself, still not happy that Hartigan had ordered the injection.

The prisoner's eyes locked on Brook's. There was fear there, and anger. Brook gave him a reassuring pat on the shoulder.

"You'll be okay," he said, detecting something in Lind's fixed stare that worried him. It was the look of someone losing control. The guards had noticed it too; they hadn't budged from the prisoner's side.

Hartigan and Krill were staring at the computer screen, watching for a rapid staccato of sharp waves and spikes over the right anterior temporal lobe, the telltale sign of a seizure.

Alpha activity continued to dominate the trace, but that was normal in such circumstances; bilateral activity across both sides of the brain's midline, with the maximum amplitude present in the frontal lobes. There was no evidence of seizure.

After two minutes, Hartigan terminated the test. Sweat bathed Lind's forehead. He hadn't taken his eyes off Brook.

*   *   *

Waters sat in a comfortable reclining chair in front of a movie screen that had been set up in his room. A yellow wire protruded from the fly of his jeans. Jenny had plugged it into a longer wire attached to a Grass-7 polygraph machine.

Cuffed and shackled, Waters had just returned from the bathroom, where he'd placed a ring gauge around the shaft of his penis. The flexible rubber collar was calibrated to measure the diameter of an erection. Jenny had instructed him on how to hook it up, and was letting him get comfortable before she started the test.

Brook and Hartigan watched the scene on closed-circuit television from the control room down the hall.

"So you just want me to enjoy the show and have a good time?" Waters asked.

"That's right, Gary. The instructions will appear on the screen. It's very simple."

The results from this test were often dramatic, but one of the keys to success was getting the subject to relax.

Jenny attached a set of five EKG telemetry electrodes to Waters's right and left arms to record his heart rate. She stuck another electrode to his right wrist to monitor electrical skin-conductance levels. Antisocials consistently had lower conductance readings.

It had been a grueling three days, but Jenny hardly noticed her fatigue. As she ran down the checklist for the final time, she reminded herself that this test would soon be over. As far as it affected Waters, she didn't doubt the results. She wasn't sure yet about her own response.

"The test will be in three parts," Jenny said, going over the details with Waters. "You'll be shown a series of slides and asked to rank them in terms of sexual interest. Then we'll show you some more slides, but this time try not to think about them. Try to avoid any mental images at all. In the final part, we're going to play a tape recording that describes a sexual encounter. Just sit there and listen."

"Hey, I knew it was a good idea to volunteer to come

here,'' Waters said. ''This sounds like it's going to be a real joyride.''

When Jenny left the room, a guard released his cuffs and shackles.

Jenny went to the control room to watch the experiment. Brook had seen her only briefly during the last few hectic days. Jenny closed her eyes and massaged her temples.

''How are you feeling?'' Brook asked. He thought she looked tired.

''A long day and no lunch. My blood sugar's a wreck.''

''Do you think he'll figure out what's going on and try to fight it?'' Brook asked. Although familiar with the literature on penile erection tests, he'd never watched one before.

''It won't matter,'' Hartigan said. ''That possibility has been factored into scoring the results.''

The clinic director sat at the bank of television screens with an open notebook in front of him. He'd been working sixteen-hour days since the preliminary tests started, but didn't show it. His shirt, red stripes and French cuffs, looked as crisp as when he'd put it on before dawn. Brook was impressed by the man's energy and driving capacity for work. He was used to workaholics and considered himself one, but he'd never met anyone in Hartigan's league.

The television screens offered five views of Waters, who reminded Brook of someone who'd just taken a seat in a movie theater and was patiently waiting for the show to start. He was missing only the bag of popcorn and a soda.

Hartigan adjusted a dial, which darkened the lighting in the prisoner's room. Waters nodded appreciatively.

The first ten color slides showed attractive women in various stages of undress. In the last four, they were naked and seductively posed. Models had been used. The poses reflected what a control group of normal males had determined to be sexually provocative.

Hartigan monitored the Grass polygraph. ''He's showing moderate arousal.''

After the first series had ended, a picture of the clinic's

exterior flashed on the screen. Jenny explained that it was a neutral control.

"The second set of slides is about to start," she said.

Waters's sarcastic voice came over the intercom.

"I know you can hear me. That was great. I had a lot of fun."

The next series depicted rape scenes. Again, Brook was struck by the powerful realism the actors had achieved. Some of the scenes were outdoors, some inside. The women looked genuinely terrified. They lay on their backs or on their stomachs with their skirts up or pants pulled down. Three slides suggested anal intercourse; two, fellatio.

"Much more arousal," Hartigan said. The penile traducer was showing a strong erection, especially to the more violent images.

Jenny forced herself to watch the slides. Each was projected for a full minute. She hoped Brook hadn't noticed the effort this was taking her and wondered whether he could sense how she was feeling, or whether the strain showed in her face. She tried to concentrate on methodically writing down her clinical observations. She'd learned long ago that, no matter how she felt, it was best to keep busy.

Waters stared at the screen. He wasn't making wisecracks anymore. Jenny guessed he was on to them. He had repeatedly denied that he was a serial rapist, or that he had uncontrollable sexual urges, but this test dramatically showed otherwise. The mercury-filled ring around his penis couldn't be fooled.

He sat in his chair, watching another series of ten slides. This time there was no sexual imagery at all. Each slide showed a man beating, slapping or kicking a woman. As before, Brook found the realism excellent.

Waters had an erection before the second slide was shown, by far his most powerful response. The pattern continued throughout the sequence.

Brook knew what it meant. Waters's sexual-arousal patterns were strongly keyed to violence. Sex or eroticism had little to do with it. The act of violence was arousing in itself.

"I'd say we've got a sadist on our hands," he said.

"Who rapes and degrades women," Jenny said. "And likes to hurt them." She glanced at the polygraph readings. She'd never seen such an explosive sexual response to violent stimuli. The rape itself was of secondary importance. Waters was a true sadist, and she felt chills as she watched him sitting there—physically deformed, skinny, his eyes wide with almost drunken excitement.

"He's trying to fight it," Hartigan said. He was also closely monitoring the polygraph readings. "He knows what's happening."

Another striking confirmation of Waters's sadistic tendencies followed. With the screen blank, he was told to listen to a recording that described a nonsexual attack on a woman. A technician had prerecorded the tape, narrating how the attacker meets a woman on a hiking trail, pulls her into the woods and starts slapping and beating her. He strikes her face and body repeatedly, beating her bloody.

The tape ran for thirty more seconds. When it was over, Waters just sat there. The polygraph had recorded another erection.

Suddenly, he stood up and pulled off the rubber ring and its wiring.

"It's not going to work!" Waters shouted. "This doesn't prove a fucking thing!"

FOURTEEN
‡>─‡

AT ELEVEN P.M. THAT night Hartigan called Jim Serra to his office. Most of the staff had already gone home. Hartigan motioned Serra to a chair and slipped a cassette tape into a VCR. Serra sat down and suppressed a yawn. He'd been working since five that morning and was living on coffee and extra-strength Tylenol for a recurring headache. He figured Hartigan wanted to talk about the PET scans they'd scheduled for the next day.

"I want to show you something," Hartigan said, pushing a button on his desk. It turned on a television built into a bookshelf.

Serra soon forgot his throbbing head. It was a tape of Frank LePonty, pacing back and forth in his room, moving rapidly from wall to wall like a caged animal. He was wearing white shorts and a T-shirt, and he kept rubbing his hands together as if they were cold.

"That was taken a day after we gave him his last neuro-stim treatment and nine hours before his escape," Hartigan said.

It was the first time Serra had seen the film. LePonty's face had taken on a wild, crazed expression. It almost didn't look like him.

Hartigan stopped the video.

"Check his eyes," he said.

They were blazing with frantic excitement. Serra also saw how LePonty's lips were clenched, the face grotesquely contorted.

"Is he saying something?" The sound was nearly inaudible.

Hartigan frowned. "Unfortunately, the audio was turned down when this was recorded. We enhanced it as much as we could. It sounds like some kind of chant."

Serra watched LePonty move rapidly across the room, eight steps, pivot and turn, eight steps, pivot and turn.

"My guess is he's having some kind of psychomotor attack," he said. Excitability and rapid pacing were hallmarks of these extremely rare seizures, which could also be violent. Sometimes the abnormal behavior lasted for hours, even days, after the initial attack. The patient usually wasn't even aware of what was happening.

"He may even be hallucinating," Hartigan said. With a true psychomotor seizure, that wasn't unusual either.

Both men studied LePonty's frantic movements a few minutes longer, then Hartigan turned off the tape. For weeks he'd been trying to figure out what had happened to LePonty, but lately he'd drawn some conclusions and wanted to discuss them with Serra.

"Have you finished your redesign of the coils?" he asked.

Serra nodded. Thanks to the film, he was fully awake. Hartigan offered him a cup of espresso. He kept an Italian espresso maker on the console in his office, and was capable of living for days on the strong, syrupy-thick coffee. Serra declined. He didn't dare pump any more caffeine into his overcharged system.

For the last week, he'd been working almost nonstop to redesign the electromagnetic-stimulation coils. He'd used a circular 90-mm coil for LePonty and had recently switched to a double-coil design. Thanks to computer-generated, three-dimensional imaging techniques, he'd been able to reconfigure the shape of the copper coils in only a few days. A double-coil achieved a wider, deeper magnetic field and had the additional advantage of offering lower electrical resistance and more heat dissipation, which meant the device wouldn't get as hot after repeated stimulations.

"We went too far the last time," Serra said irritably. "We did way too many stimulations and probably wound up with a major kindling event." In other words, an electrical forest fire had spread beyond LePonty's limbic system into other parts of his brain, triggering a seizure of unusually long duration. That would explain LePonty's compulsive pacing, his nervousness and trancelike facial expressions. A close-up also showed that his pupils were dilated, another telltale sign of a major seizure.

"I know what happened," Hartigan snapped, putting down his espresso. Their tests with cats had graphically demonstrated the danger of kindling that spread through the brain. "I don't want it to happen again." Serra's tone had set him on edge. He pushed another switch on his teak desktop, which he somehow managed to keep clear of books, papers and other clutter, despite his crushing work load. The lights dimmed, and a wall panel slid up revealing a movie screen. A projector blinked on.

Serra immediately recognized the color diagram of the hippocampus. Located deep in the amygdala and rolled up in the temporal lobe, the organ got its name from its seahorse shape. It was one of the most primitive parts of the cortex, connecting the different neural pathways of the limbic system. It played a crucial role in learning, memory and attention span.

"Can your magnetic fields reach that area?"

"It's deeper than we've ever gone before."

"My question is can your electromagnetic pulses hit that part of the brain?"

"That's not the problem," Serra shot back. "The problem is we haven't figured out yet how to keep the kindled seizures from spreading from the limbic region into other neural structures."

"That's why I want to use the hippocampus as a trigger."

Explaining the concept to Serra helped Hartigan think it through again. The literature on kindling and the results of his experiments on cats were conclusive. Someone had used the analogy of jump-starting a dead car battery, an idea that had stuck with him. The hippocampus represented a set of cables, the limbic system the dead battery; in this case, the cables were hooked up to Serra's neuro-stim machine. Or, to use another comparison, the hippocampus was one of the brain's main switchboxes, plugged into other structures in the limbic system through a complex neurochemical wiring network.

Hartigan's idea was to kindle the hippocampus, hoping it would work like an electrical switch and "turn on" kindling in the rest of the limbic brain, their primary target. Because of its sensitivity, the hippocampal switch could also be thrown with fewer stimulations.

Hartigan picked up his cup and emptied it. "That way we won't risk overstimulating, which should help us confine the kindling to the limbic system. The fire won't get out of control and start to spread."

Hartigan regretted that he hadn't tried this approach with LePonty. The fact remained, however, that they had kindled his limbic brain, setting off a series of self-sustaining seizures that had totally altered the man's personality. It still chilled him to watch that film. LePonty looked like he wanted to jump out of his skin—or kill someone. The problem had come near the end of the treatments, when his seizures started firing in a kind of chain reaction.

Hartigan remained confident they could have extinguished them with anticonvulsants. Al Silver was working with PCZ Pharmaceuticals, the drug lab affiliated with the clinic, to perfect just such a compound. But then LePonty had escaped.

Serra listened to Hartigan's analysis, his annoyance increasing. The experiments had turned a second-rate con with no history of violence into a monster. And Hartigan wanted to resume them.

"Let's not forget here that he also had some IQ deficits," Serra said. "The intelligence tests showed that pretty clearly." The tests measured how LePonty had performed simple mental tasks like counting or sorting.

"Big deal," Hartigan said, unable to stifle his anger at Serra's objections. "So it took him a few seconds longer to add and subtract some numbers. Those results were insignificant. The fact is the man was using different parts of his brain to process information."

The final series of PET scans had proven that beyond any possible doubt. Nothing had so encouraged Hartigan or buoyed his conviction that they were on the right track than those striking computer-generated pictures, which had captured how LePonty's brain actually worked when he performed those adding and subtracting tests. When he was injected with a radioactive material, the areas of his brain most involved in those mental processes "lit up" on the PET scan.

Hartigan pointed out that different areas lit up after kindling than before. The kindled seizures had somehow changed the way his brain worked, how it processed information.

Serra wasn't ready to drop it.

"But something went wrong. It all comes back to that, doesn't it? Kindling did change LePonty's brain: It made him a homicidal maniac."

Hartigan wasn't about to let that last comment pass unchallenged.

"In case you've forgotten, Doctor, we didn't have a chance to finish with LePonty."

Despite his near exhaustion, Serra's anger boiled up.

"In case you've forgotten, neither did Mark Ulman."

FIFTEEN

A DAY LATER JENNY interviewed Waters. She'd just come from a staff meeting in Hartigan's office. Everyone was excited. The PET-scan analysis wasn't finished, but the preliminary results for all three prisoners showed intense blood-flow activity in their pyriform lobes—the entire temporal-lobe portion of the limbic system. The area had lit up repeatedly during the tests and was precisely where Hartigan had placed so much emphasis. It was clearly the part of the brain most actively involved in criminal thoughts.

The test results differed significantly from those of the control group; with a few exceptions, the students hadn't exhibited any limbic brain activity at all.

Jenny had brought along a life-sized model of the brain for her session with Waters. She wanted him to understand what had happened with the PET scans. Waters was sitting at a desk in his room. He hadn't shaved, and his short, blond hair needed combing.

"This whole limbic area was involved," Jenny said, tracing the cingulate gyrus, cingulum, fornix and amygdala. "So was the thalamic nucleus."

"I've got all this figured out," Waters said, staring at the model with a smug half-smile. Jenny sensed his pent-up hostility. "You're still trying to prove that I'm good for killing those whores in Kansas City and you'd like to trick me into admitting it. Isn't that what this is all about?''

"I think you've raped and killed a lot of women, Gary, but that's not the point of these tests. We're trying to find out how your brain works."

Waters shook his head. He wanted to make sure she understood that he was on to her.

"I haven't killed anybody."

Jenny opened a folder and took out a sheet of paper that listed an inventory of everything police had found in a Kansas City storage locker Waters had rented. The items included an eight-foot stack of hard-core pornographic magazines, many of which emphasized bondage and torture—some of the roughest stuff she'd ever seen. There were also three boxes of bondage paraphernalia: halters, whips, chains, ropes.

Jenny read some of the magazine titles aloud—''*S&M Erotica. Bound and Gagged. Tough Love.*''

She leaned back in her seat. It was starting to happen again. She kept forcing herself to stare at Waters as she fought against it, tried to turn it off.

The mental images had switched on like a movie.

She remembered how she had opened the door of her Hyde Park apartment and stepped out into the sultry air to walk to the biology lab next to the Fermi science building. It had just stopped raining. Wearing shorts and carrying a canvas backpack, she started up Woodlawn Avenue. Normally crowded with students and faculty members on their way to and from the pubs and secondhand bookshops along Rush Street, the sidewalks were still deserted after the hard rain.

The air was pungent with the smell of rain, mowed grass and wet pavement. The Gothic spires of the quadrangles stood out in dark silhouette against the gray sky.

Thinking about her bio-chem exam, Jenny was working through a complex analogue when she passed a row of overgrown shrubs near a bus stop. Something tripped her, and she went down hard. Then he grabbed her by the legs and pulled her into a clearing in the bushes.

"You scream, you're dead, bitch."

His mouth was next to her ear. His warm breath smelled of wine. He pinned her hands to her sides and straddled her waist. She tried to scream, and he hit her across the mouth, stunning her. He yanked down her shorts. She kicked wildly, and he hit her again.

"Shut your fuckin' mouth!"

She couldn't see his face in the darkness, a young black man with a gold chain around his neck and a bushy Afro. Wiry, strong, vicious. He ripped off her underpants, rolled her over, and pushed into her. Twisting frantically with all her strength and clawing at his face, she pulled away. This time he hit her so hard, white lights flashed in her eyes. He slammed her face into the loamy ground and spread her legs and thrust deep into her. He was panting. Then she lost consciousness. She woke up in City Hospital, lying on a gurney, with two residents and a cop staring down at her.

Jenny took a few deep breaths to steady herself. She didn't think Waters had noticed what had just happened to her. It was her worst flashback in years.

She had thought she was over them for good, and in control of her feelings and memories, but for days she'd sensed an attack coming on, building slowly like a serious depression, stalking her, waiting for the moment when she was most vulnerable.

Jenny was sure that her long sessions with Waters had something to do with it. She had never met anyone who troubled her as much as he did. He was the worst sexual predator she'd ever encountered, and he'd managed to get under her skin in a way she hadn't thought possible.

She'd been trained to prevent that very thing from happening, and trained well. Every time she met him for an interview or a test, he was searching, probing for a weakness, a way to ingratiate himself or get inside her head. Jenny was confident she could handle him, but she conceded that he worried her.

He was giving her that arrogant smirk again. He was toy-ing with her, trying to find out how much he could get away with and whether this conversation could be turned to his advantage. Waters was following his usual pattern, admitting to something only when it suited his purpose.

She took a cassette tape from the fanfold file and inserted it into the tape recorder she always used during interview sessions. She hadn't intended to do this. Waters looked puzzled.

"This might sound familiar," Jenny said, pushing the start button.

The voice on the tape was high-pitched, soprano, almost a banshee wail: "Fuck my ass, say it. Say how much you like it, bitch. Say it! Say 'Fuck my ass'!" The speaker repeated the words five or six times, changing the modulation from high to low pitch.

The tape had been seized by the police who raided Waters's apartment. It chilled Jenny to the core. She knew what Waters was doing—rehearsing words he intended to make his victims utter as he tortured them. She wondered how many women had listened to them in the depths of terror.

"That's you, isn't it, Gary?"

She turned off the cassette. Waters hadn't moved.

SIXTEEN

BROOK PULLED ON A pair of plastic gloves and slipped his radiation detector into the front pocket of his lab coat. About the size of a transistor radio, it would emit a shrill beep if he got too close to something dangerously radioactive. The white badge pinned to his lapel, another warning device, would light up if the radiation levels got too high. Such accidents were almost unheard of, but everything in the clinic's PET-scan room was considered potentially hot, and that included the big, gray PET scanner that filled one wall, the radioisotope calibrator that functioned as a sophisticated Geiger counter—even the IV drip bag.

Marty Conner, the clinic's PET expert, had drilled Brook repeatedly on that subject. Radiation was usually well within safe levels, but if either of Brook's on-line detectors went off, he was to clear out fast.

Positron emission tomography had revolutionized the study of the brain. PET images were far more detailed than an X ray or other imaging techniques. And, unlike them, each scan represented a snapshot that captured not only how a specific part of the brain looked at a particular moment but also how it was working, how it processed thoughts and emotions. As a way of visualizing the inner workings of the mind, nothing beat PET.

Hartigan liked using the analogy of an orchestra to explain

the theory. Just as the winds, strings and other sections worked together to play a symphony, specific brain areas worked together to produce human behavior. PET showed which areas were active when certain tasks such as reading or adding numbers were performed.

Hartigan was among the first to use the computer-generated scans to try to map the brains of convicts. The idea was to highlight the parts of their brains most involved when they had criminal thoughts.

For the last three days, Brook had worked closely with Conner, learning the clinic's complicated PET-scan procedures. Hartigan wanted him to help run the scans on the prisoners, and the impromptu seminar with Conner had been a good experience. Conner had written two books on PET. He had a talent for patiently explaining the science, and never tired of discussing it.

Conner favored a look that was unvarnished L.L. Bean. Under his lab coat, he invariably wore flannel-lined denim jeans, a woolen shirt and a pair of expensive hiking shoes with lug soles. Conner was a big man, six four and well over two hundred pounds, with most of that weight in his chest. His steel-gray beard and sense of humor helped soften his imposing physical impression.

Ready to do the first scan on Waters, Conner had added a pair of yellow suspenders to his ensemble. The straps were decorated with mallards.

"Let's bring him in," Conner said. He made a telephone call, and a few minutes later Waters arrived with Jenny, Hartigan and a technician who would monitor the scans by computer. The tech smiled at Brook and Conner as she sat down at the terminal.

Another technician was stationed downstairs with the linear accelerator, which produced the radioactive positron emitter, or "marker," that would make Waters's brain light up.

Brook had come to appreciate the brilliant simplicity of the procedure. The clinic used Oxygen-15 for the marker—a radioactive isotope of oxygen, with a safe, two-minute half-life. After the oxygen gas was converted into a clear liquid, or "water," a high-speed pneumatic tube shot it up to the PET-scan room on the third floor. Injected into the subject's arm, it took about twenty seconds to reach the brain, where it formed an image of blood flow, which was the best indicator of brain function. Increased blood flow translated as increased brain activity.

The scans—computer-generated pictures, or images, of blood flow taken at different times—showed which parts of the brain worked hardest when certain mental tasks or activities were performed. In the case of criminals like Waters, the idea was to see what parts of the brain lit up when they watched a film that graphically represented their preferred crimes. It was like injecting a red dye into their brains and then waiting to see where it showed up. The parts that turned red were the hot spots for criminal mental activity.

With Conner's assistance, Hartigan had spent over two years gathering control data for the experiment they were about to run. They'd used volunteer medical students. Once the word was out, they'd had no shortage of students willing to earn five hundred dollars for a couple of hours of watching "dirty movies." PET scans of their brains looked considerably different from those of criminals watching the same X-rated films.

Jenny nodded to Brook. Her dark hair was combed back. Brook thought she looked tired. He certainly was. They'd all been working brutal hours preparing for the PET scans. He'd seen Jenny every day, but lately they'd rarely had a chance to say more than a few sentences to each other.

Waters had on the usual clinic attire—tan chino slacks, a blue pullover, Nikes. As always, his ankles were loosely shackled. Two guards helped prop him up. He wore a sort of drunken grin and was unsteady on his feet.

Brook knew why. An hour earlier, Hartigan had injected Waters with 30 cc of Valium to calm him down before they started the scans.

Conner introduced himself to Waters, smiling his broadest country smile and offering his hand. "Mornin', Gary. We'll get started in a few minutes, but first I want to explain what's going to happen so there won't be any surprises. This is gonna be a piece of cake.''

Waters grinned and said, ''You're lyin'.''

Brook and Conner helped him up on a gurney. Still smiling, he waved to Jenny, who'd stayed in the computer control room with Hartigan and the technician. They were watching through a thick plate-glass window.

''We're going to inject a chemical into your right arm,'' Conner said. ''Then we're going to take some pictures of your brain while you get to lie here, relax and watch a movie. It's a heck of a deal. But, Gary, listen to me.''

Conner put a big arm around Waters's shoulder.

''It's very important that you lie perfectly still and don't move your head. That's critical. Before we're finished, you'll hear me remind you about that a couple hundred times. Any questions?''

''What kind of movies? I like Walt Disney, *Snow White,* family shit like that.'' Waters smiled at his joke.

''One other thing, Gary. To help you keep your head still, we want you to wear a special mask. You won't even feel it.''

That was news to Waters. ''You never told me about a fuckin' mask.''

Conner nodded to Brook, who strapped Waters to the padded gurney. They put a cushion under his legs to reduce the strain on his back and rolled him over to what looked like a large, green CO_2 cylinder. The metal canister produced a soft, plastic gel that orthopedic surgeons use to make casts for broken bones. The substance came out in a foam that Conner rubbed on Waters's forehead, cheeks and nose, expertly sculpting out the eye holes. In less than a minute, the goo had hardened into a stiff, white mask that covered the top half of Waters's face. The sides of the mask extended past the ear and were attached to slots in the gurney, effectively holding his head in position.

''How does that feel?'' Conner asked. He and Brook moved the gurney to the PET scanner, easing it forward until

Waters's head was just inside the big machine's circular opening.

"What about that movie, Doc?"

"It's coming, Gary," Conner said, giving the prisoner a reassuring pat as he tightened the blue velcro straps that held his right arm to a splint. They were ready to attach the IV shunt that would pump the radioactive Oxygen-15 "water" into his veins.

Brook swabbed Waters's arm with alcohol and inserted the IV needle. Each scan lasted about forty seconds. It took twelve minutes between scans for the accelerator downstairs to produce another "water." Hartigan had scheduled nine scans for this first session.

Conner carefully placed a black visor over Waters's mask. Completely covering his eyes, the bizarre-looking device was a virtual-reality, head-mounted display, or HMD. It was designed to project three-dimensional images that would wrap around Waters's entire field of vision.

The prisoner showed more uneasiness, twisting his body.

"I don't like this," he said.

"Don't move. I repeat: Do not move, Gary," Conner said. "You've got to lie very still, or we're going to have big problems."

He made a hand signal to the technician in the control room. Moments later a red light flashed on the wall over the PET scanner. It meant the "water" was on its way. Brook took his position by the pneumatic tube. The clear fluid arrived within seconds in a plastic syringe. Brook slipped the syringe under the device that served as a Geiger counter. The digital reading indicated that the water was still a little hot: 30 millicuries. He waited until it dropped to 20, then injected the liquid into the IV at Waters's right elbow. A green line on the technician's computer terminal traced its rapid journey to Waters's brain. When the line suddenly climbed, she announced over a loudspeaker, "Begin now!"

Conner stood by the gurney, his eyes focused on his own computer screen and a television monitor that showed what Waters was seeing.

"Concentrate on what you're seeing," he told Waters, speaking into a microphone. A receiver was clipped to the prisoner's ear under the mask.

Brook glanced at the monitor screen and saw cars driving down a city highway. That was the "control" image, projected on Waters's HMD for five seconds. It was followed by the ten-second "task" image.

Even though Brook knew what was coming, it was still tough to take. The scene depicted a man anally raping a half-clothed woman. He was shown throwing her down and raping her on a wooden floor as she struggled. For Waters, the effect would be even more powerful. The HMD made it look like he was watching the attack from a few feet away.

During the forty-second scanning period, three complete sequences were shown. Blood-flow readings taken during the control state would later be subtracted from those recorded during the task state. The results—compiled by high-speed computers using complicated logarithms that Brook didn't pretend to understand—would highlight those parts of the brain that had become most active, or "lit up," while Waters watched the rape scene.

They were going to use a similar approach—but different task images—with the two other prisoners. Lind would watch a man about his age robbing a bank; Billings, two men fighting in a bar with knives. As with Waters, the emphasis was on violence.

"That's it, Gary," Conner said when the first session ended. "You did great. We'll start the next scan in twelve minutes. How was it?"

Waters didn't answer. Once again, Brook was struck by his grotesque appearance. Strapped to the gurney and wearing a mask and HMD visor, Waters looked like something out of the pages of wildest science fiction.

"Why did you make me watch that?" the prisoner asked, his speech still slurred from the Valium.

"We want to see how your brain works," Conner said.

"Fuck you. You want to see if I'm a sex pervert," Waters said in an incongruously dreamy voice. "The lady doctor was trying the same thing when she had my dick hot-wired a couple days ago.''

After a few more minutes, the red light flashed again. Brook moved to the pneumatic tube to catch the next Oxygen-15 water sent up from the linear accelerator. This one came in at 25 millicuries, almost the perfect 20 they were aiming for. When the digital radioactivity counter indicated the proper reading, he injected the solution into the butterfly shunt in Waters's arm. As before, the technician who sat at the computer terminal in the control room told them when the water reached the brain.

Waters's lips, visible under the lower edge of the plastic mask, curled back from his teeth. Brook knew the PET scans wouldn't lie, that Waters wouldn't be able to fool them. The images shot during the experiment would provide an unmistakable portrait of how his brain responded to violence, how the neurons and their elaborate networks processed thoughts and emotions involved with sex, rage and anger. He couldn't wait to see the PET scans. Gary Waters's brain couldn't hide.

SEVENTEEN

JIM SERRA MADE THE final adjustments on the BAT-12, the electromagnetic stimulator he'd spent nearly two years designing and perfecting. He and Hartigan were about to run their first series of neuro-stim tests on Waters and Lind to try to induce a kindled seizure in their limbic brains. Animal experiments had indicated that a minimum of seven to ten such seizures were needed to produce permanent changes in the brain's electrochemical circuitry. Hartigan figured they'd probably need to do considerably more with humans.

They were working alone in Serra's lab on the third floor. No one else had been told, and they had taken precautions to move the men to and from the third floor by way of a back stairway that was usually kept locked. They'd also scheduled the procedure for six in the morning, before most of the medical staff arrived at the clinic.

Serra checked the discharge switch on the energy-storage capacitors. He was using his new double-coil applicator wand and wanted to run a test to show Lind that the procedure was harmless. The lab room—one of the smallest in the clinic—was jammed with equipment, including the digital EEG, a portable EKG and the bulky stack of capacitors, which stored and reused the energy generated by the neuro-stim machine.

The BAT-12 was a powerful instrument, capable of generating up to five-million watts of impulse power, and Serra had worked hard to shape the coils to help dissipate all that heat. Coil design was critical.

Waters and Lind lay on gurneys, with their wrists and ankles strapped down. They wore heavy sweaters, as did Serra. The room had been cooled down to help keep the capacitors from overheating.

"Close your eyes, Ed," Serra said. He placed the neuro-stim wand a few inches from the back of Lind's skull and touched the switch. The machine made a soft clicking noise.

"What do you see?"

"Flashing lights popping all over the place," Lind said.

Serra did the same to Waters.

"Like fireflies," Waters said, grinning.

"Those are phosphenes," Serra explained. "We stimulated your cerebral cortex, which affected the retina. That's why you're seeing all those bright dots. Did it hurt?"

Lind shook his head, but he was still mistrustful.

As previously agreed, they wanted to kindle the hippocampus, hoping it would trigger kindling in the rest of the limbic brain. The main objective hadn't changed: These kindled, self-sustaining seizures were expected to produce anatomical changes that might eliminate or considerably lessen criminal thoughts and behavior.

They'd already described the procedures to the two men several times without going into the specifics. They repeatedly emphasized that it would be painless and that they were just running some routine tests to see how their brains worked.

What they didn't tell them was that they were going to stimulate part of their limbic brains until they elicited a mild seizure. They would continue these seizures until they got the neural changes they were looking for, a process expected to last four or five days.

"Are you going to do some more of those PET scans?" Lind asked. He'd already had one PET session; others were scheduled.

Serra nodded and said, "If you have questions about any

of this, just ask. We'll do our best to explain things to you.''

A set of Lind's PET scans were clipped to a wall-mounted display. They showed how his limbic brain had lit up like a Christmas tree during the virtual-reality test. The areas of increased blood-flow activity were highlighted in colors. The spectrum ran from purple, representing the least neural activity, to red and white, representing the most intense. The brightly colored scans were beautiful, almost a work of art.

The fifteen horizontal slices of Lind's brain showed the entire cingulate gyrus as a pulsing white light. The amygdala and hippocampus were bright red. The results, with some variations in shading and location, had been similar with Waters and Billings, although Waters had shown the most limbic blood-flow activity.

They needed to run two or three more PET sequences and do a full range of neural and intelligence tests after kindling, to measure the degree of change. Hartigan and Serra anticipated a marked decrease in blood flow in the limbic brain. The experimental evidence with primates suggested this would be accompanied by a lessening of aggressive tendencies. But the great unanswered question remained: Would it produce similar results with the infinitely more complex human brain and, more specifically, with ASPD criminals?

"So I've got nothing to worry about, right?" Lind asked again, rubbing his eyes. His face told the two doctors that he suspected they weren't telling him the complete truth about what was going to happen. He was jumpy.

"You'll be fine," Hartigan said. "We'll stop this if you feel any discomfort."

His main worry was left unsaid—the fear that the seizures would spread to other parts of Lind's brain. Al Silver's work suggested that some of the newly developed anticonvulsants could curtail a kindled response, putting it out like water dumped on a fire. Silver was perfecting just such a drug. If need be, they were ready to intervene with aggressive drug therapy if the kindling began to spread beyond Lind's limbic system.

The trick was allowing it to proceed far enough to achieve the desired neurological effects, yet not so far that it ran wild. Hartigan and Serra understood the risks of this incredibly delicate balancing act. But they weren't about to tell the prisoners.

"This isn't going to hurt, is it?" Waters had been only half listening as Serra had gone through the procedure with him step by step.

"Hold out your hand," Serra said. He put the neuro-stim wand a few inches from Waters's right hand and administered a single pulse-wave.

The machine clicked.

"How was that?"

"It felt like static electricity," Waters said.

"Then, no sweat, right?" Serra said, smiling.

"Why does it make that noise?" Lind asked.

"There's about a thousand amps of current going through those copper coils. When they heat up and expand, they start knocking around."

Serra had worked hard to reduce the noise, but the decibels were still pretty high, especially at the stronger pulse-levels.

They were going to do Lind first, and Serra had already marked his scalp with the small, red crosses that corresponded to the international "ten-twenty" system of electrode placement for the EEG. The term derived from the fact that each electrode was spaced within 10 or 20 percent of the total distance between a given pair of skull landmarks. Serra would use specific ten-twenty landmarks to target the electromagnetic stimulations. The hippocampus, the target of the first neuro-stim series, was represented by a specific cluster of four electrodes arranged in a kind of triangle.

Serra daubed Lind's scalp with an electrolyte jelly and attached the twenty-three gold-disc electrodes to record the crucial EEG readings. The EEG would provide the first indication of a seizure.

"All right, Ed. Let's get started," Serra said. "This won't take long." Lind lay with his head on a pillow; they released his arms from the restraints. Serra reminded him to keep still so he wouldn't twist the EEG leads.

The ever-present guards stayed by the door. The four of them made no pretense of looking interested.

"This could be a little loud at times," Serra cautioned. "You're going to hear that clicking noise."

The first sequence of twenty-five stimulations would occur at a rate of one stimulus every three seconds—the fastest speed possible that would still allow the capacitors to recharge. Serra held the neuro-stim wand about an inch from Lind's head, right over the electrodes that marked the location of the hippocampus. He had designed the coil windings to direct the maximum magnetic strength to that precise part in the brain.

"Okay, it's showtime," he said, turning on the machine.

Lind winced at the rapid series of clicks.

"Does that hurt?" Serra asked.

Lind shook his head. "It stings a little. Nothing bad."

Hartigan was monitoring the EEG. Lind's brain showed a series of sharp alpha waves but no evidence of the continuous spike-wave pattern associated with a seizure. So far, the prisoner's hippocampus was absorbing the neuro-stim without kindling. Like a pot of water on a low flame, it would take a while before it started to boil.

During this first session, they planned to do at least ten neuro-stim sequences. They would increase the intensity of the stimulations, building gradually over several days. They would do at least two sessions a day.

All went smoothly, better than they'd hoped. Then midway through the tenth and final sequence, Serra glanced at Lind's left hand, which had begun to twitch as if in spasm. The fingers were shaking, quivering.

Almost at the same moment, Lind's eyes opened. "I feel strange," he said.

"Describe it," Serra said. "Talk to us, Ed."

"It's like I'm seeing something that I've already done. I'm right there, watching it happen. I've never . . ."

He noticed his hand.

"What the fuck!"

He tried to get up. A guard hurried forward, but Serra ordered him back and gave Lind a reassuring pat on the shoulder.

"We're almost done," he said. "You've got to lie still."

Lind swallowed and looked at Serra and at the guard. He took a breath and promised not to move.

They had to redo the last sequence. With the magnetic pulse increased for these final stimulations, the metallic noise from the heated coils was louder than ever.

Click!
Click!
Click!

Lind gasped out, "I'm telling you, I can see it clear!" He turned toward Serra, who saw a look in his eyes that he'd never forget.

Click!
Click!

Lind's left hand stopped twitching the moment the neuro-stim wand was turned off. He opened and closed it, making a fist. "I didn't have any control over my hand. And that damn feeling . . ."

Serra and Hartigan knew that hand-trembling was one of the telltale physical reactions that often preceded a seizure. So they'd come a long way during this first session. They weren't sure at all about Lind's other complaint. Whatever he'd seen, or had imagined seeing, troubled him a lot more than his hand.

It was Waters's turn.

"No fucking way am I going to do that." He'd watched the entire procedure lying flat on his back, and was trying to pull loose from the leg and arm restraints.

Hartigan motioned for the guards, who got next to the gurney.

"If you keep it up, we'll have to hold you down," he warned.

Waters looked up at him, his eyes open wide.

"It's your choice," Hartigan said. "But one way or another, we're going to go forward with this."

EIGHTEEN

THAT AFTERNOON BROOK VISITED Lind's apartment in the clinic's subbasement. Lind had already eaten lunch. No matter what else might have happened, the treatment certainly hadn't affected his appetite. The meals at the clinic were catered by a good restaurant in the West End, and Lind had chowed down on a pepper steak, fried potatoes, salad and cheesecake.

When Brook arrived, he was sitting on the comfortably upholstered sofa, watching a movie on the room's VCR. Before the interview, a guard had shackled Lind's right leg to an eyebolt in the floor. Tethered there, he could stand up but couldn't take more than two steps.

Brook wanted to talk to Lind about their next PET-scan session and discuss the results of the last series of scans.

The two men sat at opposite sides of a low coffee table piled with magazines and newspapers. Brook had taken off his lab coat and loosened his tie. It had been a long, wearying day, but he hardly felt his fatigue.

Lind sat there sullenly, eyes locked on the television screen.

"What's going on, Ed?" Brook said. "You look upset about something."

"You people promised I wouldn't feel anything, that there wouldn't be any side effects," Lind said with a scowl. "It's been six hours and my fuckin' hand is still tingling.''

Puzzled, Brook asked what he was talking about. "Six hours since what?"

"Guy who runs this place and another doctor put a bunch of wires on my head and shot some kind of electricity into me," Lind said.

"When did this happen?"

"Early this morning."

It sounded to Brook like they'd given Lind an EEG exam, but he wondered if something else might have happened.

"And you say something's wrong with your hand?"

"Yeah, but that's just part of it," Lind said angrily. "I saw something that happened to me fifteen years ago. I saw it in my head. Like somebody had slipped a tape into my brain and punched the start button."

"What was it you saw?" Brook asked, becoming more puzzled. "Can you describe it?"

Lind sat there without answering.

Brook sensed that his show of anger was partly a facade to cover up what was really bothering him. Whatever had gone on this morning still had him on edge. Brook didn't have much time with him and needed to break the ice.

Taking a big risk, he unlocked Lind's ankle shackle. He was allowed to carry a key in case of a medical emergency, but was under strict orders not to use it without an armed guard present. Brook knew he was committing a major security violation.

So did Lind, who stared at him. His face remained neutral, but Brook saw the change in his eyes, a softening of the anger. Lind recognized the good-faith gesture for what it was. Several seconds passed.

Brook sat back down. "We'll probably have visitors any minute. I'm afraid you're going to have to put that shackle back on, so you better enjoy it while you can."

As Lind leaned over to rub his right ankle, Brook noticed the thick pack of shoulder muscles move under his loose-fitting sweater. It would be easy for Lind to jump him. He wondered if Lind was weighing those chances even now.

"So what do you want to know?" Lind asked, straightening back up.

"I'd like to hear more about what went on this morning."

Before Lind could answer, the door flew open. Three guards rushed into the room with their guns at the ready. Each carried a black, short-barreled automatic weapon that Brook guessed was an Uzi.

"Doctor, the prisoner will have to be shackled," one of the men said.

"Leave him alone," Brook said. "I'll take responsibility."

"No can do," the guard said. As the other two men kept their automatic weapons leveled at Lind, Brook refastened the prisoner's leg shackle to the bolt in the floor. The task accomplished, they withdrew without saying another word. The whole thing had lasted barely a minute.

"You're gonna hear about that, aren't you?" Lind said when they were gone. He started to smile.

"I can handle it," Brook said, realizing the two of them had made it over a hurdle—a small one, but a hurdle nonetheless. "Let's get back to this morning."

Lind massaged the fingers of his left hand, staring off into space as he considered what to say.

"Fifteen years ago I robbed a bank with a guy here in St. Louis. Someplace down in Lemay. First Mississippi Bank. We emptied three or four cash drawers and got away clean. I was carrying the moneybags and, when we get to the car my partner pulls a gun on me. He has it right in my face, and I can hear the hammer snap when it misfires. I shot the sonofabitch twice in the guts and left him lying there."

Lind kept massaging the palm of his left hand. His already pale skin had an unnatural pallor.

"When they were zapping me this morning, it all flashed in front of my eyes, the whole scene." His hands balled into fists, then relaxed. "It was weird. I could see the bastard's face when he squeezed the trigger. It was so goddamn real. And then my hand starts to feel strange. All prickly and tingling, like it had gone to sleep."

"Zapping you? What do you mean?" Brook asked.

"They explained it, but I don't remember the name. Too many long words. They held this thing shaped like a Ping-Pong paddle near my head. Christ, it was loud."

Brook realized what Lind was talking about; Hartigan and Serra must have given him electromagnetic stimulation. He hadn't known anything like that was planned for the prisoners.

"You can't believe how real it was," Lind said. "I could see the guy's face, the guy I shot."

His eyes were wide but focused on something Brook couldn't see. His voice almost broke when he said, "I swear to god, I almost screamed."

"How do you feel?" Brook asked.

"Kinda shaky. I've been better."

"Have you ever had one of those flashbacks before?" Brook asked.

"No way," Lind said. "I'd think about it every now and then in the joint, usually when I was lying in the rack at night. But never like this. This was different. I was pouring sweat. I could see Joey's eyes when I shot him. It was that close up."

"How does your head feel?"

"Not too bad. Maybe a little achy."

Brook took Lind's wrist and checked his pulse. It was well within the normal range. He checked his eyes. They looked fine.

"Did Doctor Hartigan or anybody explain what happened to you, explain it so you understood it?" he asked.

"If they did, it didn't sink in, 'cause I don't know shit."

Brook told Lind he'd find out and get back to him.

"And I'll get you something for your headache," he said, getting up to leave. "Anything else you need?"

"Is it going to happen again? Can you tell me that?"

"You're going to be all right, Ed," Brook said. "You've got some of the best doctors in the country taking care of you." He managed a smile. He wanted to look confident for Lind's sake. Maybe it helped. Lind seemed to relax a little.

"Can I take that to the bank?" Lind asked.

"Sure, as long as you don't rob the place once you get there."

Lind laughed.

Brody was waiting in the corridor with Dr. Hartigan when Brook left the prisoner's room. Brody wore his usual black turtleneck and blue jacket. Hartigan had on a dark pinstripe suit. Standing under the track lighting in front of the mounted paintings in the corridor, the two men looked like patrons at a private art showing.

"Follow me," Hartigan said. He was livid.

They went into the security-control room. Brook followed the two men past the closed-circuit television monitors and the other electronic equipment into a small office. It was Brody's. The furnishings were spare, a metal desk and two chairs.

"You were incredibly foolish in there," Hartigan said, lashing out as soon as the door was closed.

"I know it was a risk, but I wanted to establish a rapport with him so he'd talk to me," Brook said. He'd decided to lay out the facts, and wasn't about to throw himself on a sword. "He's really worked up about whatever happened to him this morning."

He looked at Hartigan, waiting for an explanation.

The clinic director hesitated, but only for a beat. "That's no excuse for violating a fundamental security regulation," he said. Brook had never seen him so mad, and suddenly wondered whether the display was meant more for Brody's benefit.

"It sounds like you gave him a neuro-stim treatment," Brook said, pressing ahead.

Hartigan's irritated expression didn't change. "We're running some neuromuscular tests to see the effects of magnetic stimulation on the motor cortex and other deep neural structures. We're going to do the same EP tests on all three prisoners."

Brook knew that EPs—"evoked potentials"—consisted

of applying an electrical stimulus to nerve fibers to see whether current flowed through them without obstruction; the idea was to measure the responses of pathways in the nervous system to see if there were any disturbances. It was like running a voltage-meter test on the electrical wiring in a home to check for short circuits. They wanted to see if the prisoners had any neurological impairment.

A routine test—but Hartigan was apparently using neuro-stim to trigger the current. That was an entirely new technique.

"He had a striking occurrence of *déjà vu*," Brook said when Hartigan didn't volunteer any more information about the procedure. "His recall to an event that happened fifteen years earlier was extraordinary. And it scared the hell out of him."

"I'm aware of that," Hartigan said, nodding his head dismissively as if to suggest it was a matter of no importance. "Our neuro-stim tests are none of your concern. I'm more interested in making sure you understand that our security regulations have to be obeyed."

"That man could have broken your neck before you knew what hit you," Brody said. "You know about anatomy, Doctor. One good handchop in the thorax, and you're dead."

"I made a mistake," Brook said. "It won't happen a second time. So spare me the melodramatics." The answer was flip, but he couldn't help it. Something about the man grated on him.

Brody leaned over, placing both hands on the table so that his face was only inches from Brook's. The whites of his eyes were etched with delicate red lines. He had a hard, well-conditioned body, but Brook noticed for the first time how old his eyes looked.

"I wasn't trying to be melodramatic," Brody said. "I just wanted to let you know how easily accidents can happen."

NINETEEN

BROOK MET JENNY FOR a hurried dinner at a popular Welsh pub on McMaster Avenue, where the waitresses moved at warp speed and the green walls were covered with German and English beer posters. Jenny had a burger with Welsh rarebit sauce, a house speciality. Brook ate the "Plowman's Special"—an assortment of cheese, fruit, boiled ham, rye bread and chutney sauce. He washed it down with a mug of Watney's pale ale. The air was pungent with cigarette smoke and the smell of fried onions.

Brook found Jenny preoccupied and troubled. She hardly spoke, even though the meal had been her idea. Over coffee she abruptly suggested that they return to the clinic. She had something to tell him, but didn't want to discuss it in public. Brook had planned to head back to work anyway. He also wanted to tell her about his disturbing session with Lind and the conversation he'd had with Hartigan.

They were each driving their own cars, and Brook had trouble keeping up with Jenny as she pushed her red Geo Prizm well over the speed limit down the dark West End side streets. Five minutes after they had left the pub, they parked in the clinic's well-lit back lot, which was surrounded by a tall chain-link fence with an automatic security gate. A pair of rotating cameras were pointed at the brightly illuminated doorway.

Jenny pressed a button on an intercom. An impersonal male voice requested her to punch her security code into the key pad. She touched five digits and the door clicked open.

They took the elevator to her office on the third floor. Jenny switched on the lights. It was still early by clinic standards—ten-thirty P.M. Like the other offices, hers was book-lined and elegantly furnished. A computer terminal sat on her desk. Jenny slipped off her overcoat and let it drop on a chair.

Brook couldn't help but stare. He was struck by Jenny's dark-green eyes, black hair and high cheekbones. He liked the sound of her voice and how she smiled and moved her hands when she spoke. He liked the way her cheeks reddened when she laughed, but there had been little laughter the past few days. Jenny seemed preoccupied, and Brook guessed it was the pressure of her sessions with Waters and the lingering effects of Mark Ulman's murder.

He still meant to make some inquiries about the circumstances of Ulman's death, but hadn't had the chance.

Jenny took a looseleaf binder off a shelf. Brook noticed that it contained about a dozen 8- by 12-inch, black-and-white photographs encased in protective plastic sheets.

"This is my scrapbook," she said, flipping it open. "These are some of the serial sexual offenders I've worked with over the years. My rogues' gallery. I thought you might want to take a look."

Three of the men had been executed, she said. They were in their late twenties and thirties. All but two were white. One of the exceptions was Lejuan Miller, who had raped, bludgeoned and strangled eight elderly women in a wealthy suburb of Ames, Iowa.

"You interviewed Miller?" Brook was impressed.

"Twice. He even agreed to give me some of his blood. The testosterone count was sky high, but so was everything else. He had elevated blood histamine, elevated krypto-syrroles in his urine, high levels of lead and cadmium. Chemically speaking, Lejuan was a walking animal farm."

Jenny turned to the last picture. The name was Edward

Preston. He was thin, with small, close-set eyes. He had a wide, slightly off-center nose and a frowning mouth. Not pleasant to look at. Unlike the other photographs, this one didn't have a list of known victims and dates of assault neatly typed at the bottom of the page. Just the name, age and a date—June 16, 1988.

"What did he do?" Brook asked. His question was almost perfunctory.

"Before he was shot to death, he raped four young women in Chicago in the early 1980s. All of them were co-eds. One of them was me."

Brook looked up at her. He was sitting on the edge of her desk. She stood next to him. Stunned, he didn't know what to say or do.

"It's all right," Jenny said. Her eyes were clear, unflinching. "I've wanted to tell you for days. I didn't know how."

For a brief, wrenching instant, she wondered whether she'd made an unforgivable mistake. Brook sensed that, and reached out and took both her hands firmly in his. They were smooth and strong.

"Jenny, I'm so sorry," he said.

Everything made sense. Why she'd dropped him, why she'd never answered his calls, why she'd transferred to another school. The instant he took Jenny Malone's hands in his own, he suddenly realized that everything that had happened between them would be forever colored by this moment. The strong tug of his feelings, the way he'd instinctively reached out to her had startled him. Nothing like that had ever happened to him before. He cared for Jenny, and was worried about her. He was a psychiatrist, for crissakes. He knew how rape affected its victims.

Jenny guessed what was running through his mind. She'd expected it.

"I felt violated for a long time, and escaped into my work," she said. "I went to one doctor who told me to get out of forensic psychology. He thought I was only asking for trouble, that working with sex offenders would open up too many bad memories for me. But somehow I convinced myself that I was really over it. That I was an excellent therapist who could handle what had happened." A bitter smile crossed her lips. "Now I know better. I'm not sure I can handle it at all."

Brook couldn't think of anything even remotely comforting to say. He knew from personal experience how much strength it took to come to terms with a horror that never fully receded from memory, the dull ache that became as familiar as your face in the bathroom mirror. He had firsthand knowledge of the price you paid to keep moving forward.

Finally, he asked, "Is it Waters?"

Jenny nodded. "That's part of it. He's deadly, John. He's gotten under my skin in a way I never expected. I've discovered that the strong, always-in-control doctor is a lot more vulnerable than she thought."

Listening to herself say these words, she wondered, again, whether she was making an unforgivable mistake, telling him all this. She didn't want Brook or anyone to think that she was weak and easily hurt. She'd fought that battle with herself for years and had been winning—at least until very recently. She looked at Brook, not doubting that he was overwhelmed, and feeling a little sorry for him. She hoped she'd done the right thing. But that was her way. Direct, up front, no hidden meanings, no games. Not even with her life's story.

Brook stood absolutely still, trying to think of something to say that might make sense.

It was her turn to touch his hand.

"My god, Jenny."

She entwined her fingers in his.

Without prompting, Brook found himself discussing his father's murder, thinking it might help her understand that she wasn't alone. He told Jenny about the nights he'd sat up in bed, drenched with sweat.

"Did you try therapy?" Jenny asked.

Brook said, "I wound up talking to a psychiatrist a few times. I thought it was an expensive waste of time." He couldn't help smiling at the professional irony.

"I had a good doctor," Jenny said. "She specialized in treating rape victims. A wonderful lady. She helped me stop feeling unclean. I know that probably sounds like something out of a bad movie, but a rape victim really feels like that. You feel dirty. You keep telling yourself that somehow it's all your fault. Those were such strong, all-consuming feelings."

For the most part, she'd been able to face down those thoughts and hold them at bay. All but one. Ever since the attack it had been impossible for her to have a meaningful relationship. But she wasn't going to talk about that; she'd already gone much further than she had intended.

Jenny closed her book of photographs. She understood that she and Brook had reached a turning point, and guessed that he recognized it as well. She sensed that he wanted to help her. She saw that in his face. If she could only let him.

"We'd better get some sleep," she said, trying to smile.

As he helped Jenny on with her jacket, Brook finally mentioned his strange meeting with Lind. He described Lind's déjà vu episode, which still puzzled him.

"I've never run into anything quite like that," he said. "What he saw scared him. The details were that real, that vivid."

Brook was about to say more, when he noticed that Jenny was staring at him. She'd started to pick up her briefcase, but put it back down. She hurriedly scribbled a note and handed it to Brook, who read in silence, then nodded that he understood.

He helped her on with her jacket and followed her back outside to her car, where Jenny explained that she was worried their offices might be bugged.

"Why do you think so?" Brook asked. Her comment startled him.

"It's just a feeling. We're so security-conscious with that man, Brody. I wouldn't be surprised if he listened to everything we said." She mentioned that Brody had recently questioned her about Mark Ulman. He was talking to every member on staff—the doctors, technicians, secretaries, everyone.

Brook thought she might be overreacting, but after his own recent encounter with Brody and Hartigan, he was willing to give her the benefit of the doubt.

"Tell me again what happened to Lind," Jenny said. They walked in the glare of the parking-lot lights. A cold wind had picked up.

Brook quickly went through the details once more. When they reached Jenny's car, he noticed how her expression had changed; her eyes told him that she was troubled.

"Mark said that LePonty was acting strange before the escape," Jenny said. "He kept having these wild déjà vu episodes. They were as scary as Lind's. Mark had never seen anything like it. A couple of nights before he was killed, he came to my office and we talked it over."

Brook was struck by the coincidence of the two prisoners having the same kind of sensory experience, but didn't know what to make of it.

Jenny slipped a key into her car door and slid behind the steering wheel. She was trying to act as natural as possible for the benefit of whoever might be watching them. But, up close it wasn't working. She looked worried.

"Mark said he'd gone to Hartigan to complain, to find out what was happening to LePonty," she said. "He wasn't happy about how their talk turned out. Hartigan pretty much kept him in the dark about what was going on."

Brook told her that Lind's problems had apparently started after Hartigan and Jim Serra had given him an evoked potentials test.

Brook said. "Did you know that they'd used neuro-stim for the test?"

Jenny shook her head. She didn't remember Mark Ulman talking about it, either.

Perhaps she'd put the thought in his mind with her comment about a bugged office, but Brook felt that someone was watching them. He noticed that the outdoor security cameras were pointed in their direction.

Jenny hesitated. "Mark was certain that someone was talking to LePonty, making secret visits to his room," she said.

"Somebody on staff?"

Jenny nodded yes as she started her engine. "I'm pretty sure he had an idea who it was, but he didn't want to tell me. I think that person may have helped LePonty escape."

TWENTY

IT WAS ALMOST MIDNIGHT, nearly an hour since he'd left the clinic and walked to the MetroLink stop, three blocks away on Euclid Avenue. On the way out of the building, he had run into Dr. Brook and managed to crack a feeble joke about leaving work so early.

He often left the clinic for late, head-clearing walks in the cold air, and enjoyed buying a cup of coffee and a bagel at the station's sandwich shop, where he browsed the newspapers and magazine racks arrayed at the kiosk. He thought it was one of few things St. Louis offered that remotely resembled an urban experience like the ones of his years growing up in New York City.

He'd been thinking about Mark Ulman again. He could never completely put him out of mind. He had respected Ulman, admired him right up to the moment he decided to have him killed. There was no other way. Ulman was bright; he was starting to figure out what they were doing to LePonty.

He still remembered how frightened he'd been during that shaky period. None of it seemed possible now, but back then he'd been almost too uptight to focus on his work. He was that sure Ulman was going to turn them all in.

It hadn't taken him long to realize they had only one option. He decided to turn LePonty loose, knowing what would probably happen. He'd done it on his own, without telling anyone else.

Still holding his steaming coffee cup, he turned away and slowly walked down Euclid toward Forest Park Boulevard. He had a lot to think about and not much time.

Hartigan's experiments were moving along more rapidly and successfully than anyone had anticipated. He wasn't sure how many others on the staff knew that fact. Two or three at most, he figured. Hartigan was always careful to limit knowledge to only those who absolutely needed to know, and even then he restricted how much they were told.

It all added up to one thing: He had to be ready to act—to do the same thing as before. Only this time, he'd set loose two prisoners instead of one. The irony wasn't lost on him. With LePonty, he was trying to save the experiment. Now, he was trying to end it, and it didn't matter to him how far that meant he had to go.

The reason for this 180-degree change was pretty straight-forward. Mainly he wanted revenge. The fact he was going crazy just made it easier.

He had to be honest with himself. His disintegrating mental state was the main reason he was pushing ahead with this. His depression was worsening. His latest bout had already gone two months without remission. He thought he'd hidden it well at work, but the gray flatness of his mental landscape had become almost unbearable.

He'd stopped taking the tricyclic antidepressants iproniazid and imipramine, even the MAIOs. Prozac and one or two of its chemical clones had offered temporary relief, but a few weeks earlier he'd turned to lithium. He'd always considered lithium, not Prozac, the true miracle drug of mental illness. An element on the periodic table, it had been around since 1949, and remained the treatment of choice for his kind of manic depression. His brain's ability to function—even heavily medicated—continued to astound him. He could still do his job better than anyone else in his field. But he was reaching his limits.

As he headed down Forest Park, he pulled up his collar

against the cold November wind. With characteristic precision, he started working over the details of what had to be done—sorting, filing, mentally cataloging them.

The only clean way to make his plan work would be to reprogram the clinic's computer system. He'd recently turned his attention to that problem, reading every paper and technical abstract he could find on the subject. The Internet, as usual, had been a superb research tool, sending citation after citation to his PC terminal. It was incredible. Almost every detail he needed, no matter how arcane, was there at his fingertips, waiting for him on the information superhighway. All he had to do was click onto it. He was rapidly mastering the practical programming applications. But, eventually, he'd need the right log-on password.

That was the key. He'd have to figure out how to steal Hartigan's. The director was the only staff member allowed to access the system, and he could do so from his office terminal. He knew this important fact because Hartigan had once been careless enough to mention it to him in private.

There was another difficulty to consider: He might have to kill some people. He hadn't given up on the idea of injecting them with a fast-acting sedative. But that might be unrealistic. He might not have time, or the chance to get close enough.

He kept returning to one inescapable fact: He had to be certain that he could kill, up close and without hesitation.

As he walked along the deserted street, his right hand was thrust into the pocket of his parka. He was gripping a Smith & Wesson 9 mm. He'd paid nine hundred dollars for the gun and had been test-firing it in his soundproofed basement every night for a month. The weapon helped ease his mind.

TWENTY-ONE

THE BAT-12 MADE its strange clicking sounds, which provided a bizarre counterpoint to Lind's deep breathing.

Click!

Jim Serra had just given Lind a series of twenty-five short-burst electromagnetic stimulations, targeting the hippocampus. He'd reduced their intensity as they rapidly neared kindling. When they finished with Lind, they would bring in Waters, who was still down in his room.

Click!

Lind's eyes bulged wide in sudden fear.

Click.

"I can feel it coming!" He looked at Serra. "What's happening?"

"You'll be fine," Serra said. "Hang in there a little longer. It's almost over."

Lind swallowed and said, "I've heard that before."

Sweat poured down his cheeks. His hand began to tremble. Hartigan and Serra had been watching for that. He was having another "sensory focal attack," one of the physical tip-offs that preceded a seizure.

"Look at the monitor," Serra said. "I think we've got one."

The EEG's computer screen showed a distinctive series of spikes. The "after discharge," or AD, phase had lasted a good thirty seconds. Serra knew that Lind had just experienced a mild seizure in his limbic brain and that the AD had lasted longer than the stimulus. That was key. So was the fact that, over the last two days, they had systematically reduced the intensity of the electromagnetic stimulations, which meant they were getting stronger responses with less magnetic current.

There was only one possible explanation for what had just happened· They had succeeded in kindling Lind's brain

Hartigan glanced at the wall clock. It was six thirty-eight A.M. He wanted to remember the time, even though it was anticlimatic. Two days earlier he'd kindled Billings. Still, he wanted to savor the moment.

Hartigan looked tired, but was immaculately groomed in a pale-blue shirt, paisley bow tie and freshly starched lab coat. He hadn't spoken more than three sentences since they'd gotten started, but now permitted himself a broad smile.

"Let's try for one more seizure," he said. "I'd like to try to sustain this a while longer."

Serra gave Lind another stimulation, holding the double-coil wand close to his scalp. Again, he greatly reduced the amplitude and lowered the peak coil energy. Lind immediately had another mild seizure, which told them that his limbic brain had experienced a convulsive sensitization to the electromagnetic stimulus—another unmistakable indicator of the kindling phenomenon.

Hartigan's attention had been focused on the EEG, but he glanced at Lind, who continued to sweat heavily. They had known all along that the trick would be to hold the kindled seizures at moderate levels of intensity and not have them spread to other parts of the brain.

"How about a beer after this is over?" Lind said.

"You got it," Serra answered.

Checking the EEG monitor again, Hartigan saw something that caught his attention. Initially, the onset of kindling had been accompanied by a gradual increase in Lind's delta-wave activity—2 to 2.5 waves per second. But the electrodes that focused on the hippocampus showed pronounced theta-wave activity in the 4-to-7 Hz range. The peak-to-peak measurement indicated high velocity. What was remarkable here was that theta waves were rarely seen in awake adults.

"He's got a strong theta rhythm," Hartigan said.

"It must be a muscle artifact," Serra said, joining Hartigan at the EEG.

"I don't think so," Hartigan said. "There are no muscle contractions No evidence of paroxysmal spiking. Here, take a look."

The two men stared at the digital machine's oversized color monitor. Lind's strange brain-wave pattern continued a full forty seconds. Theta waves usually suggested a diffuse organic disease or some kind of metabolic disorder, but that was generally at low amplitudes. Lind's EEG was showing amazingly high amplitude thetas. Kindling, even in its early stages, had altered Lind's brain-wave pattern in a way they couldn't explain. It clearly indicated that neurochemical changes were occurring deep in his limbic brain, but no one could say what it meant beyond that. It was baffling.

Lind's face glistened with sweat. He tried to say something, but couldn't get out the words.

"What's wrong, Ed?" Serra asked. He stood next to the gurney.

Lind took a few breaths. "I don't want any more of this." His face changed, moving from concealment to anger and now to fear. The sequence was remarkably swift.

"Does it hurt?"

"No."

"How do you feel?"

"Like I told you before, I keep seeing things." He looked angry and confused, and his face went through another strange transformation, revealing something Serra had never seen before—something dark and ugly.

"What do you see, Mr. Lind?" Hartigan's voice was solicitous, measured.

Lind stared at his left hand, which had stopped trembling. The way he looked worried Hartigan. It also worried the guards, who moved in closer to the gurney in case something happened.

"I'm not telling you a damn thing. Just make it stop. And the same goes for that smell."

Hartigan was immediately interested. A change in the sense of smell was important, indicating that powerful reactions were under way in the limbic system. Hartigan had been ready for that possibility. The olfactory bulb, with its hair-cell receptor neurons, had strong limbic connections to the amygdala, septum, even the hypothalamus. A recurring odor could sometimes accompany sharp memories of the past, or indicate an abnormal mental or emotional state.

As he rapidly catalogued the possibilities, Hartigan kept coming back to the "aura" that often precedes an epileptic seizure. An olfactory aura was almost always associated with the rare kind of fit that could manifest both auditory and visual hallucinations.

Lind broke out in laughter. "You like that, don't you? You're probably wondering what's going on in that poor fuck's head."

Serra looked at Hartigan as if to say, maybe we ought to call it a day. He thought they'd pushed Lind far enough for one session.

"Ed, what are you smelling?" Hartigan spoke in that same quiet, soft voice that the lab staff had learned to be wary of. "Does the smell accompany or precede what you're seeing?"

This time, Lind didn't answer. Hartigan decided not to press it, and had him escorted back to his room, where he could rest and have lunch. Serra called down to security to have them bring up Waters.

As soon as Lind was gone, Hartigan said, "He's manifesting a vivid aura. First the focal hand response, then whatever it is he imagines he's seeing. And that smell. It's all linked somehow to his theta-wave activity. I've never seen anything like it."

Neither had Serra. Lind's neural response was more explosive than he'd anticipated, much more dramatic than those exhibited by Waters and Billings. Those two had recently begun to exhibit mental agitation as a result of neuro-stim, but neither compared with Lind; and they'd shown absolutely no theta activity. Serra didn't need to look at another set of PET scans to know that the neural structures that controlled Lind's most powerful urges, emotions and feelings were being altered.

The kindling was doing exactly what Hartigan had predicted, but with several unforeseen and troublesome complications. They still didn't know what to make of the bizarre theta waves, and it bothered them that Lind was exhibiting some of the more unusual symptoms of an epileptic seizure.

A few minutes later, two guards escorted Waters into the room. He was already on edge, even before they told him to climb up on the gurney.

"I don't want any more of this shit," he said.

Waters had continued to tolerate kindling better than Lind, but not as well as Billings. He was starting to exhibit some side effects similar to Lind's—increasing irritability, mood swings, nervousness. But he was still willing to answer questions.

"What's wrong?" Hartigan asked.

At first Waters didn't answer. "I know about those flashbacks Lind's been bitching about," he said. "It's been happening to me, too."

"Can you describe it?" Serra asked. He was recalibrating the BAT-12 for another round of neuro-stim.

Waters started slowly, explaining how he'd cut a woman once, a prostitute who hadn't put out enough. She'd complained when he refused to pay her, and he slashed her across the face and chest.

"Was she dead, Gary?" Hartigan asked.

"Maybe. I'm not sure," Waters said. "She wasn't moving when I fucked her. I keep playing that scene over and over in my mind." He looked up at Hartigan. His head sagged forward, and he pulled it back.

"It happened to me again this morning. It was so damn real I creamed in my pants." Waters stared at Hartigan again and smiled. "No sense lying about it."

TWENTY-TWO
⊳◁

BROOK TOOK A SHOWER, shaved and changed clothes. After staying up until four that morning, he badly needed all three. The hot shower and the slow, half-hour jog he'd taken through his West End neighborhood had helped loosen his stiff muscles. Feeling better, he drove back to the clinic to pick up Jenny for a late dinner. After his day, Brook had a deep need to talk. He needed to get his mind off the PET-scan experiments, even for a couple hours.

His thoughts kept returning to Ed Lind. He was troubled by the inmate's increasing agitation and irritability, and he kept thinking about Jenny's comment that Mark Ulman had been worried about LePonty's strange déjà vu episodes. It sounded a lot like what was happening to Lind, and Brook doubted it could be written off as a coincidence.

He still wanted to talk to Ulman's widow, hoping she could give him a clearer picture about what had been going on at the lab just before her husband's death. In particular, he wanted to know if she could tell him how LePonty had been acting.

But, hell, he didn't know when he'd find time for that. He hadn't had time to do much more than work and grab four or five hours of sleep a night. It was the roughest grind of his life. As he pulled up in front of the clinic, he glanced at the dashboard clock. It was seven forty-five. Jenny was waiting for him at the front door, gripping her heavy leather briefcase. It was the earliest they'd left the clinic in days.

"I've got another suggestion for dinner," she said, sliding into the front seat.

"Great," Brook said, happy to see her and immediately feeling his tension start to ease.

"Why don't we go to your place and send out for pizza? I'd love to see where Doctor John Brook lives." Jenny smiled but felt her cheeks tingle.

"That takes courage," Brook said. Her proposal caught him by surprise. "My place is a mess."

"I'm not worried," Jenny said.

Brook's apartment was on the top floor of a two-family structure on Westminster Place, near Forest Park, a once-fashionable area in sharp decline. Most of the buildings on his block had been torn down; his apartment and several boarded-up homes across the street were all that remained.

The desolate urban setting was a little eerie, but Brook liked the isolation. And the space—the apartment had two commodious bedrooms. He paid only two-fifty a month for the place.

He attributed the low rent to his landlady Rita Stell. Rita usually stopped by to see him once a day to talk about her problems, which generally involved one of the men she was seeing. And Rita, an attractive divorcée in her late forties, often had much to discuss. Brook liked her, and figured she gave him a break in the rent because of these rambling consultations.

They drove back to his flat and found a parking place in front of the building. Getting out of the car, Jenny kept a wary eye on her surroundings, even as Brook opened the door for her. She made sure she always knew whether anyone was near her. It was reflexive. Jenny never let her guard down on the street. Never.

They had just reached the front steps of the two-story flat when Rita Stell opened her door and greeted them. She was dressed in a tight-fitting evening dress and short jacket. She wore spike heels and her red hair hung to her shoulders.

"Jenny, this is Rita," Brook said, grinning.

Rita stared at Jenny, giving her a brief but intense inspection.

"You've done well, John. Better than a dull, stay-at-home like you deserve."

"Thank you," Jenny said, taking Rita's offered hand, and smiling.

"Big date?" Brook asked, fishing his door key out of his coat pocket.

"I'm not sure how big it'll be—not yet anyway." It was vintage Rita—loud, impromptu and off-color. "I'd like to chat with you two and really pry, but I'm outta time."

With that she was down the steps and walking rapidly to her car, her heels clicking on the sidewalk.

"Whew," Jenny said softly.

"I meant to warn you about Rita," Brook said. "She improves with exposure."

Brook ordered a pizza over the telephone, a "Chicago Special," which was delivered within minutes. They ate in his cramped kitchen, washing the pizza down with two bottles apiece of Rolling Rock beer. There was just enough room for a trestle table, two chairs, the refrigerator and a sink stacked with dishes.

After they ate, Brook gave her a tour of his apartment. Medical books and scientific magazines were stacked in bookcases; other books and magazines were piled haphazardly on the floor. He apologized for the clutter and layers of dust. He couldn't recall the last time he'd given the place a good cleaning.

Later, Jenny helped him put away the dishes.

"Thanks for letting me come here tonight," she said, stacking the plates in a cupboard. She wasn't sure yet what was going to happen between them, or even what she wanted to say.

"That was some session you had with Waters yesterday," Brook said. She'd had another one-on-one interview with the prisoner. Brook had watched it later on videotape. Jenny had handled the prisoner with skill and had looked strong and self-confident doing so. Considering her recent mental state, the performance had been all the more remarkable. Brook was worried about how Jenny was holding up, but if that session with Waters was any indication, she was doing great.

"What do you think of him?" Jenny asked. She'd been working that afternoon on her notes from the interview.

"A classic sociopath and plenty dangerous," Brook said.

"What I want to know is how many women he's killed," she said, wiping her hands on a dishcloth and sitting down at the table. She didn't want to go into the living room, where there was only one sofa. She felt more sure of herself at the kitchen table.

Brook sat across from Jenny. For days he'd been trying to sort out his feelings for her. He'd tried not to let his mind dwell on what had happened to her and the fears it produced in him. Better to stare them down. Instinctively, he knew that this meant taking a big chance. His life had been largely risk free. But, now, he was looking into the depths of Jenny's green eyes.

"What do you think about us?" she asked, reading his thoughts perfectly.

"I've been asking myself the same question."

"And have you come up with an answer?" She was simultaneously embarrassed, excited, defiant.

Brook slowly nodded his head and took her hand. "I'd like to try again," he said. "But what do you think about that, Jen?"

A smile illuminated her face. "Walking out on you was the hardest thing I ever did, but I didn't know what else to do." Her eyes were moist. She'd said it all. It was up to him.

Brook didn't trust himself to speak as a knot formed in his throat. He didn't dare.

Jenny laughed and said, "I overheard some interns talking about me once in New Haven. They were eating lunch in the hospital cafeteria and didn't know I was just around a corner. One of them called me 'Miss Ice Sculpture.' He had it so right I almost walked up to him and patted him on the back."

Brook could identify with her. He'd been called aloof,

indifferent, an egoist. All with good reason. He'd considered the ideal woman someone who wouldn't complain when he beat it back to work, the gym, wherever, after they'd had sex. He knew he was one of those never-spend-the-night guys.

"My longest affair lasted two months," Jenny said. "He was," she hummed a little flourish, "an intern! What a disaster. We tried to make love once in my apartment. I closed my eyes and kept telling myself, 'Come on, you can do it.' Then I started laughing. I couldn't help it." She groaned at the memory. "What a scene for a movie. This nice-looking guy is doing his best and I'm pretending I'm Ingrid Bergman, all dewy-eyed with passion in *Casablanca*—and then I start laughing. I never saw him again. We both made sure of that."

Brook's laughter helped break the emotional wave that had paralyzed him. He wanted to take her in his arms, but sensed this wasn't the right moment.

"All I know is that I don't want to lose you again," Brook said.

"You'll have to be patient with me," Jenny said, a plea from the heart. She knew this wasn't going to be easy. "You were always such a patient guy back in Chicago." A faint smile crossed her lips. They both knew better.

She stood up. "I guess I'd better be going."

Brook walked her to the car for a ride home. Jenny squeezed his hand. They had made a good start and realized the next time would be easier.

TWENTY-THREE
>⊸<

HE WAS ON HIS way to visit his wife's grave on a glorious late-fall morning in St. Louis. Cold, clear, crisp—the kind of day Elizabeth had delighted in. She was from New Mexico and had never gotten used to the city's humid weather. Fall had always been her favorite time of year.

She was buried in Calvary Cemetery, once the resting place for the city's elite. William Clark, of the Lewis and Clark expedition, was buried there. So was General Sherman, plus assorted tycoons from the Gilded Age in their elaborate marble mausoleums. And now Elizabeth. After she found out about the cancer, she'd picked the spot herself, a shaded hill that offered a view of the Mississippi River.

The problem was that the once-elegant cemetery was on the edge of Walnut Park, a cemetery of another kind. One of the worst slums in the country, the neighborhood was filled with single-story frame homes splashed with gang graffiti. You had to be careful going there. But this time the doctor wasn't worried; he'd taken to carrying his 9-mm pistol everywhere—even to pay a visit to Elizabeth.

As he pulled off Interstate 70 and drove up West Florissant to the cemetery's gated main entrance, he considered what he'd accomplished so far and what he still needed to do.

Stealing Hartigan's computer password had been easier than he'd imagined. He had quickly mastered how to create a hidden file that would mimic Hartigan's sign on screen and capture his log-on password. Once he'd figured out how to do it, the task required only ten key-strokes, which he practiced over and over until he could do it blindfolded.

After testing his program to make sure it worked, it was a simple matter to sneak into Hartigan's office and record the hidden file on his work-station PC. Hartigan was careless about locking his door and was often away from his office for extended periods—especially in the evening, when he paid unannounced visits to the medical staff. They were all careless about locking doors, moving frequently among their labs, each other's offices and the library.

Fortunately for him, the clinic's vaunted security system was woefully substandard in that regard, even with all the recent tightening up. He'd read about new systems that required every employee to wear a badge with an embedded microchip that transmitted a digital ID code whenever the wearer passed a door equipped with a radio receiver. It was an easy, effective way to track everyone's movements in a building.

His plan never would have worked with something like that in place.

As he headed up the winding, tree-lined driveway to his wife's grave, he smiled at the thought that he could later point out the lab's security failings to Hartigan and Brody. There would be delicious irony in that.

It had taken him just over two minutes to get in and out of the director's office. He had copied his program onto Hartigan's PC, then turned the machine off so that the next time Hartigan sat down at his terminal he'd have to restart it, using his password to sign back on.

Yes, he'd been clever and lucky. In another life he might have enjoyed working exclusively with computers. He was particularly proud of the error message he'd programmed to flash on the screen after Hartigan had logged back on. "SecurNet Error: A protocol error has occurred. Restart your work station." He could imagine how Hartigan would curse the idiots who designed the clinic's SecurNet software as he relogged onto his PC, totally unaware, of course, that in doing so he'd just let someone steal his password.

He had slipped back into Hartigan's office the following evening, copied the captured password, then deleted the hidden file.

It had been instructive to sign on to Hartigan's PC later and leisurely read through his directory files. He'd discovered that the director kept a running commentary on the individual performances of everyone at the clinic. With so many hackers around these days, that wasn't smart. Hartigan's comments about him had been perceptive: arrogant, opinionated, unwilling to accept criticism, exceptionally competent.

Then, finally, he found what he'd been looking for all along. He knew that, alone among the staff, Hartigan had computer access to the program. And there it was, under the file innocuously slugged "ETOM."

He'd taken a long look. It was everything he had expected.

The doctor got out of his car and walked up to the knoll where the simple stone marker bore his wife's name and the dates of her birth and death. She was forty-one, two years younger than he. The grass was soft. He stood there, holding his hat, remembering how she had died. He felt himself starting to lose control. She'd been lucid up to the last hour, when she finally slipped into a coma. By then her eyes were yellow from the morphine that entered her veins through an IV drip bag.

He was crying, sobbing uncontrollably, letting the tears come, as they always did on such visits. It hurt. God, how it hurt. He saw his wife's face and cried out to her. She'd been so beautiful.

He asked her forgiveness for what he was about to do.

The clock was ticking. He knew there would be no chance for a dry run. This had to work the first time.

TWENTY-FOUR

THE NEXT NIGHT, LATE, the telephone rang in Brook's office. It was just after midnight and he was trying to catch up on paperwork.

"Glad you're still there." It was Marty Conner. "Better get down here. You'll want to see this. Meet me in the control room."

Conner sounded worried, which wasn't like him. Brook had never seen him get rattled, and more than ever he'd come to appreciate Conner's skills with the PET scanner. He was a genius with the complicated nuclear technology and at interpreting the data. A good man. Brook liked him.

He rode the elevator down four levels to the subbasement. When the door slid open, the sound stopped him cold: a loud, yelping wail.

Ouuuuuuuuu!

It reminded him of a wolf howl. He'd heard that haunting sound in the backwoods of Montana, during a hike in the Rocky Mountains near the Canadian border. He'd camped for the night in a remote trail shelter almost at the frost line. The shrieking howls, carrying up through the valleys, had kept him awake for hours. He remembered how they'd cut right through him. He felt the same way now.

For once, even the security guard stationed in the hallway looked tense. "He can stop any time he wants," he said. It was unusual for one of Brody's people to say anything at all.

Brook pressed the buzzer to the security-control room. Again, the sound.

"Ouuuuu!"

The door unlocked automatically. Conner was waiting.

"He's been doing that for the last fifteen minutes in his sleep," he said.

The guard monitoring the clinic's security cameras didn't look up from the panel of television screens. He, too, appeared edgy.

"Here, check the boy out. What do you make of that?" Conner asked. The picture was slightly out of focus and fuzzy with snow. The horizontal hold-line flickered up and down once or twice.

Lind was lying on his bed. The overhead lights in his room were dimmed. He wore a red sweatshirt, shorts and a pair of white cotton socks. His eyes were closed, his breathing rapid and labored. Mouth gaping, his head suddenly snapped back as he emitted another howl.

"Ouuuu! Ouuuuuuuuuuuu!"

"I've called Hartigan," Conner said. "He's on his way in."

"He looks somnambulent." Brook said.

Amplified over the audio system, the sound was chilling— the loudest shriek yet.

"I've heard of something like this happening on death row," Conner said.

Brook was also aware of the phenomenon. Prisoners condemned to death who howled at the moon like dogs in heat, even though, locked away far from a window, they couldn't see it. Such inexplicable outbursts were rare. But what Lind was doing was even more unnerving.

"Are we getting any of this on tape?" Brook asked.

Conner nodded.

"Do you have his chart?"

Conner handed him a metal clipboard. Brook scanned the pages. The chart included a daily log of Lind's lab tests, CAT scans and the other medical treatments he'd received since his arrival. Nothing looked out of the ordinary.

"I want to talk to him, maybe do a mental status," Brook said. "I need to find out what's going on in his head."

He followed Conner into the hallway and waited until two guards shackled the prisoner.

"Be careful in there," Conner said as Brook entered the room.

Lind, wide-awake and sitting up in bed, glanced at the young doctor—and experienced a sensation so strange and overwhelming that he almost cried out. He knew as he sat there, aching in every muscle and joint and—god, yes,—in his fucking head, that something was happening to him.

He was glad to see Brook, who had always taken the trouble to explain things to him in as much detail as he wanted. Lind felt that Brook hadn't lied to him. He'd slowly begun to open up to him ever since that night Brook had broken the rules and unlocked his leg shackle.

But now he wanted to kill him.

The urge suddenly surged through him so powerfully that it made him shake. He was grateful that his legs and wrists were shackled. If he could get up . . .

"You were howling, Ed," Brook said. "You sounded like White Fang. Do you remember any of that?"

Lind drew a blank, and wondered what the doctor was talking about. He rubbed his eyes and figured he must have fallen asleep and had another of those strange flashbacks. They were almost like daydreams—but, the more he thought about it, they weren't daydreams at all. They were too detailed, too real.

"How are you feeling?" Brook asked when Lind didn't answer.

"I'm tired, and I hurt," he said, trying to clear his head.

He looked up at Brook with wide, unblinking eyes and was suddenly overpowered by rage. He'd never felt this way before. Never.

"I'm thinking about killing people, and it scares the shit out of me," Lind said, forcing out the words, still not sure why he was saying them. "Then sometimes a light goes off in my head, and I feel like crying in shame."

"What kind of light?" Brook asked. He wasn't concerned about Lind's threat; he just wanted him to keep talking. He moved closer to the bed.

"It's warm. Bright, like a flash." Lind shuddered. "I don't feel so crazy then."

"Can you describe it, tell me what it's like?"

Lind looked at him with suspicious eyes. His sweatshirt was soaked through.

"You think I'm fucking wacked out, don't you?" he said.

"Tell me about the light, Ed. Is it a person?"

Lind nodded. "It's more of an image, a blur. It tells me not to hurt people."

"You can see it? Can you tell me what it looks like in any way?"

Lind shook his head. "Not really. I can't make out a face. The voice comes out of the light or maybe right after it. I'm not sure about the timing. It's like a bolt of lightning going off in my brain. All my senses are in overdrive, but then the light calms me down."

"You said you were thinking about killing someone," Brook said. "Can you talk about that?"

Lind closed his eyes and rubbed them with his fingers.

"I wanted to kill you," he said finally.

From the way Lind was staring at him, Brook was convinced he still wanted to do it. With his bare hands. The look was measured, cold, deadly. Brook chose his next words carefully, forcing himself to stay calm.

"Have you ever had any feelings like this before you came here?"

Lind laughed. "No way," he said.

Brook glanced again at Lind's medical chart. He noticed that every morning at six A.M. Lind was given an evoked potentials test, using electromagnetic stimulation. Hartigan had told him about the EP tests.

Brook asked Lind about the neuro-stim procedure.

"I could do without it," he said, lying back on his bed.

Brook hadn't been able to shake off the thought that Lind's déjà vu episodes and these strange visions or hallucinations had started soon after his first neuro-stim treatment. Ever since then he'd wondered about the possible connection. He remembered how Hartigan had blown him off when he tried to discuss it.

"How often do you get them?" Brook asked.

"About every day."

TWENTY-FIVE
><

BROOK AND JENNY DECIDED to go see Mark Ulman's widow as soon as possible. They had talked it over during a noon-hour walk to a neighborhood delicatessen. They were taking care to avoid such conversations at the clinic. Brook hoped he could get a clearer idea of how LePonty had been behaving shortly before his escape. In particular, he wanted to know if Ulman had mentioned any neuro-stim treatments to his wife.

Brook kept coming back to that. Maybe it was just a coincidence, but the fact was that Lind's behavior hadn't changed until Hartigan and Serra began to run those early morning neurological tests on him.

Jenny made some telephone calls and learned that Liz Ulman had sold the big home near Tower Grove Park shortly after her husband's murder, and had moved across the river to the East Side. Jenny called some mutual friends and found out she'd bought a condominium in Belleville, a commuter burb about fifteen miles from St. Louis. Her parents still lived there.

Jenny eventually tracked down a telephone number and called her. Liz Ulman reluctantly agreed to meet them.

Late the following afternoon, Brook and Jenny left the clinic and took the Martin Luther King Bridge over the Mississippi. They were in Belleville twenty minutes later. Neither of them was familiar with the town, so it took a while before they found Liz Ulman's address in the darkness. They were a few minutes late when they arrived at her building, an expensive-looking condo with cedar siding, large patio decks and a private pool.

The night air was cold and damp. Brook pulled up his coat collar. He took a deep, nerve-steadying breath and pressed the white button to the right of the door. A moment later an attractive woman opened it a crack and peered out over the security chain, looking at them warily.

Recognizing Jenny, she opened the door. Liz Ulman was in her early thirties. She stared at Brook a moment, and he couldn't help but feel that she was somehow comparing him to her dead husband.

"I've been told I was Mark's replacement," he said.

She led them into a comfortably furnished living room and motioned them to a sofa by the fireplace. She didn't offer to take their coats. It was clear she didn't plan for this to be a long meeting.

"What can I do for you?" she asked, sitting across from them. She wore black slacks and a woolen sweater with a snowflake pattern. Her hair was tucked behind her head. She watched Brook closely. He detected hostility.

"Mrs. Ulman, I know your husband was working with a patient named LePonty."

Her face momentarily clouded. She twisted the fingers of her left hand.

"Can you tell me if he ever mentioned having any problems that he was worried about? Serious problems."

"I've already discussed this with Doctor Hartigan," Liz Ulman said. She looked suddenly annoyed. "He came by the day after Mark was killed. I told him everything I could think of."

"I'm sorry. I didn't know that," Brook said apologetically. He was afraid she was about to tell them to leave.

"Liz, we don't mean to be asking the same questions," Jenny said. "But it would be a big help if we could find out what Mark was thinking. He and I had some conversations before he . . .'' She caught herself.

"Go ahead. You can say it," Liz Ulman said. Her voice was frosty. "You and Mark talked just before he was killed."

"He was worried about what was happening to LePonty," Jenny said.

"You want me to tell you what he thought was going wrong, is that it?" Liz Ulman was staring at them with eyes that flared, suspicious eyes, eyes that could detect any lie.

Brook nodded. "I think something might have happened with an experiment. Something that worried him."

Liz Ulman straightened in her seat, her eyes boring into his.

Making her decision, she said, "He knew something strange was going on. He went to Hartigan and begged him to stop the treatments. He was so worried he was losing sleep. He was a wreck."

Jenny asked for specifics.

"LePonty had become mentally unstable. That was Mark's main concern. The man's behavior was explosively erratic. He also claimed that he was seeing things, all kinds of weird stuff. Mark said he'd never encountered anything like it. He wanted to change the experiment's protocol, but Hartigan wouldn't hear of it."

Explosive violence, hallucinations, perhaps other psychotic manifestations. That pretty well summed up Lind as well.

Brook glanced at Jenny, who had drawn the same conclusions.

Liz Ulman caught their look and smiled. "Does that sound familiar? Is something like that happening there now?"

"Yes," Brook said. He wanted to say more, but hesitated, worried about how far he should go.

"Let me guess. You're afraid to get too specific." Liz Ulman grinned. "I know all about the need for secrecy. The disclosure agreement Hartigan made you sign. Mark didn't start telling me what was going on until right before he was killed.'' Her eyes came back to Brook. Her voice had momentarily softened, but the edge returned. "Of course, by then it was too late.''

"Did Mark ever mention any magnetic-stimulation tests they may have been running on LePonty?'' Brook asked.

Liz Ulman's head slowly went up and down. "That was one of the things he wanted to talk over with Hartigan. Mark said it had something to do with setting up electrical fields in the brain. He'd found out about it somehow, and didn't like what was happening. He'd argued with Hartigan about it.''

"Do you know why they argued?'' Jenny asked.

"He thought it was one of the reasons LePonty was acting so strange.'' Liz Ulman paused a moment to reconsider what she'd just said.

"Mark thought it was really messing him up. He'd started to do a lot of reading on electromagnetic stimulation. He'd brought home a pile of papers and journal articles on the subject. He was up until two and three in the morning, reading them.''

Brook felt suddenly adrift. This was worse than he'd imagined. He realized that Hartigan had been aware of problems with the neuro-stim tests, but had gone ahead with them anyway—on Lind and the others.

"Mark even went to see Al Silver,'' Liz Ulman said.

"Why was that?'' Brook asked.

"Somehow he'd learned that Silver was working on a new drug that he thought might help LePonty. It had something to do with changing the chemical balances in the brain. The results looked very promising, but Silver wouldn't talk to him. He wouldn't even give him the time of day.''

Brook recalled that Hartigan had briefly mentioned Silver's work to him after he'd stumbled onto their kindling experiments with cats.

"Can you tell me how Mark found out what Silver was doing?'' he asked.

Liz Ulman shook her head. "No, I just know he was angry that Silver wouldn't talk to him.'' She took a breath and looked straight at Brook. "The night he died, I think Mark was going to try to stop the experiment. He was scared. Now I know why."

Jenny asked her whether Mark suspected anyone of paying secret visits to LePonty shortly before his escape.

"He did, but he had no idea who it could be," she said. "I thought about going to the authorities later, but I didn't have any proof and who would have believed me? We're talking about the world-famous Hartigan Clinic, and I was just a hysterical widow whose husband had been killed in an unfortunate accident."

She folded her hands on her lap. She'd mentioned none of these suspicions to Hartigan after Mark's death.

"I've got a question for you," she said. "Who do you think is running the clinic? I mean, really running it?"

The answer seemed obvious.

"Doctor Robert Hartigan," Jenny said. "He never lets us forget it for a moment."

"Mark had started to have doubts about that," Liz Ulman said. "He thought someone else was pulling the strings. Someone with serious money and influence. He was planning to look into it. He ran out of time."

Again, Brook wanted to know more. He couldn't imagine anyone but Hartigan calling the shots. The man had too much ego to play second fiddle.

"You're on your own on that. Mark's dead, or he would have helped you."

Brook told her how sorry he was that he'd never met her husband or had a chance to work with him. He hoped she believed him.

They stood to leave. They'd talked for twenty minutes. There was no more to say.

"Something's going on, isn't there?"

"We're having some problems," Brook said. He didn't want to go into the details. He didn't have to. Liz Ulman understood.

"Mark waited too long before he decided to get out," she said. "Please, don't make the same mistake."

Brook carried those words with him as he and Jenny walked back to his car. No sooner had Brook settled into the seat and tried to get control of his fragmented thoughts than Jenny locked her eyes on him.

"I'm worried," she said.

Brook felt a cord pull tight on his chest.

"So am I," he said. He was beginning to understand why Mark Ulman had been scared.

TWENTY-SIX

HE SAT IN HIS front room and went over his final preparations. He had mentally rehearsed every move a hundred times and gone over them repeatedly on paper. It was going to be risky, but he thought he had a chance—if he kept his nerve, if he got lucky, if he didn't snap before then.

Once he logged on to Hartigan's computer directory, he would have to work quickly and not make any mistakes. The moment he signed on, he'd leave a "transaction log," a record that someone had accessed the system. That's why he didn't dare use his own PC. He'd have to borrow someone else's. He smiled, knowing that he already had the right candidate in mind.

He pulled out his lower desk drawer and picked up the Smith & Wesson. He liked the feel of the handgun and could anticipate the upward kick. The five-inch silencer that fit over the vented barrel had cost five times as much as the pistol. At first he'd worried about getting one, but it was easy. This was the United States after all. You could buy anything you wanted.

As he had done before, he slipped the pistol into the overlarge pocket of his lab coat, to make sure it fit and to get used to the feel of carrying it. Hartigan had become a fanatic about the security at the clinic, but so far he hadn't installed a metal detector that would pick up the weapon. His plan would be difficult but not impossible. He would have surprise on his side.

He thought once again of the irony in all this. The last time, he'd set LePonty loose to make sure Ulman didn't ruin their experiments. Now he wanted to do the same thing, only the motivation was different: He wanted to get even with his esteemed colleague Dr. Robert Hartigan. The man who had given him a job, backed him to the hilt, pushed him to do cutting-edge research that would soon pay huge dividends. The man who was about to sell him out.

The explanation for this radical shift in viewpoint was actually so simple: As he'd long suspected, hatred was a more potent emotion than fear.

There was no question that he had to keep pushing himself. He calculated that he had only about a week, or less. If he waited much longer, the neuro-stim treatments were almost certain to work. It wasn't a sure thing, but he was betting the procedure had an excellent chance of altering the brain's complex neurotransmitter network in a way that drastically reduced criminal behavior.

On the very eve of success, Hartigan was claiming that the procedure was all his idea, his work, his breakthrough. It was incredible the way the man was talking, how he was taking all the credit. The fucking bastard. The crucial ideas had been his, not Hartigan's. There were others on staff who could verify this, but of course they wouldn't open their mouths.

He'd been thinking about it almost nonstop for over forty-eight hours. He'd considered marching into Hartigan's office and just killing him. He'd even thought of another approach—calling a television crew to the clinic and making a statement about their secret experiments.

But the plan he'd finally settled on was exquisitely more focused: He wanted to humiliate, both professionally and privately, his brilliant mentor. Nothing less. For a man like Hartigan, that would be a fate worse than death.

He'd always reserved his greatest scorn for those who hesitated to do what was absolutely necessary. He coldly figured there was an even chance that he wouldn't survive, that something would go wrong. And surely something *would* go wrong. Chaos theory almost guaranteed it. No matter. The moment had come to prove that he was a virtuoso.

TWENTY-SEVEN

THE SPINAL TAP HAD been Brook's idea. He wanted to get some insight as to what was happening to the prisoners neurologically.

Jenny knew she didn't have much time. She'd be alone with Waters two, maybe three minutes at most. Hartigan had scheduled another PET-scan series for the prisoner that morning. So at seven o'clock Jenny had given him an oral dose of benzodiazepine. They'd found that Waters tolerated the procedure better if he was mildly sedated; it took some of his edge off and made him more cooperative.

When Waters was strapped to the gurney, two guards joined her for the trip up from the subbasement. She had timed it so they arrived for the test a few minutes early. Conner was still fine-tuning the scanner, so Jenny told the guards to push the gurney into an adjoining room, where Waters would be more comfortable. The scanning room was kept cool.

The guards stationed themselves in the hallway. Jenny joined Conner, who was alone and preoccupied. With no one paying any attention to her, she went back into the room where Waters lay half asleep.

She managed to roll him over on his side and draw off 10 cc of the clear fluid from his lumbar spine with a large-gauge hypodermic she'd brought. Waters was already under the effects of the sedative, and didn't even notice the needle prick.

Later that morning Jenny slipped Brook Waters's cerebro-spinal fluid sample. Over his lunch break he took it to a friend at the state hospital who had the analysis run.

A few hours later, Brook sat in his office staring at the faxed results, not believing what he was seeing.

A striking neurochemical change was under way in Waters's brain. The clearest indication was the enhanced glucose metabolism; at the same time there was a decrease in the protein marker GFAP. Protein synthesis had decreased nearly 60 percent compared with the results of the spinal fluid tests they'd run when Waters had first arrived at the clinic.

A significant change in tissue density was also apparent. Cellular structures were being altered in the brain, as were synaptic pathways—changes that appeared to reach even into the cell's complex RNA and DNA.

Brook dropped by Jenny's office and laid the printout on her desk without saying a word. She scanned the paper and looked up at him.

"I don't understand," she said.

Brook suggested they take a walk.

When they were outside the building, Jenny blurted out, "My god, what's going on?"

"I'm not sure," Brook said. He'd never seen values like this. Not even in the textbooks.

"There's nothing in his medical chart to explain what's happening, and I've been checking it every day," Jenny said.

"I don't trust those charts at all anymore," Brook said. "For all we know, they've been altered." That seemed more than likely, considering the results of the spinal tap. Nothing in the men's medical records could account for what was happening to their brain chemistry.

Jenny and Brook walked to the end of the block and slowly headed back toward the clinic. The cold air helped Brook think.

"Jenny, I want to do an EEG on Lind tonight," he said. "I want to check his brain-wave activity."

They made their plans quickly. Brook would use an ambulatory monitor. The digital device was about the size of a large transistor radio and required only three electrodes. It was easy to hook up, easy to carry.

"When will you do it?" Jenny asked.

"I'll go down late this evening. He'll be asleep then."

After Lind's howling episode, Hartigan had put him on a light dose of Valium to make sure he slept through the night. It was essential for the long battery of tests and PET scans that he be well rested. And like many chronic offenders, Lind had complained of chronic insomnia. So had Waters.

Brook quickly firmed up his plans. Before they went back to the clinic, Jenny pressed his hand.

"Call me when you're finished," she said.

Brook went down to Lind's room just before midnight. He'd been to see him at night several times before, most recently a few days earlier, when Lind was howling in his sleep.

The guard on duty recognized Brook. He looked surprised to see him.

"I'm going to peek in on Lind for a few minutes, see how he's sleeping," Brook said. "We don't want a repeat of what happened a couple nights ago."

"You got that right," the guard said. He entered the room first to make sure Lind was shackled to the bed. Returning to the hallway, he said, "He's out cold. Guy didn't budge."

Brook thanked him and went in, carrying the portable EEG monitor in his briefcase. The recessed lights were kept dim even when the men were asleep. The bed was in the corner, in shadows. Lind lay on his back, breathing easily.

Brook knew from watching the monitor screens that it would be hard for the guard to see exactly what he was doing in the dim light. Standing with his back to the mounted surveillance camera, he attached the electrodes to Lind's scalp. He'd already applied the electrolyte gel to the leads, which he taped to Lind's forehead and right temple. He placed the cassette-style monitor under the blankets, and departed. He'd been in the room less than five minutes.

"I'll drop back a little later tonight, before I go home," he told the guard on his way out.

Brook returned to his office to catch a few hours' sleep on the sofa before going back to Lind's room.

Brook had removed the leads and was wiping the gel from Lind's head, when the prisoner woke up. He stared straight at Brook, but didn't move. His eyes slowly focused on Brook's face in the dim light.

"This shit's starting to scare me," Lind said, his voice groggy. He sounded half asleep. "I already told that to Hartigan."

"What scares you?" Brook asked.

"The way I feel," Lind said. His eyes opened wider as he looked up at Brook.

"You still feel like you want to kill me?" Brook asked.

"I just want it to stop," Lind said. "Can you make it stop?"

"You're going to get better," Brook said, trying to reassure him. "I want you to believe that."

He thought for a moment about telling him there were drugs they could give him to help control his powerful urges. He remembered what Liz Ulman had mentioned—that Al Silver was working on a new drug apparently designed to do just that.

Quickly reconsidering, Brook decided it wouldn't be a good idea to tell any of this to Lind.

"It won't be much longer before you'll feel yourself again," he said.

"You make sure of that, Doc. Promise me." He was drifting off again.

"You've got my word," Brook said.

Lind took a few shallow breaths, closed his eyes and turned his head to the side.

Brook stood there, staring at him a moment. Then he departed with the EEG monitor in his briefcase.

*   *   *

He called Jenny from his office and told her he'd be right over. Fifteen minutes later he was in her apartment.

She'd put on a sweatshirt and a pair of jeans, and stood there in her living room watching quietly as he hooked up the EEG monitor to her computer printer.

He liked the way she didn't look nervous; it helped calm him down as he ran off the EEG readouts. When he sat down at Jenny's desk and laid the data out in front of him, he noticed that his pulse was racing.

Lind's brain-wave activity stunned him.

"Look at this," he said, still not quite believing what he was seeing. "He's having one seizure after another."

Jenny stared at the printouts. "How long was the monitor hooked up?" she asked.

"Over ninety minutes. More than enough time to get a good reading."

The distinctive peak-and-valley spike pattern showed that Lind was experiencing repeated, low-grade seizures. What was unusual here was that these mild seizures lasted only a few seconds each but were recurring.

"They're coming in back-to-back clusters that last ten to thirty seconds," he said.

Jenny kept looking at the printout. "Clusters followed by long intervals of normal brain-wave activity," she said. "He keeps flipping back and forth."

Brook had never seen anything like it. There was no indication that the seizures were of grand mal or even generalized intensity. Nor was there any sign of convulsions.

Brook noticed something else on the EEG printout. "His theta waves are off the charts," he said.

That was bizarre. Lind's theta-wave pattern was unusually powerful. Generated by the hippocampus, the brain waves indicated neural discharges deep in the limbic system. Brook knew that theta waves were more common in sleeping adults, but these were coming at an unusually high velocity.

Seated at Jenny's desk with the papers spread out in front of him, Brook's initial shock gave way to a sickening realization. He couldn't bring himself to admit what he thought might be going on. And yet the data was right there in front of him, staring him in the face. A clear portrait of Lind's brain waves.

"It looks like they've kindled Lind's brain," he said.

Jenny stared at him, incredulous.

"My guess is they've probably used electromagnetic stimulation as the triggering mechanism." His voice was tired but the words were controlled. "Based on what the CSF test showed, I'd say the seizures have already started to alter the neurocircuitry of Lind's brain."

Jenny slowly rubbed her eyes. It was as if she didn't want to hear any more of this.

"Jen, it's the only possible explanation," Brook said, fighting the swimming feeling in his head. "Look at the readouts . . . the repeated brain-wave activity. . . . That's exactly what kindling does."

"But how *could* they be doing anything like that?" Jenny asked, finding her voice. Her words were sharp. "How *could* they, John? It doesn't make any sense. I know they're kindling some cats . . ."

"Jenny, I don't want to believe it, either. But look at this brain-wave pattern. You tell me what else could be happening here."

"It's totally illegal," she said, pounding her fists on the table. Her composure had shattered. "How could they do anything like that to humans?"

The implications of what they were discussing were too grotesque for words. It was getting hard to focus.

"If you can change the brain chemistry of prisoners by kindling them, maybe you could also change their criminal behavior," Brook said, trying to piece together his fragmented thoughts. "You could do it without surgery or expensive drug therapy. You could go a long way toward solving the nation's monumental crime problem, not to mention prison overcrowding. Those would be huge breakthroughs."

He remembered Liz Ulman telling them her husband thought someone besides Hartigan might have been calling the shots at the clinic. Brook didn't doubt it, considering what might be at stake if Hartigan was really kindling prisoners. The risks were immense, but so was the potential for making a fortune, for dictating public policy. Hartigan might easily have outside backers for a project so massive in scope—people who might expect to benefit financially, or in some other way.

Brook now understood why they'd been running the secret kindling research on cats up on the fourth floor. He wondered how much Krill and the other key staff members knew about all this.

He tried to force himself to think coolly. In med school they used to call it "thinking like a doctor." Brook tried to comprehend the enormity of what was going on, but he was getting too bleary-eyed. Fatigue and stress were starting to catch up with him.

"So what do we do?" Jenny asked finally.

"I'm not sure," Brook said. "For starters, I don't think we do anything."

"But we've got to let someone know about this," Jenny said, her anger flashing again.

"I agree, but we need more proof. There might be another explanation for all of this. I don't think so, but there might be. We need to hang in a while longer. You can be damn sure they'll have some plausible explanation for what's happening, some contingency plan in case they need deniability. They could crush us like bugs unless we've really got our shit together."

Jenny sat in her chair. She looked drained, but he could tell she agreed.

"We've got to be sure we're right about this if we're going to take on someone like Hartigan," he said.

Another thought kept intruding into his tired brain. Mark Ulman had started to figure all this out but hadn't lived long enough to put the pieces together. If someone had considered Ulman a potential risk that needed to be eliminated, what about them?

TWENTY-EIGHT
>◁◁

BROOK FINISHED HIS THIRD diet soda of the evening, crumpled the can and tossed it in the wastepaper basket next to his desk. It was the day after he'd run the EEG test on Lind, and he still didn't know what to do. It was clear that kindling had triggered changes in Lind's brain that none of them fully understood.

The whole thing scared him. He wanted to halt the neurostim treatments immediately, but didn't know how. Complicating matters even more, Hartigan had left town for the day. His sudden departure was unannounced and puzzling, considering that he had to be at a crucial moment in the kindling experiments. Brook wondered what could have been so important as to make him leave, even for a few hours.

It was almost ten-thirty P.M. Brook planned to work for another hour or so, then drop by Jenny's office and head home. He'd seen her only briefly that morning. She didn't look any better than he did.

They'd talked about taking a trip together, maybe to the Great Smoky Mountains. He'd told Jenny about Mount LeConte, the second highest peak in the mountain range. You had to hike or ride a horse five or six miles up. They would sleep in a log cabin with a wood stove and awake before dawn to watch the sun rise over blue ridges stretching to the horizon. She seemed eager to go.

Of course they'd had that talk before all this blew up in their faces.

Brook was gathering his papers when the alarm went off, a shrill blast one floor up that almost made him jump out of his chair. This had happened several times before. They tested the security system at all hours, and it was getting to be a damn nuisance.

Brook went to the door, expecting to find that it had locked automatically. All the doors in the building were set to lock when the alarm was triggered. But when he inserted his key, the handle turned in his hand. The door was unlocked.

Brook met Ted Krill, whose office was just down the hall. The racket was ear-splitting.

"I'm getting tired of this," Krill shouted over the noise. "Every time it goes off, I damn near have a heart attack."

Brook nodded.

The alarm stopped. A moment later the lights went out.

"Now what?" Krill said impatiently. "This is a new one."

Another voice said, "Where's a pretty girl when you need her?"

It was Marty Conner standing in the darkness at the far end of the hall. The burly biochemist also worked on their floor. As usual, he'd found something to joke about.

They heard a door open and saw a flashlight beam probing the walls. Brook squinted as the light hit his face. A man was moving quickly toward them, one of the security guards. Brook noticed that he carried what looked like an Uzi.

"Get back in your offices and lock the doors!"

"What the hell's going on?" Conner said.

Ignoring the question, the guard shone his flashlight in each of their faces to check identities. He barked out his order again and hurried to the opposite end of the hall. He hit the stairwell door on the run, pushing it open and disappearing down the steps.

The lights blinked once or twice, then came back on. Brook took off as soon as the guard left them. He wanted to get up to Jenny's office. This wasn't a test. Something was wrong. He'd just stepped into the stairwell when he heard the first gunshot, a sharp crack that echoed up from a lower floor.

More shots followed. Loud, ringing blasts. He counted them: three, four, five. Then silence.

Brook pushed open the door on the third floor and sprinted down the hall to Jenny's office. He let out a breath when he saw her standing in the doorway.

"What's happening?" she said.

"I don't know. Lock your door and stay inside. I'm going downstairs."

Jenny shook her head. "No. I'm coming with you."

"Let's go, then," he said. "We'll take the elevator."

They rode straight to the subbasement. The door opened and they stepped into the hallway. The lights were on. Brook felt his mouth go dry when he saw that the doors to Lind's and Waters's rooms were ajar. He checked both. They were gone.

Jenny looked in on Billings, who was still in his bed. His door was also unlocked.

Brook tried to stay calm and think clearly. He kept repeating to himself that this couldn't be what it seemed. He thought that perhaps Serra had taken the prisoners to one of the labs for some unscheduled tests.

Then he saw that the door to the security office was open. Jenny stepped toward the door.

"Get back!" Brook shouted, surprised at the scratchy sound of his voice.

He pulled her away and pushed open the door. He tripped over the body without seeing it. He looked down at the guard's face. There was a dark, gaping hole where the nose had been. It looked like an exit wound. He'd been shot from behind. Blood was still spreading out in a thick pool from the back of the skull.

Brook was standing in it, slipping as he backed away.

"Where are the guards?" Jenny said. Her voice had a

tense, nervous edge, but she hadn't panicked, not even after seeing the body.

"They've got to be around," Brook said.

He noticed that the elevator had ascended to the fourth floor and had stopped there. He didn't want to be caught in the subbasement. He went to the stairwell and opened the door to listen, but couldn't hear anything. They'd better move.

"Let's go up."

Jenny was right behind him. They quietly climbed the steps to the first floor. Brook opened the door a crack and peered out into the lobby. The lights were dimmed. It looked empty.

"I want you to leave the building," Brook whispered.

"Forget it. I'm staying."

There was no time to argue. Besides, he knew he couldn't win. Brook pulled Jenny by the hand and headed for the front door. It was open. He could hear traffic on the street.

They were halfway across the polished floor when a voice stopped them.

Waters.

He was alone and holding a pistol, which he brought up from his side. He'd been rifling papers in the receptionist's office. He cut in front of them and pulled the door shut. Brook noticed his eyes—they looked slanted and burning, like those of a snarling cat.

"Nice to see you, Doctor Malone."

He smiled at Jenny.

"This isn't going to work," Brook said, staying in front of Jenny, trying to shield her with his body. He steeled himself to keep his voice steady. It was important to keep talking. He wondered where Lind was.

"That's your opinion," Waters said. "We've already killed a couple people. I'd say things are working out just fine."

"How are you feeling?" Jenny asked. She sounded perfectly at ease, and natural.

"Except for my head, real fine," Waters said. The sleeves

of his cableknit shirt were rolled way up. Tattoos went from wrist to shoulder.

"Is Lind with you?" Brook asked, desperately trying to keep him talking.

"Yeah, he's around somewhere. The boy decided to tag along with me."

"Where is he?"

Waters smiled again. "Why don't you shut the fuck up." He jammed the pistol into Brook's stomach, doubling him over. Brook staggered backward, aware only of his clawing need to breathe and to keep thinking. Somehow he had to keep trying to focus.

"Lady Doctor, there's something you can do to make me feel better," Waters said, grabbing Jenny's arm when she moved to help Brook. His voice had hardened. "Why don't you strip. Then I want you to go down on your knees and suck me off. I've been thinking about what that would feel like for days."

Jenny's expression didn't change. She pulled her arm free.

"You really don't want to do that, because you'd have to kill me first," she said. "I'd suggest you go back to your room."

The words were softly spoken and firm. There was no terror in them.

"Just take off your clothes, bitch! You got to know, after all our nice talks, that it makes no difference to me whether I fuck you dead or alive."

Waters had taken his eyes off Brook just long enough for him to lunge forward. Brook caught him hard around the waist and pushed him into a wall, sending the pistol flying. He drove a knee into Waters's crotch and smashed a fist into his face. Waters went limp. Jenny snatched up the pistol.

"Drop it! Do it now!" Lind pounced through the stairwell doorway, holding a pistol and a small gym bag. Jenny let the gun fall to the floor.

"Don't do this," Brook said, panting, trying to fill his lungs with air. "We can help you."

"Don't talk about helping me. You bastards have fucked

up my head!'' Lind shouted. He looked different. Like Waters, his eyes were blazing slits and, for an instant, Brook
glimpsed the murder lust that was burning there. He managed
to pull himself up straight; his limbs were leaden as he staggered to his feet. His chest ached from having the wind
knocked out of him. He knew that he had to make a connection with Lind. He started to say something, but Lind cut
him off.

"I went upstairs to get Hartigan," Lind said. "He wasn't
there, so I killed one of those fucking guards."

Lind's flaming eyes told Brook that he was going to kill
him, too. Whatever was about to happen, he knew there was
nothing he could do to stop it.

Struggling to his feet, Waters started to pick up the pistol
Jenny had dropped, but Lind reached down and got it first.
He slipped it into his belt. Waters shot him a look, but said
nothing.

"Let's get out of here," Lind said.

"Sure, like I told you, I know where we can get a car and
money. You stick with me, you'll be on your way out of this
fucking city in half an hour."

Brook almost groaned out loud with hope. His heart was
pounding.

"Then let's move," Lind snapped. "I want to see that
money."

"No problem," Waters said. He spat blood on the floor.
"But first, I'd like . . ."

Brook didn't hear the rest of the sentence. A heavy, crashing blow knocked him down, flat on his face. Everything
went black. It was a moment before he could see and hear
again.

He recognized Jenny crouching over him.

"Don't try to move," she said. Her fingers touched his
head, probing. "It's not fractured, but we'll want to get an
X ray to make sure you don't have a concussion."

Brook realized what had happened. Waters had hit him
with a bronze flower vase he'd snatched from the reception-

ist's desk. Yellow and white mums were all over the floor.

When Brook tried to get up, his legs buckled beneath him. He sat down hard and rubbed the back of his head. A lump was starting to swell. He looked at Jenny.

"I'm fine," she said. "Nothing happened to me."

"What about Lind and Waters?"

Jenny touched the side of his face. Her hand felt cool. "They're gone."

TWENTY-NINE

ONE OF BRODY'S MEN lay dead just inside the door of the security office, the back of his head blown off.

Another had been shot in the stomach, on the second floor, where he'd encountered one of the prisoners in the hallway. He was alive, barely.

They had carried the wounded man to an examination room. Conner and Krill were working on him when Brody arrived. The two doctors moved with the speed and quiet efficiency of ER veterans. Conner had already started an IV line with normal saline.

"His skin's cool to the touch," Krill said. "He's lost a lot of blood."

"What's his pressure?" Conner asked. He didn't look up as he jabbed the IV needle into the guard's left wrist.

"Seventy over thirty. Pulse is one-twenty and irregular. We could lose him."

"We're going to need four or five units of blood typed and crossed," Conner said. "He's hemorrhaging. He's almost bled himself out."

Conner glanced up and saw Brody watching from the doorway. "Call an ambulance. We don't have enough blood plasma here. If we can get him over to Barnes, he might have a chance." Barnes Hospital, only seven blocks away, had one of the best-equipped ERs in the country.

Brody looked at the wounded man's pasty, death-mask face. They'd opened his shirt, exposing the chest and stomach. The dark hole was just above the navel. Brody tried to remember the kid's name. He thought it was Roberts, but wasn't sure.

"The pressure's still dropping," Krill said, adjusting the drip rate on the IV bottle. He tightened the blood pressure strap around the man's left forearm.

Conner glared at Brody. "Didn't you hear me? We need an ambulance!"

When Brody didn't respond, Conner reached for the telephone mounted on the wall. Brody pushed his arm away.

"No calls. If you can save him here, do it."

"He's going to die!"

"We're not going to break security on this," Brody snarled. "If we get another hospital involved, the secrecy of this project could be jeopardized. I'm not going to let that happen."

Conner was a strong man a couple of inches taller than Brody. But when he reached for the phone again, Brody grabbed his right wrist and bent it down and back. Conner went to his knees. His eyes opened wide in pain.

Krill hadn't stopped working on the wounded guard. "We need to get another IV line started. I'm worried about his respirations. He's hardly breathing."

Brody shrugged. He disconnected the telephone and stepped back into the hallway. Conner slowly straightened up, holding his right hand in his left palm as if it were a broken cup.

Brody still didn't have a clear idea how Waters and Lind had escaped. He couldn't believe someone had gotten out of the place a second time, especially after they'd increased security.

Someone had helped, someone on the clinic's staff. It was the only explanation that made sense.

Brody's chief assistant, Rob Eliot, walked up, clutching a cellular telephone. Two men were with Brook and Dr. Malone, taking statements, he said. Eliot had called in six more to help with the manhunt.

Brody had asked him to call the senior medical staff and have them at the clinic no later than six o'clock that morning.

Brody had personally called Hartigan, who had gone to Jefferson City to talk to Len Beckworth, the state-prison warden. Hartigan had handled the call better than Brody had anticipated, and was on his way back to St. Louis.

Beckworth wouldn't be pleased, and Brody would have to explain what had happened. He decided to put that call off as long as possible.

"I'd better go talk to our two doctors," Brody said.

Eliot's cell beeped as they started for the stairwell. One of their men was calling; he was monitoring the police scanner.

"A couple guys just stole a car five blocks from here," Eliot said. "White boys."

"We know anything else?"

"They shot the driver. He's still alive."

"Get on over there and see what you can find out," Brody said.

Eliot hurried off without saying another word.

Brook sat at the receptionist's desk, holding an ice bag on the swelling at the back of his skull. He had decided against an X ray, despite Jenny's urging. It wasn't any worse than some of the head-busting knocks he'd taken playing high school football. Just a slight hematoma.

Brody approached, motioning away two of his men. He wanted Brook and Jenny to tell him exactly what had happened.

"Which one of them was giving the orders?"

"Lind," Brook said. "Waters said he knew where they could get a car and some money."

He was starting to have a splitting headache. He remembered how Waters had looked at him, and tried not to think about how close he'd come to being killed.

"I don't think we should continue this discussion," Jenny

said. "John got knocked pretty good in the head. He should be having an X ray, not doing an interview." She looked upset.

"You wouldn't have any idea how they got out, or how they got that pistol?"

"Do you think we should?" Brook said, irritated by the question and tone. His head was spinning. More than anything, he wanted to try to sleep. And after that, figure out what he and Jenny were going to do next. First they discover that Hartigan is kindling prisoners, then two of those men escape. It made him queasy just to think about it. He needed to work the details through with a clear head.

Before Brody could answer, Conner descended the stairwell. His lab coat was splattered with blood.

"Your man's dead," he said. "As far as I'm concerned, you killed him. Don't think I'm not going to report what happened."

"You think we're calling the police?" Brody asked scathingly.

"Yes I do, and right now," Conner said.

"Not a good idea," Brody said. His dark, too-small eyes focused on Conner. "We bring the cops in on this, they'll fuck it up and you'll have a bloodbath. Lind and Waters aren't going to give up without a fight. What if they take hostages? The next thing happens is the press and television people are camping outside your doors, asking what the hell were you doing with prisoners in the first place."

Brook looked at Conner, wondering if he knew about the kindling experiments. Is that what Brody meant? Or was he referring to the PET scans they were running on the three men? Considering the escape, that was bad enough. Brody was right about how the media would react, the kind of questions they would ask.

"Is that what you want?" Brody continued. "Look, we're better off going after Lind and Waters ourselves. That's my business, and I'm good at it."

"You let him die!" Conner boomed out. He stepped toward Brody.

"If I were you, I'd try to get some sleep. We'll have a staff meeting in a couple hours and discuss some of the dos and don'ts."

Fists at his sides, Conner glared at Brody. Two guards moved in behind him in case of trouble. Without saying another word, Conner turned and climbed the stairs.

"We'll talk again," Brody told Brook.

Cutting the interview short, he took the elevator to the subbasement. They had removed the body and were using a Shop-Vac to clean up the blood. Whoever planned this had been damn good. Somehow they'd managed to tap into the clinic's security system and virtually shut it down.

Someone yelled to him that him Eliot, one of his key men, was calling, and handed him a telephone. The news was about as bad as it could get.

Eliot was at the intersection of Boyle and West Pine, six or seven blocks from the clinic. A family had been returning home in their car around midnight. The father, a thirtyish lawyer, was driving. His wife sat next to him. Their two small children were sleeping in the back.

Two men, both white, had come up to the driver's side as the man stopped to park in front of his home.

A thin man with short, blond hair had shot the lawyer in the left shoulder when he tried to pull away from the curb.

"Here's where it gets interesting," Eliot said, continuing his story. "The other guy rabbit-chops the shooter from behind and knocks him cold. He gets the screaming wife and kids out of the car, and does the same for daddy. He lays him on the ground, then tosses his pal into the back seat, and they drive away."

Brody took a moment to absorb all that. Then he told Eliot, "Get the number of the stolen car and haul ass back here."

THIRTY
➤◆⊲

WHEN HARTIGAN ARRIVED FROM Jefferson City a few hours later, Brody met him privately in his office. Things were going to get messy and he would need Hartigan's help to hold the staff in line. That wasn't going to be easy. To his practiced eye, a couple of those overeducated brains looked ready to crack. Connor for one.

"I want you to find out who's responsible," Hartigan said as soon as Brody gave him a brief overview of the escape.

"You got any ideas who it was?"

Hartigan sat at the table, staring at his hands. He shook his head. Brody wondered if he was telling the truth. He couldn't be sure that the great man wasn't holding something back, that he did have some suspicions but wasn't sharing them. He would almost bet even money that he was.

"What did they say in Jeff City when they got word about the escape?"

Brody glanced at his watch. Five-ten. He'd find out soon enough. After a hurriedly called meeting with the medical staff, set for six o'clock, he was supposed to give Beckworth a full report. The warden and Paulus had probably exploded. They'd spent a fortune revamping the security system. They'd brought him in on a big retainer. They'd let him spend a ton of money to hire staff. And now they had two people dead and two freaks loose. It was ass-reaming time.

His career was as much on the line as the shits with the
medical degrees.

"They want us to keep working on Billings," Hartigan
said. "At least I convinced them of that much. But everything else is to come to a standstill until we can find Lind
or Waters, or until . . ."

Brody finished the sentence for him. "Or until we kill
them."

Hartigan didn't answer. "My guess is both are having
spontaneous, intermittent seizures that could keep flashing in
their brains like a strobe light. These could go on indefinitely
and spread from the limbic system into the rest of the brain."

The prospects with Waters were particularly frightening.
Lind hadn't been prone to violence before he was kindled.
Waters had been a sadistic serial killer. There was no telling
how deadly he would become as a result of his treatments,
or what crimes he'd be capable of commiting with his limbic
brain doing a slow burn.

Hartigan's eyes looked cold. "They escaped at the worst
possible time," he said. "In a few more days we would have
finished the kindling treatments and controlled their seizures
with drugs." He smiled at Brody. "We were that close to
success."

"We've got a couple psychos running the streets, don't
we? And I've got to risk my ass to bring them in."

"You're getting paid." Hartigan's voice had a biting edge.

"Not enough, Doctor. Not nearly enough. I've seen both
of those bastards up close."

THIRTY-ONE

BROOK AND JENNY LEFT the clinic shortly after Hartigan and Brody met with the staff and discussed how to handle the escape. No point in sticking around. They both needed to get away. They were supposed to come back tomorrow and start catching up with their patient load. Hartigan wanted them to keep busy.

Brook suggested they go to his place for breakfast. They took his car. Neither spoke more than a few words during the short drive to the West End. Everything seemed changed. Even the streets looked and felt different.

Brook parked his car and led her upstairs to his flat. It smelled musty when he opened the front door.

Jenny leaned against a wall.

"It's awful," she said. She was emotionally wrung out, and touched Brook's hand. "How did all of this happen?" She sat down on a chair in the kitchen. "I'm scared, John."

The scene at the clinic was as close as he'd ever come to being killed. Waters would have done it. He wanted to do it. He'd be dead if Lind hadn't stepped in.

He would never forget that. The reality of what had happened had gone off like a delayed fuse in his head. He sat down across from Jenny and hunched over the table, no longer in the mood to eat.

It had all seemed so right when he signed on at the clinic.

It was exactly what he wanted to do, exactly the kind of research he'd dreamed about during the long slog through med school. But now he and Jenny were caught up in something that scared the hell out of him.

"What's next?" Jenny asked. She almost sounded herself again.

"We wait and hope Brody finds them," Brook said. It bothered him that a man he so intensely disliked appeared to be their best chance. If by some miracle Brody found Waters and Lind, and managed to bring them back alive, they still might be able to salvage their experiment.

Even as he played with this thought, he couldn't help but smile at its fantasy aspect. Reality was otherwise. Reality was the pained, uncertain look in Jenny's eyes and the lead in his stomach.

It wasn't going to be easy capturing either man. He'd seen them, heard them, spoken to them. And yet, as far as he could, he wanted to help them.

He had to find them first. Not easy. If he called the police for help, there would be carnage. Brody was probably right about that. He could see the whole chain of events play out in his mind.

He put a pot of water on the burner to make tea, while Jenny sat on the sofa in the light that poured through the flat's dusty front windows. The water had just started to boil when the telephone rang. Brook picked up the receiver, thinking someone at the clinic was calling.

It was Lind.

"They've found the car." Brody passed the word straight to Hartigan hot off the police scanner.

It was four in the afternoon. Hartigan hardly responded to the news as he sat in his office, staring at the enlarged PET scans of Lind's and Waters's brains. He had the latter set out, and he looked distracted.

"It's parked on Tamm Avenue outside an old radiator factory. Homicide's been called and some of the top brass are on their way. Sounds like it could be rough."

The brass included Jason Dunning, chief of detectives. Over the years, Brody had met Dunning a couple of times on business. He was a good, tough cop.

Brody hoped Dunning would let him nose around a little. He'd have to be careful, though. He didn't want to raise any suspicions.

Tamm was about two miles from the clinic. Elliot drove. When he found the place, it was lit up like Christmas. "Man, will you look at that," he said, stopping a block away.

Squad cars, red lights flashing, blocked the street in front of the factory. A couple dozen blueshirts were standing around, keeping passersby and residents behind the yellow crime-scene tape that had been strung across the street. The spectators were out in force, thirty or forty of them. Most were drinking beer.

Brody noticed the battered green van parked just up the street. The crime-scene truck. That usually meant a homicide case.

"Stay here," Brody told Elliot. "I'm going to try to get inside."

He crossed the street. The building's facade was covered by thick vines, dead and winter brown. A pair of planters framed the entrance. The small, one-time factory had been rehabbed and converted into a private residence. The front was artfully floodlit.

Two plainclothes detectives stopped Brody before he got to the door. He flashed his U.S. marshal's ID, holding it out just long enough for them to focus on the letters. He kept his thumb over the date.

He asked to see Major Dunning, using his first name.

"We're old friends."

"The major's busy."

"He'll want to see me," Brody lied.

The man disappeared inside the building. He was short, thick-necked and wore a fedora. His checked sports coat looked a size too small in the shoulders.

"We hear you found the car from that shooting in the West End," Brody said to the other detective.

The cop nodded. "The lab boys towed it away a few minutes ago. Brand-new Chrysler."

"What's going on?" Brody asked. "This is a pretty big show for a car recovery."

The detective spat on the sidewalk. "This is a bad one. A gay guy lived here. From the looks of the place, he must have had big bucks. Somebody carved the shit out of him."

Lind's words were clear and hard.

"Aren't you gonna thank me for saving your life?"

Brook had one thought: He's got my telephone number! He knows where I live!

"I didn't have a chance, Ed. Waters tried to brain me."

Jenny looked in from the kitchen, saw Brook's startled expression and hurried into the front room.

"Yeah, sorry about that. Gary's really fucked up. First he shoots that poor sonofabitch for his car, then he kills another guy. He's a worse head case than I am. He and I decided to go our own ways."

Brook bit down on his hand and braced himself against the wall. He almost cried out.

"Ed, I want to help you. You don't have any reason to believe that, but I think I can make you feel better." Saying it, he realized he meant every word. "There are some things we . . ."

Lind's laughter was unlike anything Brook had ever heard—shrill, loud, a laugh from hell.

"I don't think so. No fucking way."

Brook forced himself to keep asking questions, to keep him talking. He didn't want him to hang up. "Can you tell me where you are? I'd like to come and talk to you. Just you and me, alone."

"Is somebody tapping your line?"

At first, Brook didn't understand what he meant.

"Is someone listening in to this? From all the questions you're asking, makes me think you're trying to keep me talking."

"I am trying to keep you talking. But I'm not recording this conversation if that's what you mean."

"If they're not listening, they will be," Lind said.

Holding the receiver tight to his ear, Brook made a decision. He gave Lind his beeper number.

"In case you're right, maybe it would be better not to call me here again," Brook said. "If you want to talk to me, use the beeper. I'll find a secure phone."

"You do whatever you want. It doesn't make any difference one way or another."

Lind still sounded amused. "You want my advice? Go find Waters. He likes to hurt people. That's why I figured we better split."

"Why was that, Ed? Tell me why you wanted to get away from Waters." He sensed a hint of guilt or uneasiness in Lind's voice, something he was trying to cover up.

The telephone went silent for a few moments. Brook heard Lind breathing. When he spoke again, his words were hard, metallic, dead.

"Maybe we'll talk later. Maybe I'll kill you. I'd like to kill you." His focused rage came through over the telephone. It terrified Brook.

Lind had something else to tell him.

Jenny was watching Brook's face. She put her hand on his shoulder when he hung up.

"He told me Waters killed a guy and they took his car. They ditched it in South County. Lind said we ought to go find it. He gave me an address."

Major Dunning approached Brody and stuck out his hand. He was about Brody's size but had gone soft in the middle. He wore a baggy Irish-tweed jacket and a gray hat with a narrow brim straight out of the 1950s. He also wore a pair of latex surgical gloves.

"What brings you here, Tom?" Dunning asked. "Last I heard, you were still with the feds."

Brody shook his head. "I saw the light a few years back. I'm working as a security consultant these days. We heard that you had a problem. We've got contracts with some companies over this way. I was in the area and thought maybe we could help out.''

Dunning looked at him a moment with unblinking eyes. Brody hoped he wouldn't press him with questions. He'd already stuck his neck out with a story that was purest bullshit. Another lie would be pushing his luck.

Dunning said, ''Thanks, Tom. Maybe down the road. We got a bad one here. Somebody who really likes to kill. You wanna look?''

Brody followed him into the foyer. The sudden transformation from factory to home was stunning. The foyer opened into a large, open living room with a vaulted ceiling and skylights. Next came an elegantly furnished dining room and the enclosed patio and swimming pool.

Beat cops, suits and technicians were gathered out by the pool. Cameras flashed. Everyone was wearing gloves.

Dunning got a pair from one of the techs and gave it to Brody.

''Better put these on. You're gonna see blood like you've never seen it before.'' He led Brody through the dining room, where china and crystal glittered under recessed lighting. ''Watch where you step.''

''Who owned all this?'' Brody asked, admiring the layout.

''A guy named Gregorio. A well-connected builder. Rich. About eight years ago we picked him up with some other homos in a rest room at Forest Park. He got a good lawyer and the charges were dropped. He had quite a setup here. Lots of parties. A real fairyland.''

Brody understood why everyone wore gloves.

''Is this a gay killing?'' He knew from experience that homosexuals liked to use knives, the murder weapon of choice in the gay community. They dug slasher attacks. The victim was usually tied up with ropes and tape like a stuffed pig.

''Worse,'' Dunning said.

They went out on the patio. It was roofed over and shielded from the street. African masks and other primitive artwork decorated the brick walls, which had been left exposed. Brody got a whiff of chlorine and sandalwood.

The pool ran the length of the patio. It was shaped like a phallus.

Cops stood in small groups, smoking and cracking nervous jokes. A bad sign. The techs—all in white coats—were working with tape measures and clipboards.

A guest apartment was at the far side of the patio.

"He's in there," Dunning said.

Brody saw the blood just inside the doorway. A couple of crime-scene boys were trying to get a footprint from one of the stains. The gore had soaked down into the carpet.

Brody followed Dunning into the apartment.

"Hold it here," Dunning said.

It would have been impossible to go any farther without stepping in blood. The beige carpeting was black with it. The furniture, walls and ceiling were splashed with blood. The place was a slaughterhouse.

A detective with plastic bags over his shoes came out of a bedroom.

"They're bringing him out," he said. "Everybody back. Give them some room."

Two men pushed a collapsible metal stretcher into the living room.

Without flinching, Brody looked at the naked body, or at what remained of it. The face had been carved off—mouth, nose, eyes, forehead. The facial features had disappeared into an oozing red hole. The killer had eviscerated the trunk, opening the chest cavity like a doctor performing an autopsy. The genitals were missing.

"We can't find the guy's pecker," Dunning said.

Brook waited until it was dark, then he and Jenny got into his car, drove down Skinker Boulevard and headed east, toward downtown St. Louis. They picked up Interstate 55 and turned south. The highway followed the Mississippi, and they could see the lights of towboats moving on the black water, pushing long tows of fuel and grain barges downstream.

Lind had told Brook that the car was parked near a country-and-western bar on Telegraph Road in South County. Before they'd left his apartment, Brook had checked the address on a map. The quickest route was to take I-55 south, to Telegraph. The bar was a few blocks from the highway exit ramp.

Jenny had insisted on going along. Brook had tried to talk her out of it. Waters was out there somewhere, and he'd made clear what he wanted to do to Jenny. Brook had been dead set against her coming, but there was no changing her mind.

"Why do you think he wants us to look at this car?" Jenny asked, trying to break the uneasy silence.

Brook said, "He laughed when he told me about it."

He tried to imagine what was happening inside Lind's head. They'd been aware all along that kindling might trigger violent outbursts like those associated with psychomotor seizures. Brook was worried that spontaneous, kindled seizures might grow in intensity or spread into other parts of Lind's brain and affect his entire temporal lobe.

He considered the risks: Lind could flip back and forth from extreme violence to moments of goodness, even religiosity. He could have blackouts, memory loss, strange otherworldly visions. He could become a Jekyll and Hyde. There was a good chance this was already happening.

The picture was even bleaker with Waters. Brook didn't want to think about that man's potential for killing. He'd been deadly *before* they'd kindled his brain. Now he'd become something even worse.

"We've got to take precautions, Jen."

Just forty-eight hours ago, he was trying to figure out what Hartigan was up to at the clinic. Now he was worried about whether one of their patients was going to kill him. The palms of his hands were sweaty.

At the Telegraph Road exit, he turned off the interstate and drove south on a wide, four-lane highway lined with fast-food restaurants, twenty-four-hour gas stations and strip malls. Cars and pickups jammed the parking lot for the country-and-western bar The Singing Cowboy. Brook had lived in St. Louis long enough to associate South County with rednecks, line dancing and long-neck beer.

Fortunately, the car they were looking for wasn't on the parking lot. Lind had given him precise directions. It was parked behind the building in an alley. A big Buick. Dark green.

Brook pulled behind the one-story bar and nightclub. The alley paralleled a quiet residential street that ended in a cul-de-sac.

"There it is," Brook said, stopping. Jenny slid out of the front seat before he could object.

It was dark, but the glow from the nearby parking lot made it bright enough to see. He also had a flashlight.

He took Jenny's hand and they walked to the car. The air was cold, but he was pouring sweat. The front door was slightly ajar. Brook hesitated. He had the strong sensation that someone was watching them. The hairs on his neck started to tingle.

He opened the driver's-side door. His flashlight showed dark stains all over the tan upholstery of the front seat. He knew what it was. So did Jenny.

A blue gym bag was on the floorboards of the rear seat. It was the bag Lind had carried during his escape.

The zipper wasn't fastened. Brook opened the bag and shined the light inside. It contained something like a coil of rope. It glistened in the light. Then he realized he was looking at someone's intestines. They were wrapped around a shriveled, pink sac: A penis and scrotum.

THIRTY-TWO
><

THE ENVELOPE ARRIVED AT the clinic three days later, addressed to Dr. Jenny Malone. The block letters were neatly printed and underlined in red pencil.

Jenny took the envelope off the stack of mail on her desk and opened it as she sipped her third cup of coffee that morning. She was downing way too much caffeine.

She almost dropped the cup when she saw the contents. Coffee splashed onto her desk.

The four black-and-white Polaroid photographs showed a woman gagged with a pair of nylon stockings and bound to a chair with duct tape. Her hands were tied behind her back. She had a nice figure, slender legs, and looked in her mid-twenties.

The photographs had been taken in sequence as someone methodically stripped her. Jenny knew why the photographer had used a Polaroid camera—no photo lab would have developed pictures like these without calling the police.

In the first photo the woman was shown fully dressed in a short, black skirt and long-sleeved white blouse; next with her panties and bra; then with just her panties. In the last she was naked except for a pair of high heels.

The clothing apparently had been cut off her. It lay in pieces at her feet.

The woman's hysterical, frightened eyes made Jenny want

to cry out. They were white and bulging out of their sockets. She was looking straight into the camera.

The last photo carried an inscription on the back. Printed in the same neat letters, it said: "I couldn't get the bitch to say cheese."

Waters.

Jenny didn't have the slightest doubt.

He'd already gotten a victim. So, it had started.

She called Brook to her office and showed him the photographs.

"She's probably already dead," Jenny said.

"We better let Hartigan see these."

Left unsaid between them was the decision they had reached about Lind.

Brook had been going over it virtually nonstop ever since Lind had called him. He was gambling that Lind would try to get in touch with him again and that he could talk him into a meeting.

Brook hadn't given up on the idea that he could help Lind. He kept thinking about the drug Al Silver reportedly was working on, the one Mark Ulman had mentioned to his wife.

Silver worked at PCZ Pharmaceuticals, the private lab in West County that had a contract with the clinic. A day earlier, Brook had called an old med-school friend, a genius in biochemistry who worked for a large drug company based in St. Louis.

His friend told him that the word on the street was that PCZ was heavy into research on peptides, the bond between adjacent amino acids. Brook had burned the midnight oil reading up on peptides. The substance served as a kind of naturally forming anticonvulsant. If Silver was working with peptides, it wasn't too much of a stretch to think that maybe he'd come up with a drug that could extinguish kindling.

Brook hoped he could find Lind and treat him with whatever compound Silver had developed; if that didn't work, he'd try one of the proven anticonvulsants, like carbamazepine or clonazepam.

Their first order of business was to find and treat Lind.

The next step would be to tell authorities about Hartigan's kindling experiments.

If Brody or the police got to Lind first, it would almost guarantee a slaughter. The trick would be finding Lind before they did. And Lind wasn't going to come in voluntarily, or easily.

Brook wasn't sure that Lind even wanted to be helped. In fact, just the opposite was likely. Lind had expressed it with blunt clarity when he told him: I'd like to kill you!

Even as he opened the door and let Jenny walk ahead of him into Hartigan's office, Brook got another bad shot of the jitters.

Hartigan took one look at the Polaroids and summoned Brody, who spread the photographs out on a small conference table and carefully examined the envelope.

"It's got a Sullivan postmark," Brody said. "That could mean he's still in the state." Sullivan, Missouri, was a small town on Interstate 44 about a hundred miles west of St. Louis.

"He's doing just what Robert Berdella and James Pace did," Jenny said. She explained that both serial killers routinely took photographs of their victims during torture and kept them in scrapbooks. The pictures gave them a sexual kick.

But Jenny guessed Waters was using them for a different reason. "He's trying to taunt us."

Waters may have tolerated kindling better than Lind, but his complaints about nervousness and headaches shortly before his escape were disturbing, indicating possible mood swings. Already deadly, he would become even more unstable.

Something in the pictures caught Brody's eye for detail. An elaborately carved crucifix hung on the wall, just visible to the left of the woman's head. That told him that Waters wasn't using a motel, which wouldn't decorate its rooms with religious articles. The furniture was also distinctive. The woman was tied to a chair that looked like an expensive antique.

"I'll get some blowups," Brody said. "You're sure this came from Waters?"

"No question," Jenny said. "It's his way of telling us he's going to start killing again. He's almost daring us to try to stop him."

"You think the woman's already dead?"

Jenny nodded. Serial killers usually kept their victims alive for days, weeks. Flies trapped in the spider's web. But on the run, Waters couldn't afford that luxury.

"What do you think he did with her body?"

"I don't know. Getting rid of one isn't as easy as you might think. If you dump it, you run the risk someone might see you. Berdella's solution was to cut the bodies into small pieces, which he put in plastic bags and set out at the curb for the trash pickup. Nobody ever caught on."

Brody asked her how long she thought it would be before he killed again.

"Hard to say. He's probably going through a period of depression. A serial offender will crash hard after he comes down from the high of killing someone. It might take weeks before the urge to do it again starts to build. Berdella lasted six to eight months. The only thing I can say for certain is that Waters is going to start trolling for another victim. And sooner, not later."

Brody leaned back in his chair. He'd shifted his eyes from the grisly photographs to Brook, who fought the urge to look away. He met Brody's gaze and held it.

"Have you been in touch with Lind?" The abrupt question was accompanied by a hard-assed frown.

Brook wasn't sure he could trust himself to answer.

"Why do you ask?" He worried that his voice would betray him.

"No reason. It's just that you spent some time with him. You two had a couple nice long talks. You even visited him the night before he escaped. One of my men left a note that you stopped by to make sure Lind was sleeping all right. I thought Lind might try to make contact with you the same way Waters sent these pictures to Doctor Malone." Pausing, he dropped the next shoe to see how Brook would react. "You better let us know if that happens."

Brook pounded the table. "Brody, I'm tired of your threats and insinuations. If you think I'm lying, put me on your fucking polygraph!"

The outburst startled Hartigan. It also momentarily surprised Brody, who continued glaring at Brook. He kept playing the eye-contact game. Neither man blinked or looked away.

Hartigan swung into his role as conciliator. After his recent glumness, he became friendly, almost warm.

Brook read the sudden change in personality as an act. It was a revealing moment. With a flash of intuition, he realized that Hartigan was playing a role. They all were. They were acting because they no longer trusted each other.

"I'm sure John would have told us if Lind or Waters had tried to contact him," Hartigan said to Brody. His words were soothing. "But I agree with you. We've got to be prepared for that."

He rose and showed Brook and Jenny to the door. The meeting was over. He put a hand on Jenny's shoulder.

"What would you like us to do to help?" Brook tried to sound as sincere as possible.

"This is a psychiatric clinic," Hartigan said. "You've got your patients. As soon as Mr. Brody finds our runaways, we'll get back on track."

Brody didn't get up from his chair.

"He's lying," Brody said.

"Tell me again what your man saw," Hartigan said.

Brody glanced at his notebook, flipping the pages. "He saw Doctor Malone and Doctor Brook get into a car at ten-thirty, Tuesday, three nights ago, and head south on Interstate 55. They appeared to be in a hurry. He kept them in sight until they pulled off at Telegraph Road. That's when he lost them. An old man in a beat-up hauling truck pulled out in front of him from a gas station. Damn near ran my man off the road. By the time he got around the bastard, Doctor

Brook was gone. I think I know where they went.''

Hartigan waited for more and wondered why Brody hadn't told him this earlier. He'd never trusted the man, never liked him. It was hard to accept that he'd become his closest ally.

"We got word today that the cops found the car of the gay who was sliced up like lunch meat. It was abandoned in an alley a half block off Telegraph Road. About the same area where we lost our two doctors.''

"That doesn't prove anything,'' Hartigan said.

"No, but it's a coincidence, wouldn't you say? I mean, out of the blue they leave the West End and drive all the way out to South County, and we lose them right about where the dead guy's car is found.''

"The police are sure it's the right car?''

Brody laughed with something almost resembling real mirth. "Yeah, Bob. It's the right car. The guy's penis was inside.''

Hartigan didn't respond. He looked as if he hadn't even heard Brody, that his mind was miles away.

The moment passed. Then he asked, "What do we do if he's been talking to Lind?''

"We'll keep him under surveillance,'' Brody said. "I'm going to put a tap on his telephone. Nothing elaborate. We'll use an exterior bug. If there's more contact, eventually we'll get him.''

"Is that necessary?'' Hartigan didn't like the idea of a tap.

Brody nodded. He gave Hartigan a patient look. "It's necessary.''

Brody mentioned that he was following some other leads that involved the gay builder. "During the escape, Waters told Lind he knew where they could get a car and money. He must have known this guy. We're working hard on that.''

THIRTY-THREE

LIND LOOKED UP THE address in a telephone book in an all-night convenience store. There was the name, Les Winkler. He had a house on Iron Street in Lemay, a blue-collar neighborhood of small tract houses built in the fifties. Pickups and bass boats jammed the driveways.

Not long after he and Waters had split up, he stole a car, an unlocked Olds Cutlass he found in the parking lot of a strip mall in South County.

It surprised him how quickly his old skills returned. He popped the cowling on the steering wheel, jimmied a few wires and *presto*: Ignition! He pulled onto Lindbergh Boulevard and headed north on Interstate 55. The engine missed badly. It needed a new set of plugs.

Lind didn't care. He wouldn't need it long.

He found Winkler's house within thirty minutes. He couldn't read the addresses and had to keep stopping to get out and look. The house was white with red shutters, just as Nancy had described it in the one letter she'd written to him in prison.

He parked down the block and waited. He figured that a guy like Winkler would have a gun in there, probably three or four. He took the Smith & Wesson .357 magnum out of his belt and slipped it under the front seat. He wasn't going to bring a pistol. He didn't want to risk firing it, for fear someone would hear the shot. The walls in these chickenshit houses were paper thin.

Lind had a Buck knife he'd found in the queer's home. The five-inch blade was beautifully honed. The queer had quite a knife collection, which was too bad for him considering what happened.

Waters had had a lot of fun with those knives. He'd tied the fag down to a table, cut off his shirt and stuffed a napkin in his mouth. The guy was still very much alive at that point. He'd shitted himself.

Lind had walked out of the room before things really got rolling. Going there had been Waters's idea. He knew the address and had promised the fag was loaded, which he was. Lind had left the place with a couple hundred bucks in his pockets, plus the knife. They drove the guy's car into the county and ditched it. He had no plans to lay eyes on Waters again.

He looked at his watch. It was nine fifty-five P.M. He'd wait until ten o'clock.

A headache was torquing up as he sat there, staring at the house with the big van parked under the car port.

He could stand the headaches.

The face was another matter. A black face from a black hole in his brain. The thing—it was more of a shape or silhouette—had made its first appearance when they were messing with his head at the clinic.

He'd finally figured out what it was: his personal monster. Maybe his personal devil. They'd become good friends.

The monster was sitting with him in the front seat, telling him what to do. As long as he didn't see a flash of light or feel its strange warmth, they'd be fine.

The monster couldn't stand the light.

When it screamed, he screamed.

The strange smell always came first. The overpowering scent of cut flowers, roses. Almost at the same moment—he still hadn't figured out the timing—the light would pour over him and he'd wack out and feel the presence of something otherworldly. Maybe God.

Lind didn't want that to happen. He didn't want to worry about remorse or pity, which were entirely new feelings to him. He didn't want to change his mind. Not until he'd finished with Les Winkler and made his other paybacks.

He looked at the van. It had a custom paint job. Winkler made good money selling auto parts for a used-car dealer. He could afford a few luxuries.

Lind had been in prison when Winkler married Nancy, his former wife. She'd moved in with their six-year-old daughter Amy. Lind had never met the child. He was behind bars when she was born. Every year or so Nancy sent him a photograph. A cute kid, big almond-shaped blue eyes and curly black hair.

At first he thought Winkler would be a good deal for Nancy. A solid guy with his steady job and paycheck. For the first couple years, maybe it worked. Then a friend wrote him that Nancy had left Winkler. The auto parts man turned out to be a wife beater.

He'd worked her over good one night and she'd finally gotten frightened enough to leave. She climbed out the bedroom window with Amy while Winkler was watching the tube.

A few days later Nancy called Lind in prison. She'd never done that before. She was crying. She told him that she suspected Winkler had abused their daughter sexually. He told her to see a doctor and call the cops. The doctors thought the girl probably had been molested, but couldn't prove it. A cop from juvenile checked Winkler out, but nothing came of that either.

That had been two years ago. Amy was eleven years old and seeing a psychiatrist.

The lights were on in Winkler's front room. The flickering television glowed blue in the window. Lind looked at his watch. Winkler was probably watching the ten o'clock news.

He got out of the car and took the empty pizza box from the back seat. He'd found it in a Dumpster.

He went to the front door and knocked. He stood under the yellow porchlight, holding the pizza box.

Winkler peered out a small window in the door. It opened a crack.

"I've got your pizza."

"I didn't order . . ."

Lind grabbed him by the throat, pushed him back into the house and slammed the door. It took only seconds.

Winkler was a heavyset man with a small head and black hair that he combed straight back and wore in a short ponytail. Beefy and tall. Big Boy. The kind who enjoyed throwing his weight around. A mean-looking wife beater and child molester.

Winkler wore jeans and a Western shirt stained with ketchup. Lind squeezed the throat so hard he could feel the neck bone.

"Are you alone?" He loosened his grip.

The small head nodded up and down. Eyes bulged. The voice croaked.

The monster said: Hurt him.

Lind kneed him in the balls. Winkler went down with a howl.

The monster said: Break the fuck's nose.

Lind gave Winkler a hard shot to the face and heard cartilage snap like a dry twig. The nose flattened like a wad of putty.

He took out the Buck knife and shoved the blade into Winkler's left nostril. He flicked his wrist and slit the nose wide open. Blood splattered.

Winkler was blubbering.

He picked Winkler up by his head, twisted his left arm around his back and got him up on his toes. He led him down a hallway to the bathroom. A striped bass was mounted over the bathroom door. Nice touch.

He pushed Winkler into the bathroom, trying not to step in the blood that was pouring on the floor.

Lind kicked him in the ass toward the bathtub.

"Get in!"

Winkler was so big he looked like he was squatting in a

barrel with his legs pulled up against his chest. Blood spread out on the bottom of the tub.

Lind closed the drain and turned on the water.

He let the tub fill up to the top. The water sloshed over onto the floor.

Winkler was crying, begging. He offered money. He offered his rifle collection. He offered his bass boat.

Lind grabbed Winkler's ponytail and drove his head under the bloody water and held him there. The man flailed his arms. Bubbles rose. His face started to turn blue.

Lind yanked the head out, let him fill his lungs, pushed him back under.

Winkler didn't put up much of a struggle. It was surprising how little he fought to stay alive. On the fourth or fifth dunking, the bubbles got bigger. The neck and face turned a darker shade of blue. Winkler went limp.

Lind left him lying in the water.

THIRTY-FOUR

He took the signed Andy Warhol print down from the living room wall—the lurid Marilyn Monroe with platinum hair and luminescent lips. Elizabeth had bought it in New York twenty years earlier for an obscene amount of money.

He'd always hated it. He hated Warhol, an albino geek.

He smashed the glass frame to bits on the edge of the coffee table, tore the print to shreds and jammed the wadded pieces into the trash can in the kitchen.

With Marilyn gone, he studied the light-gray wall, an expanse of open space about ten feet long and ten feet high. For what he had in mind, it would serve perfectly.

He'd bought four gallons of premium-grade paint from a hardware store in Crestwood. Yellow, blue, red and green. He opened the cans with a screwdriver and sat on the thick pile carpet and stared at the wall until he had the dimensions right in his mind. He didn't bother with drop cloths.

Dipping a brush into the red paint, he outlined a human head on the wall. He painted it big, about seven feet high. He used blue and yellow paint to draw the various parts of the brain—cortex, cerebellum, brainstem, frontal lobe, temporal lobe. He used green to shade in Broca's area.

When he finished, he stood back to admire his handiwork. Something wasn't quite right. He painted a long red line from the brain to the far end of the wall, then continued the line

201

to a wall in the bedroom, where he painted a crude microscope.

He laughed out loud. The microscope represented Science.

In his more giddy moments, and this was one of them, he still believed that science would lead to an understanding of the brain, and, ultimately, of the mind. He'd long since discarded most of his other beliefs.

He painted a date on the wall next to the microscope: Dec. 24, 1994. Christmas Eve.

An important moment in his life. At eight-twenty that morning—for reasons that continued to torment his days and nights—he'd swallowed a foul-tasting concoction of amino acids. He diluted the enzyme solution in a cherry-flavored soft drink and drank six ounces from a paper cup. Within a day his serotonin levels plunged, which was exactly what he'd expected. What he hadn't expected was his complete inability to ever get them back to anything approaching normal.

A twenty-four-hour urine sample showed the damage. As had every subsequent sample.

He'd splattered the carpet with paint drippings and ruined a pin-striped Hermès shirt that had cost nearly three hundred dollars. A gift from his wife.

He sat down and continued to stare at the brain. He popped a Red Dog and followed it with a chaser of Old Overholt, swigging straight from the bottle. The alcohol would hit him like a wrecking ball, but not for a few minutes.

Somehow he'd knocked his brain's delicate neurochemistry permanently out of balance. He looked at his watch. It was just after six o'clock. Almost time for another clozapine injection. He took 20 cc in four injections daily to try to regulate his fouled-up serotonin levels. Serotonin was one of the key neuroreceptors in the brain linked to aggression; the lower the serotonin, the more aggressive the behavior.

He had inflicted himself with the very brain deficiencies that marked violent antisocials, who often had chronically low serotonin levels. He used to laugh at the irony, sometimes scream. His particular deficiency didn't lead to violent outbursts aimed at others. Fortunately, it was turned inward. As Freud liked to say, violence directed outward was aggression. Directed inward, it was depression, or craziness.

He'd really fucked himself up. No question about it.

Fucked up serotonin receptors, fucked up neurons, fucked up chances of survival.

He'd been taking clozapine for two months, hoping the drug would push his serotonin back within the normal range. Without much luck so far. Buspirone and Prozac had worked well for a while, nearly a year. But then something had gone wrong.

His latest blood tests indicated the clozapine wasn't doing much better.

He took another sip of the Red Dog and rye. His painting was pretty good. A great brain. Outstanding symmetry. Broca would have loved it.

It had been a rare good day. After much thought, he'd finally resolved how to get the right information to Dr. Brook. He'd simply mailed a letter to him at the clinic. The downside was that he wouldn't be around to watch him open and read it. He'd love to see how he'd react, but he could guess.

He had originally planned to tell Brook the whole story, at least as much of it as he knew or had been able to deduce. Then he dropped the idea. No sense making it too easy on the boy. It would be more rewarding to let him work for the answers himself.

Mark Ulman had gotten this far on his own; he'd almost found out about their kindling experiments, and in a few more weeks or months he would have figured out the rest of it. That's why he had him killed. Ulman had become a threat to their work. No, correct that. A threat to *his* work.

In one of those wonderful flipflops so common to science, he was going to help Dr. Brook put it all together. He'd feed him bits and pieces of the story along the way. But it would be Brook's job to draw his own conclusions.

Brook was bright and tough. He liked him. But, more important, Hartigan might find the young man dangerous, which was just what he hoped.

He'd taken delicious pleasure in observing the clinic director of late. The pompous bastard looked thoroughly deflated.

If he hadn't been so heavily medicated, he would have found the last four days exhilarating. Even juiced up on clozapine, he'd been able to take a polygraph and submit to a long interview with two of Brody's brutish lieutenants. Most of his colleagues had already submitted. For appearances' sake, he had protested long and loud.

He'd found it strange that a doctor of Hartigan's experience and talent would put any credence whatsoever in polygraph tests, knowing, as he surely did, how easy it was to cheat. He'd answered all the questions, lying when necessary, fully aware that the machine wouldn't detect any of his lies.

If they really wanted to find out the truth, a phenobarbital injection would have done the trick nicely.

As he felt the alcohol kick in, he wondered what Lind and Waters were up to. How many people had they killed? He'd watched Waters the night of the escape. Not long, twenty seconds at most. The man needed to kill like others needed to breathe.

Another moment of artistic inspiration hit. He'd paint Waters's chemically reconfigured brain.

He picked up the gallon of red paint, tripped and stumbled. The heavy bucket tipped over. The paint pooled on the carpet. His alcohol receptors were hot on the re-uptake. He dipped his hands into the bucket up to the wrists.

Late the next evening, Brook finally got around to opening his stack of mail. An unmarked white envelope contained a single sheet of paper with eight names. Each name was numbered, one through eight. Numbers five through eight were LePonty, Edward Lind, Gary Waters and James Billings. Brook didn't recognize the first four names.

Brook was afraid to mention the list on the telephone—

assuming at all times that someone was listening—so he drove over to Jenny's apartment and showed it to her. She didn't recognize the names either.

"Who do you think sent you this?" she asked.

Brook had been thinking about that ever since he'd opened the envelope.

"It's got to be someone on staff, but I don't have a clue who." Another big question he wanted answered: Did this person, whoever the hell it was, know he was wise to the kindling experiments?

Brook was pretty sure what the list meant. He had a friend who worked at the state's psychiatric forensic unit in Fulton, Missouri. Roger could pull the records for him. Brook had gotten to know him when he was doing competency hearings for the state hospital.

Early the next morning, Brook drove to the Pike University med school library on Euclid Avenue. He didn't want to use an office telephone or call Roger from his apartment.

He parked on the street. It was raining. As usual, he couldn't tell if anyone had followed him.

It was just after eight, but every seat in the library was already occupied by a grim-faced med student. He walked around, browsing the books and periodicals until he was sure no one was watching him. He made his call from the faculty lounge.

He got Roger on the first try. After a few minutes of shooting the breeze, Brook casually asked him if he could check the status of four men he believed were inmates in the state system.

"You got their IDs?"

"No such luck."

"No problem," Roger said. "We can do it with the names. It'll just take a little longer."

Five minutes later he was back on the line.

"I hope you weren't planning on treating those boys," Roger said.

"Why's that?" Brook asked.

"They're all dead."

THIRTY-FIVE

BRODY REFUSED TO BELIEVE that Waters had found and killed the builder Michael Gregorio by chance, especially on the same day he'd escaped from the clinic. He'd had his men start a detailed check on Gregorio's background. He even asked a return favor from a Missouri highway patrol captain he'd helped once with federal wiretap information. The captain promised to get him Gregorio's telephone records.

Brody also attended to another urgent piece of business that he hadn't looked forward to. He called Beckworth at the prison on a secure line and took an ass-chewing for the fuckup with Waters and Lind.

Beckworth never raised his voice but made it clear that Brody better track the two down. Brody took it for a solid ten minutes. He offered no excuses.

Brody asked Beckworth for Waters's and Lind's prison records. He also wanted a list of every visitor the men had had over the last three years.

He sent Eliot to Jefferson City to get the files. By six o'clock that evening, he had the records spread out on a table in his office. In the last sixteen months Waters had had only one visitor, but he'd come frequently: A prison chaplain named Brother Timothy Watkins of the order of the Brothers of the Most Precious Heart, OMC.

Brother Timothy had taken what appeared to be an unusually deep interest in Waters. Eleven visits in six months was heavy traffic, even for a chaplain. His last visit was two weeks before Waters was transferred to the clinic.

The records showed that Brother Timothy lived near Viburnum, a hamlet one hundred twenty miles southwest of St. Louis. Brody remembered the Sullivan postmark on the envelope Waters had sent to Jenny Malone; Sullivan was about thirty miles from Viburnum.

Brother Timothy didn't have an address or listed telephone number in Viburnum. Thanks to his friend with the highway patrol, Brody got the unlisted number. He called and got a recording—a warm, friendly, male voice. No one answered.

Brody and Eliot were on their way to Viburnum by seven that evening. The weather was good for a change. Cold and clear. They made the drive in just over three hours, most of it on twisting two-lane country roads that could be deadly if you took your eye off the blacktop for even a moment.

Viburnum was on the western edge of Missouri's Ozark leadbelt. Most of the mines had long since shut down, and the town was a weather-beaten assortment of closed stores and clapboard homes that needed paint.

They asked about Brother Timothy at the town's one operating gas station. The pump jockey told them to find the parson. The parson knew everybody.

The parson's house was just down the street. The old cracker who met them at the door had watery blue eyes and was about seventy. His thick hair was still black. The parson explained that he was head of the town's revivalist church. He was also chief of the volunteer fire department, acting deputy and county mailman.

He smiled when Brody flashed his well-used U.S. marshal's badge and asked about Brother Timothy.

"I wondered when someone would come around askin' about Brother Tim," he said with a crinkly grin.

"Why's that?" Eliot asked.

"He runs some kind of retreat house, at least that's what he calls it," the parson said. "It's up near Taum Salk Mountain, in the middle of nowhere. A nice place, too. Somebody spent a ton of money building it. But it all seems kinda strange.''

Brody took the bait. ''Why's that?''

''The only people who ever go there are single men. Mainly young men.''

He winked at Brody.

''You think Brother Tim's light in the sandals?'' Eliot asked.

''I don't rightly know, but he sure do like to visit with men. He'd bring 'em into town sometimes for dinner at Ruby's Chicken Wing. Out here in the country, folks notice that kind of thing.''

Brody and Eliot thanked the parson, who gave them precise directions to Brother Timothy's. They reached the turnoff on Rural Route B twenty-five minutes later. They almost blew right by the road marker the mayor had told them to look for—a mailbox with a white cross painted on the side.

A gravel road wound up through the trees at a steep grade. Eliot slipped the Jeep Cherokee into four-wheel-drive and started climbing. Brody told him to cut his lights. He wanted this to be an unannounced visit.

They pulled into a wide clearing in the trees a quarter mile later. They were on the crest of a hill. The moon lit up a spacious two-story home that looked like a ski lodge. It had a peaked, Swiss-style roof, skylights and large picture windows that must have offered a superb view of the surrounding countryside.

A green BMW and a white Volvo sedan were parked in front. Brother Tim had a taste for expensive cars.

''I'll go in the front,'' Brody told Eliot. ''You go around back.'' Since the cars were there, Brother Timothy was probably at home, but it was too quiet. Brody figured that on a cold night like this, he'd have a fire going. He couldn't smell any woodsmoke.

He climbed the flight of wooden steps, drawing his Glock-17 from the shoulder holster under his jacket. The Austrian-made automatic held seventeen rounds of 9-mm parabellum ammunition.

He knocked on the door. No answer.

He knocked again, harder, but with the same result. Then a light blinked on. The door opened.

Eliot.

Brody exhaled and lowered his pistol.

"The back door was unlocked," Eliot said. "There's another place out there. A small cabin of some sort, maybe a guesthouse. It looks empty."

"Let's check this first, then we'll do the cabin."

Brody felt his heart beat and stop, beat and stop, beat and stop. Walk-ups were the screaming worst. He'd seen a partner catch it that way, serving a writ. A guy popped out on a dark landing and shot him through the forehead.

But this wasn't a walk-up. He had a dose of the big-time shakes and couldn't explain it.

The ground-floor level was airy and spacious. A large living room, galley kitchen and a dining room that faced a wall of windows. The furniture, all Danish modern, looked expensive. A staircase led up to the second floor.

Brody went first, followed by Eliot. Both had their guns drawn. Brody wished he had his .12-gauge Ruger. He'd left it in St. Louis.

He found a switch and turned on the hallway lights. Four doors. Probably bedrooms. A bathroom was at the end of the hall. Moonlight poured through a skylight in a silver pool on the hallway floor.

Brody signaled for Eliot to check the rooms while he covered. The first two were empty.

Eliot reached inside the third and flipped on the light. He stepped back into the hallway.

"What is it?" Brody asked.

Eliot didn't answer. He was leaning against the wall.

"What the hell is it?"

Brody pushed around him. He stepped into the doorway and froze. It took an act of will to keep from throwing up. He squeezed down hard on his bladder.

It was the woman whose picture he'd seen at the clinic. He recognized her immediately. She was tied to the same chair. She was naked except for a pair of red high heels. Her throat had been cut, a gaping wound. And that was only the beginning.

She was sliced open from neck to crotch—a long, straight, deep cut that had almost split her in two.

A knife with a tapered, twelve-inch blade was stuck into the floor between her legs. Brody was sure the killer had left it there on purpose. It was a kitchen knife with a stainless-steel blade and a black handle.

When Eliot got his voice back, he said, "I hope she was dead before he did that."

The carpeted floor was soaked with blood. Brody noticed the splattered blood pattern on the walls and ceiling. He took out a pocket camera, a Minolta with a 35-mm lens, and snapped some pictures.

A crucifix on the wall caught his attention. Elaborately carved and nearly two feet high, it was the one in the Polaroid.

Flecks of blood had landed to the right of Jesus' head.

Brody wondered how long he'd kept her alive after taking the photographs. When had he gone to work on her? How had he done it?

The intricate cuttings on her breasts looked like scrollwork. The bastard had drawn the curlicue pattern with a blue felt-tip pen and then traced the lines with a knife, making shallow cuts. Blood had obscured the design.

"Let's check that cabin out back," Brody said. He wanted to get out of this place. He needed to breathe cold air. His shirt was soaked through. Little chest palpitations almost cut his breath off. He wanted to find Waters and kill him.

They went downstairs and out through the rear. A brick walkway led to the cabin. Like the main house, it was built to resemble a mountain chalet.

Brody tried the front door, which opened at his touch.

He had a good idea what to expect even before he turned on the light and saw the dead man. Like the woman next door, he was naked; he sat in the middle of a large room with his hands tied to the back of a wooden chair.

He looked about fifty years old. Thin with a paunch. He was balding and had short, gray hair. The face was tanned, as was the rest of the body. He liked to sunbathe in the nude.

Coming closer, Brody saw that the hands weren't tied at all. They were nailed to the chair's wooden back. The feet were nailed to the floor. The killer had tied a rope around Brother Timothy's neck and twisted it from behind with a stick. He'd been slowly strangled.

The face was contorted. The last scream frozen.

A towel lay nearby. Brody placed it over the dead man's head.

They searched the cabin, then returned to the main house. Brody remembered seeing an open address book next to the telephone. Under the *G*s, he found the name, telephone number and address of Michael Gregorio, the gay builder who'd been slaughtered in St. Louis four days earlier.

Taking the address book with him, Brody turned off the lights. On the way out, he stopped in the kitchen. He found a bottle of Jack Daniel's in a cupboard. He'd already taken his first long drink before Eliot started the engine.

THIRTY-SIX

LIONEL FRANK, DOB, 8-12-67. Died January 3, 1990; COD, stabbing puncture wound inflicted while in prison.

William Kisker, DOB, 1-15-56. Died July 12, 1990; COD, coronary embolism.

Marcel Washington, DOB, 5-4-62. Died September 8, 1991; COD, coronary embolism.

Thomas Pettit, DOB, 10-10-68. Died October 21, 1991; COD, lung cancer.

All four had died within less than twenty months of one another. The time frame was suspiciously compact. It was also highly suspect to have two young men in the same population segment die of something as exotic as a coronary embolism. The odds of that happening were pretty remote.

Barely a week had passed since Lind and Waters's escape, but it seemed like a month. As Brook drove to his apartment, he wondered for the hundredth time who had sent him that list. And, more important, were those four dead men somehow linked to the kindling experiments performed on LePonty, Lind, Waters and Billings? Or were they involved in another experiment, one he didn't know about?

Brook had already told Jenny about the four names. He'd slipped her a note. Glancing at it in the hallway, she'd closed her eyes. It had rocked her as much as it had him. Even more.

The possibility that Hartigan may have been involved in other medical experiments that left four men dead was as troubling as Lind and Waters's escape. And that was saying something, because the thought of those two on the streets scared him sick.

He and Jenny had to be at the top of their hit list.

If their brains were spontaneously seizing as a result of kindling—or, even worse, if the seizures had spread to both brain hemispheres—they were going through the tortures of the damned. A hellish mixture of emotional responses could be stirring in their cerebrums—everything from blackouts and depression to murderous rages. Brook figured that Lind and Waters were often in psychic and physical pain. The effect on their thresholds for fear, anger and other moods—all by-products of the limbic system—were staggering.

All of these facts continued to assail Brook as he wearily climbed the steps to his apartment. It was nearly seven P.M. Jenny was coming over a little later. They needed to talk. Brook took a shower, changed into jeans and a loose-fitting sweatshirt and drank a bottle of Rolling Rock.

On impulse, he went into the bedroom and took the quilted guncase from the back corner of the closet. He unzipped it and picked up his father's Winchester shotgun. It was the old model 1001, a .12-gauge pump. His father had bought it for $120 shortly after he got out of the Army. He'd given it to Brook on his fourteenth birthday.

A side pouch in the case held a .44-caliber Colt revolver, another gift from his father.

They'd spent a lot of cold fall mornings hunting ducks along the Nolachukee River near Bryson City, Tennessee. Thanks to his dad, Brook knew how to handle a shotgun. He was a good, instinctive shot.

He sighted down the barrel, the walnut stock snug against his right cheek and shoulder.

He had the weapon out when Jenny arrived. He left the Winchester on the sofa in the front room and went down the stairwell to let her in. She set her briefcase on the landing and took a deep breath.

"I know," Brook said. He took her in his arms and held her tightly. At first her hands stayed at her sides, but then Jenny returned his embrace, hugging him around the chest. He raised her chin and kissed her. She pressed close against him.

Brook helped Jenny off with her coat and followed her upstairs. She wore a navy-blue dress that showed off her figure. Worried that his apartment was bugged, Brook cranked up the volume on his CD player. Jenny understood—they would talk in whispers.

She saw the shotgun on the sofa and looked at him in surprise.

Brook tried to smile.

"I did some shooting when I was younger."

Her eyes started to glisten. He could see her fear.

"It was my father's, Jen."

So why do you have it out, her eyes asked him.

"Two men who've got a hell of a good reason to hurt us are on the loose. I'm pretty sure that Brody has some of his goons following me, and it looks like Hartigan was kindling Waters and Lind and may have been doing some other experiments on prisoners. It all starts to add up, Jen."

"And that gun helps?"

"A little, yes." For some instinctive reason that he couldn't explain, the Winchester did comfort him.

They were in real danger. That was the new reality. No matter how much he tried to explain it away or tell himself that he was overreacting, his mind kept returning to that unavoidable fact.

Jenny sat down on the sofa. Brook stood the shotgun in a corner.

"Don't you just want to get in the car and drive away from here?" she asked.

"All the time."

"We could go out West."

"I'd love to see Santa Fe and the Grand Canyon." He'd never been any farther west than St. Louis.

"Let's go."

Brook took Jenny's hands. "You're serious, aren't you?"

"We turn in our resignations and leave," she said. "We don't even give them notice."

Brook tightened his grasp on Jenny's hands. He hadn't wanted to mention this. It loomed behind all his other worries.

"What if they won't let us resign?"

"What do you mean?" She sensed Brook's anxiety, felt it touch her like a shot of electrical current.

"They may have found out that we know about the kindling experiments."

He was right. They did know too much, Jenny admitted. She hadn't considered that.

She sat perfectly still. The furnace in the basement suddenly kicked in. The blasting music made her head throb. She was aware of other sounds in the flat. She couldn't focus on Brook's conclusion.

"I've been thinking about it for days," he said. "Too much is happening. We're not in control, and that worries me a lot."

"Then what do we do?" she asked, swallowing hard.

"Maybe we hang in a while longer and hope that Brody and his people find Waters and Lind, or that Lind calls me again. But you're right. We better start thinking about getting out."

Jenny made a decision. With Brook still holding her hands, she stood up and quietly kissed him on the lips. "I'm not hungry." He'd promised dinner.

"Neither am I," Brook said, reading her eyes. He put his hands around her waist and pulled her against him. She melted into his body, and then they were kissing each other hungrily, hands touching, exploring, fumbling for buttons and zippers.

Brook lifted her up and she clung to his neck as he carried her toward the bedroom.

"Let's take our time and not worry about this mess we're in," she said.

"Who's worried," he said, managing a smile.

When he laid her down, she was already out of her dress.

She trembled at Brook's touch. She closed her eyes as he lay next to her and kissed her breasts.

This moment was all that mattered. She was going to make love with him. She wasn't afraid.

THIRTY-SEVEN

ON THE NIGHTSTAND, THE beeper went off—the sound shrill and abrasive. Brook rubbed sleep from his eyes and stared at the digital display. He didn't recognize the number.

"Who is it?" Jenny asked. She'd rolled over in the bed and was facing him.

"I don't know," Brook said.

He'd given Lind his number and told him to dial it twice in succession if he ever wanted to reach him. That way he'd know who it was.

He doubted Lind would ever do that, but he still found himself waiting, hoping.

Twenty-five seconds later, the beeper went off again.

It was just after six o'clock. A heavy, cold rain was falling.

"I guess it wouldn't do any good for me to ask to come along, would it?" Jenny said, speaking in a whisper.

"Maybe next time. I think I'd better go alone on this one." Brook had already slipped into his clothes. He bent down and kissed her on the cheek, then walked out to his car. He tried not to rush, in case anyone was watching. He drove over to the Pike University med-school library to return the call.

He parked at a meter in front of the building and looked up and down Euclid Avenue. The early-morning traffic was heavy. He couldn't tell whether anyone had followed him.

He found a telephone booth on a second-floor mezzanine and dialed the number. Someone picked up the receiver on the third ring.

"I killed a guy a couple nights ago."

Ice water in the face couldn't have hit Brook harder.

"Where are you?"

Ignoring the question, Lind said the dead man was an old friend of the family's.

"I want to see you, Ed."

He didn't know what else to say.

"I didn't even remember how I snuffed him until the next morning," Lind continued. "It's like you wake up from a dream and suddenly remember every detail. Only it wasn't a dream."

"How are you feeling?"

"You did this to me. You and those other bastards in the white coats."

Brook bit down on the back of his hand. "Are you having any seizures?"

"I see a face that doesn't have any eyes or mouth and tells me to kill people. Does that mean I'm having a seizure?" Lind laughed and choked and kept laughing. His voice was taunting, sarcastic.

He was hallucinating. There must be limbic involvement.

The line went dead. Lind had hung up again.

Hartigan sat at his power desk staring at Brody with tired eyes. He straightened a trouser crease and waited impatiently for him to begin.

Brody skimmed over a two-paragraph report. "About six-thirty this morning Doctor Brook leaves his flat and drives to the library at the Pike University medical school. One of my men, who's dressed like a med student, follows him inside. He makes a telephone call that lasts forty-seven seconds. When he hangs up, our boy looks plenty upset."

"Why would he drive all the way over there to make a telephone call?"

"Good question."

"You think he was talking to Lind?"

"That's a reasonable guess. Another is that he figures we might be listening to his calls."

Which they were. They'd already bugged his flat. It was easily done. A man dressed like a Southwestern Bell repairman had spliced into the telephone line and installed a small receiver and transmitter behind the guttering. The receiver picked up the conversations, and the transmitter sent them two miles to an antenna on the roof of the clinic. The bug was risky, but it would take a pro to spot the wiring job and they didn't plan to use it long.

Brody was convinced that Brook was their best bet for tracking down Lind. Brook had befriended him. If the prisoner was going to call anyone, it would be Brook. Brody doubted that Lind had left St. Louis. He was relying on intuition and nearly twenty years' experience chasing assorted shitbums.

With the exception of a long prison stretch, Lind had spent most of his adult life in St. Louis. His parents were dead. He still had a few relatives here, an uncle and a cousin, both of whom were being closely watched. It was familiar ground. He knew how to get around, where to go for help, how to disappear.

Brody was leading up to the next item of discussion.

Beckworth had called him first thing that morning. The warden had learned that a man in prison records named Roger Helms had looked up the files on four dead inmates. Beckworth had been electronically monitoring those names and had noticed that someone had accessed the files by computer. He checked the log-on and tracked down Helms.

"Turns out, Roger pulled the records as a favor for Doctor Brook."

Brody took out a slip of paper and read the names.

"Any of those sound familiar?"

Hartigan sat in his chair. The room slipped in and out of focus. It bothered him that Beckworth had spoken to Brody without mentioning it to him first.

Brody let him squirm. He enjoyed this part of it. "Beckworth told me about your secret project. He didn't go into the details, but I got the general drift. You had some, ah, problems.''

Hartigan buttoned his jacket. He was freezing and yet sweat was running down his sides. He wondered if he was coming down with something, or if he was just badly frightened.

''I don't give a shit about whatever it was you were doing up at the pen,'' Brody went on. ''I *do* give a shit about whether you have any idea how Doctor Brook found out about those four men.''

''It has to be the same person who let Waters and Lind go.''

''Good boy. But who? Who knew about your work with those other prisoners? Is it a long or a short list?'' Brody's anger slipped out. It still infuriated him that he'd only just found out about all this.

''No one knows,'' Hartigan said.

But what if you're wrong? Hartigan thought. *What if someone has found out?*

He didn't think that was possible. Beckworth and Paulus were the only others who knew about the protocol and the results. They'd approved the ''final solution.'' He still blanched at those words with their suggestion of the Holocaust.

He began to catalog his staff and their access to information.

Brody interrupted him.

''Beckworth thinks we ought to make preliminary preparations to take care of Doctor Brook.''

The words hit Hartigan like a slam in the head.

''What do you mean?''

Brody didn't blink. Their eyes met.

''He's worried our boy may be on to the kindling experiments, which means he's a big liability.'' He didn't mention that Beckworth had already made him a cash offer. Fifty thousand dollars if the job had to be done. He had agreed to it.

"Good god. It's much too early to consider anything like that." He needed to talk to Beckworth himself . . . as soon as possible. "If anybody should be . . ." He didn't use the word. ". . . it's the person who set Lind and Waters loose."

"My sentiments exactly," Brody said. "But what if that person is Doctor Brook?"

"Impossible! Waters almost killed him. And how would you explain LePonty's escape? John Brook wasn't even on staff then."

Hartigan was jolted out of his listlessness. The heavy, unreal feeling he hadn't been able to shake for days.

Brody said, "I admit we've got some unanswered questions, but you can see how Beckworth and Paulus are looking at all this. If Brook and the girl do know about your experiments, they might decide to tell someone else, and then we've really got a problem. You, me, your wonderful clinic. You get the point."

"I'll talk to them both this afternoon," Hartigan said angrily. "We have no proof. Just some crazy, unfounded suspicions." He felt the floor lurch under him as he spoke. "I don't want to hear any more talk about preliminary preparations."

He wasn't ready yet to believe that might have to change.

Brody didn't tell him that they were already past the preliminary stage.

THIRTY-EIGHT

HE HAD GONE BACK out to his wife's grave in Calvary Cemetery on a raw day, but was having trouble thinking about Elizabeth. He hated himself for that. As he knelt at the foot of her grave, bare-headed in the wind that howled off the Mississippi, he was certain that she'd understand. He had much on his mind.

Maybe it would be easier to kill Hartigan and have done with it. Before the latest security crackdown, he'd smuggled several handguns into the building.

It wouldn't be difficult. Hartigan was always there late. He'd pay a visit to his office, put the gun to his head and squeeze the trigger. Then another bullet and it would all be over.

He dusted the powdery snow from his trousers and trudged back to his car. The folder lay next to him on the front seat. It contained two pages.

He would have preferred to keep slipping Dr. Brook an occasional clue and let him work up to the grand finale on his own.

A shame that had become impossible. He was spiraling downhill too rapidly. His periods of extended lucidity were becoming more infrequent.

He'd let Brook take a good look at the most damning evidence so he could draw his own conclusions. He wanted another doctor on staff to know about some of the clinic's darker secrets. It would be fun to see how hard the facts jolted the boy.

He'd taken the last of the clozapine two days earlier. It wasn't working at all any more, so he'd switched to tryptophan.

Barring some genetic defect on his part, the tryptophan would produce a protein called tryptophan hydroxylase, which might perform a little miracle in his unbalanced brain by boosting his dangerously low serotonin levels.

He wasn't convinced it would work, but he couldn't afford to be choosy so late in the game.

He was reminded that study after study had shown the link between low serotonin and aggressive, violent behavior.

What sublime irony. It served his scientific ass right.

He turned up the heater full blast and slipped out of his overcoat. He rolled up his right shirtsleeve.

What was her name?

Marci? Molly? Mary?

That was it, Mary McBride. A classic borderline. One of his most difficult cases. Intense, erratic feelings, aggravated by lesbianism. She was afflicted by the certainty that she was all alone in her pain, that absolutely no one was there to help her.

She was the worst self-mutilator he'd ever encountered. He didn't catch on to her for months. He should have figured something was wrong when she kept wearing sweaters and long-sleeved blouses to his office in July and August.

He finally noticed a trickle of blood on her wrist. He told her to roll up her sleeves, then took a breath: She'd scored her forearms with a knife. Scars on top of scars.

She'd been doing it for years and that morning had cut herself a little too deeply. The blood had seeped through the bandages.

Mary inflicted pain to convince herself that she was real, that she really existed.

Her sense of her own unreality and nothingness was that strong.

He suddenly remembered how she looked. Plain, boyish features, overweight, a dumpling with a butch haircut and hot-pink lipstick. She wound up killing herself with a drug overdose.

Here's to you, Mary.

He took out a Swiss Army knife, a birthday present from Elizabeth. He'd never used it before. He raised his right arm, made a fist and dragged the stainless steel blade from wrist to elbow. The line of blood looked like a piece of red string.

He felt a sting. He'd made a good shallow cut. For a first try, a nice job.

He made another cut, then another and another.

THIRTY-NINE

BRODY'S LUCK STARTED TO change when he sent Eliot and three other men back to Brother Timothy's hideaway in Viburnum to clean up fingerprints. Sooner or later the cops were bound to stumble on those bodies. Brody didn't want them to get a print that would point to Waters, who was supposed to be doing twenty years in Jefferson City. If they started down that road it was bound to lead straight to the clinic.

The break came while Eliot was searching the home. He found some papers in an office file drawer that indicated the dead builder, Gregorio, was a leading benefactor to Brother Timothy's religious order. Gregorio had thrown fund raisers for the order, which had a reputation for having a large gay membership. Brody figured it was likely that Brother Timothy had told Waters about the rich St. Louis builder during one of his many visits to see Waters in prison.

The records showed that Gregorio had even built the order four or five nice places in the country. One of these retreat homes was run by Brother Timothy. They were trying to locate the other homes, figuring there was a chance Waters knew about them and might be using one for a hiding place.

Now, three days after Eliot's discovery, Brody put down his glass of Cutty Sark—he allowed himself one shot a night—and stared at the map of Missouri taped to the wall.

He'd circled Steelville, Licking and Bourbon in red. A methodical check of the telephone numbers in Brother Timothy's Rolodex had provided leads on retreat homes near those three rural Missouri towns.

Studying the map, Brody saw that all three were south of Interstate 44. So was Viburnum, where Brother Tim's place was located. Rugged country. The Ozark foothills. It wouldn't be easy tracking them down. And, of course, they were only guessing that Waters was hiding in one of them.

Brody had tied up Eliot and three teams trying to find the homes and hoped he wasn't wasting his time. He had another reason to hurry. On a hunch, he'd ordered his men to make some more missing-persons inquiries with the appropriate police agencies. The Crawford County sheriff's department reported that two days earlier a twenty-three-year-old waitress had disappeared.

The woman's husband had reported her missing. She had worked the evening shift at an all-night truck stop on I-44. She got off at midnight and never returned home. The truck stop was midway between Steelville and Bourbon.

Brody had sent a man to talk to the husband, an unemployed trucker who lived in a trailer with two small kids just outside Bourbon. He'd provided a color photograph of his wife, a slender, pretty women with frizzy blond hair.

Brody had done a double take as soon as he saw the photo.

The woman bore a striking resemblance to the dead woman they'd found near Viburnum. Both had nice legs, full breasts and blond hair. They were about the same size and had a similar facial structure.

Brody knew that serial killers often selected victims who matched their ideal image of a woman. Ted Bundy had done this. Photographs of his victims, dozens of them, revealed close similarities in hair style, build, even educational background. Bundy had preferred slender college co-eds with shoulder-length hair.

Waters seemed to like young blondes with nice bodies.

As the night wore on, Brody kept waiting for his men to

report, relying on coffee and jagged nerves to keep him awake.

Shortly after five in the morning, Eliot called. He was ten miles south of Steelville and had found one of the retreat homes. He and his partner had parked their car off the road and hiked up through the woods. The place was on a hill overlooking the Meramec River. Another Swiss chalet.

Eliot was using a cellular telephone, so his words were guarded. "I think you better get out here."

"What's happening?" Brody asked. He'd already slipped on his shoulder rig.

"We got two cars parked in front. A guy just went out to one of them and took something out of the trunk. It's still dark, but it looks like it might be our man."

Brody arrived by seven-thirty. He'd tried to catch a few minutes' sleep during the ride out from St. Louis, but the Jeep's tight suspension and his driver's lead foot made that impossible.

The morning sun had started to burn off the fog and mist that rose in clouds from the river and lay on the surrounding hills. Eliot gave Brody an update as he squatted behind a tree and scanned the house through binoculars.

Like the place near Viburnum, it was a stunningly modern design with a pitched, cedar-shake roof tucked into a rectangular clearing on high ground. The rear deck offered a sweeping view of the Meramec River valley. The back of the house was built into the side of a hill that dropped like a wall to the river.

From their position in the trees, they could see most of the deck.

A Honda Civic and a GMC Jimmy were parked near the front door.

"Except for that one trip to the car, he's been in there the whole time," Eliot said.

"Is he alone?"

Eliot shrugged and said, "Hard to say."

"Did you cut the phone lines?"

"The first thing."

The forest setting was eerily quiet. A wisp of smoke rose from a metal chimney on the slanted roof. The wood fire smelled pungent in the cold air.

"I can get up on the deck by going along the riverbank and working my way up the bluff," Eliot said. "There's good cover. Maybe I can get a look inside."

Brody bought the idea. "Take a radio."

Eliot slipped a two-way into the pocket of his fatigue jacket and disappeared into the trees. He wore camouflage, green and brown. They all did. Brody and his driver stayed up on the ridge. Six others with scoped rifles were scattered around the cabin.

Eliot reported from the riverbank in the time it took for Brody's feet to go numb. "I'm a hundred yards below the house. I'm moving in closer."

"Stay under cover," Brody said into the radio.

"I don't like the feel of this," said his driver.

"I don't either, pal," Brody said. Not one damn bit. If Waters was really in there, he was armed and probably wacked out. You couldn't anticipate how he'd react. His brain was a blow-out.

Ten minutes later, Eliot called again. He'd moved along the riverbank until he was directly below the house. The deck supports were sunk into the side of the steep hill about fifty yards up from the river. It was a rough climb. He'd have to scale the rock ledges without benefit of a rope.

"I'm coming up," he said.

"Copy," Brody said. "Watch yourself."

Five minutes later Brody was astonished to see Eliot shinnying over the balcony railing.

"Christ, he's already there," he said.

Eliot flattened his back against the wall and inched his way to the sliding glass doors that opened onto the wide deck. He glanced inside.

"The room's empty," he whispered into his radio. "Looks like some kind of rec room. There's a big fireplace in there. I'll try the door latch."

"Hold your position. Confirm!"

Eliot didn't answer. Through his binoculars, Brody saw him jiggle the door handle. He watched him slide the door open about a foot.

"What's the crazy sonofabitch doing?" Brody said.

Eliot took a pistol from his belt.

"Is he gonna do what I think he's gonna do?" the driver asked. He also had a pair of binoculars trained on Eliot. He thought he was a stupe who took way too many chances.

With his Beretta semiautomatic held at a right angle from his body, Eliot crabbed sideways to the opening. He took another look inside, and disappeared into the house.

"Fuck it!" Brody said. He tried to raise him on the radio. Eliot had turned it off.

"You want me to go on down there?" the driver said, tightening his gloves. He was ready to move out.

"No, goddammit! Nobody goes down there!"

Long minutes passed. An age. Eliot's radio clicked back on.

"Thanks for sending a guest."

Brody immediately recognized Waters's deep baritone voice.

"I needed somebody to talk to. I have Mr. Eliot seated right in front of me. I've also got the most amazing tool I ever saw. It must be some kind of blow torch for stripping paint. Fits right in your hand. I found it out in the garage."

Eliot's scream was so ear-piercing that Brody almost dropped the radio.

Waters called Brody on the radio and reminded him about their deal. He didn't want any confusion. They had talked three times during the day, each call accompanied by screams from Eliot.

Waters provided running commentary to accompany the torture scenes.

Your friend really doesn't like this.

I'm burning his thumb.

Let's try another body part. (Laughter.)

Eliot's screams had gotten progressively worse during the day—if that was possible.

Brody had held off sending in a SWAT team. He didn't want to provoke Waters into a shootout. There was no telling how far the sound of gunfire would carry. They had to let him play with poor Eliot.

Their deal was that Waters could leave after dark. He'd take the Honda. Eliot would go with him as insurance. No one would try to stop them.

Brody looked at his watch. It was eight-thirty. Time for Waters to make his move.

He blew on his hands. It was cold as a bitch so close to the river.

"They're coming out," said his driver, who was watching the house with a pair of night-vision binoculars.

"Let's do this right," Brody said. He wondered if Waters had really believed him. He doubted it.

Eliot's feet were hobbled with a cord. He could barely move. His mouth was taped.

Brody was concerned about taking Waters alive—if possible. He'd drilled his people repeatedly. No head shots. If they had to shoot, they were to try to bring him down at the legs.

Waters made Eliot get into the front seat. Waters's collar was up and it was hard to see his face. He got in and started the engine.

The car would have to swing right at the end of the clearing, then start down a narrow road that made a hairpin turn to the left. Brody had had his men pile logs at just that point, which was out of sight of the cabin. They were going to stop him there, one way or another.

The car backed up slowly, then started down the driveway.

Brody suspected something was wrong even before the car lurched to a stop.

The driver's door flew open and a man tumbled out.

"Hold your fire!" Brody shouted. He kept looking back toward the cabin as he ran down to the car. This didn't feel right.

One of his men picked up the driver by the shoulder and shone a flashlight on his face. It wasn't Waters.

"Who are you?" Brody shouted.

The man shook his head.

"What's your name!"

The man opened his mouth. The flashlight beam showed a dark stump flapping where the tongue had been cut off. He grunted. Spittle flew. He pitched forward on the ground.

Brody figured he was probably the religious brother who ran the place. He was about fifty. His skin was a pasty white color. He was going into shock.

"Get a blanket on him," Brody said. He checked on Eliot. Waters had burned him on both palms so that he'd scream on cue. His skin was blistered there, and he looked ready to pass out from fear and exhaustion, but he'd been lucky. Waters had been more interested in torturing the brother.

Brody broke for the house with two of his men right behind him.

Waters had probably gone out the back. That meant he was heading toward the river.

One of his men broke away to search the cabin. Brody and the others started descending the hill. It was tough, dangerous going in the darkness.

Brody stumbled twice. He bruised his elbow and cut his hand on a rock.

Somebody shouted, "He's in the river."

Brody got down to the bank just in time to see Waters reach the middle. The Meramec was only twenty yards wide there, and shallow. He was trying to wade across in water up to his knees. Waters fired three shots at them, then lost his balance and went under. He'd hit a deep pool.

Brody was already in the river. The current had pushed Waters up against a submerged tree on the opposite bank. One of Brody's men caught up with him there and held his head under until he stopped struggling. He pulled him up, Waters gasping for breath. Then, as Brody watched, Waters butted his man in the face with his forehead and broke free.

He was halfway up the sloping riverbank, clawing his way

up the muddy slope, when Brody made it across the river. He charged up the bank behind Waters, grabbed him by the waist and spun him around. He saw the butcher knife in Waters's hand.

"You really want to try that?" Brody said, smiling.

When Waters slashed at him, Brody grabbed his knife hand and bent it up behind Waters's back. He applied more pressure. He didn't give a shit if the arm broke.

Waters screamed in pain and dropped the weapon.

"You'd think with all that practice you've got with knives, you'd learn how to use one in a fight," Brody said.

He kicked Waters hard in the back, knocking him onto the riverbank. He lay facedown in the mud, not moving.

One of Brody's men scurried down the steep hill from the house, grabbing onto rocks and tree trunks to keep from falling. An avalanche of stones tumbled into the water. Brody was going to reprimand the stupid bastard—until he saw the look on his face.

"You better get back up there," the man said. "We just found one of those missing women."

FORTY

THE ELECTRONIC MESSAGE WAS only two lines. The first was a list of numbers. The second mentioned a book in the clinic library and a page number.

Brook had logged onto his office computer and was checking his e-mail when he got the message. It could have been sent from anywhere.

He recognized the numbers as Missouri prison system IDs and he had a feeling they involved the four men who had died at the prison.

Minutes later he was in the library. The book—*Advanced Neurosurgery*—was on the shelf in a corner of the room farthest from the door and out of view of the librarian.

His hands shaking, Brook opened the book to page 250, the one mentioned in the message. A small key was folded in a piece of paper. A note scribbled in pencil said it would open a file cabinet in Hartigan's office.

The key had a number—E104.

It was late in the afternoon, but Brook decided to go home early.

Rita Stell was waiting at her door when he walked up.

"Have you noticed that car parked down the street with two men in it?" she asked. "I think they're watching this place. They'll sit there a while, then leave."

"How often have you seen them do that?" Brook asked.

He looked up and down the street. A couple of unoccupied cars were parked at the far end of the block.

"Three, maybe four times. I wasn't sure about it at first."

She lingered at her open door, wanting his advice.

"It's probably a couple of bill collectors," he said.

Rita frowned. "It would be more fun to think that someone's having an affair and hubby's got the detectives out."

Brook suggested she call the police if she saw the car again.

Rita started to step back into her apartment, then remembered something else. "How's it going with you and Jenny? Don't screw that up, Doctor."

Brook smiled. "Don't worry, Rita. I promise."

When he got upstairs, he sat in his darkened kitchen and drank a beer. He tried to think clearly. He wanted to get into that file cabinet in Hartigan's office, but he didn't have the slightest idea how to do it.

At seven-thirty P.M., still unsure of his next move, Brook telephoned Jenny. He'd already promised to call her then. He said he'd pick her up in ten minutes. He made it sound as if they'd already agreed to go back to the clinic together to catch up on their paperwork.

Jenny played along. Brook explained nothing over the telephone.

He changed into a pair of jeans, wolfed down a sandwich and drove to her apartment. He assumed someone was following him.

Jenny met him at the door of her building. Brook made sure she had her briefcase. During the walk to the car, he hurriedly explained what had happened and what he had in mind.

Jenny would stop by Hartigan's office for an unannounced visit. She'd talk to him about her job, her future, whatever.

"I'll drop by after a few minutes and say that I need to have an important talk with him," Brook said. "One way or another, I'll get him out of that office."

Jenny said, "Let me guess the rest: That's when I'm supposed to open the file cabinet."

Brook said, "I'll try to give you five minutes."

"Do I take anything?"

"Only if it looks interesting."

"No problem," Jenny said, trying to smile. "They taught me all about breaking and entering in med school. It was one of my best courses."

"It's your call, Jen," Brook asked. "There's probably a better way to do it. I just can't think of it."

As they drove to the clinic, they talked about maybe catching a late movie after they finished their work. They assumed the car was bugged.

Brook parked on the clinic's back lot, and they took the elevator to Hartigan's office. The outer door was open and the lights were on. As usual, he was working late. He rarely left the building anymore.

"Let's do it," Jenny said. She knew that, if she didn't, she might not be able to work up her nerve later.

Brook slipped her the file-cabinet key and squeezed her hand.

Brook went to his office and tried to shore up his own nerves. He looked at the clock on the wall. It was seven-fifty. Jenny had been with Hartigan nearly ten minutes.

He hurried down the steps to Hartigan's office. The door was open. Jenny was seated in front of his desk. The clinic director was smiling.

He noticed that Jenny had her briefcase open. She was ready.

He took a breath, knocked and stepped inside.

"Excuse me, Doctor," he said. "I'm sorry to interrupt. I need to talk to you right away."

"I'm busy," Hartigan said. "What about dropping by in, say, twenty minutes." He was leaning back in his chair with his legs crossed, hands folded. Except for his tired eyes, he looked relaxed.

"This can't wait, Doctor," Brook insisted. "I promise it will take only a minute. We can talk out in the hallway."

"I don't mind," Jenny said.

Hartigan excused himself. He promised Jenny he'd be right back.

Brook let Hartigan precede him into the hallway. He shut the door behind them.

"All right, John. What's so important?" Hartigan faced him. He looked irritated.

Brook's plan was crude and simple: Make a scene.

"Someone's following me," he said with an explosion of forced anger. "I want it stopped."

"I don't know what you're talking about, Doctor," Hartigan said. Brook's outburst had startled him.

Brook caught something in the doctor's surprised expression.

"I'm not making this up," he said. "Brody and his security people are responsible, and I resent it."

"I resent your tone," Hartigan said, going on the offensive himself.

"Tell me it's not true."

"This is absurd. You're being irresponsible as hell. I didn't expect that of you."

Brook changed tactics. He apologized and tried to look contrite.

"Let's talk to Brody and put it to him directly," he said in a tone that suggested he'd come to his senses. "Maybe there's an explanation. Something you're not aware of."

"I see no need to do that at all," Hartigan said angrily. "I'd never allow anyone on my staff to be followed."

"It would clear the air."

"I'd like to finish my conversation with Doctor Malone," Hartigan said.

Brook pushed the red panic button on the wall opposite Hartigan's office, a security alarm. The clinic had several on every floor.

A bell clanged. Loud, jarring noise. Within seconds, three security guards came running down the hallway, pistols drawn.

Hartigan threw up his hands in disgust. "This is inexcusable!"

Brook didn't have to worry any more about pumping himself up for the show. Hartigan's enraged expression gave him all the adrenaline he needed.

An hour later, Brook didn't ask what Jenny had found, although he was busting to know. When she whispered the answer during the short walk to his car, he shot her a confused look. It wasn't what he'd expected.

They drove straight to his flat. When they spoke it was for the benefit of whoever might be listening. They discussed a change of plans about the movie. They agreed that they were too tired. It didn't take much acting.

They arrived at Brook's flat and went upstairs. Brook turned his CD player on loud. Without saying a word, Jenny opened her briefcase and took out a specimen jar.

"When I opened the file drawer, this is what I found," she explained in a soft voice. The quart-sized jar contained part of a brain floating in a clear formaldehyde solution. A sectioned cortex. "There were five other jars in the drawer, each with a cortex. Each jar was labeled with a number and date."

Surprised, Brook examined the cortex. Part of the amygdala, hippocampus and optic nerve were exposed.

He needed better light. He picked up a gooseneck floor lamp and found a pair of surgical gloves in a bedroom drawer.

They went into the bathroom and shut the door.

"Talk in a whisper," he said.

The bathroom was unusually large. Gleaming white and pink tile. He unfolded a towel and laid it over a small wicker table. He set the lamp next to the table and took off the shade.

He unscrewed the specimen jar and removed the brain. The cortex had the gray color and consistency of liver. It was spongy and smelled of the chemical solution.

"How many jars did you say were in that drawer?" he whispered.

"I counted six," Jenny said softly.

Examining the label, Brook instantly recognized the prisoner ID number in the upper left-hand corner. It was written in blue ink along with a date, which he also recognized: September 8, 1991.

The specimen was from Marcel Washington, one of the four inmates who had died under strange circumstances at the state prison. He remembered the cause of death: coronary embolism.

The numbers Jenny had copied off the other specimen jars in Hartigan's office matched the men's IDs, which Brook had memorized.

But his mystery informant had sent him only four names. Jenny had copied down six ID numbers.

Brook wondered about the identity of the two others as he readjusted the lamp to shine the maximum light on the brain segment. That's when he noticed the dark line that ran at an oblique angle through the cortex into the amygdala. The cluster of nerve circuits between the amygdala and the hippocampus had been obliterated.

Brook realized that someone had used a surgical laser to slice deep into the cortex and snip away the neural connections between those sections.

The dark line marked the laser's track through the brain. They had used either a laser or a high-intensity microwave. It was hard to tell. Both would have achieved the same results. The techniques were used increasingly for stereotactic brain surgery, delicate eye and heart operations and for other procedures.

But never on prisoners, and never to cut away important nerve circuits.

The hippocampus was crucial to memory and emotion.

Jenny knelt next to him as he examined the brain. When he told her his suspicions, she closed her eyes.

"But why?" she whispered. She was as stunned as he was.

Brook was still trying to figure it out. "It's like doing a lobotomy, only a lot safer and quicker. You could probably do it on an outpatient basis."

It was obvious that Hartigan had used laser surgery to try to alter criminal behavior by operating on the brains of a small group of inmates, all of whom were dead.

"I can't believe Hartigan would have gone that far," Jenny said, forgetting to keep her voice down. *First kindling and now this. How had they gotten away with it?* she thought. It was inconceivable to her that anyone could carry out such procedures.

"I know," Brook said. "And it shouldn't have killed them."

FORTY-ONE

LIND SAT IN THE back pew of the church, staring at the flickering candles. He'd been waiting nearly two hours, hoping
to see the light again, or feel its warmth. The latest car he'd
stolen—an old Plymouth—was parked outside.

His .357 magnum was tucked into his belt, concealed under his jacket.

The monster wouldn't come into the church. He didn't
know why that was true—or even where he'd gotten the idea
to come here—but he believed it absolutely.

He needed help. It was the first time he'd admitted that.
He was so scared that it took an act of will to keep him in
the pew.

It was out there somewhere, waiting. A dark face. If it
appeared again, he was afraid he would wind up wiping out
some people. He'd go to the clinic and kill every doctor he
could. That had been his plan all along.

He'd start the massacre with Dr. Brook.

One more bitch of a headache was stoking up to white-
hot intensity. He wasn't sure he could stand another one.

He hadn't been in a church since he was a kid. And never
a Catholic church. The place, St. Anthony of Padua, smelled
of incense. It felt peaceful to sit there in the cool darkness.
He wondered if the strange voice would talk to him again.

It always seemed to come with a burst of light that seemed to radiate outward from deep within him.

An old woman knelt by the statue of the Blessed Virgin in the front of the church.

She looked eighty. Parchment face, deep folds and creases, sunken eyes.

Or did she?

Her profile seemed to be changing before his eyes.

He began to smell flowers. He was starting to hallucinate again.

His tears flowed. He experienced a bizarre lightness of spirit. He fell on his knees and looked up at the stained-glass window high above the main altar. Jesus risen. The last light of the day illuminated the ruby and emerald colors of his crown.

The voice spoke to him. He sensed the words rather than heard them. They left an imprint on his brain, as if an invisible stylus were tracing them on the cortex a letter at a time.

The voice suddenly told him to call someone. It provided a name.

Lind almost cried out.

It was perfect.

He'd tell this person what had happened to him, how they'd fucked up his head at the clinic. He'd make a public confession.

While thousands listened.

The light poured through the crown like a laser. It was all over him. His pistol fell on the pew.

The woman turned and smiled at him. She no longer looked old. To Lind's hallucinating eyes, she looked twenty. She was beautiful.

FORTY-TWO
◄►

Brody put down his notebook and unfastened the handcuffs. Waters stared at him bug-eyed. He was already hyperventilating and dripping sweat. His face and hair were soaked.

"Who helped you escape?" Brody asked.

Terrified, Waters sat there, squeezing his thighs.

Brody suddenly picked him up out of the chair by his head and neck, and held him at arm's length. "Who helped you, asshole!"

"I don't know." The words were a gasping croak. He clutched Brody's forearms, legs kicking in air.

"Wrong answer. Who let you out?"

"I . . . don't . . . know." The voice rasped. His lips were flecked with spittle.

Brody began to believe him, which didn't improve his mood.

"Why didn't you clear out of Missouri?"

"Nowhere . . . to go." Waters's face was turning sunburn red.

"Wrong again, Gary. You knew those fag brothers had a couple nice hideouts where you could play butcher shop."

Brody dropped Waters hard. The emaciated body crumpled on the floor. Brody's arms fluttered from the lift. Over a hundred and fifty pounds held straight out. Not bad.

"You mess with my head anymore, I'll kill myself," Waters screamed, after Brody pulled him back into the chair.

Waters was wild with fear, twisting, jerking, begging.

He'd been sedated ever since they'd brought him back to the clinic under heavy guard two days earlier. This was Brody's first chance since then for a private talk.

The man with the missing tongue had died of cardiac arrest.

Eliot was in good shape, considering what he'd gone through. Waters had played the terror game with him for hours, holding the blowtorch near his eyes, telling him he was going to give him a new mouth and nose, touching the blue flame to his palms to make him scream. Hartigan had personally treated Eliot's burned hands. He was back at work with both of them bandaged.

So far they'd kept the rest of the staff in the dark about Waters's capture. But that would have to change soon. Hartigan wanted to give him another series of PET scans. The blackouts, rage and confusion he'd experienced ever since his escape were symptomatic of limbic kindling.

Diagnosis: Waters's brain was still seizing.

Brody had to stop his fun when Hartigan arrived. He'd managed to have five minutes alone with Waters. It wasn't enough.

Hartigan pried up Waters's right eyelid. The whites were bloodshot. A crack addict's eyes.

"He's not ready yet."

Waters screamed when he saw Hartigan take out a hypodermic from the pocket of his lab coat. Brody squeezed down hard on the prisoner's wrists while Hartigan injected 20 cc of lorazepam deep into the muscle of his right forearm.

The prisoner jerked his head back and forth. He screamed, "Kill me! Just kill me!"

Brody backhanded him across the face. The slap popped like a broken lightbulb.

"That's enough!" Hartigan angrily ordered Brody out of the room. The lorazepam was already working. Waters's eyes closed. He'd sleep a few more hours. Then they would start the peptide injections.

But first they needed to calm him down. He was still too agitated.

FORTY-THREE
⊳━◆━⊲

BROOK HAD BEEN UP since four-thirty, reexamining the brain specimen Jenny had taken from Hartigan's office. His uncertainty and dread deepened every time he looked at the scorch mark that ran down the midline of the cortex.

He tried to make notes as he thought through all of the conflicting implications and possibilities. It was hard to hold the pencil. His hand was shaking too much.

Had the prisoners died as a result of the laser experiments? Or were the results so disastrous that Hartigan or someone else killed the men and then had Beckworth change the records to cover it up? The warden had clearly been an active participant. Who else had been involved? Silver? Someone outside the clinic?

The mystery source who'd twice given him information on the secret project had provided ID numbers that matched those on four of the specimen jars in Hartigan's office. But Jenny had counted at least six jars, leaving two unaccounted for.

At around nine A.M., Brook went out to call his friend Roger in the records department at the state forensic unit in Fulton. To vary his routine of driving to the med school library, he walked four blocks to a grocery store. A mom-and-pop operation, it even had an old-fashioned telephone booth with a door that closed for privacy and a seat to sit on.

He asked Roger to check the two new ID numbers. He wanted to match them with names.

"Hold on, while I check the files." Roger sounded worried, and Brook sensed something was wrong. He heard Roger punching the keys of a computer. In less than a minute he was back on the line.

"Here's a change for you," Roger said in surprise. "The IDs belong to a Mary Sargent and a Joyce Jones. Sargent is white. Jones, African-American. They were both doing long stretches at Green Island for robbery and other assorted charges. Jones shot a guy during some drug deal that went bad."

The Green Island women's prison was in northern Missouri near the Iowa border.

Brook hadn't expected them to be women. He asked Roger for the date and cause of death.

More key punching.

"Both ladies died of brain embolisms in October and December of 1991, respectively," Roger said.

That made four of six who had died of embolisms, which meant there'd been quite a run on ruptured blood vessels. In a population segment as small as a prison, it seemed statistically impossible that two men and two women could have died of embolisms in such a short time span.

This seemed to confirm Brook's suspicions that someone had falsified the records to cover up the real cause of death.

Roger said, "John, I've got to tell you something. Maybe I should have called you earlier on this."

Brook sat still in the telephone booth. He was aware of the fan whirring over his head and the cool breeze on his face.

"What do you mean, Roger?"

"Every time you access a file from one of our on-line workstations, you leave a computer trail. I got a call three days ago from Beckworth. I couldn't believe it."

Brook leaned back against the wall of the booth. He closed his eyes. Roger was still talking.

"He wanted to know why I was looking up data on your four dead cons."

"What did you tell him, Roger?"

"The truth. That it was a routine request. I do record checks for docs all over the state." Roger's voice underwent a slight change. "It was routine, wasn't it, John?"

Brook heard his own breathing. Time stood still.

"Talk to me," Roger said.

Brook wondered what it would be like to go completely unhinged. That had never happened to him before.

"Routine as hell."

"Glad to hear it," Roger said.

"Did Beckworth say anything about why he was so interested in those names?"

"He didn't. I figured if he wanted me to know, he would have told me."

"So what about this request? Are you going to tell him you looked up some more records for me?"

The pause on the line answered his question. Almost.

"I don't want to know what's going on here. I'm not going to call Beckworth. But if he calls me, I've got to tell him the truth."

"That's fine, Roger," Brook said. "You can never go wrong if you tell the truth."

Brook and Jenny went jogging that afternoon. The temperature was in the upper thirties, the sky overcast. It was almost too cold to run, but that way they could talk without fearing anyone could hear them.

Brook picked up Jenny at her apartment and drove to Forest Park. They got out at the Jefferson Memorial. It was a two-mile run to the art museum and back. They looked across the deserted golf course, and could see the roof of the main building up on Art Hill.

Jenny told him about the way Hartigan had kept watching her during a routine patient-evaluation discussion. She'd detected a suspicious coldness, almost hostility, from a man she had once admired.

"Hartigan suspects something," she said.

"I know," Brook said. "My guess is he's figured out we know about the kindling experiments on Lind and Waters. He's probably thinking we've also found out about the other prisoners."

He described his morning conversation with Roger. "Hartigan and Beckworth know that I've been trying to get information on those dead inmates."

Jenny dropped her hands to her sides and closed her eyes. Brook slipped his arm around her waist and pulled her toward him.

He made a decision: They weren't going to be apart any more. He'd spend the night at her place, or she would stay with him. For whatever was coming, they needed to be together.

"We've got to get away from here," Brook said.

"Where do we go?"

He began to run, slowly at first, his eyes watering in the wind. They jogged on the paved bike path, heading toward Skinker Boulevard and the Washington University quadrangles half a mile away. A few other runners were out, fighting the wind and cold. Fellow hardcores.

Brook found himself continually looking over his shoulder to see if anyone was following them.

"Why not drive to the Smokies?" he said, running next to Jenny. He'd been working that idea over hard the last few days. The mountains and backwoods hollows were as remote as anything in North America. You could lose yourself there. He knew the Smokies like a native. He could hide in that country.

"I know where we can find a cabin. Spend a few weeks and figure out what to do next."

He wasn't fooling himself. He was scared shitless—for himself and for Jenny.

Jenny was breathing harder as they picked up the pace. She was ready to leave.

It appeared that Hartigan was responsible for the deaths of at least six prisoners. And Hartigan and his powerful friends realized that he and Jenny knew some of the details about their experiments.

Brook hadn't heard from Lind for a few days. He still wanted to help him, and felt it was his ethical duty to do so, but he didn't want to get killed for his trouble. After all, Lind had made it clear he wanted to kill him. He'd do it if he got a chance.

He and Jenny jogged back to their car twenty minutes later, lungs burning from the cold air.

"When do we leave?" Jenny asked.

"Tomorrow. We don't tell anyone. We just go."

Brook drove to his apartment. When they got to the top of the steps, Jenny kissed him.

Inside, they started undressing as they stumbled toward the bathroom. Brook turned on the water in the tub full blast. As they waited for it to fill, Brook and Jenny stripped off the rest of their clothes.

Jenny slipped out of her bra and panties. She was warm from the run. Her face was still flushed.

She put her arms around Brook's neck. He felt her nipples against him and smelled the sweat on her shoulders as he kissed her breasts. Knowing what he wanted, she pushed her nipples up to him so he could take them in his mouth.

He slid his hands down, and she opened her legs, letting him touch her. He felt her body spasm. He picked her up and got into the tub.

They knelt in the warm water. She leaned back and her hips came up and he tasted her. She quivered and thrashed off his mouth, spilling water over the top of the tub. He took her by the waist and tasted her again.

He tasted her hair and the soft, moist folds. She cupped her hands over her mouth.

He kissed her, and she arched her back and held him there so he could taste all of her.

She shivered again and again. She started to cry and spasm as he entered her.

He held her by the waist, not wanting to let her go, afraid of losing her.

Later, he dried her in a thick towel and carried her to bed.

When he woke up, it was dark and Jenny was kissing him. She moved lower and touched him with her hair, then with her lips. He closed his eyes and let everything fall away from him. He gasped, and let her take him. She did it with a boldness and passion he hadn't expected. He touched her hair, curling it in his fingers.

FORTY-FOUR

A CAB DRIVER DELIVERED Lind's note at eight-thirty that evening.

Brook read it as he stood by the front door: "Listen to Bill Masterson tonight. I'll meet you later at 2238 South Broadway. It's an old warehouse down by the river. Come alone."

Brook showed it to Jenny. He was sure it was from Lind. He recognized his back-slanted printing. "Who's Bill Masterson?"

She looked at him with a strange expression.

"Jenny, what's the matter?"

"He's got a radio call-in show. He's like Rush Limbaugh."

Brook grasped Lind's intent, and the potential.

"My Lord! When's he on?"

Jenny glanced at the clock.

"In twenty minutes."

Krill ran to Hartigan's office and shouted for him to turn on the radio.

"It's him. It's Lind. He's on KPDN."

By the time Hartigan switched on a radio with shaking hands, they'd gone to a top-of-the-hour news and commercial break.

Krill explained in breathless, almost incoherent sentences that Lind had been the last caller on the Bill Masterson Show. He'd announced that he was a convict and that he wanted to make some kind of public confession.

Masterson had promised to start with him as soon as they returned.

Hartigan called Brody in and they stood stone-faced and tense in front of the radio, waiting for the show to resume.

When the last commercial ended, Masterson reintroduced Lind.

Hartigan recognized the voice. He had to sit down as Lind calmly told Masterson that he'd been an inmate at the Men's Club at Potosi, Missouri.

"And I guess you just got paroled?"

"Not exactly. They sent me to St. Louis to have my brain fixed." He laughed. So did Masterson, the nervous laugh of someone who didn't know what was coming next but realized he was playing with fire.

"It works like this, Bill. They zap your head with an electromagnetic field. It was really messing me up, so I got the hell out of there."

Hartigan was on his feet. This could finish them.

"Wait a minute here. What do you mean, you got the hell out? Are you telling me you're an escaped con?" Masterson sounded incredulous. His arrogant tone and vocal mannerisms let it be known he thought of himself as the great lord of the airwaves.

"That's what I'm telling you, Bill. But I didn't escape from the pen. I broke out of a medical clinic here in St. Louis. Another guy went with me. I'll tell you a secret. You're getting this first. Before TV or the newspapers. I killed a guy. I hurt him bad, then I killed him with my hands. Know what, Bill? I'd like to do it again. It felt good."

The tone of Masterson's voice changed. At first he'd been talking to Lind as if he were trying to humor him. He sounded startled and unsure of himself.

"Can you tell me your name?"

"No can do, Bill. I've got some unfinished business to

attend to. If I told you my name, it might get the police on my . . ."

The station's sound man dubbed out the rest of the sentence, which was sprinkled with obscenities.

"My big worry is the security guys. If they find me, I'm . . ."

More words were bleeped.

Brody was shaking his head. He nervously began to pop the knuckles on his right hand. Hartigan's face was gray.

Lind said, "That's about it, Bill. I hope that helped your ratings."

"Please, don't hang up." Masterson sounded desperate. "I'd like to talk to you off the air. Please stay on the line."

"Maybe I'll call again, Bill."

Masterson, confused and shaken, broke for another commercial. He came back a minute later and apologized to his listeners for the troubling call. Then he abruptly and uncharacteristically changed the subject. He wasn't going to talk about what had just happened. In the nutland of call-in radio, it was too risky.

"He's playing a cat and mouse game with us," Brody said, letting his anger pull him along. "He's going to dribble it out a piece at a time on the goddamn radio. If we don't get to him, this place is finished and all of us with it."

Within twenty minutes Hartigan's private telephone rang. It was Beckworth, who was in a rage.

Hartigan said very little, then hung up and repeated the orders for Brody's benefit.

Beckworth's plan, hastily developed with Paulus's agreement, called for the prison to release the details about Lind and Waters. Within an hour, Beckworth would tell the media that the two men had escaped from a private clinic in St. Louis, where they'd been sent for psychiatric treatment. He would tell the reporters that one of the men had already been recaptured and that the other suffered from paranoid delusions and wasn't a risk to the public.

Brody wanted to know what Beckworth had said about Brook and Jenny Malone. He knew the subject had come up.

Hartigan said, "You're to find Doctor Brook as soon as possible and bring him back here. He's no longer considered trustworthy."

All right, you smug bastard, so you don't want to say it, Brody thought with disgust. You want to keep your precious deniability intact. I'm supposed to bring him in dead or alive.

Preferably dead.

He had another question. "What about Doctor Malone?"

Hartigan sat in his chair in frigid silence.

FORTY-FIVE

JENNY HAD CINCHED HER robe around her waist. They were in the bathroom and they had music blasting in the background. She was trying not to raise her voice above a whisper. Brook wasn't buying any of her arguments.

"I've got to meet him, Jen. I owe him that much. He trusted me."

"I know all that." She felt a thickness in her chest. She'd said all this before.

Ignoring the comment, Brook said, "We'll leave as soon as I get back. You'll love the Smokies." Taking her face in his hands, he kissed her lips, swallowing hard when he tasted her tears.

He took her into the bedroom and got out his father's .12-gauge and the Colt. He loaded both weapons, slipping four shells into the Winchester's pump-action magazine. He showed Jenny the safety and demonstrated how to snap it on and off with her thumb.

"Soon as you do that, you're ready to shoot. Just squeeze the trigger." He handed her the pistol. She looked at him with wide eyes and shook her head.

"Take it, Jen." He showed her how to grip the pistol with both hands.

"Aim for the chest and keep both eyes open."

She did as she was told, cupping the butt of the pistol in

her hands and extending her arms so she could sight down the barrel. One thing surprised her. The weapon felt good in her hands. The weight comforted her.

Brook put the pistol on the dresser. He checked his watch. It was nine-twenty-five.

Lind hadn't been precise about the time. His note said only that he'd meet Brook after the radio show, which had just ended. Brook could imagine what the response to Lind's comments had been at the clinic. He couldn't help admire what he'd done. What better way to strike back, to keep them guessing, to let the terror build?

"I've got to go."

He took Jenny in his arms. Her robe came open, and he slipped his hands inside and pulled her against him.

"This is going to work," he said, whispering in her ear, trying to sound confident. A doctor was trained to talk that way, but he was definitely out of practice. "I've been in tougher jams, although I'll admit I can't think of any just now."

Jenny didn't laugh.

Brook snapped on a Gore-Tex parka. He wore a black watch cap, Lycra ski pants and a pair of running shoes.

A few days earlier, he'd asked an old friend at the state hospital to make his car available. His friend's Tempo was waiting in the parking lot, with the key under the driver's-side mat. Brook knew he'd be followed if he drove his own car.

All he had to do was get there. Five miles.

He was going to run for it.

Brook kissed Jenny once more and slipped down the back steps to the basement. He took a few deep breaths, opened the side door and sprinted across the yard. He hurdled the fence, nearly stumbled and hit the ground running.

"He's making his move!"

The news crackled over Brody's radio as he sat in the front seat of the Jeep. It was a cold night, a roaring twenty degrees, and his feet were starting to feel it.

They could have whacked Brook the moment he stepped outside the back door. He had two men in position. An easy shot. Thirty yards, max. But gunfire in this neighborhood was sure to draw cops, and he was betting Brook would lead them to Lind. They were paying him a lot of money to handle this job properly. He'd already blown one detail, when his men hadn't stopped the escape. If he fucked the recovery—well, Beckworth and Paulus weren't the forgiving kind.

"Eliot and Kemp are on his ass."

Both men were in excellent shape. Both were runners. Each wore a lightweight headset radio. They were supposed to keep Brook in view and not let him see them. Brody and three other teams would follow in cars.

"They're heading for Forest Park."

Brody told his driver to get moving. He'd anticipated this. He picked up his cell phone and punched in the numbers, cursing the winter and his cold feet. Hartigan answered.

"I'd get him over here . . . now!" Brody said.

"We're on our way," Hartigan said.

Brook cut into Forest Park and ran across the golf course. He'd deliberately picked this route because it was out in the open. Anyone trying to tail him would have to show themselves. The ground was uneven, and it was damn dark. He didn't want to break an ankle. He climbed a steep hill and stopped at the top to quickly tie a shoelace. He noticed movement at the bottom of the hill where the sloping ground fell off into a lagoon basin.

He couldn't see anything, just the streetlights reflected on the water.

Someone was down there. He was sure of it.

Sprinting, he started up a rutted, gravel road that wound through the Kennedy Forest. The dense patch of trees was notorious as a pickup zone for hookers.

He came out of the woods by the city zoo, hopped a fence and ran across Interstate 40, clearing the median divider with two feet to spare. A big semi heading east at seventy miles an hour came within a few feet of splattering him. The trucker laid on the horn.

The blast was still ringing in Brook's ears when he jumped the fence on the other side of the highway and started up Tamm Avenue.

He was in Dog Town, an old part of St. Louis south of the park. Straining on a steep upgrade, he looked back over his shoulder. He saw a man jumping over the highway median. He was running hard.

Brook's lungs burned. He ran through an alley, took one wire fence, then another and another, and came out on a street behind a church. The highest ground in the city. To the east, he glimpsed the cupola of the state hospital silhouetted against the black sky. He was halfway there.

The guy behind him was getting closer, maybe fifty yards back. Brook hadn't shaken him off. The bastard was a hell of a runner.

Brook ducked between two garages and waited. He heard someone running down the alley. The man was breathing hard. Brook picked up a trash can and waited, chest heaving, then cut in front of him, driving the heavy metal container into his face. He went down on his back. Brook smashed the can down on his head. He followed with four strong kicks to the side.

The man lay still, groaning. Blood trickled from his nose and mouth. He was wearing a pair of night-vision goggles and had a radio receiver strapped to his head. Brook ripped off the goggles and radio and threw them over a garage roof.

At Arsenal Street, he turned east. He was almost there.

He ran down the middle of the street in the yellowish glow of the sodium-vapor lights. If they tried for a shot now, someone might see it. He was leaving a chorus of dog howls in his wake.

He bolted across another yard, angling toward the hospital from the side. He cleared a fence on a dead run, nearly sliced open a calf muscle on the barbed wire, and reached the parking lot.

His friend's car was waiting right where it was supposed

to be. White. Four doors. Brook collapsed into the front seat.

His chest felt like it would explode. He groped under the floor mat and found the key.

His arms were leaden. He finally got the engine on and backed up hard. He hit a post, smashing out a taillight.

Brody screamed at Eliot over the radio.

He had a map spread across his lap. His driver was accelerating. They were roaring down Hampton Avenue. Kemp had been knocked cold in an alley and Brook was gone.

"Slow down, you asshole!" Brody barked at his driver. "We don't want to have an accident or get pulled over."

The other teams were racing in the same direction. They'd fanned out along a grid pattern so they could cover the widest possible territory.

Brody looked at his watch. Five minutes had passed since Eliot's last transmission. That damn idiot! They were supposed to stay out of sight and just follow him.

His radio came to life again.

"I see him."

Eliot!

"He ran . . ." Eliot was gasping, out of breath.

"Come on, spit it out!"

"State hospital. Arsenal and Southwest. He's got a car."
Damn!

Brook tore out the main gate of the hospital parking lot, turned onto Arsenal and gunned it. He glanced in the rearview mirror. The street stretched long and dark behind him framed by rows of vapor lights. He didn't see any cars back there, but one was coming toward him. He shot by it and nervously looked in the mirror again, praying it wouldn't turn around and chase him. He started to breath more easily when he saw the car brake and slowly turn into the hospital parking lot. It was probably someone reporting for the late shift.

He took another look behind. No headlights. He was in

the clear, with maybe an hour to meet Lind and pick up Jenny.

The plan was for her to wait an hour back at the apartment, then dial 911 and report a fire. When the trucks pulled up in front, she'd bolt out the back door. If anyone was still out there watching, maybe they'd be diverted long enough to give Jenny a chance to get away undetected.

At least that's what he hoped.

She would run to the Lafayette Hospital medical complex. Brook would pick her up outside the ER room. Then they'd head to Tennessee.

It hurt every time his chest moved. He still hadn't caught his breath. Strong winds blasted the Tempo. He turned up the heater. There were more cars now that he was on glittery Kingshighway. Used-car lots, fast-food joints and all-night convenience stores lit it up daylight bright.

In ten minutes he was on South Broadway. He found the right address easily enough. A vacant warehouse that fronted the Mississippi.

He parked on a side street. He was near the river. He could smell the water and heard barges slamming together at their mooring couplings. A towboat was in mid-channel, its powerful spotlight playing across the dark water in a long, white line.

The decrepit, abandoned warehouse was in a gone-to-seed neighborhood.

Brook went around to the side of the building, a long, one-story, brick structure that dated to the turn of the century. He tried a door. It creaked open on rusty hinges. A few lights were on, high up in the exposed rafters. The pungent smell of oil, dust and chemicals hit him in the face.

Brook stepped inside. Someone spoke behind him.

"I didn't think you'd be stupid enough to come."

"They may have followed me. I'm not sure," Brook said, turning around.

Lind sat on a bench, hands deep in the pockets of a hooded jacket. There wasn't much light, and Brook couldn't make out his face.

"I don't doubt it," Lind said, his voice hoarse, a low growl. He went outside and returned a minute later. "I didn't see anybody, but that don't mean shit. Come with me. We'll keep this short. I've got things to do."

Brook followed him to a freight elevator.

"I heard you on the radio," Brook said, trying to start a conversation. He wanted to get him talking. "Why did you call . . ."

"I'll get to that," Lind said, cutting him off.

The elevator wasn't working. Lind swung around the cage and climbed down a ladder to a lower level. A single light burned in the blackness.

"Sit down," Lind commanded. Brook sat as directed, on a pile of boards and plywood under the lightbulb.

Lind kept standing. "I came close to killing you. I went by your place twice, but a couple fucks from the clinic were watching from a car down the street. Anyway, let's just say I changed my mind."

"Why didn't you get out of the state?"

"I figured my best chance was right here. I was raised in this neighborhood. This warehouse was the first place I ever broke into. I know every inch of it."

Brook explained what had happened at the clinic, that he and Jenny were probably under suspicion. He told Lind they were going to Tennessee . . . to the Smoky Mountains. They were going to leave tonight.

He felt like he was taking this too fast, but he was running out of time. He had to do it.

"I want you to come with us," Brook said. "I can help you. You sure don't have any reason to believe that. But I think I know what's happening in your brain . . . the sudden seizures . . . the hallucinations and strange smells. There's a new drug that . . ."

Lind's laughter echoed off the cavernous brick walls.

"Fuck you. No more drugs. Let me tell you what this has been like. This morning I had to hurt myself again." He opened his palm. It was wrapped with a bloody bandage. "I pushed a nail through it. Pain's the only thing that makes it stop.''

"Makes what stop?" Brook was sure he already knew the answer. Uncontrollable rage—explosive, abrupt, deadly rage. It was a distinguishing characteristic of psychomotor seizures. Lind's brain was still kindling. He'd gone wild-eyed sociopathic.

"The voices," Lind said.

Brook saw the gap teeth in the wide mouth when Lind smiled, squinted, blinked.

"I was going to drive to the clinic a couple of days ago and come in shooting. The voices were screaming: Do it! Do it, Eddieeee! I wanted to kill you, that shit Hartigan, anybody I could find. Only way I broke it off was to shove that nail through my hand.''

He took a long-barreled pistol from the pocket of his jacket. He placed the muzzle against the side of Brook's head.

Brook stared at him. So this was it.

He clenched his teeth and swallowed.

He gulped air.

Click.

Lind had squeezed the trigger, but the round wasn't chambered. Brook sagged his head.

"How'd that feel? You almost shit your pants, right? That's how I feel when it starts to come on me. You really think you can make that stop?"

Sweat had popped on Brook's face. It took a moment to tamp his nerves down so he could speak.

"You mentioned seeing a light once," Brook said. "You said it gave you a feeling of comfort. Does that still happen?"

"That's why I didn't kill you. That's why my brain's going flip-flopping, wacko nuts. When that light goes off in my head, I feel safe, sorry. I start to cry."

He explained that he'd been sitting in a church when the idea came to him to call a radio talk-show.

"You asked why? Easy. I figured I could scare them.

Make them worry about what I'd say the next time.''

"You're going to call again?''

Lind laughed. The echo that bounced back from the dark wasn't of this world. It was like nothing Brook had ever experienced.

They had been lucky as hell.

One of the teams was approaching the hospital on Arsenal just as the white Tempo sped by in the opposite direction. They'd played it cool, turning into the hospital parking lot and waiting until they were sure Brook was a good four or five blocks down the street. Nosing out of the lot with their lights off, they saw him start to turn onto Kingshighway and tore after him.

Within fifteen minutes, Brody got the radio message he'd been hoping for: The doctor had parked his car and gone inside an old warehouse. He hadn't come out.

Brody arrived at the site with three other teams, and sent two men to flank the building and watch the rear. That left him with four others to make the sweep. They wore black jumpsuits over their bulletproof vests and had smeared their faces with black greasepaint.

"Make sure you got flashlights,'' Brody said.

He pulled out his piece and checked the clip.

Just before Brody moved out, he got another radio message: They'd brought Waters over to Brook's apartment and turned him loose. He'd jimmied a door on the first floor and was already inside.

"Honey, could you come down here . . . here . . . a minute?''

Rita Stell was yelling up the back stairway.

"I've got me a terrible headache . . . Could you come . . . come take a look!''

It bothered Jenny to leave the flat, but Rita definitely sounded distraught. Not at all characteristic. She went down the back stairs. A door on the first-floor landing opened onto Rita's kitchen, then continued to the basement.

Jenny heard a radio.

"Rita, what's wrong?" she asked, entering the kitchen.

Rita stood by the refrigerator. She was naked. Her bathrobe lay on the floor. Her eyes were wide open.

Jenny saw Waters.

He was in the hallway. He wore jeans and a brown leather bomber jacket. He had a pistol pointed at her.

He was grinning.

"Try to run, I'll kill you," he said. "Truth is, I'd rather fuck you dead. But you already know about that weakness of mine, don't you, Doctor Bitch?"

"Let her go, Gary," Jenny said in a soft voice. Her throat was as dry as sand. Her heart fluttered.

"Sure, I'll let her go," Waters said. "She's a little old, but I got to admit she's still got a nice ass. Come here, bitch."

Rita was frozen. Waters pulled her head back and fired a shot through her temple. Blood and a blur of pink pulp hit the ceiling and wall. Rita shuddered, and fell against the kitchen table.

Jenny bolted for the back steps, ducking low. Two ear-splitting shots exploded behind her. The flashes lit up the dark stairwell.

She threw herself against the door on the second floor and fell into the kitchen. Waters was charging up the steps behind her. She bolted the door just in time. He hit it on the run.

She grabbed the telephone. Her hands were shaking.

Call the police! Dial 911!

The line was dead.

Waters hit the door again—he was kicking it. The latch was starting to go.

Brook didn't hear it at first. He strained to listen.

"There it is again," Lind said in a whisper. "Upstairs. Fuck!"

He slammed the pistol into Brook's stomach, knocking his wind out like a burst balloon. Brook keeled over on the floor. Lind put the gun under his nose.

"Did you bring them? Is this a setup?"

Brook could only shake his head. A little higher and the blow might have cracked a rib. Lind's eyes were focused on the top of the ladder.

Brook finally stammered: "I told you . . . They've . . . been . . . following . . . me."

"How many?"

"I'm not sure." He heard the sounds above. Footsteps. Wood creaking.

Lind said, "Come with me. Watch yourself. There are holes down here. They used to be for the conveyor belts. You could fall two stories."

Brook staggered after Lind, who disappeared into the shadows. The musty space was filled with overturned work-tables, benches and trash.

Brook ran straight into one of the tables. Something hard and metallic hit the floor and went rolling.

He stopped in his tracks. It was quiet upstairs. Maybe they hadn't heard. Then he saw a spotlight playing on the far wall. Then another light and another. The beams were angling down from the floor above them.

One of the lights painted him. He squinted into it, throwing up a hand against the bright glare.

Wood splinters hit his face simultaneously with the blast of gun shots.

Lind shouted at him from a doorway.

"Over here!"

Brook rolled under a table and came up running, head down. He found the door as another ripping burst sent brick fragments flying above his head. They were on a staircase. Brook stumbled down in total darkness. At the bottom, Lind grabbed his shoulder, pushed him around a corner and shoved him down on his knees.

"Crawl. Stay behind me."

They were in some kind of tunnel. Brook felt cold air on his face. He crawled over cinders and what felt like brick fragments.

After ten yards or so, Lind stopped abruptly. He took out a pocket lighter.

"They used to unload coal right off the barges through these chutes."

The orange-yellow flame illuminated a metal grate that blocked the tunnel.

Brook heard and smelled the Mississippi. They were that close to the river.

"This gate wasn't here when I was a kid," Lind said. "We gotta go back."

Jenny slammed the kitchen table against the door and ran into the living room. She went down the front stairwell off the living room in three long jumps. She tried to open the door. She turned the lock and pushed.

The door was stuck.

She pushed again. He'd jammed it from the outside.

She pounded against the thick, beveled glass with her fists. She screamed.

Upstairs, Waters hit the back door again. Jenny heard the wood frame breaking apart.

She remembered the guns in the bedroom.

She ran up the steps just as Waters pushed open the back door and shoved the table out of the way. He saw her and fired.

The bullet splintered glass in a butler's pantry into a hundred pieces. Fragments flew. A glass shower.

There was no way she could make it into the bedroom. He was going to cut her off. She threw herself into the bathroom and locked the door. The doors in the apartment were all made of thick, heavy wood with strong locks.

A moment later, Waters knocked.

"Doctor. There's no need to fight this." The baritone voice was pleasant, friendly, amused. "Let's make it easy. Here's my deal: You make it easy on me. I make it easy on you."

Jenny didn't answer.

"Listen, bitch. I'm going to fuck you, then I'm going to kill you, but it doesn't have to hurt. At least not too much."

Jenny sucked air through her teeth and tried to think. The

bathroom window was too small to squeeze through.

She slammed open the medicine cabinet. A pair of barber's scissors was on the shelf. The long, tapering blade was pointed like a dagger and was covered by a plastic sheath.

She picked them up.

"You should already be scared shitless, Doctor!"

Waters laughed at his joke.

She had to figure out a way to surprise him.

"Doctor Bitch, I'm going to count to ten, then I'm going to shoot this lock off."

One . . .

Jenny started taking off her sweater, shirt, bra, pants.

Four . . .

She was down to her panties. She fought even harder to control her breathing.

Seven . . .

Carefully, she slipped the scissors—point first in the sheath—up her rectum until only the handle showed.

Eight . . .

Convicts did this all the time in prison to conceal metal shanks and knives. Maybe it would work.

Nine . . . Ten!

She stepped away from the door just as the three gun shots obliterated the lock. Waters kicked it open. He saw her standing by the radiator, and he smiled.

Jenny felt his eyes rake her body. She covered her breasts with her hands.

"I know what you're going to do," she said, lowering her hands and standing up straight. "I'll make it easy. I'll do whatever you want. Just don't torture me."

"Well, I don't know, Doctor." Waters grinned. "You got a pair of high heels?"

Jenny shook her head. Waters was splattered with Rita's blood.

"Too bad. You'd look great in heels." With the pistol, he motioned for her to step forward. "And, hey? What makes you think I want this to be easy?"

*   *   *

Brook and Lind backed up the entire length of the tunnel, about thirty yards. They heard steps on the stairwell and saw two flashlight beams stabbing down toward them.

Lind reached up into the stairwell and fired three shots. The bullets ricocheted on the stone walls. The noise reverberated in the closed space like cannon fire.

Gunfire boomed above them. Automatic fire. Brick fragments flew like hail. A piece nicked Brook's cheek. Feet hit the metal stairwell. They were coming down after them.

"Let's go! Go!" Lind said.

Brook had trouble seeing, and stumbled. He heard voices behind them. The bastards were already out of the stairwell. If someone caught them with a flashlight, it was all over. They'd be perfect targets.

He could see the flashlights, probing up, down and across the walls and floor.

Moving in a crouch, Lind hurried along the wall. He came to another waist-high opening. The brick entrance was arch-shaped.

Lind crawled in first. Brook bent down and started to follow. The tunnel was similar to the first.

Someone shouted, "Over there!"

Rapid fire. Another shower of stone and powdered dust.

Brook scampered along the sloping passageway on all fours like a monkey.

"If this one's locked, we're screwed," Lind said.

Brook skinned the palms of his hand on the brick floor. He started to smell the river again.

The opening was grated.

"Get back and get down!"

Lind lay flat, extended his arm and fired a magnum round at the grill's metal lock. Sparks flew. The lock held. Brook's ears rang. He spat out dust and gunsmoke.

Lind fired three more times. Cascading sparks—white, red, orange. The lock shattered. He kicked at it. The grill swung open.

They were on the slope of a hill that dropped sharply down to a long-abandoned railroad siding and overlooked the riverbank. The Mississippi spread before them in a wide, black band. A big towboat, lights blazing from three decks, moved past them pushing a long line of barges upstream.

Brook slid down behind Lind to the closest trackbed, digging his heels into the muddy hillside to keep from pitching forward. They started up the tracks, hugging the hillside, which was sheer as a bluff. The cold air and the dank river smell hit him like a bucket of water.

Lind was a few paces up ahead. He suddenly ducked into the trees and brush that lined the hillside. They'd gone about fifty yards up the tracks, which started to curve away from the riverbank. They were so close to the water, Brook heard the waves lapping against the rocks.

Lind signaled to Brook with his pistol.

Brook ducked down and crouched next to him behind a tree.

Lind whispered, "Up ahead."

The hillside fell off abruptly to level ground. The railroad tracks crossed a gravel road on which a green car pulled up and stopped. A man got out, the engine still running. He was alone. He was looking up the tracks in their direction, talking into a radio.

Brook saw flashlight beams on the hillside behind them, at the entrance to the tunnel.

Lind said, "We either go for the guy with the car or we swim, and I don't know how to swim."

"Put your arm around my neck," Brook said. "I'll tell him you're hurt. That we're giving up. If we can get close enough, maybe we can jump him and get the car."

Lind slipped the sleeve of his jacket down over his hand and pistol. He grabbed Brook around the neck and shoulder and leaned against him.

Brody crawled up the tunnel, following two of his men. When he reached the entrance, he looked out at the river. A long row of barges—dark, hulking, rectangular shapes with corrugated decks—were tied up five-across against the shore.

They slammed and banged together in the current like freight cars, and made a hell of a racket.

A horn blew somewhere out on the water.

Brody hoped the loud river noises had drowned out the sound of the shooting. There'd been way too much shooting.

His anger was at blast-off levels. They were blowing this bigtime. They'd lost the element of surprise from the first moment they got into the warehouse. And they'd let Lind and Brook get clear of the building.

Just as he came out of the tunnel, he got a radio call from the team he'd sent around the back of the warehouse.

"I see them. One looks hurt."

Brody barked his order: "When they get close enough, shoot them."

Waters grabbed Jenny's left breast and throat. He squeezed her breast and twisted it. She screamed, and he pulled her out of the bathroom. He made her kneel in the hallway, forcing her down with both hands.

"We're going to take up where we left off."

He backhanded her across the side of the face. She went down, seeing popping white lights and caught herself with her hands. Her nose was bleeding.

Waters pressed the pistol against her head. She was on her knees. He pulled his zipper down and tugged at his shorts, revealing his erect penis.

"Take it, Doctor Bitch!"

Jenny hesitated.

He slapped her again.

She held him rigid with her left hand and did what he wanted. He grabbed her hair and groaned. She turned slightly away from him, holding him in her mouth.

With her right hand she reached down between her legs and withdrew the scissors, cupping them in her palm. She slipped off the protective sheath with her fingers, got a firm grip—then lunged, stabbing the point into Waters's right side. She hit him as hard as she could, driving the steel blade in deep, just under his armpit.

He screamed and dropped the pistol. Jenny bolted for the bedroom. Brook's pistol was there. She slammed the door shut, turned the lock and pushed a dresser in front of it.

Waters was roaring in pain—and in rage.

Gunshots blasted. The doorjamb exploded.

Waters screamed, "I'm going to carve you like a pig!"

Jenny bit down on her tongue to keep from crying out, and reached under the bed. She pulled the shotgun out by the barrel. It was already loaded.

Waters fired more shots into the door. Smoke clouded, wood splintered, chips flew.

Jenny pushed the safety off. She was breathing so hard it hurt.

"I'll cut you, bitch!"

Waters started to get the door open. He had a hand in. It was covered with thick blood. He pushed the dresser back.

The bed was in a corner. He wouldn't be able to see her until he got all the way into the room.

Jenny threw a blanket over the shotgun. The barrel was pointed at the doorway. She crouched between the bed and the wall. Her right hand was under the blanket, gripping the stock. She'd grabbed the Colt off the dresser. It was at her knees.

The door opened.

He staggered into the room, blood pouring from the wound under his arm. He gripped his pistol. Time dragged. Seconds.

Jenny screamed, "Stop right there!"

Waters's face was twisted, grotesque, enraged. He took a step, then another.

Jenny was almost hyperventilating. She waited until he was in front of the bed, then squeezed the trigger. The shotgun went off in roaring fire.

Waters went down, missing most of his left leg. He lay on his stomach, blood jetting up from the huge wound. He looked her in the eyes. He moved his lips, but nothing came out. He started crawling.

She had the pistol.

She flicked off the safety, and steadied the Colt with both hands.

Waters moved again. He was sliding along in his own blood, his arms clawing the floor as he pulled himself toward her. His pistol was on the floor right by his hand. He was trying to reach it, reach her. A cry—piercing, guttural, from beyond hell—tore from his throat.

She knelt up straight and swallowed. She remembered to keep her eyes open. She fired into his back. The slugs sounded like eggs hitting a wall. Blood flew.

He stopped moving.

She shot him again and again.

Brook stepped from the trees and shouted to the man with the radio.

"I've got Lind. He's shot."

Brook and Lind got to within ten yards of the man before he raised his pistol. A big one.

But Lind fired first. The shot made the man drop down behind the car for cover.

Brook hit the ground and rolled into some brush.

Lind ran straight for the car. He dived up on the hood and took the man down with a flying tackle as he tried to get off a shot.

Brook got to his feet and caught the whole show.

Lind hit the man in the face with the pistol. He jammed the barrel deep into his mouth and pulled the trigger. His head erupted like a shattered melon.

Lind rifled the guy's pockets and found a set of keys. He spun around when Brook approached and stuck the pistol in Brook's face. It was clotted with gore.

Brook knocked the gun away with his hand. "If you point that at me again, you're going to have to kill me."

Lind's eyes focused on him slowly, half lucid. Killer eyes. He was panting.

"I came here to help you," Brook said. "I risked my fucking life. You don't want my help, fine. It's your choice."

Lind lowered the pistol.

Brook saw Lind fighting himself. He didn't give a damn
how it turned out. He'd gone as far as he could, done his
best. He didn't want to die. But he'd reached the end of the
line. He was beyond fear.

Lind smiled. He handed him the keys. "You drive."

Instantly, Brook felt the release. His legs almost went to
jelly.

Lind wasn't going to kill him. Not right now, anyway.

They heard voices up the tracks. Flashlights were coming
their way.

Brook jumped behind the wheel, slipped the car into gear
and took off down the gravel road. Lind sat next to him.
They were heading back toward Broadway. The narrow road
curved to the left.

Brook gunned it. The car, a new Dodge Intrepid, fishtailed
left and right. He was tearing up the road with his lights off.
Lind ejected a clip from his pistol, pulled another from his
pocket and snapped it into the magazine.

Bright flashes up ahead. White.

Somebody was shooting at them!

The guy was out in the middle of the road. They'd come
around a curve and there he was. Up close and shooting. A
bullet shattered the windshield. A jagged hole.

Brook ducked down in his seat and punched the gas pedal.

A black shape tried to jump out of the way at the last
moment, but didn't make it. The left bumper caught him.
The Intrepid shuddered at the impact.

FORTY-SIX

BROOK HURRIED THROUGH THE Lafayette Hospital waiting room. Almost every one of the thirty metal seats was taken. Mostly women and children. Coughing. Hacking. Stifled groans.

No sign of Jenny.

He checked the time again. He'd done that repeatedly. He was over half an hour late meeting her. He jogged back to his car. He'd left the engine running.

"Better get back to your apartment," Lind said, staring straight ahead.

Brook hesitated. The strange, detached expression on Lind's face bothered him.

"Better go there. Now."

Brook pulled away fast, almost broadsiding an ambulance as it turned into the ER entrance with its siren winding down. He stood on the accelerator, pushing seventy up Kingshighway. He turned onto Lindell and gunned it over to Euclid through heavy traffic.

"Pull over."

They were a block from his apartment.

Lind got out of the car, slipped two guns into the waistband of his trousers and jogged up the street. Brook followed. He was worried about Lind's mental instability and didn't like this at all. He didn't know what Lind was doing and didn't trust him. The man could flip out at any moment and turn on him. They stopped at the far end of his block.

Brook looked around a building and saw the car parked in front of the flat. He could make out at least one person in the front seat.

Lind said, "Gotta figure somebody's around back, too. I'll check that out."

"How about giving me one of those pistols?" Brook felt an acute, immediate need to arm himself.

Lind pushed one on him, butt first. "Don't hurt yourself."

Lind disappeared into the darkness. Brook almost shouted for him to stop. He didn't know where Lind was going, and worried that he was trying to clear out. It wouldn't have surprised him.

Brook moved closer, crouching behind the trees that lined the sidewalk. A man got out of the car. Brook heard the static from his radio. One of Brody's people.

He watched him walk toward the building.

Brook glanced up at the darkened windows of his apartment and experienced a strong rush of fear. It looked wrong, felt wrong.

He sprinted into the street and made it halfway across before the man turned and started reaching into his jacket. Brook tackled him around the shoulders and drove him to the ground.

The guy was shorter than Brook, but strong. Brook got him in a headlock and slammed his face into the sidewalk. Once. Twice. He left him there unconscious but still breathing. He removed the pistol from his shoulder holster and threw it across the street.

Lind approached quietly from the back of the building. He looked at the man and growled, "Not bad."

Relieved, Brook took a deep breath. Lind hadn't run off. "Did you find anybody?"

Lind nodded. "He had a nice spot back there. He was ready to blow the shit out of anybody who went out the back door."

"What happened to him?"

Lind smiled. "He's in about the same shape as this guy."

Brook was already up on the porch. He noticed the chock of wood stuck in the base of the doorframe. He kicked it out and opened the door. The stairwell was dark.

"Jenny!"

He shouted her name again and ran up the stairs. He was almost to the top when the lights suddenly came on. Jenny swung around a corner. She had the Winchester leveled at his head.

Recognizing him, she dropped the shotgun and threw herself into his arms. She'd gotten dressed.

Brook noticed the bullet-shattered bathroom door. He glanced into the bedroom and saw Waters's lower torso. He knew who it was without having to see the face.

Lind stuck his head into the stairwell. "We better get out of here. Move it!"

"Are you ready?" Brook asked Jenny.

She couldn't believe she'd killed a man. But there was no guilt. Only relief, gratitude. She was aware that Brook was holding her by both shoulders.

"Jenny, are you all right?"

"Yes!" she said. "Yes! Yes!"

He lay in his bedroom, staring at the crude microscope he'd painted on the wall in red and gold. It was nine feet high, six across. He'd drawn a long red line, connecting the microscope with the brain he'd already sketched on his living room wall.

Nice.

Except for one thing: The symbolism was all wrong.

What arrogance to think that science, as represented by his microscope, could ever explain the mysteries of the mind or understand its complex chemistry and biology. It couldn't be done. Freud had come to realize that; so had Jung, Fromm, all the others.

It could drive you mad even to try to decipher the smallest piece of the puzzle.

He took a deep breath: He knew a little about madness.

He got up from his bed. Naked, he caught a glimpse of his sagging belly in the dresser mirror. He dipped a paint brush into the open can of paint and scrawled a red question mark through the microscope.

Artistically, it wasn't bad. He'd taken a few drawing courses in college for grins. Who knows, his mural might even be worth money later.

Impulsively, he dipped a finger into the red paint and drew a heart on his bare chest. He'd always been a good anatomist. The heart was perfectly placed, each valve drawn to proportion. He painted two concentric circles around it and looked in the mirror.

Excellent.

The heart was at the center of a bull's-eye.

It was nearly time to have that last talk with Dr. Hartigan. An exit interview.

Earlier that evening he'd almost paid him a visit to settle matters. But something was wrong. Hartigan had appeared distracted, out of sorts.

The timing wasn't right. He'd always respected the importance of good timing.

Better to wait.

He sipped Old Overholt straight from the bottle. Another rocket went off in his head in a shower of cascading red and blue lights.

He'd stop by to see Hartigan in the morning. With a little luck, he'd make it through another night.

FORTY-SEVEN

⊳◼⊲

IT TOOK BROOK FIFTEEN minutes to drive to the PCZ Pharmaceutical lab in West County. He pulled into the parking lot and turned off the lights. The building was cube-shaped and plated with bronzed glass.

They'd gambled that Al Silver would be there. Actually, not much of a gamble. Brook had found out that he was at the lab almost every night.

Brook had the barest outline of a plan: Force Silver to give them some of his antikindling medication, and hope it worked on Lind. He planned to give it to him as soon as he could get him someplace safe; then they'd wait a few weeks and see what happened. If it didn't work, he was going to try an anticonvulsant. Provided Lind cooperated.

Over the last ninety minutes, Lind had been rational, even reasonable, but Brook wondered how much longer this interlude would last. He didn't hold out much hope that Lind had suddenly turned a corner.

The convict seemed to trust him, at least a little, and that was enough. Brook wanted to do whatever he could to make sure that fragile bond continued to grow between them. Whatever happened later would depend on it.

"So what do you want to do?" Lind asked impatiently.

"We get him to come out to the car, and I'll invite him inside," Brook said.

Jenny called the lab on the car's cell phone. A security
guard transferred her to Silver's office. She stated that she
had something important to tell him and that she was parked
on the lot next to his silver BMW.

Moments later Silver strode out the front door. Brook and
Lind kept down in the backseat as he approached the car.

Jenny waved at Silver and rolled down her window. When
he came over to the driver's side, she pointed a pistol at his
face and told him to get in the back.

Lind reached up and opened the door. He pressed his own
pistol into Silver's crotch as he climbed in.

"Nice to see you," he said. "How many guards you got
in there right now?"

"One."

"Where's he at?"

Silver's voice trembled. "He could be anywhere in the
building."

Brook told Silver what he wanted. "Just tell me one
thing," he said. "Will your new drug work on humans? Will
it keep them from kindling?"

For a moment Silver looked surprised that Brook knew
about his work. Recovering some of his natural arrogance,
he said, "I'd stop this right now before it gets any worse."

Lind tapped Silver on the back of the head with a pistol
butt. The light blow produced an immediate attitude change.

"Don't hurt me, please," Silver begged.

Lind said, "If you try anything in there, I'll kill you."

"Have your drugs been tested on human subjects yet?"
Brook asked.

Silver nodded.

Brook took a breath to steady himself. So Ulman had been
right; somehow he'd found out that they were going to use
Silver's antikindling drug on LePonty.

"Is it some kind of peptide?"

Again, Silver looked surprised at what Brook knew.

"A polypeptide chain. We're using protein molecules to
produce the. . . ."

"Fuck the science, you bastard," Brook said, cutting him off. "Just tell me, does it work?"

Silver looked frightened.

"In two or three days. The results have been excellent with Billings."

Brook told Silver to get out, and followed him to the door. Jenny and Lind stayed inside the car. Silver inserted a plastic ID card into a slot; the glass doors opened automatically.

Brook fought back his fear. The guard wasn't at the front desk.

The corridor was narrow, clean and dimly lit. The floors practically gleamed. It was so quiet the sound of their footsteps reverberated. Brook hadn't taken his hand off the pistol in his jacket pocket.

The guard came around the corner. He wore a blue jacket and gray slacks, the same uniform as the clinic's security staff. Young. Hard-looking.

"Forget something, Doctor?" he asked.

The guard eyed Brook, a strange face to him.

"Thomas, this is Doctor John Brook," Silver said, introducing Brook. "He's a colleague of mine. We wants to check some documents in my office."

Silver pronounced Brook's name slowly and distinctly. The guard seemed to catch something in the tone. He looked again at Brook and started to leave, then turned suddenly, reaching for his pistol. Brook already had his gun out. He pressed the barrel against the man's chest.

Brook opened a door in the hallway. It was a broom closet complete with a sink and set of mops. Brook took the man's gun and shoved him into the small space. He turned the doorlock.

He glared at Silver. "That was a smart stunt, Al."

Silver hadn't budged. "Don't . . . don't hurt me."

"What's going on?" Brook asked. "As soon as that guy heard my name, he was on full alert."

"They've warned the entire staff to be on the lookout for you," Silver said.

"Where do you keep the drugs?"

"In my office."

It was down the hall, which doglegged to the left.

Brook struggled to control his nervousness. It was everything he could do to keep from grabbing Silver by the neck and forcing him to run. If Brody showed up now, they were finished.

Silver's office was more like a private lab. A circular worktable with a black-laminate countertop dominated the center of the room. There were trays of reagents, a computer terminal. The most impressive item was a binocular microscope.

A steel cabinet was in the corner.

Silver didn't have to be told. He unlocked the door. The cabinet was filled with trays of 10-cc injectable bottles. Each contained a pink liquid.

"What temperature?"

"Room temperature. Don't let it freeze."

"How often do you give it?"

"Two injections a day, morning and night. Like I said, you should start to see results in two or three days, four maximum."

Brook took twice as many as he thought he'd need. He stuffed them in the pockets of his parka.

"What else can you tell me, Al? What's really going on at the clinic? What's the program, the real one? Just for starters, who's paying for all this research?"

Silver didn't answer.

"You want Lind to ask you that question?"

Silver frantically shook his head—no, no, no.

"It's the Paulus Foundation," he said. "A man named James Paulus runs it, a rich conservative from New Mexico. Paulus thinks we can make a fortune offering kindling as a cheap, effective treatment for hardcore criminals. The demographics are on our side. The country's crime problem is only going to get worse. We know that. The criminals are getting younger and more violent all the time. There's going to be a big market for noninvasive procedures like kindling."

Again, Ulman had been right. Brook remembered how Ulman's wife had told them her husband thought someone was calling the shots from offstage, someone with money.

There were footsteps outside.

"You were taking a long time," Lind said, entering the room.

Silver looked like he was having a heart attack. Drenched with sweat, his face was that ashen.

Brook told Lind he'd gotten what he came for.

"What about the guard?"

Brook explained what had happened. They were in the hallway.

Lind asked, "Where is he?"

Brook pointed to the closet.

Lind took out a magnum.

"Ed, no!"

Brook grabbed him by the shoulder. Lind turned fast. Silver caught the look in his eyes and began to scream like a child.

Brook saw it too. He'd never seen a man's face contort so horribly before. Lips, teeth, eyes. An expression diabolic and murderous. Then it was gone like the passing of a shadow.

"Don't do it!" Brook said. "Don't kill him!"

And don't kill me, he thought. He sensed that it was possible this time, that Lind was balanced on a wire between reason and that other place he'd visited.

Lind grabbed Silver by the throat and shoved him against a wall. The scientist wailed and threw up his hands. Lind pushed him inside the closet with the guard and locked the door again.

He looked at Brook and said, "If you've got something to give me, you better do it soon."

Brody surveyed the carnage in Brook's apartment. They were lucky the place was so secluded. Otherwise somebody might have heard the gunfire and called the police.

The bedroom where they'd found Waters was unbelievable. A chunk of his leg had been blown back into the hall-way.

They had already removed his body and Rita Stell's. They'd found her after they checked out the shot-up rear stairwell that connected the two apartments. They took the bodies out the back. They'd pulled a panel truck right up to the door.

Brody's anger was at full throttle. They'd missed Lind and Dr. Brook at the warehouse. He'd lost two men in the process. And now this mess with Waters.

A call on his cell phone distracted him.

It was one of his men back at the clinic's security office. He was monitoring the surveillance cameras at the PCZ lab.

The camera had just picked up Brook and Silver's entrance into the building.

Brody immediately dispatched two teams to the lab. He told them to speed. They would run a risk of getting pulled over, but maybe one of them would make it in time.

The man watching the television monitors told him that repeated attempts to raise the guard had failed.

Brody took off with Eliot and headed for the lab. This time there could be no mistakes. They had to stop them.

Fifteen minutes later he got another call.

One of his teams had arrived in time to see the Intrepid pull away from the lab's parking lot. Two men and a woman were inside.

"You want us to stop them?"

"Negative," Brody said. They were right on a major intersection, for crissakes. The place would've been crawling with cops right after the first shots were fired.

"Just stay with them."

FORTY-EIGHT

IT WAS NEARLY TWO in the morning. They were on Missouri Route 21, a two-lane blacktop that ran south out of St. Louis, one twisting mile after another, all the way to the Arkansas line. The road rivaled some of the worst stretches in the Smokies—killer curves, no shoulders, plunging drop-offs into thick woods.

Brook was driving. He was groggy from fatigue, and his eyes were burning, but he thought he could hang on a while longer.

Lind sat next to him, wide awake and alert. Jenny was asleep in the back seat. The car's steering was quick, sure. The problem was holding the speed down on the curves and not overdriving.

Brook's plan was to take 21 as far as Poplar Bluff, then head due east across the Mississippi River into Tennessee. Once he crossed the state line, he could make it to the mountains blindfolded.

He'd settled on Route 21 because he thought it would be easier to spot someone following them on a rural two-lane.

He glanced in the rearview mirror. It had become a habit. Four, maybe five cars were back there. Most of them would probably turn off at the Potosi exit, the last town of any size until you reached Poplar Bluff.

Brook nodded when he saw the illuminated exit sign for

Potosi, home of the state's largest prison. He'd been there more times than he could remember, to do mental-status evaluations on death-row inmates.

They passed the turnoff.

Brook, eyes riveted in the mirror, saw three sets of headlights angle off to the right. The road ahead curved in a long arc, then straightened out for several miles.

If anyone had continued past the exit, he'd know in a moment.

He crested a hill and looked behind. He saw the high beams first. Then a car came around the curve, moving fast, rapidly closing the gap between them.

Lind looked through the rear window.

He grinned and said, "They found us."

Still not sure, Brook punched the gas pedal to the floor. The burst of acceleration snapped his head back. He came out of a tight S-turn and hit a long, climbing straightaway. Gripping the wheel, he nudged the speed to eighty-five.

They reached the top of a hill. The lights were still there, maybe a mile behind them.

Lind looked at Brook. "No offense, but maybe I better drive."

Brody put down his cell phone. He'd just spoken to Beckworth, who'd promised to send a helicopter from Jefferson City as soon as the weather improved. It was lousy. Thick cloud cover, light rain and fog. You couldn't see more than two hundred feet. They had a good pilot, a former highway trooper hot to trot. But there was no way he'd take off in this weather.

The forecast didn't show any improvement until late the next morning.

Eliot drove the Jeep. Three cars followed them. They were thirty miles out of St. Louis, heading south on Route 21.

Eliot kept the speed at sixty-five miles an hour. They would play it safe until they were farther out in the country. The odds of running into a cop with a radar gun out in the sticks at two in the morning was almost nil.

Brody's thoughts scatter-gunned. He didn't want to find out what would happen if he didn't stop Brook's car.

The stakes had skyrocketed in the last three hours. Beckworth had reminded him that he was in charge of security. He was being paid big bucks. He was responsible.

The warden had made it all abundantly clear. The bastard had almost been ranting.

Brody wasn't going to let that prick rattle him any more than necessary. After a few minutes, he hung up on him. Beckworth wouldn't like that at all.

The cell phone beeped.

It was Crance, who was driving the car chasing Brook. He'd been steadily pulling closer.

"Permission to use automatic fire."

"Get as much room on them as you can. Then stop the car."

"Forget it."

Jenny was wide-awake, leaning forward in the backseat.

"You're gonna have to stop soon anyway," Lind said. "You're falling asleep at the wheel."

He took out his pistols and checked their loads. He also picked up Brook's shotgun, which lay on the floorboards at his feet.

He tested the pump action and smiled. "Nice gun."

Brook said, "It was my father's."

"My old man had a shotgun, too," Lind said, "I remember when he sawed off the barrel and taped the handle. I musta been eight years old. He was on his way to hold up a grocery store."

Brook saw the headlights again. Whoever was following them was gaining ground on every straightaway. Lind was right. He couldn't hold out much longer. His reflexes and concentration were shot.

Jenny said, "Let him drive, John. I trust him."

Lind laughed and said, "I wouldn't go that far, lady. You rob banks, you learn how to drive. It's an acquired skill."

"All right," Brook said. "As soon as we're out of this curve."

He hit the brakes in the middle of the road. The front of the car nosed down hard. He slid across into the passenger seat while Lind got out and ran around to the driver's side.

As soon as he was behind the wheel, Lind floored it. They pulled off like a shot, the rear tires screaming and pouring a trail of smoke.

The car behind them had gained. It was only a couple hundred yards back.

"That guy's really coming on," Brook said.

"No problem," Lind said.

He leaned back in the bucket seat, both arms extended straight as he gripped the wheel. Brook saw him smile.

"Hot car," he said. "I could have used one of these on the last job I pulled."

Brook glimpsed a yellow caution sign flash by as Lind tore into a thirty-mile-an-hour curve. He took it at sixty, swinging out over the center line.

"As soon as we're far enough ahead, I'm going to stop," Lind said. "I want you two to get out fast."

"Are you crazy?" Brook said.

"Yeah, I guess I am," Lind said, breaking into a lopsided grin. "Crazy as hell, compliments of the best medical science you folks have to offer."

"Forget it. We're not getting out of the car."

"Suit yourself, but I'm going to kill those bastards behind us. If you and Doctor Malone want to stay here and enjoy the show, that's your business."

One hand on the wheel, Lind reached over and picked up the loaded Winchester and set it between his legs, stock up. He kept the speed well over eighty.

Brook was no longer aware of the trees outside, the shapes a dark blur.

Lind adjusted the rearview mirror.

"When I stop, get the fuck out of this car and off the road."

Lind shot over another hill, then slammed on the brakes. The Intrepid fishtailed and swerved to the left. He barely kept it on the road. The ground dropped off sharply on both sides of the blacktop.

Lind shouted, ''Get out!''

Brook and Jenny threw open the doors and ran. When Brook turned around, Lind had blocked one lane entirely and most of the other. He'd positioned the Dodge well below the crest of the hill.

Brook understood what he had in mind. A chill went through him.

The other driver wouldn't see the car until it was too late. By the time he came over that hill, he'd have only a few seconds to decide whether to broadside the Dodge or go off the road into the trees.

Brook gauged the distance. He and Jenny were still way too close, about ten yards. He saw a pair of headlights coming over the top of the hill.

They started running down the blacktop just as the car hit the crest, nosed down and went into a long slide. The driver, braking hard, was desperately aiming for the narrow gap of open pavement between the Intrepid and the side of the road, but there was no way he'd find it.

Lind sat in the car with the window down.

Brook heard shotgun blasts and, glancing back, saw flashes coming from the driver's side.

Somehow the driver of the other car managed to make it through the opening, but the back wheels hit the edge of the blacktop. The car flipped on its side and cartwheeled end-over-end down the shoulder of the road. Brook saw it coming, two tons of twisted steel hurtling right for them. The sound of grinding metal was earsplitting.

Brook pushed Jenny off the blacktop. There was no place to take cover. They both hit the muddy slope and fell on top of each other as the wreckage went off the road a few yards behind them. It rolled through the thick trees, snapping them off with a sound like rifle shots before plowing to a stop.

The car didn't explode or burst into flames as Brook had expected it would. He got up and looked down through the channel of broken trees and saw it lying on its side; the roof was caved in and one of the doors had sprung open. There were no survivors as far as he could tell.

He and Jenny climbed back up to the highway. A few moments later, Lind pulled up next to them. The Intrepid wasn't even scratched. The interior smelled of gunpowder.

Lind opened the passenger door for Jenny. "Hey, folks, how about a round of applause?"

FORTY-NINE

HARTIGAN MET WITH HIS senior staff to update them on the search for Lind. Marty Conner, Jim Serra, Ted Krill and Al Silver listened in silence in the clinic's third-floor conference room as Hartigan described what had happened during the previous eight hours.

Silver was nursing a swollen left eye. He told the others that he'd accidentally walked into a bedroom door. It was almost the truth. He'd smacked his eye on the doorknob when Lind shoved him into the lab's broom closet.

Hartigan had ordered Silver to keep his whimpering mouth shut about what had happened, then he told the others that Lind had apparently kidnapped John Brook and Jenny Malone. Brody had practically his entire security force out looking for them. They would be getting additional help soon from Warden Beckworth.

What he didn't tell them, not even Silver, was the latest news: that Brody had lost two men in a car wreck sixty miles south of Potosi. Nor did he tell them that Lind and their two colleagues had disappeared.

Everything he'd struggled to accomplish during the last ten years was slipping away. It was as if he could feel the ground moving under his feet. The sensation of disequilibrium was that real, that frightening.

He'd achieved a medical breakthrough in the treatment of

ASPs. No one could doubt it. He would prove that kindling was a successful behavior-altering procedure. It had worked with Billings. It might have worked with Waters and Lind as well, if they hadn't escaped before he could inject them with Al Silver's peptide to stop the kindling process.

At the very end of it all, he had to trust men like Beckworth, Paulus and Brody to keep everything from falling apart. It was incomprehensible.

No one asked any questions. The men took the news in almost drugged silence.

The session lasted less than five minutes. Serra lingered after the others had departed. He asked to meet with Hartigan privately.

"I want to go over those latest PET scans on Billings," he said.

Hartigan nodded. The work with Billings was the one break in the gloom. They went to his office. Serra closed the door behind them.

Hartigan sat down at his desk and looked at Serra as if seeing him for the first time. The man looked ill. His face was drawn, feverish.

"Are you all right?" Hartigan asked.

Serra shrugged. "Just a touch of the flu. Nothing serious."

They had reached the foothills of the Smokies as they drove east on Route 64 into Chattanooga. Across the Tennessee River, Signal Mountain rose in the mist. A few miles to the south, they could make out the knobby shape of Lookout Mountain. The North Carolina line was only forty miles to the east.

It had been ten hours since they'd left St. Louis. Their route had taken them from Poplar Bluff, Missouri, east into Tennessee, where they'd picked up 64.

Even distracted by worry, Brook felt old stirrings in the blood as he approached the mountains.

The Smokies were the East Coast's most massive geological uplift. They were over five hundred million years old, beyond prehistoric. A mix of rock, sand and sediment in layers twenty thousand feet thick. Sheets of rock so ancient they didn't contain a speck of plant or animal life. Rocks harder than granite. The mountain chain consisted of sixteen summits over six thousand feet, a ridge line that didn't drop below five thousand feet for thirty-six miles. And, creating their own mystery, the brooding peaks were almost always covered by a blue, smokelike haze.

Brook was headed to the south of the main chain in the Yellow Creek Mountains, where the peaks wouldn't be much over four thousand feet. Still, nothing to sneeze at during the winter, especially in a storm.

Brook worked over everything that needed to be done. At the top of his mental checklist: He still wasn't sure how he was going to give Lind a peptide injection.

He still had the 10-cc injectable bottles in his coat pocket. He'd also taken a dozen monoject syringes from Silver's office and some disposable butterfly tubing.

He'd been worrying for hours about how he would get Lind to do this. He doubted he'd be able to force the issue. Not with Lind, who was dozing in the backseat with the Winchester within reach and a .357 in his belt.

Brook had relieved him at the wheel an hour earlier. He wondered how much longer Lind could hold out without an explosion. In a strange way, wrecking that car back in Missouri had helped calm him down.

Jenny sat next to him, sipping coffee they'd bought earlier at a truck stop.

She was trying to take it an hour at a time. So far, there had been no aftershocks. No signs of depression, confusion, anger. Nothing like the hours of hell she'd endured immediately after her rape in Chicago.

She still wondered how she would handle it long-term, how she would adjust to killing Waters. But she already sensed that she was going to come out of this emotionally intact.

"We'll need some equipment," Brook said. "Sleeping bags, a cookstove, lanterns, backpacks, food, clothes, good boots."

Balancing her coffee cup on her lap, Jenny studied the map.

"We better get them here in Chattanooga," she said. "The towns after this look pretty small."

Her eyes were red and puffy. Brook touched her leg. She laid her hand over his.

"How are you doing?" he asked. They hadn't had a chance to talk about what had happened back in St. Louis.

Jenny smiled. "I'm trying to pretend we're on a vacation." She hesitated before she said, "Do you think they're following us?"

"If they're not, they will be."

He pulled off the interstate at a Wal-Mart. They could get whatever camping equipment and winter clothing they needed there.

Lind woke up with a sleepy groan as Brook hauled into a space in the huge parking lot.

He explained why he was stopping.

"Where are we?" Lind asked.

"Chattanooga."

Lind yawned. "This is a good time to tell us where we're going."

Brook said, "We'll be in the mountains just south of the Smoky national park. Near the upper end of Fontana Lake. My family's owned a hunting cabin up there for years."

Brook pointed out the location on Jenny's map. The Yellow Creek Mountains and the long, stringbean-shaped lake were about a hundred miles northeast of Chattanooga as the crow flies. Rugged country.

They went into the store together. It took half an hour to gather everything: winter parkas, Hollofil sleeping bags, boots, a double-burner Coleman stove, lanterns, flashlights, food. The gear, over three hundred dollars' worth, filled a big shopping cart to overflowing. Brook paid cash.

When he got back to the car, he was soaked with sweat. Lind had carried two guns into the store under his jacket. If he'd decided to take off or do something violent, Brook knew there was absolutely nothing he could have done to stop him.

Hartigan's eyes were clamped down hard on the pistol that Serra had leveled at his head.

"We need to talk," Serra said. "I know about those buttons on the bottom of your desk. If you touch one of them, I'll kill you."

Stunned, Hartigan sat there, transfixed, as Serra blurted out in a few sharply worded sentences his accumulated rage.

"You made me do it, you bastard," he said. "You're responsible."

Hartigan didn't know what he was talking about. He couldn't believe the way Serra looked, the twisted smile, how his eyes were lit up. He'd never seen him like that before.

"Remember two years ago when I'd hit a dead end with my neuro-stim design? You wanted to shift gears and run some tests on how serotonin levels affect aggression. You were pushing me hard on that."

Hartigan kept watching him, still not understanding. He did remember that they'd talked about having some med students drink a special chemical solution to lower their serotonin levels. That way they could test to see if the drop in serotonin increased their aggression levels. Afterward, they were going to give them a dose of tryptophan to get their serotonin back to normal.

"We couldn't get enough volunteers, so we dropped that idea," Hartigan said. He kept staring into the muzzle of the pistol. The dime-sized black hole in the barrel had a way of focusing his thoughts.

"No, we didn't drop it," Serra said. "You were so desperate for a breakthrough, you kept pushing me to run that experiment. Don't you remember telling me that if I didn't get it done, you'd cut the funding on my neuro-stim research?"

"Can we discuss this, Jim?" Hartigan's one thought was to keep him talking and distracted. Maybe he could hit a panic button if Serra turned his head.

"You kept pushing me, and so one night after I'd had too much wine with dinner, I drove back to the lab and made myself a cocktail. Six ounces of a concentrated amino-acid solution mixed with cherry cola." That lopsided grin again. "I found out later I should have diluted the mixture, but I was pretty drunk then. I basically short-circuited my brain's neurochemistry." He drew closer to Hartigan's desk. "You made me drink that poison as surely as if you'd held a gun to my head and ordered me to do it."

"Jim, I had no idea." Hartigan had never heard any of this before. Serra was having a breakdown. The man was raving, which frightened him more than the pistol.

"I can't get my serotonin and other neuroreceptors back into any kind of balance. I've been medicating myself for months. I'm really fucked up."

"But what you're saying isn't true," Hartigan said. "I never . . ."

What Serra said made Hartigan freeze. His chest constricted. The pistol wove slow circles in front of his face.

"What do you think people will say when they find out about that solo project of yours? The laser experiment on prisoners at the Men's Club." Hartigan's unblinking eyes convinced him he was hitting all the right buttons. "Four men dying so young. And two women. The black girl was very attractive. I've seen her picture. Was that the one you were fucking while you were fucking with her brain?"

Jenny pulled the car off Interstate 74 at a state-maintained rest stop twelve miles west of the North Carolina border. The closest town was Ocoee.

The only other vehicles in the parking lot were three or four tractor-trailers. The drivers were using the restroom.

Jenny parked at the far end of the lot away from the eighteen-wheelers. It was early afternoon. A rain was falling—light, soft, gray.

Brook sat in the back of the car next to Lind. He'd filled a syringe with 10 cc of the peptide, which was mixed in a sterile solution, probably something containing sodium chloride.

Brook needed to push him. They were running out of time. He wanted to get Lind on the peptide before they reached their final destination. He still wondered whether Lind would really go through with this and stay with them up in the mountains.

Whatever happened, they wouldn't force him. Brook doubted they could, even if they wanted to. His hope was that the peptide would make him more docile.

Lind said, "This scares me."

Brook tried to keep his voice in neutral as he covered all the old arguments: It helped Billings. It can help you. "We've got to try, or your brain will keep kindling."

Lind bit his lips. He stared with wide-eyed intensity at something no one else could see.

Brook sensed something was happening to him. Maybe his brain was about to have another seizure. "I'll inject this into your arm, and it's all over," he said.

Lind's face was twisted. Brook saw something else in his bitter eyes. Behind the fear, a plea for help.

"All right, do it," he said, rolling up his jacket sleeve.

Brook uncapped the injectable bottle, inserted the needle into a vein in Lind's right forearm and pressed down on the syringe.

"You'll probably feel a sting, maybe a slight burning," he said.

Lind kept staring at him, eyes on fire.

Now that he had Hartigan's undivided attention, Serra hammered at him. It was a pleasure. He momentarily forgot the depression that had been cranking up all morning. He even forgot his worsening tremors. His gun hand was jerking in spasm.

He explained how he found out about Hartigan's secret project.

"All good scientists need a little luck," he said.

Nearly a year ago, he'd interviewed a former prisoner at

the Green River women's facility, a twenty-four-year-old from St. Louis. It was a routine competency evaluation. She had stabbed her boyfriend and nearly killed him. Her lawyer was arguing temporary insanity.

"She had a cellmate who told her the most amazing story," Serra said. "How she'd been involved in some crazy medical experiment."

Hartigan flinched but kept his composure as Serra described how the woman had been promised a couple years off her sentence. They drove her to a small building in Fulton, where they shaved a two-inch patch in her hair above her right ear and clamped her head in a padded metal device so she couldn't move it.

Serra said, "When she woke up, they told her they used a special beam of light to see into her brain." He grinned. "That was a nice touch, doctor."

The woman remembered only one thing about the procedure. When she woke up in a darkened room, a man was on top of her. She couldn't get a good look at him.

"She said he had white hair," Serra said.

Hartigan tried to say something.

Serra almost struck him with the pistol barrel. "Shut your goddamn mouth!"

Hartigan winced at the blow that wasn't delivered.

"The woman died under the most mysterious circumstances. Imagine someone that young dying of a brain embolism. Remarkable, wouldn't you say?"

His face only a few inches from Hartigan's, Serra said, "Why did you do it? What made you think you could do laser oblations and get away with it, or expect that they'd work?"

Hartigan didn't answer.

Serra said, "The inmates developed these strange side effects. One of them couldn't stop crying, so you sedated him. And when that didn't work, you killed him. You killed all of them. How did you do it, doctor? A drug injection straight into the heart? A bolus of air shot into a vein?"

Hartigan puffed his chest in anger. Serra enjoyed the effect.

He explained how he found it curious that the only files Hartigan kept under lock and key were in cabinets beneath his bookcase. He wondered what kind of documents were stored there. Then one day Hartigan left the keys on his desk.

Serra said, "I borrowed them for half an hour and had copies made. Did you know they can do that in the drug store across from the MetroLink on Euclid? I came in here one night at two in the morning. It was a couple months before we upgraded our security system, or I couldn't have done it. I read all your files. I examined those incredible brain specimens."

Some valve had opened behind Hartigan's eyes. They were pulsing with pure hatred.

"So what do you want?" he snapped. "An apology? Do you want me to say I'm sorry that some chronic offenders died because I was trying to find a way to treat them? You can go to hell."

"I've already been there," Serra said, slamming the gun down on the table, shattering the glass top.

"There was something else I stumbled on after I stole your computer log-on. I was surfing through your files when I came across the most amazing document. A rough draft of a scientific paper you were preparing on our neuro-stim experiments. It read like it was all your work. I was hardly mentioned."

Serra straightened. His hands were trembling. Another tremor. And this time something else. The mild buzzing in his head that had bothered him intermittently for days began to roar. A cascading, churning white noise.

"You were going to claim all the credit for yourself, weren't you?" Serra put his hands to his head and pressed viselike as if trying to squeeze out the sound. He clamped down his eyes in pain. The neuroelectrical wires in his brain were unraveling, breaking apart, short-circuiting.

This was his worst attack.

"Something else occurred to me when I was reading that

paper,'' Serra said. ''I realized you were going to have me killed. If you were going to say the breakthrough was all your idea, I'd have to be dead.''

His eyes were pressed shut long enough for Hartigan to hit the button on the bottom of his desk top.

Brody had reached Poplar Bluff, Missouri, with four of his security teams in tow. He was waiting for Beckworth to arrive by helicopter. The warden was bringing extra men, and Brody had sent for six more of his own people.

Brook's résumé said he was from a small town near Knoxville and had spent a lot of time hiking in the Smoky Mountains. It was possible he was hauling ass back home. Brody had already sent a two-man team on ahead to Tennessee to check out Brook's mother and make sure he didn't show up in his hometown.

Brody doubted he would be that stupid. The galling truth was that Brook, Malone and Lind could have headed just about anywhere on the map.

As he ate a quick breakfast with Eliot in a cheap diner, Brody felt the pressure steadily building in his head. He'd been fighting back his anger for hours.

He was used to being in charge, defining the moment, making his own professional arrangements. It infuriated him that he wasn't in full command of this situation.

How in christ's name could he be? He knew he needed to wait for Beckworth and his people before they committed themselves.

The warden had already sent a bulletin out on the NCIC system, alerting police agencies, especially sheriff's departments, in a four-state area to look for a green Dodge Intrepid with Missouri plates that had been stolen in St. Louis. On Brody's advice, Beckworth had sent bulletins to every law enforcement agency in Tennessee on the chance that Brook might be heading back to familiar territory.

If the warden wanted to run this show himself, fine. It didn't please Brody, but what could he do? After last night's sorry performance, he wasn't exactly inspiring confidence.

It didn't help his appetite that he'd taken a look inside the car that had plunged off Route 21. They'd located the wreckage shortly after dawn. It wasn't hard. The last radio message from Crance had included a mile marker, which helped them pinpoint the location. So did the skid marks.

They'd buried the two bodies in shallow graves a couple of miles away. He'd soaked the car inside and out with gasoline and torched it. It went off in a fireball of orange flames and black smoke.

From the length of the skid marks, Brody figured the fools must have been doing eighty miles an hour when they sailed into the trees. He doubted they'd lost control. Crance was a good driver. It seemed more likely that someone had forced them off the road.

It was nine in the morning, and the sky was slowly clearing. Beckworth wasn't expected to take off from Jefferson City for another hour. The overcast was still too soupy to fly.

Meanwhile, Brody's men were spread out in town two to a car so as not to draw attention.

Brody was finishing the last of his scrambled eggs when he got a call from Beckworth. They'd just gotten a hit on Brook. A caretaker at a highway rest stop thirty miles northeast of Chattanooga had noticed a new car with Missouri plates. Two men were in the backseat and a young woman was in the front; the men appeared to be arguing.

It looked odd, so he mentioned it to a sheriff's deputy who'd pulled into the rest stop half an hour later. The caretaker had taken the trouble to jot down the car's license number.

The door slowly opened. Hartigan saw one of the security guards peek in. So did Serra.

He stood up straight and fired three unhurried shots into the wooden door. The bullets went *thwack, thwack, thwack.* He heard a man scream and fall.

"We're going for a walk," Serra said, pushing Hartigan toward the door. Serra gave the door a hard shove to open it. A leg blocked the opening. A young man in a blue jacket lay there not moving, eyes wide open. He'd been shot in the upper chest.

In the hallway, Serra pressed his pistol against the back of Hartigan's head. Another guard came pounding up the steps, carrying a submachine gun.

"Get back!" Hartigan shouted.

When the man hesitated, Serra fired at him. Two quick shots. The guard tumbled back down the staircase.

Serra and Hartigan rode the elevator up to the fourth floor. Serra led Hartigan to the animal lab, ordered him inside and locked the door.

As soon as Serra switched on the lights, the kindled cats began to wail and hiss.

"Open the cages," Serra said.

"You've lost your mind," Hartigan said.

A bell was ringing, the sound blasting in their ears. There were heavy footsteps in the hallway.

"Open them," Serra repeated. "Or you'll die here. I swear it."

Hartigan opened a cage, but the small white cat inside didn't even move. He opened two others. Both cats jumped out. One sprang up on a work counter and went into a frightened crouch; the other disappeared around a table.

"That's good. Keep going," Serra said.

A voice outside from the hall ordered him to open the door and release Hartigan.

Serra pushed Hartigan to another cage. He recognized the animal. It was the killer Tommy.

"Open it," Serra said.

"You've got ten seconds," the voice outside repeated.

Hartigan released the latch on the cage as a burst of gunfire shattered the doorlock. The lab door flew open. Hartigan ducked behind a table. In the small space, the gunshots sounded like claps of thunder. Hartigan put his hands over his ears and flattened himself on the floor. He didn't see Serra fall across the table.

Then Hartigan was aware of what he thought was water

dripping on his face and neck. It was spilling over the edges of the table. He wiped his cheek, and looked at the blood and clotted gray matter on his hand.

When he stood up, he noticed that his lab coat was splattered with Serra's blood.

Two guards, weapons drawn, were in the lab.

"Man, that last shot took off most of his head," one of them said.

Hartigan wasn't looking at James Serra. He'd just remembered Tommy. The cage was empty.

"He's out!" he shouted, frantically searching the narrow confines of the lab for the escaped cat.

The guards looked at each other, not understanding.

Hartigan lunged for the opened door, trying to close it, hoping he wasn't too late. From the corner of his eye, he glimpsed Tommy hurtling at him from the top of a cabinet.

The frenzied animal was trying to get out of the lab. It hit him chest-high and clung to his jacket, raking his face deeply with its claws. Hartigan tried to throw the cat off him, but it held on tenaciously, slashing again and again at his face, lacerating his cheeks.

Hartigan finally managed to knock the animal to the floor.

One of the guards fired and missed as the cat scurried out of the lab. The two other cats had also bolted.

"What the hell was that!" the man yelled. The animal's ferocity had stunned him.

Hartigan held a handkerchief to his bloody, mangled face. He was unable to speak.

FIFTY

HOTHOUSE. RANGER. MARBLE. Topton.

The names of the small North Carolina towns raised a hundred ghosts, mainly of his father and their hunting trips into the Yellow Creek Mountains. He remembered long nights sleeping by campfires; the sun rising over blue peaks that rimmed the horizon; his father's stories about duck hunting before World War II.

Brook knew that he was back in familiar country long before he pulled into Fontana Village in the late afternoon. The small resort town, a colorful assortment of cabins and summer homes perched in a mountain gorge near the western tip of Fontana Lake, was almost deserted at this time of the year. Only a few locals stayed on. The crowds showed up in the spring when the striped bass started running in the lake's deep mountain-fed waters.

It had been raining ever since they left Chattanooga. The rain and gloom matched everyone's mood. There hadn't been much talking since they'd left the rest stop.

Brook kept waiting for the peptide solution to hit Lind. The main risk would probably be to his endocrine system. The drug might shoot his blood pressure sky high.

It was late afternoon and they were well up in the country. The Great Smoky Mountains National Park was five miles away, across Fontana Lake. The closest tall peak, Shuckstack, rose up in front of them, over four thousand feet.

Brook parked by a grocery store. Most of the stores—
mainly bait-and-tackle and souvenir shops—were closed.

Jenny went in alone and bought food and other supplies,
mainly canned goods: coffee, meat, vegetables and other
items that wouldn't spoil. She also bought a set of cookware
and utensils, something they'd forgotten to do in Chattanooga, an oversight Brook regretted. He wasn't happy that
they had to stop. He would have preferred to pass through
the village without anyone seeing them.

Brook helped Jenny load her purchases into the trunk. He
drove north out of the village on Highway 28, which climbed
steadily. About three miles out of town, he turned onto a
gravel side road. It was steep, deeply rutted and in worse
shape than he'd remembered it.

"Tell me again where we're going?" Lind asked.

They had already passed two small cabins. Each looked
deserted, but Brook vaguely remembered them.

"My dad's uncle built a place up here back in the thirties.
We used to come up during the deer-hunting season. One of
my mother's relatives still owns it. I don't think anyone uses
it much any more."

The cabin was near the summit of one of the highest balds
in the Yellow Creek chain.

The road steepened and dissolved into a logging trail. A
few times the Intrepid's rear tires caught in a rut and spun,
and Brook had to roll back and try again.

Through gaps in the trees, they saw the silver glint of
Fontana Lake in the distance—and, beyond it, the tallest
peaks of the Smokies.

"It's beautiful," Jenny said. She laid her hand on Brook's
right arm.

Even Lind had perked up at the scenery. He was leaning
forward in the back seat, staring out the front window. "Do
you get nosebleeds up here?"

Brook went another quarter-mile, then stopped.

"There it is."

The house was carved into the mountainside. A plank

stairway climbed to the screened front-porch. His father had liked to sit on the porch and watch the sun go down. He would be out there even in cold weather, sipping bourbon and smoking his pipe.

The place looked unchanged from Brook's last visit. How long ago? Sixteen, seventeen years?

He took two sleeping bags from the trunk and climbed the steps. The cabin windows were securely shuttered. He went to the woodpile in back and found the key in an old Prince Albert's tobacco tin wedged under the iron slat that supported the wood.

Brook couldn't believe it. He didn't think the key would still be there. He wondered if anyone in the family had been up here since his father's death.

He opened the front and rear doors to let the place air out. The cabin had two large rooms, each with a wood stove. The furniture consisted of four wooden chairs and a big table made of hewn boards.

Leaves were scattered on the floor, probably brought in by squirrels that had climbed down the chimney.

Brook got fires going in both stoves. The place warmed up quickly, but it would take a while to get the dampness out of the air.

Brook and Jenny prepared dinner on the Coleman they had bought in Chattanooga. The main course was canned stew with bread, applesauce and sweetened instant coffee.

Lind ate heartily. He appeared in a good mood. After dinner, Brook gave him his second peptide injection. This time he submitted without protest.

"You're not going to feel anything for two or three days," Brook reminded him. "Think you can hang in that long?"

"What choice do I have?" Lind said.

There was no way they could force him to do anything. Lind had two pistols and a .30-caliber rifle he'd pulled out of the wrecked car back near Poplar Bluff. Brook wasn't about to try to make him stay put.

If Lind wanted to leave there was nothing they could do to stop him, and he knew it. Even if Brook could have sedated him, Lind would have considered it a betrayal.

The only thing they could hope for was that the raw, rainy weather and the cabin's remoteness might work in their favor.

Brook loaded four D batteries into the back of their portable radio and fiddled with the dial. All the local stations were running weather bulletins.

An unusual storm front was working its way toward the South Carolina coast. The hurricane season had ended months earlier, but the front was packing winds of nearly hurricane strength, almost seventy miles an hour. The freak storm had been building all day.

Forecasters were worried about what would happen when all that warm, moist Gulf air worked inland and collided with a cold front moving into the Tennessee Valley. Brook instantly grasped the risks. They could have a whopper of a winter storm on their hands.

Thursday, at seven P.M., Brody's convoy hit Chattanooga. He had five two-man teams, including the one he'd already sent into the state. Counting Eliot and himself, twelve men. Not nearly enough, but Beckworth had chartered a plane and was sending another six from Missouri. The plane would arrive at Chattanooga's Lovell Field by ten o'clock that night.

As they waited, he'd spread his men out in three motels along Lee Highway. They needed to get some sleep.

Brody and Eliot had checked into a Sleep Tight Inn. They'd bought a sack of burgers and milkshakes and were eating in front of the television when they caught a news broadcast. The talking heads were leading with the latest weather report. The storm center had moved to within seventy nautical miles of Cape Fear. Sustained winds topped hurricane strength.

In western North Carolina, forecasters were worried about rapidly falling temperatures and blizzard conditions.

"That sounds bad," Eliot said.

"It might help us if it snows," Brody said.

"How's that?" Eliot didn't understand. The thought of confronting a heavy snow in mountain country didn't warm him. He hated cold weather, cold hands.

Brody finished a cheeseburger, crumpled the wrapper and threw a strike into the wastepaper basket. "A bad storm will keep people indoors, and that includes the cops. The fewer cops we've got to deal with the better."

He lay down on one of the too-soft double beds and tried to sleep. He figured he'd need every minute he could snatch. This was going to get mean, fast.

At ten o'clock—nine P.M. St. Louis time—Lind used the cell phone from the car to call the Bill Masterson show on station KPDN.

Brook didn't like the idea, but Lind was so insistent on calling Masterson again that Brook didn't want to make an issue of it. If Lind wanted to bait Hartigan and the clinic on the radio, what difference did it make? The story was going to get out soon enough anyway. When the time came, he'd see to that himself.

Lind asked him to put an ear close to the phone, so he could hear what Masterson said. The reception wasn't great, the sound fading in and out. He turned up the volume control.

As soon as Lind identified himself, he was immediately put through to Masterson's producer. Evidently, they'd been expecting the call.

A young woman told Lind that Masterson was on the air, but wanted to talk to him. She begged him to hold on.

After a minute or so, Masterson came on the line.

"Thanks for calling," he said.

"When am I going on, Bill? I've got a lot to tell your audience."

"The station management has decided, uh, that it wouldn't be a good idea." Masterson was picking his words with care.

"Why's that?"

"I'm sorry. I can't say."

"Then maybe I better hang up, Bill. Be seeing . . .

"No, please. I do want to talk to you."

Brook picked up the desperation in Masterson's pleading voice. It was obvious that he wanted to continue their conversation.

"Then tell me what's going on, Bill."

Masterson said, "They said they'd sue us. Hartigan's lawyers threatened the station with a five-million-dollar slander and defamation suit if we let you discuss the clinic's work on the air."

"Doesn't slander mean somebody's lying about another person?"

"That's right, Ed."

"You think I'm lying?"

"No, not at all. It's just that . . .

"Are you recording this, Bill?"

Brook caught the hesitation, before Masterson said, "Yes, I am. Is that all right?"

Lind laughed. "I heard that you were a pretty gutsy guy, Bill. That you weren't afraid of nothing. I guess I heard wrong."

Masterson said, "I'm sorry. Maybe there's a way we could get some of this on the air. If you could just tell me what happened in your own words. Then . . .

Lind stopped him. "It's been nice talking to you, Bill. But I've got nothing more to say."

"Please, don't hang up." That same pleading voice.

"Bye, Bill. I'll try you again, maybe tomorrow, maybe the next day. You put me on, I'll make you famous. Meanwhile, see if you can buy some guts someplace. Maybe one of your sponsors sells them."

The wind that night was unlike anything Brook had ever experienced in the mountains. It shook the cabin back and forth. He and Jenny were in the back room. Brook had zipped their sleeping bags together.

Jenny leaned over and kissed him, a soft touch on the lips. Eyes bright, a smile forming. She knew that Lind was still on his mind.

"Maybe he's doing a little better," she said.

"I hope I haven't made a mess of all this," Brook said.

He didn't have a clue about the peptide's effect on Lind's kindled brain. He'd watched him carefully throughout the afternoon and evening to detect any subtle behavior changes, so far without noticeable result. Lind appeared to be more subdued, less edgy, but Brook doubted that had anything to do with the medication. It was still too early.

"You've done more than anyone else could have for him," Jenny whispered.

"You had a lot to do with it yourself," Brook said.

Jenny's legs pressed against him. Her presence was a warm comfort, a hope for the future.

He loved her. She would help him figure out what to do.

"Listen to the wind," Jenny said. Howling over the mountain crags, it sounded as if it was trying to peel away the cabin's plank roof.

She lay there listening. Closing her eyes, she murmured a silent prayer of thanksgiving for the strength that had helped her survive Waters's attack. She could still feel it coursing through her, stronger than the flow of her blood. She'd killed a man to save herself, and it didn't bother her. She'd been changed in a way she didn't understand but felt in the core of her being. It filled her with a sense of awe, gratitude and the certainty that she was going to come through this.

She kissed Brook on the cheek. "Is it going to snow?"

"Looks like it," Brook said.

Jenny moved against him.

"Are you scared?" she asked.

"Out of my wits."

"Me, too."

His main fear was that Lind would have a seizure in the middle of the night and come into their room and kill them in their sleep. There was no latch on the door and no real way to barricade it. Lind would be totally oblivious to the whole thing.

The wood fire in the stove glowed through slats in the iron grate and made flickering shadows on the walls. The flames were almost out when the snow began to fall. They lay there, unable to sleep, listening to the wind and watching the door to their room. Brook had his father's Winchester at his side.

They dozed off. By around one that morning the wind had subsided, but a muffled sound from the other room awakened them. It got louder, a choking wail. Something crashed to the floor.

Brook got up and went to the door. He held the shotgun.

"Don't even think about going out there," Jenny said in a whisper, getting up.

Brook motioned for her not to move.

"Don't do it," Jenny hissed.

Brook cracked open the door. In the dim light he saw Lind crouched on his knees, beating his fists against the floor. Lind threw back his head and moaned and bit down hard on his hand as if fighting against whatever had taken possession of him. Brook remembered the wild, unearthly howls he'd heard Lind make that night back at the clinic.

Lind looked up and saw Brook in the doorway and screamed between clenched teeth. He clamped his hands against his head and groaned.

Brook felt Lind's eyes scorch him like acid. He released the safety on the shotgun. If Lind came for him, he'd have to shoot.

Lind got up stiffly and kept staring at him, his chest heaving.

Brook wanted to say something, but the words wouldn't come. His mouth was too dry.

Lind turned and staggered to the front door. He threw it open and went out onto the porch and disappeared into the darkness. Brook didn't try to follow him. He was paralyzed with fear.

A scream shattered the silence, followed by another scream, then another. Brook forced himself to move toward the door and look outside.

Lind had taken an ax from the front porch. Brook had noticed it leaning in a corner the day before. He cursed himself fiercely now for not having hidden it.

Lind approached a pine tree and began to attack it with the ax. The sound of the chopping echoed in the darkness. Lind hit the tree in a rapid succession of wild, frantic blows. He swung over his head and from the side, slashing at the tree as if locked with it in mortal combat; he fell to his knees and still he kept up the savage chopping. The dulled blade thudded into the bark.

Lind finally fell backward into the snow and lay there, gasping in exhaustion.

Brook wanted to go out after him but didn't dare. He went back into the bedroom with Jenny and sat near the stove with his shotgun across his lap, watching the door. Waiting.

A few minutes later, it began again. The sound of an ax slamming into a tree. Lind was howling with almost every blow.

FIFTY-ONE

THAT NIGHT THE WIND blew at near hurricane strength across much of the Carolinas. The storm front, triggering powerful thunderstorms as it moved inland, was gaining strength by the minute. Barometric pressure had fallen off the charts. Tidal-force waves were pounding the Outer Banks, and evacuations were ordered.

The rapidly widening storm also played havoc with air flights. The Chattanooga airport was closed all night and was still officially shut down when a chartered Learjet landed just after six in the morning in a driving rain.

Beckworth was the first out of the plane. He was five feet six inches tall and weighed a trim one hundred forty pounds. Somewhere just past forty, he looked fit, and his hair had turned prematurely white. He wore a dark-green parka, khaki trousers and hiking boots. Six other men similarly outfitted followed. They all carried oversized bags, which they quickly put in the trunk of waiting cars driven by Brody's men.

By seven-twenty A.M. they had all assembled in a private banquet room at Uncle Ed's Pancake House. The restaurant was across Lee Highway from the Sleep Tight Inn. Brody had rented the room and arranged for breakfast for twenty-five.

Beckworth had brought a team of his most trusted prison

guards. They wore an assortment of hunting coats, rain gear and boots, and looked like a group of good-old-boy duck hunters who'd gathered for a morning feed before setting out for the blinds. All were armed with high-powered rifles, which they carried broken down in suitcases.

Sitting in fatigued silence, they ate plates piled high with pancakes and sausage links as Beckworth and Brody talked in a corner.

"Paulus wants this concluded as soon as possible," Beckworth said.

The warden reminded Brody of a banker, the neatly trimmed white hair, horn-rimmed glasses, manicured nails, the constipated voice.

"So do I," Brody said.

"What's your plan?"

Beckworth's rapid-fire questions irritated Brody. He hated the man's arrogance, the puckered dry mouth, the iron-lidded stare.

"We hope for another sighting. Meanwhile, we spread out through the mountains. If need be, we check every town. We keep looking until we find them. Brook knows this area. It's where he grew up. He's here somewhere."

"Just find them," Beckworth said.

"It's not going to be easy. This is some of the roughest country in the United States."

"That's your concern, Brody. That's why we hired you. We'd been told you were worth the large fee."

Fuck you, Brody thought.

"What do we do with Brook and the woman?" he asked. They'd already gone over plans for Brook and Malone back in St. Louis. But he wanted to make Beckworth spell it out again.

As far as Brody was concerned, killing two young doctors was the most problematic part of the operation, the one most likely to carry the biggest risks.

The warden fixed his unflinching eyes on Brody. "Do we really need to discuss that?"

It took all of Brody's self-restraint to not say something

he knew he'd regret. He shrugged, and got a plate of pan-cakes.

Two hours later, Beckworth's office telephoned him with another NCIC report. The car had been spotted in a place called Fontana Village. A grocery-store owner had gotten suspicious when a woman bought a lot of canned food and avoided giving a specific answer when he casually asked where she was staying. The guy got a look at the car, and at Brook and Lind, and told the village's part-time cop. He passed the description on to the local sheriff.

Brody found the town on the large map he'd spread out on the table.

"How long will it take to get there?" Beckworth asked.

Brody frowned. "Two, three hours, if we don't run into a blizzard."

Sunday, eleven A.M. Lind sat by the stove, staring at Brook with burning eyes. His back rested against the wall. He hadn't moved for over an hour, and except for the wide, staring eyes, he almost looked asleep.

Sometime during the night, he'd come back inside the cabin, his demons momentarily exorcised. He looked in bad shape. His hair was matted from thrashing in the snow and mud, his cheeks gaunt and sunken. His knuckles were crusted with blood. He'd kept slashing at the tree until the ax handle broke off in his hands; then he'd beaten the trunk with his fists.

Wanting to do something, anything, Brook got up from a chair and checked the ancient window thermometer bolted to the weather-beaten sash. Thirty-six degrees and falling. A good six inches of wet, heavy snow covered the ground. The snow was mixed with sleet.

Jenny was making a pot of fresh coffee.

After what had happened, it still amazed Brook that Lind had agreed to another injection. He'd given him a shot of the peptide shortly before breakfast.

Brook's nerves were stretched to the breaking point; he was constantly on guard, watching Lind carefully as he tried to gauge his mood. For the moment, a strange calm had settled over Lind. But Brook had already seen how violently the sudden attacks hit him. It worried him sick. He doubted the injections would do any good; Lind's brain had kindled too long.

Lind checked his watch. He started lacing up his new boots.

He said, "I think I'll drive into that town. Maybe buy some magazines and paperbacks. Give me something to do."

Brook and Jenny both looked at him.

Lind finished tying his boots. He stood up and jumped up and down a few times to get the feel of them.

"Nice fit."

"What's going on? What are you doing?" Brook felt a sickening numbness come over him.

Lind said, "I want to go to town. You got some problem with that?" He picked up his two pistols and stuffed them into the deep pockets of his overcoat. He also got the rifle.

Brook said, "You don't need to arm yourself like a commando just to buy a couple magazines."

Lind hesitated as if he'd just remembered something important. He unloaded one of the pistols, a .45 and dropped it on his sleeping bag along with a box of ammunition.

Jenny was doing a better job at concealing her emotions. She managed a smile. "It's still snowing, Ed. You might have trouble getting back."

"No problem," Lind said. "I'm not coming back."

He moved toward the door and knocked Brook's hand away when he reached out to stop him.

"I owe you for trying to help me," Lind said, not raising his voice, a frigid smile on his lips. "I paid you back in full last night."

Wires started vibrating behind Brook's eyes and in his stomach, a tingling that numbed his brain.

"I wanted to go into your room last night," Lind continued, slipping on his hooded blue parka. "I was going to shoot both of you. The voices in my head were screaming for me to kill you. I was going to do you, then the lady. I don't know why I couldn't pull the trigger.''

Brook peered at Lind through the haze his eyes were making. He told him he needed to give the medicine a chance. It sounded futile, but he couldn't think of anything else to say.

"No time. If I had to make it through another night, I'd kill you for sure, and never even know what I was doing.'' He grinned. "Sorry about the car and the fix I'm leaving you in.''

Brook lunged for him when he started for the door, grabbing him around the waist. Lind threw two fast punches. Brook ducked them.

Brook was taller, but they were about equally matched in physical strength. He blocked a hard shot to his face, staggered and caught himself on a chair.

"Don't do it, Ed. Don't go.''

Lind jammed an elbow into Brook's stomach, but Brook had a tight hold on him, and didn't go down. Lind grabbed the pistol from his pocket and swung. Brook crashed to the floor.

Dazed but not unconscious, he heard Lind roar at Jenny, "Keep him in here, or I'll kill him!''

Brody rode shotgun in the lead car as they pulled into Fontana Village. Eliot drove. Brody was pleased to see that it was a resort community that had shut down tighter than a drum for the winter.

For whatever was coming—and he could sense something was—the fewer around the better.

The snow that had fallen intermittently ever since they'd left Chattanooga blanketed the roofs, trees and streets in the deserted village. Big white flakes were dropping straight out of the gray sky.

The weather bulletins indicated the storm in the Atlantic was moving inland. The heavy snowfall was expected to continue in the higher elevations of western North Carolina.

There was only one main road in and out of town, Highway 28. And Brody figured the snow would soon close it. They had made it in just under the wire.

FIFTY-TWO
⊳◁

THE EIGHT CARS IN their convoy drew attention from the few
locals who remained in the village. They quickly located the
volunteer cop, a rangy country boy who wore a watch cap
and a down vest. He ran the one service station that remained
open.

Brody let Beckworth do the talking. The warden showed
the cop his impressive credentials and told him they had
come all the way from Missouri to track down an escaped
felon who they believed was hiding near there.

The cop was excited, just happy as hell to have the chance
to help nail a bad guy.

He quickly rousted the grocery-store owner, who had sold
a three weeks' supply of canned goods to a woman. She got
into a new car with two men. The guy in the back looked
like he was sleeping.

Brody showed him Lind's picture.

The grocer didn't recognize him. He hadn't gotten a good
look at the men in the car, especially the one in the back
seat.

"Which way did they go?" Brody asked.

"North, out of town," the grocer said. "They took the
local road."

"How far does it go?" Beckworth asked.

"Two, three miles," the cop said.

"Any turnoffs?"

"Only two. They run up to some hunting cabins. Those places are usually vacant this time of year."

"Mind if we check them out?" Brody asked.

"Hell no," the cop said. "I'll take you myself. If anybody's up there, we'll find them. Let me get my four-wheel. We don't want to get stuck."

Lind drove down the steep hill slowly, struggling to keep on the narrow road in the snow. He hadn't liked taking the car, but he didn't want Brook to follow him.

He didn't trust Brook's injections, didn't think they'd work. Even if they did, his brain, or what was left of it, wasn't his anymore. Something within him told him to clear out. He didn't try to fight it.

He had known men on death row who described a strange peace that settled on them once they realized all the legal appeals were over and that, sooner or later, they were going to have to walk into the death house and lie down on that gurney. That was pretty much his mood. He was resigned to whatever was going to happen.

Gripping the steering wheel, he felt a sudden lightness in his head and stopped the car. This was something new. A strange, almost soothing lifting of pressure. He was trying to focus on what was happening to himself when he heard car engines. Two vehicles suddenly came around a curve thirty yards away and stopped. A four-wheel-drive GMC and a sedan.

Lind instinctively got out of the car. Two faces stared at him from the front seat of the GMC as the wiper blades cleared snow off the windshield.

A man opened the driver's-side door and slowly stepped out. He wore a fishing cap and a tan winter jacket. A pistol belt was strapped to his waist.

A younger man in a leather jacket got out on the other side. He edged away from the GMC, working the pump on a shotgun. The slide action made a grim metallic snap.

Two other men eased out of the sedan, one from each side.

They took care to stay behind the opened doors. Lind recognized them—guards from the clinic.

The man in the fishing cap shouted up the road that he was a member of the Fontana Village volunteer police department.

"Mister, I'm asking you to put that rifle down. You give up and nobody gets hurt."

Lind kept his eyes on the other men. He raised his rifle in a smooth, unhurried motion and fired three quick shots. He felt the spasm of the recoil against his right shoulder.

The man with the shotgun looked as if he'd slipped on ice. His feet sailed out from under him. He landed hard on his back and didn't move. The bullets had hit him chest-high.

The cop looked at the man sprawled there on the snow, which was turning red under his neck. He looked back at Lind, who made a sharp motion with his head. The cop bolted into the trees.

Lind fired again, puncturing the driver's-side door of the sedan with a tight pattern. A man wearing a green poncho that flapped out in the wind pitched forward into the snow. His partner ran down the road, not looking back. He'd dropped his rifle.

Lind jogged up into the trees. He found a clearing where he could look down into the village.

It was like a Christmas card. He saw what he was looking for—four white rental vans parked in the middle of the street with men starting to pile into them on the double. Even from a distance he recognized one of them: Brody.

Lind scrambled back to the car, turned around and headed back up the road, rear tires sliding in the snow.

Brook stood out on the cabin's open porch, holding a handful of snow against the back of his aching neck. He heard gunfire and understood immediately what had happened. Lind had run into some kind of trouble. They had tracked them down faster than he'd dreamed possible.

He told Jenny to get her boots and coat on. They had to get out.

Minutes later he heard a car coming up the road, and he grabbed the shotgun. He shouted for Jenny to get ready to make a run for it.

Closer, tires crunching in the snow, the car fish-tailed around a curve and plowed to a stop. Lind threw open the door and hurried up the steps to the cabin. Brook couldn't believe that he'd come back. Maybe he'd returned to kill them. There was no telling. He pumped a shell into the Winchester and stepped forward.

"We're going to have visitors," Lind said.

Brook was still struggling to get a grip on his fear and total surprise. Seeing Lind again was the last thing he'd expected. He kept his eyes locked on him, not trusting himself to speak, trying to think through what he'd do if Lind did something. He'd already let him get way too close.

"It's Brody," Lind went on. "He and his men are down in the village. They'll be coming up this road real soon."

He looked at Brook, who noticed the startling change in Lind's expression. His face had gone softer and his eyes had lost some of their mean glitter. He was almost smiling. "I can't explain to you what's going on in my head. I feel . . . different. Maybe better. I'm not sure."

"When did it start?" Brook asked, trying to slow down all the thoughts flashing in his head.

"When I was hauling ass down the road. Something happened. The feeling that I was going to fall into a black pit eased off. You think that medicine you've been shooting into my arm is starting to kick in?"

"It could be," Brook said. Maybe the peptide injection was working after all, or starting to. He had no way of knowing. Lind's churning brain remained a lit fuse. Brook didn't doubt for a second that he could kill them.

He wanted to question Lind, but there wasn't time. If they stayed in the cabin much longer, they'd be trapped there. And probably sooner rather than later. There was only one road off this mountain, and whoever was down there in Fontana Village was sure to come up it.

In the middle of a snowstorm.

Brook went over the terrain in his mind. There was a ranger station at Twentymile, one of the more remote entrances to the Smoky national park. It was eight to ten miles north of Fontana Village on Highway 28. They could call for help from there. But they'd have to get across a narrow arm of Fontana Lake. He knew where they could get a boat—if the place was still in business.

Brook stared out toward the ridge line that on a clear day rose from the blue mists, looking so close you could touch it. The mountains had vanished in the falling snow.

He explained his idea to Lind and Jenny. Jenny had already put on an extra pair of thick socks and laced up her boots.

"How far do we have to go?" she asked.

"Ten miles, not far." Ten miles as the crow flies. In good weather, a rough descent to the lake over rough ground, then a hike along Highway 28. Not too bad in good weather. But to do it in the dead of winter, in a snow storm . . .

He remembered his father, who had warned him against the dangers of snow and cold in the mountains. How it could slow you down fast, how it could kill.

Still, he loaded a knapsack, put in some cookies and a few cans of fruit cocktail and stew. He also stuffed in extra clothes for both himself and Jenny.

He'd slung the pack over his shoulders and picked up the Winchester and the .45, when Lind called to him. He'd gone out on the porch to watch the road. His voice was urgent and carefully controlled.

"They're coming."

Brook looked out the door. A man was hiking up the steep, switchback trail about one hundred yards below them. He wore a green parka covered with snow. Two men followed him, staying to the side of the trail. They carried rifles and wore identical parkas.

Brook said, "We go out the back door and run to the right, down the hill."

Lind picked up his rifle. "Tell me where you're going to find that boat," he said. "I'll meet you there."

"No way," Brook said angrily. "We're going together."

Lind quickly checked the rifle's magazine, snapping it open. He looked at Brook. His face was set. He'd made up his mind. "We need to slow these assholes down or none of us are going to make it off this mountain," he said. "So you two get going and I'll catch up."

He turned to Jenny. "Tell him to listen. You know I'm right."

Brook hesitated, unsure of himself, but realizing he couldn't fight Lind over this and hope to win.

"Hey, if I'm really starting to get better, there's no way I want to get blown away. And if I'm not, what difference will it make?" Lind said. "So tell me again how to get to that boat."

Brook pointed to a gap in the trees; a curtain of snow obscured an arm of Fontana Lake. "Go that way," he said. "You'll pick up an old logging trail a couple hundred yards down the mountainside. Follow it all the way to the lake. There's a big boat dock half a mile or so down the shoreline. You can't miss it."

"So what are you waiting for?" Lind said impatiently. "Get your ass out of here!"

Brook grabbed Jenny by the shoulders and held her hard against him. Then he opened the door and let her out first. She ran for the trees to the right of the cabin.

He came out behind her and glanced down the road. The man out front was running.

Jenny started to turn around.

"Go! Go!" Brook shouted. He almost pushed her down the mountainside.

For a few moments they were silhouetted against the trees. He heard the flat, sharp whine of bullets. A strange, unforgettable sound. They were shooting too high. Then he heard Lind open up with his rifle. He'd moved out of the cabin and was crouched behind a tree, where he had an open field of fire at anyone moving up the road.

Brook and Jenny crashed down the sloping ground, grabbing tree trunks for balance, stumbling and frantically getting up again.

Brook yelled, "Watch out for drop-offs!" They might not see them in the snow until it was too late.

Jenny was out in front, scrambling, moving a zigzag course down the mountainside.

Brook stayed close to her. He strained to see in the snow, strained to remember the ground. After a few minutes, he stopped to listen.

He wiped the snow from his eyes. It was falling heavy and wet, out of a slate-black sky. He heard nothing but the sound of the wind in the trees. Then there was more gunfire, loud bursts coming down from the cabin.

FIFTY-THREE

WITH HIS SHOULDER BRACED against a tree for support, Lind reloaded his rifle. It was slow going as he moved farther down the mountainside. The snow had made the rocks and ledges slippery, the footing and visibility treacherous. He was getting winded.

He didn't mind the snow, which had given him the cover he needed to escape. It occurred to him that he might have gotten away entirely if there hadn't been so many following him.

Those bastards were hanging tough. They were maybe a hundred yards back. He heard them shouting into their portable radios. Their excited, strained voices carried up to him.

His own voices—the ones in his head—had gone strangely quiet. The pain had stopped. Maybe the fire in his brain had finally burned itself out. He wasn't sure yet, and wondered if he'd lost touch with that strange, fleeting sense of conscience he'd had for the first time in his life. It was the closest he'd come to an awareness of a force or power that represented good. He had never doubted there was one for evil.

He wanted to laugh. Maybe it was for the best. He'd always suspected that a conscience would only trip you up.

He stopped his descent behind two snow-covered balsam trees that formed a V at their base. Dropping to his knees, he waited for Brody and his men to come trudging down the steep slope. They'd have to cross ten yards of clearing with only a few stunted trees for cover.

He didn't have long to wait. In a few minutes he saw a man carrying a rifle and wearing yellow-tinted ski goggles come out of the swirling snow. Another man was a few yards behind him. Heads down and moving in a crouch, they looked like hunters trying to follow an animal's tracks.

Lind steadied his rifle, rested the barrel in the notch in the trees and sighted in. His cheek pressed the wet stock. He targeted the lead man's head and squeezed off a shot. The man fell over with his legs bent under him. He didn't make a sound.

Lind fired two more shots at the second man, who dropped belly-flat in the snow and didn't try to get up.

A miss, but he wasn't going anywhere.

Lind wiped snow off his rifle barrel. For the first time he felt the numbing cold that went deep into the bones. The wind had shifted to the north. Lind rubbed his hands and blew on them.

Another man came down the slope. He was moving from tree to tree, skillfully using cover.

Gunfire exploded to Lind's right. The bullets went way over his head, snapping through the branches of the trees.

They were pouring in fire so he'd keep his head down. Bullets were flying everywhere, rifle-range shooting.

Lind waited for a clear shot. A man in green jumped from behind a ledge and crouched behind a tree. When he showed himself again, Lind shot him in the guts. The man's choked scream echoed in the brittle air.

Three bodies lay in the snow in front of him. It had become quiet. Just the soft, lulling sound of the snow and sleet pelting through the trees.

He started moving again.

Brook and Jenny hit the old logging trail about twenty minutes after they ran from the cabin. Brook had worried about finding it in the snow. He hadn't been on that trial in

years, and he'd never had to find it in a blizzard. He hoped
Lind would be as lucky.

The snow was blowing down so hard that he tied himself
to Jenny by the wrist with a length of rope he'd brought
from the cabin. He was afraid they would get separated.

Brook wanted to hit the north arm of Lake Fontana at
Shore Point, where there used to be a boathouse and dock.
The place was closed during the winter. Brook hoped he
could get one of the outboards started and make it across the
lake.

He stopped to catch his breath. His lungs felt on fire.

"Listen," he said.

They could hear gunfire from somewhere up the mountain.
Lind was still alive.

"Do you think he can make it?" Jenny asked.

Brook shrugged. He didn't know. He was worried about
Lind. And something else.

"If they've got a map, it won't be hard to figure out where
we're going to come off the mountain, or what we're trying
to do. There's only one way out of here. My guess is they'll
start checking all the boat docks north of the village."

"How many are there?" Jenny asked.

Brook shook his head, trying to remember. "Three, maybe
four. It's been a long time."

The one at Shore Point was farthest from the village.

They started down again, stumbling through the thick,
matted undergrowth of dead leaves and fallen branches.
Seven or eight inches of snow covered the ground and it was
still falling.

The logging road sloped down through the pine and fir
trees all the way to the shore of Fontana Lake. Brook headed
south. In the heavy snowfall, they were almost on top of the
place before he made out the shape of the dock and boathouse. The large, low-slung building was painted a drab red,
and it jutted straight out into the water.

A cluster of boarded-up log cabins and rust-stained trailers
faced the lake in a tight semicircle. A two-lane blacktop that

ran north from Fontana Village ended at the campground's entrance.

The resort looked more run-down than Brook remembered it. The cabins had sagging front porches and torn window screens.

Brook told Jenny to watch the road and warn him if she saw any cars plowing toward them through the snow.

"Where are you going?" she asked.

"Try to find us a boat."

He jogged down to the boathouse. The double doors were securely padlocked. Brook took out the .45 and fired a round into the lock.

He swung open the door and stepped through the entrance.

There had to be fifty boats in there. He heard something scuttering above him, and glimpsed a large rat running across one of the crossbeams that supported the roof.

The boats were big, lake-going cabin cruisers that could sleep six, some house boats, and even a couple of sleek thirty-foot-long sailboats. Most were bass boats—short, stubby craft with raised seats and big outboards designed to push them across the water at over eighty miles an hour.

The boats were tied up in four long, uneven rows that faced each other across narrow channels of water. Planks of wood served as walkways between them. A wooden pier rimmed the walls of the building, which opened onto the lake.

Brook found a small fishing boat with a 25-horse Mariner outboard a few slips down from the entrance. It was exactly what he wanted, a sixteen-foot runabout with an aluminum hull. An outboard with a pull starter was the only kind of engine he had any experience operating.

He connected the battery to the terminals and reattached the fuel line to a red, five-gallon gas tank stored under the bench seat in the stern. He unscrewed the cap and smelled gasoline. He shook the tank. It felt about half full.

Outside, Jenny watched the road, which paralleled the shoreline. She couldn't see far in the snow and was looking for headlights. She climbed up on the porch of a cabin and stamped her feet in the cold. The wind was picking up again.

Concentrating on the road, she didn't see Eliot and two other men break out of the woods and take cover behind one of the cabins. She didn't see them move closer, hugging the walls.

Brody had pulled them off the hunt for Lind and sent them after Brook and Jenny. He'd anticipated the two were probably trying to reach the lake.

Jenny didn't hear them until one pressed a hand over her mouth from behind and said, "Make a sound and you're dead."

He grabbed her around the throat. Twisting around, she saw Eliot and another man run toward the boathouse. They wore parkas and ski goggles and carried short-barreled automatic weapons.

Jenny clawed at the forearm that was choking her breath away. She bit down hard on the fingers clamped over her mouth. She tasted blood.

The man jerked his hand away just long enough for her to scream Brook's name.

Then something hard crashed into the base of her skull and drove her to her knees. She didn't hear the sound of a door being kicked down or feel hands slip under her arms, pulling her backward into the cabin.

Kneeling next to the boat, Brook had just started to get up when he heard her shout. Head down, he saw two men come through the open doorway with their guns up, ready to shoot the first thing that moved. They separated, each taking a different side of the boathouse.

Brook ducked behind the big outboard engine of the bass boat that was tied up next to the boat he was trying to loosen from its moorings.

So far they hadn't seen him. But they knew he was there.

He might be able to get one of them, but not two. He choked down his panic.

If he waited much longer, the guy moving up the opposite side of the boathouse would see him. Both men were slowly coming his way, methodically searching each boat. The wooden pier creaked under their weight.

Moving as carefully and silently as he could, Brook sat down on the wooden plank between the boats and took off his overcoat. He slipped the coat and his shotgun under the sheet of canvas he'd pulled off the small boat.

Then he swung his legs into the water. The surge of cold made him gasp. He bit down on his tongue to keep from crying out. The cold was taking his breath away.

Holding high the .45, he slid into the water near the stern of the boat. The depth was up to his chest. He took a breath, ducked under the black water and came up again beneath the pier.

There was just enough room for him to keep his head out of the water and look up through the narrow spaces in the boards. He had to bite down on his tongue so his teeth wouldn't chatter.

He listened, trying to gauge the man's approach, time his footsteps. The creaking sounds moved closer. The man was right above him. Brook could make out his face. It was Eliot. He held a black weapon.

When he moved on, Brook waited a few more seconds. His heavy, waterlogged boots felt like weights. He ducked under the pier and came up next to the stern of the bass boat.

Eliot had his back turned to him. He was almost to the end of the pier.

Brook took a long breath, set his teeth and braced the pistol. He could hardly feel his numbed, trembling hands.

Eliot heard something move and whirled around. He was less than ten feet away.

Brook fired. The magnum roared, and Eliot went down. His weapon splashed into the water. He lay on the pier, tried to get up and fell back.

Brook pulled the trigger again. The hammer made a sharp metallic *click*.

A misfire.

Brook looked across to the far side of the boathouse and

saw the other man. He heard the ripping blasts of automatic-
rifle fire.

The man turned and ran in his direction.

Brook tried a quick shot. Another sharp *click*. He pulled
himself out of the water, barely able to move. He crawled
around Eliot, who was bleeding from a shoulder wound.

More shots. Loud, concussive echoes. Bullets ripping jagged holes in the wall over his head.

Brook shifted his focus to his father's shotgun.

He groped under the tarp, found nothing.

Footsteps pounding down the pier.

Brook ripped the tarp away, and saw the gun's long barrel.
He pulled it out and frantically pumped a shell into the chamber.

The man was closer.

Kneeling, Brook glanced around the prow of the bass boat.
The man was ten feet away, face contorted, running hard.
Eyes clamped, Brook swung out low and pulled the trigger
with one hand. The shotgun roared and almost tore loose
from his grip.

The buckshot threw the man backward. It was like he'd
hit an invisible wall. He was already dead. A large, raw
chunk of his upper chest was missing.

Brook pumped the shotgun again. He ran for the door,
choking back a scream as he charged through the snow toward the cabins where he'd left Jenny.

Lind kept descending the mountain. He wondered how many
were on his trail. At least ten, he figured. When the snow
momentarily cleared off like smoke, he saw them fanning
out through the trees and rocks. He knew two or three had
slipped by him and had kept going down the mountain. They
were going after Brook and Jenny. He had to get moving,
but Brody was pressing him pretty hard.

He found another good hiding place, a waist-high block
of solid granite as smooth and straight as a brick wall. He
crouched behind it and waited. When he got a target, he took
a breath, let it out slowly and fired a short, disciplined burst.

The man straightened up, dropped his weapon and fell backward off a ledge.

That slowed the bastards down. They'd all taken cover and were keeping their heads low.

Almost out of ammunition, he checked his pockets. He had six extra bullets and his loaded .357.

He started moving again, running, half staggering down the mountainside, stopping only when his leg muscles were so cramped and burning that he couldn't take another step.

He looked up and saw a blurred white stain where the sun was trying to burn a patch through the sky.

He heard his pursuers following again, heard the rock slides they started and the snap of twigs breaking under their feet. Pushing himself, he'd opened a good fifty yards on them. Then he stumbled onto the logging trail.

In the cabin the man had just started to tie Jenny up with a length of orange extension cord, when shooting erupted in the boathouse. Coming to, she kept her eyes closed, pretending she was still out cold. She heard the gunfire.

The man got up and went to the door to try to see what was happening. He'd left his rifle propped against the wall. While his back was turned, Jenny risked a look. He wasn't watching her.

Rolling over, she lunged for the rifle just as he whirled around. They both grabbed the weapon and fell down, kicking at each other as they thrashed on the floor. She gripped the barrel with both hands. An end table and lamp fell over. Coming up to her knees, Jenny grabbed the upended lamp and smashed it into the man's face as he tried to raise the rifle for a shot. He dropped back and didn't move. His forehead was gashed with a deep, red cut.

Dripping water, unable to feel his frozen feet, Brook threw himself through the open doorway as Jenny sat on the floor, frantically untying the length of cord that was wrapped around her left ankle. She hadn't expected to see him alive again.

Jenny let her head drop as Brook fell to his knees next to

her and put his hands on her shoulders. She bit down on the back of her hand to keep from crying.

"I'm fine," she said, wiping her eyes. A smile illuminated her face.

"Dead?" Brook asked, glancing at the man.

"No, but he's going to have a headache when he wakes up."

"Let's hope so," Brook said.

She explained that she hadn't seen the men until they were almost on top of her. One of them had hit her across the back of her skull, a glancing blow that stunned her. She'd pretended it had knocked her out.

"I must have got him pretty hard," Jenny said, looking at the unconscious man, who hadn't moved. She recognized him from the clinic. One of the guards.

Brook bent down and hugged her. He tried to untie the extension cord around her leg, but his hands were shaking so badly he couldn't work the knot. The last of his body heat was turning to vapor.

Jenny noticed he was soaking wet.

"My god, what happened?"

"I had . . . to take . . . a swim." Chills wracked his body, making him shudder. A burning numbness had spread to his feet.

Freed from the cord, Jenny pulled the coat off the downed man and slipped it over Brook's shoulders. He couldn't stop shaking or keep his teeth from chattering. His lips were a deep blue.

Jenny began throwing open the closets and cabinets in the cabin. She found a stack of towels and blankets wrapped in a plastic trash bag.

With difficulty, his hands almost useless, Brook stripped off his soggy clothes and dried himself off. Jenny rubbed his back and chest vigorously until the skin was a bright pink, then wrapped him in blankets.

He helped undress the man. He was in his mid- to late twenties. His pulse and breathing were steady, and he had good color.

Brook put on all of his clothing, even the underwear, which still retained some body heat. The guy was a little smaller, but the fit was close enough. Brook forced on his boots, which were also smaller but blessedly dry. Trying to work some movement into his hands, he kept massaging them, kneading the fingers and joints to get the blood circulating.

After tying the man's wrists and ankles, they checked the cabin for food. They found a few cans of tuna fish, sardines and tomato soup.

Jenny had avoided asking what had happened in the boathouse.

Brook sensed what was on her mind. "I shot two men." He tried to smile. "The good news is I've found us a boat."

"Then let's go," Jenny said, kissing him on the cheek.

"We've got to wait for Lind," Brook said. He was worried about him. It had been a while since he'd heard any shooting up on the mountain. They didn't have much time, but he was going to hang on here as long as possible. He owed Lind that much.

He didn't have to ask Jenny. One look was enough to tell him she agreed.

They piled a couple blankets on the unconscious man, wrapped the canned goods and some more blankets in a sheet, and hurried for the boathouse.

Brook stepped over Eliot's body. Another blue-eyed young killer from Brody's security force. He lay across the walkway with a hole in his right shoulder blade.

Brook assessed the wound with professional detachment. The bullet had missed the lungs, but he'd probably lost a lot of blood. The heavy flow had left a dark stain on the front of his coat. He could survive it if he didn't go into shock and they got him to a hospital.

Brook roughly pulled the other body away from the boat. The shotgun blast had almost severed his head.

Brook helped Jenny step into the boat. He glanced at his watch. He'd give Lind a few more minutes.

They stored their bag of food and blankets in the bow,

stuffing it into a watertight compartment. Brook got into the stern and squeezed the rubber bulb that primed the engine. At least he could get it started and warmed up as they waited for Lind. No matter what happened, they'd be ready to get out of there fast. He opened the choke and pulled on the starting cord. The engine sputtered, but didn't catch.

He yanked the cord a second time. The outboard kicked and blew a cloud of bluish-white smoke over the water.

"I almost had it," Brook said angrily. He readjusted the choke and gripped the starter cord with both hands. Straightening up, he snapped it back hard. The engine bucked then kicked over with a roar. Another cloud of smoke belched from the exhaust vent.

Brook pushed in the choke so the outboard wouldn't flood.

He was untying one of the mooring lines when Jenny screamed.

Catching movement from the corner of his eye, he turned just in time to absorb Eliot's crashing weight. The two of them fell hard against the boat's metal gunwale.

The right side of Eliot's face was crusted with dried blood. He had Brook around the throat with both hands, trying to push him into the churning water, into the propeller blades. His eyes were bloodshot, inflamed. He was bellowing, raging.

Brook deflected a looping roundhouse blow to his face with his right forearm, and gasped as a shudder ran through the nerves all the way to his neck. Eliot's shoulder wound was still oozing blood but hadn't slowed him down.

Feeling his attacker's grip loosen, Brook grabbed him by the injured shoulder. Screaming in pain, Eliot twisted away and drove a fist at Brook's face with his good hand.

Brook didn't see Lind burst through the boathouse door on the run. He jumped into the boat, grabbed Eliot around the throat from behind and pulled him off Brook. Eliot gasped as Lind pushed him over the stern into the water. The outboard bucked hard when a leg hit the propeller shaft. Brook cut the engine.

When Eliot's head came out of the water, Lind pushed it

back under, pressing down. Hands clawed at the air, but Lind kept holding the face under the surface until the struggle ceased and the dead man's arms came up straight from his sides.

Lind shoved the body out into the water with an oar.

"Let's get the hell out of here," he said.

This time the Mariner started on the first pull of the throttle cord. Jenny untied the line in the bow, and Brook backed the small boat out of the slip. It lurched when he switched the gear lever into forward. Gripping the rudder stick with both hands, he steered the V-bottom through the open door of the boathouse and out into the lake.

Perched on the middle seat, Lind reloaded his rifle and kept watching the receding shoreline, waiting for Brody's men to show up and start shooting. He'd gotten away from them on the trail when the blowing snow closed in, cutting visibility almost to nothing, like a sea fog. It was still coming down hard and in a few moments he couldn't even see the shore and boathouse, only the churning wake of the outboard.

Sitting in the front, Jenny glanced back at Brook and smiled.

He couldn't see worth a damn, but those mountains were out there, hidden from view, boiling up to the sky right in front of them. Old friends. For the first time since they'd left the cabin, he thought they had a chance.

FIFTY-FOUR

BRODY AND BECKWORTH GOT to the boathouse minutes later. Two of their men had found Eliot floating in the water. Brody watched in silence as they pulled the body in with an oar. A deep, jagged tear had opened Eliot's right thigh to the bone. His eyes were wide open.

Brody went outside. He hadn't smoked in years, but he wanted a cigarette.

Two out of three. Dead.

The third man, Gast, had heard an outboard pull away from the dock. Still groggy from a blow to the head, he wasn't sure of the direction. He said it sounded like it was headed north.

Brody looked at the socked-in overcast. There wasn't much daylight left. His mind had grown as gray and heavy as the sky.

How many years had he known the dumb fuck Eliot?

Two?

No, it had been nearly three years. He'd hired him right out of the FBI. Brody blew out a long breath and let the grayness keep settling over him. This was dangerous. He needed to fight it. He couldn't afford any emotion, not in these mountains.

Beckworth had opened a fold-out map of the Great Smoky Mountains and was tracing one of the roads with a pencil.

He said, "There's a ranger post about five miles to the north. A place called Twentymile. They might be able to call someone from there. Try to get help."

It was their only option. They had to be heading in that direction.

Beckworth radioed the teams that were still in the field, checking cabins and docks along the lake shore. He told everybody to start moving toward Twentymile on the double. They didn't have much time.

He'd already sent a couple of men back to Fontana Village to try to find a pickup with a snowblade. They would need the plow to push through the deep drifts on Route 28. The blacktop crossed the lake at a big dam just north of the village and followed the shoreline past the ranger post.

"If that highway isn't closed, it will be soon," Beckworth said.

Brody wasn't listening. His mind was still focused on something else.

The strong wind blowing straight down out of the mountain gaps kicked up a white chop on the water. Heading right into the teeth of it, their sixteen-foot runabout was getting pounded. With three people aboard, it sat too low in the water.

"I don't know how much more of this we can take," Brook said, shouting to make himself heard over the roar of the engine. "It's too rough out here."

He opened the throttle all the way, coaxing as much power as he could from the 25-horse outboard. The spray flew up over the bow with each crashing wave. They were taking on some water.

It was like riding in a wind tunnel. He started cutting a diagonal line for the far shore, angling across the waves instead of running into them head on, hoping they wouldn't swamp.

He yelled to Lind and Jenny, "We've got to get off the lake!"

When they finally bumped hard into the bank, several

inches of dirty water sloshed in the bottom of the hull. After they'd unloaded their gear, Brook pointed the bow of the boat downwind and, with Lind's help, pushed it off the rocks with the throttle running wide open. It might make a diversion. Send those bastards in another direction.

He wondered how much of a head start they had. It wouldn't take Brody long to figure out where they'd gone; there weren't that many options. Route 28 was the only way out. It ran right by the shore.

Pulling Jenny by the hand, he climbed a hill that sloped up from the lake. Whatever hope they had about hitching a ride ended when they reached the highway and saw the snowdrifts. They were two and three feet deep in places; plus, the visibility was practically nil. There was no way a car could move in that.

"Looks like we're walking," Lind said.

Brook was stunned. He'd never seen such a heavy snowfall in the Smokies. This wasn't snow country. It rained in winter. The days were usually overcast and wet, the snowfall light. This just didn't happen.

A loud crack—more of an explosion—made them flinch.

"What the hell's that," Lind said, snapping up his rifle.

It sounded like a gunshot—and very close. Locating the spot was like trying to track a sound under water; it could have come from anywhere.

Brook released the safety on the Winchester and strained to see in the whiteout.

Then he heard the sound again and realized what was happening: Trees were snapping under the weight of the wet, heavy snow—their trunks splintering like matchsticks.

They started hiking north in the fading light. Night was coming quickly. They slogged through the deep drifts for over an hour. Lind walked in front of Brook and Jenny, breaking trail.

Losing strength, Brook started searching the hills for rock outcroppings or hollows where they could take shelter from the storm. He wasn't sure they'd make it to the ranger station, and he worried they might have to spend the night in the woods.

He'd done that once before on a hunting trip, but at least he'd been able to cut down some saplings with a hand ax and make a lean-to to get out of the wind and rain. This time he had only a pocketknife.

Jenny saw the light first, a yellow glow that marked the entrance to the Twentymile Visitors' Center.

When they got closer, Brook smelled smoke.

Whoever was there had a wood fire going.

Nearly an hour passed before Brody's men found a pickup equipped with a snow blade, and started north on Route 28. An old Pontiac that couldn't shift out of second gear. The volunteer cop in Fontana Village told them the road was closed as far north as Chihowee and Maryville. He warned them against going out; the drifting fast-accumulating snow might bury them.

Highway crews didn't think they could start plowing until the next morning—at the earliest. The mountain country in those parts was shut down, courtesy of the monster storm still moving across the Carolina coast.

Brody and Beckworth rode in the pickup. They had rigged a tarp over the cargo bay to shelter four men hunched in back. Six others were in the car that followed the pickup, hugging its bumper.

They'd just gotten started when one of the teams still out radioed Beckworth. They'd found the boat run aground and half filled with water about three miles up the lake. The engine was running.

"That doesn't mean shit," Brody said, not falling for the trick.

As he sat in the pickup wedged next to Beckworth, he could think of one immediate problem. There were probably others, but this one would do.

What if a park ranger was stationed at Twentymile?

He answered his own question.

* * *

Brook didn't think the ranger believed their story. He had arrived on his doorstep with Lind and Jenny, snow-covered and exhausted, half an hour earlier. They'd spent every minute since then explaining what had happened, answering his questions as they sipped mugs of hot coffee.

The ranger had the wiry body and parched, hardened face of someone who had lived much of his life in the sun and wind. He was over six feet tall, large-boned, with thick wrists and forearms. He spoke with a soft East Tennessee drawl.

He had just sat down to dinner when he heard a knock on the door. His five-room cabin was set behind the Twentymile Visitors' Center. In twenty-six years with the National Park Service, he'd never had anyone drop by for an unannounced visit in the middle of a blizzard.

The truth was, he'd never seen a storm like this. Never. And he certainly had never heard a story to rival the one these people had just told him: *Medical experiments back in St. Louis. Escaped prisoners. Two people shot dead in a boathouse down by Fontana Village. Killers out looking for them.*

He was glad he'd insisted his wife, Peggy, leave in the four-wheel before the snow closed the road. He'd sent her to her mother's in Maryville. That left just him and Boomer, his three-year-old border collie. The buff-colored dog sat by the fireplace, watching the visitors with bright, curious eyes.

"What if I call the state patrol over in Maryville? Get them up here?"

He wanted to see if they would hesitate or give him some excuse for not calling the police.

"Do it!" Brook said.

The ranger got on the telephone, dialed the patrol's number from memory and laid out the story to a corporal he knew on a first-name basis. When he hung up, he put his hands in his pockets and stared at the fire that crackled and popped in the hearth.

He said, "They'll send some people at first light. Weather permitting, they might be able to get a chopper up this way."

He snapped his fingers and opened the front door. The dog

hesitated, not wanting to relinquish his privileged place by the fire. He stretched his paws out straight, rose with slow dignity, rear end first, and trotted outside.

The ranger said, "Boomer's got a great name. He'll bark like crazy if anybody turns up out there."

Hurrying and looking increasingly nervous, he took a heavy coat down from a wooden peg near the fireplace and started lacing on a pair of boots. He unplugged a cellular phone recharging in a kitchen electrical socket and put it in its canvas carrying pouch.

The ranger said, "If those people are really trailin' you like you say they are, then they aren't gonna let a little snow stop 'em. You better be ready to move out of here."

"And go where?" Lind asked. He stood with his back to the fire, letting the delicious warmth draw the lingering chill from his legs. Then, without warning, his head started to throb. He choked back a groan. It was starting again, those deadly feelings and sensations drilling deep into his brain. He glanced at Brook, who caught his look.

"Maybe you can hike up to one of the trail shelters," the ranger said. "It's rough country back there. They'd never find you. The trail starts just up the road a ways. It forks about half a mile out, at a forest-fire spotter's tower. You want to take the fork to the right."

"How far to one of the shelters?" Brook asked. He wasn't familiar with this part of the park. He kept his eyes focused on Lind, who'd broken out in a sweat.

"The first one's about two miles out. Plus, you got to climb a couple thousand feet while you're at it."

"In this snow?" Brook couldn't believe the guy was serious. They'd never make it in this weather.

"Is that where you're going?" Lind asked. He could tell the ranger didn't trust them and was eager to clear out.

The man shook his head and said, "Nothing personal, folks. But I don't want to get mixed up in this. I'll find a place near here to hunker down until morning. I'll be fine."

"Glad to hear it," Lind muttered. He was furious, but he managed not to come unhinged. He wanted to kill this guy, and saw himself doing it in slow motion, pulling his gun and pumping a round into the bastard's skull.

Brook noticed. "How are you doing?" he asked.

Lind didn't answer.

The ranger flicked a switch. The cabin lights went dark. The fire cast dancing shadows on the walls.

"What about your dog?" Jenny asked.

"He'll be all right," the ranger said. "He might even follow you up the trail. Boomer loves goin' up to the tower."

He started to open the back door. Lind stopped him.

"Mind if I borrow that telephone? I got a call to make."

"No problem," the ranger said, catching something in Lind's eyes. He quickly handed over the cell phone. He opened the back door, pulled the hood of his parka over his head and disappeared quickly into the darkness. They heard his boots crunching in the snow as he hurried away.

"He looked scared," Lind said.

"I don't blame him," Brook said. Again, he caught the unmistakable gleam in Lind's eyes and felt his stomach turn. There was nothing he could do for him. There was no way he could give him another peptide injection. He'd left all the drugs back at the cabin.

Jenny went to the front window and looked out at the sloping driveway that curved down to the road.

"How long do we stay here?" she asked.

Before Brook could answer, Lind got operator assistance and dialed radio station KPDN in St. Louis. He asked for Bill Masterson.

Brook checked his watch, realizing what Lind was doing. Materson's show was scheduled to start in ten minutes.

Brody saw the light, burning in the hills to the right of the road. They'd gone exactly four miles by the odometer, plowing with the blade every inch of the way.

They dug another couple hundred yards before the headlights illuminated the sign: Twentymile Visitors' Center.

Brody radioed to the truck following them: "Everybody out. Keep the noise down."

They trudged through knee-high snow to the cluster of small, dark structures that included the log-and-shake main building, a few restored hillbilly cabins and the rest rooms. Here and there security lights burned in the eves.

"I want every one of those places checked," Beckworth said. "They've got to be up there."

Spreading out along both sides of the road, the men started up the hill to the parking lot. They hadn't gone ten yards when a dog began barking—loud, sharp barks that echoed in the cold air.

FIFTY-FIVE

LIND WANTED MASTERSON TO put him on the air, but the talk-show host kept refusing.

Cupping his hand over the receiver, Lind turned to Brook and Jenny. "His lawyers won't let us talk about the clinic. Says he's sorry."

Brook slammed his fist against the wall. "Let me talk to him!" Lind shrugged and handed him the receiver.

Brook told Masterson who he was and what had happened at the clinic. He mentioned that they were being hunted.

"They're trying to kill us," he said, trying not to shout.

The only thing that mattered to him was that people understand the full extent of the crimes Hartigan, Beckworth and Paulus had committed.

Masterson had just repeated how sorry he was, when Boomer sounded off down below the cabin. The dog was barking like crazy.

Lind quickly motioned for Brook to hang up. He'd already zipped up his coat and looped the phone bag over his shoulder. He grabbed two rolled sleeping bags that he'd found in a closet and tossed one to Brook.

"I've got to go," Brook said hurriedly to Masterson. "I'll call back if I can. You're going to look like a grade-A shit if people find out you didn't have the guts to put me on. Think about it."

He punched the off button and tossed the phone to Lind. Grabbing his shotgun and the sleeping bag, he followed Lind and Jenny out the door.

They found the head of the trail and started hiking through the deep, heavy snow. As before, Lind was out in front, breaking through the places where drifts piled up to their knees.

After five minutes, Lind asked them if they noticed anything. Brook looked at Jenny, not understanding.

Lind said, "It's stopped snowing." He swore under his breath. It would be that much easier to follow their trail.

Jenny's calf muscles had started burning again. Fatigue pulled at her shoulders and neck like a heavy pack she couldn't put down.

"I don't think I can keep this up much longer," she said.

Neither could Brook. Both of them were played out. They would never make it to one of those back-country trail shelters the ranger had mentioned.

Fifteen minutes later they reached a clearing. In the near distance, they saw the spotter's tower, constructed of steel beams soaring upward from a wide base. All but the first twenty or thirty feet was obscured in the darkness. A stairway—metal steps and handrails—twisted up the center of the tower in a series of sharp, right-angle turns. There was a landing every ten feet or so that consisted of an open platform with a steel-mesh floor and a low railing that ran along the exposed sides.

"We're stopping here," Brook said.

"And do what?" Lind asked.

"We climb up that tower to the observation deck," Brook said. "They might not find us there. And even if they do, we've got a fair chance of holding them off. There's only one way up."

"And that means there's only one way down," Lind said. He didn't like it, and it showed.

"If you've got a better idea, I want to hear it," Brook said sharply. He was running a risk with Lind in his unstable

tate of mind, but they had to get off the trail fast, before
hey were caught out in the open.

With a little luck, they might hold out up there until morn-
ng. It was risky, but it was all Brook could think of. If Lind
ad other ideas, there was nothing he could do about it. Bet-
er to face the explosion now and hope for the best. Brook
eld the shotgun, ready for a snap shot. He'd already released
he safety. It was up to Lind. Brook knew he'd been fighting
battle with himself ever since they'd left the cabin.

Lind looked at the tower. "How high is that?"

"About a hundred and fifty feet," Brook said. "As tall as
twelve-story building. On a clear day you could see all the
ay into Tennessee from up there."

Something ran out of the darkness behind them. Lind
urned around, a gun in his hand. Brook hadn't even seen
im draw it, the movement was that smooth and fast.

Boomer charged up to them, tail wagging. He ran up to
enny.

"I guess the crazy animal wants to come, too," Lind said,
ubbing the dog behind the ears. He was barely holding on;
e knew it and so did Brook.

They walked across the clearing, and Lind started up the
teep metal stairway with Boomer scampering behind him,
aking two steps at a time.

Brook and Jenny followed.

ven with snow on the ground, it took Brody and his men
everal minutes to find the trail that led up the mountain from
e back of the cabin. The tracks showed three people and a
og. Another set of tracks, one person, veered off into the
oods.

"According to the map, most of the trails run up to a place
alled Gregory Bald," Beckworth said. "That's about five
r six miles from here." He'd turned the cabin lights on and
ad the map spread out on the dining room table.

Brody looked at the map, quickly memorizing the details.
hey would have trouble moving very fast in this weather
nd in this rugged country. But so would Brook and the

others. They needed to run them down before they found a
good hiding place.

He figured it couldn't have been easy for them, leaving
this warm cabin and going back into the cold. It sure as hell
wasn't for him.

He zipped his parka and stepped out into the snow. He'd
already sent three men ahead, following the fresh trail.

Another leg-cramping climb. For ten minutes they went almost straight up, a step at a time, stopping on the landings
to catch their breath and rub the kinks out of their aching
muscles. When they reached the top, Lind shot the lock of
the trapdoor and helped Jenny up a short ladder into the
enclosed observation deck. She fell on the floor, her lips blue.
Brook collapsed next to her.

Lind gave Boomer a boost up the ladder, followed him
inside and lowered the trapdoor in the floor, sliding the bolt
into place.

The observation deck was about eight feet by eight feet
and resembled a cramped one-room shack, complete with a
roof and a big plate-glass window in each of the four walls.
The floor was metal.

"They call this a 'birdcage,'" Brook said when he got his
wind back.

He'd been in spotters' towers before. The views were
spectacular. They were usually equipped with a good tele-
scope, mapping gear, radios and weather gauges. But all of
that had been removed from the tower, probably early in the
fall, after the end of the forest-fire season.

Lind turned over a heavy work bench and slid it against
the wall that faced the trail. If they were trapped up there,
the thick wood might give them some extra protection. Any
shooting would have to come from that side, which offered
the only real line of fire for anyone on the ground. The tower
was built on a rocky promontory; three of the four sides were
exposed only to sheer drop-offs.

Lind was starting to feel a little better about this. The more he thought about it, maybe coming up here wasn't such a bad idea.

"They'll have to shoot almost straight up, which means it's going to be tough to get a good angle on us," he said. "They won't have much of a target. From down there, the front side of the tower's about all they've got to aim at." He drew the canvas sun-curtain over the window most likely to get shot up. His hope was it would protect them from flying glass-fragments.

It was freezing, ice-house cold. The tower wasn't heated. Brook opened the two down-filled sleeping bags and laid them out on the floor, so they'd have a place to sit.

He checked his watch. Masterson's show had another ten minutes to run. Brook asked Lind for the cell phone, which he'd carried from the cabin. Lind grinned and handed it over.

"Sure, why not?" he said, understanding what Brook had in mind.

Still trying to slow his breathing, Brook dialed the station number. An assistant answered and put him straight through to the studio.

"He's doing a commercial," Brook said.

Then Bill Masterson was back on the line.

"They're coming for us, Masterson," Brook said. "Let me talk on the air. People need to know what happened while I can still tell them."

Masterson mentioned the lawyers again. He sounded apologetic.

"If what I'm telling you is true, even a third of it, do you think they'd have a chance in hell of winning a lawsuit? And, Masterson, like I told you before, what happens if it gets out I called you tonight and you didn't do a damn thing to help us? How would you explain it? Hey, I wanted to let him talk, but the lawyers said I might get sued."

Masterson was silent.

Brook said, "Let me talk, Bill."

After a long pause, Masterson said, "You're on in ten seconds."

Lind knelt in the corner, peering out the covered window.

Boomer crouched at his feet, chin flat on the birdcage's cold, metal floor. Lind was still fighting a battle with himself. He was as close as he'd ever come to sliding off into the dark. If he snapped, he'd kill Brook and Jenny. He didn't want that to happen.

The thought and what it signified made him crack a grim smile.

The sky had started to clear; moonlight shone through the gaps in the clouds. Lind was able to make out the clearing that led up to the tower. At first he wasn't sure what he was seeing; he rubbed his eyes and looked again. He detected movement, dark shapes.

"They're here," he said. "That sure didn't take them long."

He motioned for Brook and Jenny to move to the far side of the floor. He told them to sit down and try to keep their heads covered. Brook slid his back against the wall. Jenny sat next to him, hands jammed into the pockets of her coat; she had a scarf, which she'd wrapped around her neck and mouth. She pulled the end of one of the sleeping bags up over her legs to try to keep warm.

Masterson came on the radio. Brook heard him make a brief announcement. His voice seemed changed, more somber. He told his listeners that a doctor was calling long-distance and had something important to say.

Brook began by telling them who he was and what he did at the clinic. His words came without thought or plan and got right to the point. He said the man who ran the clinic, Dr. Robert Hartigan, had performed medical experiments on some prisoners in Jefferson City. He'd killed four men and two women.

Brook said: "I'm sitting high up in a ranger tower, with two other people, at Twentymile, North Carolina, and he's trying to do the same thing to us."

He heard shouting below but couldn't make out the words from that height. He continued his story, describing the clinic's kindling experiments as simply as he could, and how

omeone—he didn't know who—had helped two prisoners
scape from there.

There was more shouting and this time he distinctly heard
omeone order them down from the tower. It was Brody's
oice. Then shooting started, full automatic fire. Bullets
lammed into the birdcage's west-facing window and wall,
earing holes in the curtain. Glass shattered. The air was filled
vith the whine of high-velocity slugs.

"Keep back!" Lind shouted. He sat next to Jenny.
Boomer lay his head on his lap. Bullets pinged off the
ower's steel floor and slapped against the metal crossbeams.

Brook continued to tell his story into the cell phone, rais-
ng his voice over the ripping sound of the gunfire. "They're
hooting at us, Masterson. Can you hear it?"

"Is there anything we can do?" Masterson asked, not try-
ng to disguise the emotion in his voice. "We've already
alled the police."

"You want to do something, you repeat this broadcast
very hour."

Brook hung up and grabbed his shotgun. He looked at
Lind, who nodded. Squatting on his heels in the glass fragments and splintered wood, Lind was calmly checking the
oad in his magnum revolver.

The shooting had stopped. Brook cupped his hands and
houted that he'd just been on the radio in St. Louis. He'd
elephoned a call-in show.

"Hey, Brody. Are you down there? I told them everything.
named names. It's over."

FIFTY-SIX

BECKWORTH HAD HARTIGAN ON the cell phone within five minutes. He confirmed everything that Brook had said, and god only knows what else.

For once, Beckworth didn't know what to say or do. He stood at the base of the tower, holding the cell phone to his ear, listening to Hartigan's frantic voice, trying to calm him down as he mentally sorted through his options.

The clouds were almost gone. The moon gleamed from a dark corner in the sky.

One thing was certain. Beckworth wasn't going to waste any more precious time here. It was pointless to keep stretching their luck trying to kill the two doctors. He either had to get back to Missouri as quickly as possible, to organize a defense with Hartigan and Paulus. Or he had to get out. Leave the country.

He'd already wired money months ago to the Banco de Sud in Santiago, Chile. With typical foresight, he'd carefully checked the South American extradition laws. Chile rarely extradited anyone. His escape fund was waiting for him in two special accounts. All he had to do was get to an airport. Knoxville and Atlanta came to mind. Knoxville was closer, but Atlanta would probably be better because it had more international flights.

Beckworth was only half listening when Hartigan finally

hung up on him. He cradled the phone back into its carrying case. He was too cold. He needed to go somewhere warm and dry, and work it out logically one step at a time. That's when he was at his best.

Brody had heard everything and seen the color drain from Beckworth's face. He guessed what was going through his mind; his partner was considering when and how to sell him out.

Beckworth said, "We need to get out of here."

"Not until this is finished," Brody said, holding back his anger. He'd been cleaning up that bastard's mistakes for weeks, and now Beckworth was going to cut and run. Brody could smell it. Hartigan and Paulus had probably planned a similar double cross. Their contingency plans didn't include him. He was expendable.

Beckworth must have noticed something in Brody's eyes, a reflection of the fires raging within him.

"Everybody, listen up," Beckworth said to the men. "Things have changed. We're getting out."

He started to walk away. A few men glanced at Brody, hesitated as if unsure of what to do, then followed Beckworth.

"Nobody's leaving until I give the word!" Brody said.

Without looking back, Beckworth took three or four steps in the snow. Suddenly pivoting, he whirled around. He had a pistol in his hand.

Expecting this, Brody fired three rapid shots with his Browning 9 mm. Each bullet hit Beckworth in the upper chest, pushing him backward; the last shot spun him around. He fell on his face.

Brody didn't bother to take a look. It was a good, tight pattern. Beckworth was dead.

He slung an automatic rifle over his shoulder. Four men remained. One volunteered to go with him. Telling the others to clear out, he started up the tower stairway.

FIFTY-SEVEN

LIND HAD TAKEN A quick look down at the ground after hearing the pistol shots. He saw a dark shape sprawled in the snow. The moonlight helped. He thought he saw or heard something moving down there, but couldn't be sure.

"Maybe they've cleared out," he said. "I can't see anybody."

Minutes passed. Boomer's head came up abruptly from Jenny's lap; the dog walked to the trapdoor and put his nose down, sniffing.

Almost simultaneously Brody shouted up to them from the tower's stairwell. "Hey, up there, I've got dynamite! You don't come out in two minutes, I'll blow you out."

"I don't think he's bluffing," Lind said. He looked at Brook. "I'd better try to talk to him."

"You can't do that," Brook said.

Lind's voice hardened. "Listen to me good," he said. "We don't have much time before that man tries to kill us. I'm starting to feel it again . . . in the head. I don't know how much longer I can hold myself together, so I might as well go out and pay that bastard a visit."

Brook wondered how long it had been since Lind's symptoms had returned. He started to ask, but Lind silenced him.

"No, listen to me," he snapped. "I'm tired of fighting it. Maybe your drugs can help. I don't know. And I don't give a damn. I'm so damned tired and scared. Can you understand that?''

"You're quitting before you've even given the drug a decent chance," Brook said. "The peptide just started to work. I can help you. I know I can.'' He was angry at himself for not knowing what else to say, for not knowing how to convince him to hang on.

"We're wasting time," Lind said. "I don't want to kill you if I freak out up here." He smiled. "You two helped me. You're the only ones who ever tried, really tried, and I want to thank you. Those are two words I haven't used much in my life.''

He told Brook and Jenny to get back from the trapdoor, and lifted it just enough to peer down at the stairwell landing below them. He saw nothing.

Lind shouted, "What do you want us to do?"

Brody's answer was fierce and loud: "Get your ass out of that tower.''

Lind lowered the trapdoor and gave the dog a pat on the haunches. "You ready, boy? You ready to go smoke him out?''

Boomer yelped. His tail thumped a beat on the floor.

"If he gets past me . . ." Lind hesitated. "You use that shotgun, okay?''

Before Brook or Jenny could object, Lind opened the trapdoor. Boomer hit the landing at the base of the ladder and charged down the first flight of steps. Lind went out behind the dog, clutching his pistol in his right hand. Brook grabbed the shotgun and started after him. Boomer was barking wildly.

Brook scrambled through the hatch to the landing at the top of the stairwell. The wind that slashed off the mountains was blowing almost a gale, and he felt the tower sway back and forth. He had to grip the handrail with both hands to keep his balance. Jenny had followed him.

Automatic gunfire roared below them. Looking over the side of the tower, Brook saw Lind crouched one level down. He held his pistol with both hands, muzzle pointed up. He was looking for a target. Boomer continued to bark.

Brook, who had a better angle of vision, saw a dark figure on the landing below Lind. He was raising his rifle, probably to shoot the dog.

Brook shouted, "Hey! Up here!"

The man looked up, his face reflected in the moonlight. He had a straight line of fire right up the stairwell. Brook pulled Jenny down just as a burst of gunfire exploded below them. Bullets slapped above their heads.

Two more shots boomed out. Lind, standing, had fired when the gunman moved into the open.

Brook risked another look over the tower's side railing and saw the man lying by the stairwell, not moving. Boomer stood near him, snarling at his face. Someone else was down there. Brook thought he saw something, then heard rapid gunfire. Lind returned the fire.

Brook shouted for Lind to get back, and pumped five .12-gauge slugs down the stairs, aiming at the gun flashes, hoping the wall of steel buckshot would force Brody to keep his head down. Brook was certain it was Brody.

A moment later Lind came up the stairway; he was hanging on the railing. Even in the darkness, Brook noticed the odd look on his face, the twisted mouth.

"I'm hit," Lind said quietly. He started to fall backward.

Brook grabbed him around the waist and helped him up onto the landing.

"Can you tell me where you're shot?"

"Right calf," Lind said between clenched teeth.

Brook immediately worried about an artery. His feet slipped on the landing's grid flooring; the metal surface was slick with Lind's blood.

Boomer had stayed below and was barking again.

"Lean against me," Brook said. He got Lind up on his shoulder and lifted him through the hatch, into the birdcage. Jenny helped swing his legs inside.

"You'll be okay," Brook said as he laid Lind on one of the sleeping bags. "Try not to move." Risking a quick look with a flashlight, he probed the bullet hole with his fingers.

Lind was lucky. The slug had missed the femur and main arteries. It looked like a clean through-and-through wound.

"I'll put a tourniquet around it," Jenny said, already starting to take off her belt. "Try to slow down whoever's still out there."

Brook climbed back to the landing below the birdcage and got into a crouch. He couldn't see or hear anything. He felt the wild rush of adrenaline through his body. Then, suddenly, Boomer came charging up the stairway. Brook picked up the panting dog and lifted him through the hatch.

He heard something, the sound of a boot cleat on the steps. He fired twice down the stairwell.

"You'll have to do better than that," Brody said. "You can still make this easy on yourself by throwing down your weapons. Hey, was that the doctor I hit, or Lind? I couldn't tell in the dark."

Brook blindly fired three more times, pumping the shotgun's slide action with his left hand, ejecting the shells faster than he'd ever done in his life. The sound rang in his ears.

As he started reloading the Winchester, something hard and metallic hit the landing one level below him; it sounded like a rock. He heard it roll across the deck. Instinctively, he turned away at the exact moment a light exploded with a brilliant phosphorus flash. Clouds of white smoke corkscrewed out from the sides of the tower like flaring confetti.

It took a moment for Brook to regain his senses. He fired down the stairwell, then climbed back into the birdcage and slammed the hatch shut.

"My god, what was that?" Jenny asked.

Lind said, "Some kind of stun grenade."

Jenny was bent over him. She had his right pants leg rolled up to the knee and had tightened her belt around his upper thigh to stop the bleeding.

They heard footsteps on the metal stairs. Then Brody shouted up to them, "The next one will be a real grenade. You've got one minute to come out." The loud voice sounded like it was right below them.

Seconds later, something hit the floor of the birdcage.

"Cover your eyes!" Lind shouted. The bottle-shaped canister had landed at his feet. It burst in another flash of white light just as he hurled it back through the window.

Brook still had his eyes squeezed shut when the hatch door flew open. In the confusion, he'd forgotten to latch it. Brody sprang up through the opening, gripping an M-16.

"Nobody moves!" he shouted.

Standing up, he kicked Brook in the side—a hard, vicious blow. Brook gasped, nearly immobilized.

Brody picked up his shotgun and threw it through the shattered window. Then he yelled at Lind: "All right, asshole. Where's *your* gun?"

Lind said he thought he'd dropped it somewhere on the tower. Brody slugged him across the face with the barrel of his rifle, knocking him over on his side.

"Where's the gun, dammit!"

"It's on the floor!" Jenny screamed.

Using his flashlight, Brody found the weapon lying near the hatch, and tossed it through the window.

Jenny had stayed with Lind and was trying to retie the tourniquet, which had started to loosen. Despite the blow, which had knocked out a couple of teeth, Lind was still managing to hold on to the Boomer's leash to keep him from attacking; he growled, straining toward Brody.

Brody glanced around the cramped space. Keeping his weapon trained on his prisoners, he raised the upended worktable with his right hand and smashed out the rest of the broken window glass.

"That's better," he said. "It lets a little more air in."

He inhaled and blew out once, twice, filling his lungs. His breath made clouds of steam. "I've been looking forward to this meeting," he said.

Gasping in pain, Brook clutched his side. He figured Brody had cracked one of his ribs. He felt sick and afraid.

Brody put his rifle against the back of Brook's head and told him to stand up. "There really is one fine view up here, even at night. Come on, I want you to see this."

Brook got up on one knee, rubbing his eyes, stalling as

long as he dared. Every breath hurt, and he could still see the white imprint of the grenade flash every time he blinked. Brody poked him harder with the gun barrel, cutting his scalp.

"Up, boy," he said, pulling Brook to his feet and making him stand in front of the window. The wind stung Brook's face. He didn't dare look down at the ground.

Brody twisted Brook's arm behind him and nudged him closer to the opening, so close his head stuck through it. The slightest shove from behind and he'd go right over the side. Head first. Brook clamped down on his bladder.

"Hey, you're not afraid of heights, are you? That's nothing. You've just got to learn how to control your breathing. Take it nice and easy. That's the secret." Brody gripped Brook by the shoulders and pushed his head even farther through the opening.

"How far do you think it is to the ground?" Brody asked. Brook didn't answer; his eyes were locked on the moon, which darted in and out of the clouds.

Brody said, "Look down!"

Brook willed himself to do it. He saw trees. The white shimmer of deep snow. He took a few shallow breaths. If this lasted much longer he'd black out. He could feel it coming. His legs were already rubber.

"Isn't that just incredible?" Brody said, pulling him back inside. "The moonlight on the snow. You can't buy a view like that." Playing his flashlight on the ceiling, he noticed a small trapdoor.

"What's up on top?" he asked.

"I don't know," Brook said. His face was drenched with sweat.

Lind was tensely scratching Boomer's neck. The dog didn't take his eyes off Brody.

"Let's take a look," Brody said. "Open it up."

Brook released a latch, and the trapdoor lowered, revealing a short ladder that folded out.

"That's great. Just what we want," Brody said, tapping the ceiling with his rifle.

Brook realized that Brody was going to kill him. If not now, very soon. In the dim moonlight, Brody's white smile looked frozen.

"I can't believe people really go up on that roof," Brody said in mock surprise. "You ever done anything like that?"

Brook shook his head.

Brody grinned. "I'm going to give you a chance. All you have to do is figure out how to get down." He whacked Brook in the back with his rifle. "So what are you waiting for? Get up the damn ladder."

Jenny stood up. All of her training, her skills at negotiating and making connections with killers had deserted her. She didn't know what to say. "Why don't we end this," she pleaded. "Everything's finished. Hartigan, the clinic ... Why continue ..."

"It's called closure," Brody said. "I want to wrap it up, atone for past mistakes. So sit down."

"Do it, Jenny," Brook said. He'd already climbed up on the ladder. His head and shoulders were through the opening. He looked up and saw a few stars through the clouds.

Brody shoved him in the ass. "All the way."

When Brook was on the roof, Brody closed the trapdoor behind him. "If you start getting dizzy, remember what I told you," he shouted. "Control your breathing. You hear that?"

Squatting down, Brook felt the wind tug at his clothing. His side throbbed and his stomach felt like he'd swallowed glass. Afraid that he'd get blown off if he stood up, he crawled to the larger of two radio antennas and held on with both hands. The antenna was about eight feet high and bolted down. Clinging to it like a drowning man hanging onto a lifeline, Brook fought back the nauseating feeling that he was about to slip and fall.

The roof was covered with a grid of about a dozen lightning rods, each about six inches tall. The wires that connected them were twisted together in a thick cable that disappeared over the side and looped beneath the birdcage.

It wrapped the structure top to bottom, offering protection from lightning hits.

"I can't hear you," Brody yelled. He fired two shots that shattered the trapdoor.

Brook spun around and saw the splintered holes. The bullets had missed him by less than two feet.

"I'm here," he shouted.

"That's better," Brody answered. "Walk over to the edge."

"Don't do this," Jenny pleaded, starting to get up. Brody swung the butt of his rifle, striking her a glancing blow. He'd barely looked at her. Stunned, Jenny fell against Lind, who held her still.

Brody fired another shot through the roof, the echo cracking back from the distant mountains. Brook's eyes watered in the wind as he gripped the swaying antenna and tried not to panic.

Two more shots ripped through the roof.

"I want to hear you!" Brody shouted. He fired again, a long burst, and this time wood splinters slapped against Brook's legs. One of the fragments cut his cheek.

Figuring this was his only chance, Brook decided to try for the lightning-rod cable. Maybe he could climb down it and get below the birdcage.

It was hard for him to look at the edge of the roof, much less make his way over there. He wanted to get down on all fours and crawl, but didn't dare; he'd expose too much of his body to a rifle bullet that way. He'd have to walk to the edge, get a solid grip on the cable and go over the side. There wouldn't be much time; Brody was bound to hear the roof creak and start shooting the moment he took his first step.

Brook tried to picture exactly what he had to do, focus on it, break it down step by step and lock it in his mind so he wouldn't think about anything else, wouldn't see anything else. Then he was moving, first one foot, then the other. Three quick, soft steps to the edge of the roof.

He bent down and grabbed the thick coil of wires, forcing himself to look over the edge. The cold metal burned his hands. The wires ran along the side with the broken window. If he could just hang on, it might work.

Brody braced the M-16 on his waist and raked the roof with a spattering burst of automatic fire. He heard footsteps above him and fired again. Then the rifle hammer snapped, metal on metal. Out of bullets. He drew his pistol and fired two quick shots, emptying that clip as well.

Cursing himself, Brody remembered that he'd forgotten to reload. He angrily ejected the clip from the Browning and started to slip in another.

Preoccupied, he didn't notice Lind ease up slowly off the floor until it was too late. He drove into Brody with his head down, slamming him against a window as Boomer lunged for his legs.

Lind had him in a bear hug, pinning his arms from behind. "Get down!" Lind shouted to Brook. "Get down!"

Brook had already swung over the side when the fight broke out. Holding onto the lightning-rod cable, squeezing the thick coil of twisted wires with his legs, he went down hand over hand until he could lean out and get a foot on the window ledge. The cable passed within several feet of it. Brook had to make a choice: keep lowering himself or try to swing over to the window and pull himself through the opening.

Lind's shouts decided it. Brook leaned out as far as he dared, trying for another toehold on the window ledge. The wind was trying to rip him off the cable. He had trouble hanging on; his hands were numb with cold. Descending another foot, he gripped the window ledge with his left hand, then his right. His strength was pouring out of him like sand. Feet pedaling in air, he got his arms over the ledge and pulled himself inside.

Panting, he collapsed onto the floor, his right hand slashed from a glass fragment in the window frame. Jenny lay next to him. Boomer was barking.

Lind still had Brody in an armlock. Enraged, and twisting his shoulders violently, Brody kept slamming Lind back against one of the windows, trying to break the hold. Boomer snapped at his legs.

"I'm losing it," Lind yelled.

Wrenching himself free, Brody pulled a hunting knife from his boot. He thrust straight at Lind's throat, a vicious jab that barely missed.

Lind managed to back away. Brody slashed him across the arms and in return caught a heavy blow in the face. Brody lunged at him, stabbing him in the chest. Lind, screaming in rage, straightened up and locked onto Brody's knife hand at the wrist. He prevented him from drawing the blade, holding him close, their faces inches apart.

"Now!" Lind shouted to Brook. "Come now!"

Brook sailed in low and hard, hurtling against Brody, knocking him down. His momentum carried them both through the open hatch in the floor. Brook hit the ladder and struck the platform on his back.

He lay there for what seemed like minutes, unaware of Brody, trying to halt the sensation that he was still falling. He heard a strange rasping noise, and gradually realized his wheezing lungs were making the sound. When he tried to move, everything hurt—legs, shoulders, his right side where he'd cracked a rib.

Brody lay next to him. He was either out cold, or dead. Refusing to let go, Boomer had rolled down the steps with them. The dog lay there under the pile, not moving.

Brook got stiffly to his knees. As his mind kept flickering on and off, he remembered the man they'd killed. His body was one landing below them. Maybe his weapon was down there.

Pulsing wires of pain ran through him as soon as he tried to stand. He fell backward, wincing, choking off a scream. Almost blacking out, he knew that his right ankle was either badly sprained or broken. He grabbed the stairway railing and limped down on one leg, putting all his weight on his hands and left leg until he'd made it down the flight of steps. The pain filled his entire being, daggers that stabbed straight into his brain.

A man in a parka was sprawled on the landing, one arm dangling over the edge, his head twisted at a strange sideways angle. His rifle was still pinned under him.

Brook struggled to turn him over. He looked up and saw Brody leaning heavily against the handrail at the top of the flight of steps. He was backlit by the moon.

Brody staggered down the stairwell as Brook tugged at the dead man's rifle. Dazed but quickly coming out of it, Brody took a step and kicked savagely at Brook's head. Brook rolled with the force of the blow and made one last desperate try for the weapon. He almost had it when Brody kicked him again, driving him to the edge of the landing.

Brody pulled the rifle free and was turning around with it, when Brook summoned the last of his strength, came up to his knees like a football lineman and butted him in the chest. The impact sent Brody slipping backward on the ice-glazed deck. He hit the low railing at the edge of the platform and tumbled over the side. He managed to grab the railing with one hand, then another, and started to hoist himself up, but the wind started blasting, shaking the tower. Brody barely managed to hang on in the gale.

"I can't make it," he screamed. "I can't . . . hold . . ."

Brook had collapsed on the deck, and he saw the terror on Brody's face. Strangely detached, Brook watched him struggle to hold on. All he had to do was keep lying there and not move, and Brody would certainly fall. It would all be over. He didn't have to do a thing, just let it happen.

"Help me, please!" Brody was gripping the railing with both hands. His legs were swinging in the strong wind gusts as he tried to find something to hang on to. "I'm begging you. You can turn me over to the cops. I'll back you up about Hartigan. Don't let me fall."

Brook got up, and braced his legs and waist against the railing. He grabbed Brody by the jacket and around his back, and pulled hard. He strained for a better grip. Brody managed to get an arm up over the railing. He put a knee on the edge of the deck, then got another arm up.

"You're almost there," Brook said. "Come on, you can do it."

He was reaching for one of Brody's arms when Brody suddenly drove a fist into his stomach.

Brook fell back, unable to move, sucking air, his legs and chest throbbing. The blow had hit him like an iron ball.

Gasping and unable to focus, he patted the stock of the rifle, which lay just within his reach. At first not recognizing it, he let his fingers touch the polished, grooved wood. He touched the barrel. Then he had it, gripping it in both hands and aiming it at Brody, who had swung a leg over the railing and was stepping onto the deck.

Brook squeezed the trigger, and the lurching recoil jerked the gun from his grip. Brody's hands flew up over his head, and he went over the railing like a diver doing a backflip from the high platform. Brook heard the body hit the ground.

He let his head fall back against the deck and lay quietly for a long time, trying to get his breathing under control, listening to the wind howl through the tower. When he thought he could move without passing out, he crawled to the edge of the platform and looked down. Brody was spread-eagled in the snow.

Brook was aware of a dog barking on the platform above him. Boomer.

FIFTY-EIGHT

MOMENTS PASSED. BROOK FELT the tower's gentle sway. At first he didn't hear Jenny calling his name. She was all right.

He managed to pull himself to his feet. The pain made him wince when he put even the slightest weight on his right ankle. Using his good leg, he hobbled back up the stairway.

Lind lay on the platform under the trapdoor that opened into the birdcage. The knife was still buried in his chest. Fully revived, Boomer lay next to him.

One look at Lind was enough to tell Brook there was no need to check for a pulse. He was dead. His face was the most peaceful Brook had ever seen it.

Still dizzy from the blow to the head, Jenny joined him. Brook felt hot tears well up in his eyes the moment he saw her. The salt taste was in his mouth.

She noticed how he clenched his teeth every time he moved.

He grinned and said, "I guess my skiing days are over." He didn't want to look at his leg. The ankle felt like it was swollen the size of a watermelon.

"I'll go down and find something for a splint," Jenny said.

"No way," Brook said. "Someone might still be down there. I can make it until morning."

Together, they got Lind's body back up into the birdcage.

They didn't want it exposed overnight to the wind on the platform. Jenny managed to tie the canvas curtain across the broken window, which helped shelter them. She gently ran her fingers along Brook's ankle to gauge the extent of the damage. He winced every time she applied pressure, but he could move the foot from side to side, a good sign that the bone wasn't broken.

It was a long five hours until dawn. They wrapped themselves in the down sleeping bags. The dog slept between them. Brook dozed, numbed by pain. Awake at some point, he tried to regain his balance of mind. He'd been thinking about the fate of Hartigan and the men he'd shot in the boathouse and Lind. He prayed that Lind's voices finally had been stilled.

The sun rose in a clear sky, lighting the blue wave of the mountains. Jenny heard the noise first, the deep, staccato chop of rotor blades. Moments later, two stub-nosed Bell helicopters circled the tower. They had the red markings of the North Carolina Highway Patrol.

Jenny waved up to them through the shattered window. She felt as if she'd just come out of a dark tunnel into the brightest light she'd ever known. She was jubilant. Her face was flaming. This day—she was certain of it—had been given to her as a gift.

Brook slipped his arm around her. He wasn't worried anymore. When all this was finally over, they would have time to think about practicing medicine and doing research again. He hadn't given up on forensic psychiatry and neurology, and thought he could stake out a life in those entwined disciplines.

But first he was going to spend a few weeks away from it all with Jenny Malone. After his ankle healed, he wanted to take her on a hike to the summit of Mount LeConte. The mountain was just to the north; its sawtooth peak was just now catching the first pink streaks of sunlight.

He had hiked up there often. Every morning he would get up early in the cold darkness and find a place to sit where he could look out to the eastern horizon and wait for the radiant first signs of dawn. This was the closest he'd ever come to a religious experience. These mountains were his church. He smiled at the thought rising in him that he wanted to go there with Jenny and give thanks.

AUTHOR'S NOTE
⊳◁

THIS IS A WORK of fiction, an entertainment. At present, kindling is performed only on laboratory animals, mainly cats and primates at a handful of cutting-edge research facilities scattered around the globe. There's been no deliberate attempt, so far as is known, to kindle a human brain—and certainly not as a means of altering criminal behavior.

Could it happen? Could antisocial criminals, people like Waters and Lind, "learn" to be good? Could their brains be reprogrammed or rewired so they wouldn't want to commit acts of violence?

It's no longer an academic issue. The technical means are already at hand. Ethical considerations have ruled kindling experiments on humans out of bounds. That could change.

By the end of the decade yet another bloody crime wave is predicted as the children of the current crop of killers and thieves start hitting the streets. As public patience runs out with bankrupt solutions to crime and the staggering costs of building even more prisons, watch for an increased emphasis on the one area that's been virtually ignored in the entire debate on crime and punishment—the human brain. The shift to neurological and biological approaches to the crime problem is likely to be dramatic, widespread and searingly controversial.

Indeed, it's already happening. The scientific literature is filled with papers on the strong links between brain chemistry and violence and how new drugs are already improving antisocial behavior. Brain-imaging techniques now offer color, 3-D snapshots of how the brain works—how it processes information, how we think. The possibility of isolating "crime hot spots" in the brain or in a person's genetic makeup is no longer a matter of science fiction. It's here and now.

In the last few years, researchers into the biological causes of crime have achieved stunning results, especially in the area of brain chemistry. They've isolated such neurotransmitters as dopamine and serotonin and charted how they can increase or decrease a person's propensity for violence. They've demonstrated that criminal behavior can be predicted and modified. And they've paid a professional price, coming under attack from influential interest groups and individuals who consider such research the first step toward a society more sinister than anything ever imagined by George Orwell.

But the Brave New World has arrived. Whether it will be peopled by renegade scientists like *The Kindling Effect*'s Robert Hartigan remains to be settled.

Also to be settled is my debt of gratitude to all those who helped try to steer me straight in my research for this book.

Many people helped, among them neurologists, psychiatrists and a team of intrepid PET imagers at the Washington University Medical School; and experts on brain waves and electromagnetic stimulation at the St. Louis University Medical School. In particular, I'd like to thank Dr. John Rabun, a forensic psychiatrist, and Alan Blake, a psychologist who specializes in treating antisocial personality disorders; and their colleagues at the Missouri Department of Mental Health in St. Louis. John Rabun, widely regarded as a rising new star in criminal forensics, showed me how the twisted mind of a serial killer works. I'll never forget the journey.

I'd also like to thank Dr. Roger Gaumond of Penn State, the brightest man I know. With patience and humor, he helped me try to understand the science behind magnetic fields. The fictional leaps and errors are all mine.

I want to thank my editor at William Morrow, Henry Ferris, who performed major and minor miracles on this book, and my agent Richard Pine, of Arthur Pine & Associates, who conceived the idea and helped shape the manuscript with invaluable hands-on coaching.

For so many reasons, the last and biggest thanks goes to my wife, Janice.

STUART WOODS

The *New York Times* Bestselling Author

GRASS ROOTS
71169-/ $6.50 US/ $8.50 Can

When the nation's most influential senator
succumbs to a stroke, his brilliant chief aide
runs in his stead, tackling scandal, the governor
of Georgia and a white supremacist
organization that would rather see him
dead than in office.

Don't miss these other page-turners from
Stuart Woods

WHITE CARGO   70783-7/ $6.50 US/ $8.50 Can
A father searches for his kidnapped daughter in the
drug-soaked Colombian underworld.

DEEP LIE   70266-5/ $6.50 US/ $8.50 Can
At a secret Baltic submarine base, a renegade Soviet
commander prepares a plan so outrageous that it just
might work.

UNDER THE LAKE   70519-2/ $6.50 US/ $8.50 Can

CHIEFS   70347-5/ $6.50 US/ $8.50 Can

RUN BEFORE THE WIND
     70507-9/ $6.50 US/ $8.50 Can